CHAINS OF GOLD

Books by John McKinna
(aka John Mannock)

Iron Coffin
The Sen-Toku Raid
The War Mountains

Ben Gannon *series*
Crash Dive
Tiger Reef
Shark Lake
Chains of Gold

For more information
visit: www.SpeakingVolumes.us

CHAINS OF GOLD

John McKinna

SPEAKING VOLUMES, LLC
NAPLES, FLORIDA
2020

Chains of Gold

Thank you, Kurt Mueller and the whole Speaking Volumes staff for keeping John's books alive. We know he would be as pleased as we are with your representation of his work. The McKinna family.

ISBN 978-1-64540-116-2

All my love and gratitude
to my wife, Teresa,
for whom all my books are written.

Acknowledgments

John's parents, who kept their home filled with books for their children. Because of that, John fell in love with storytelling at an early age and felt the written word was mankind's greatest invention. How lucky we are.

Thank you, Mum and Dad.

Our combined families, for their love and encouragement through the years. From the publishing of his first book, John received lots of support from all of you and it means more than you know.

John's readers, for letting him know how much you've enjoyed his books and for keeping his work alive for years to come.

Thank you!

Prologue

The storm is upon us.

Ben Gannon shifted in his chair, momentarily distracted by the soft tinkle of ice cubes as the waiter refilled the water glasses at the next table. Outside the restaurant, through the ornate ironwork framing the balcony, the gentle midday din of the French Quarter wafted up from Bourbon Street. Refocusing his attention on the tattered, age-stained manuscript page, glossy between its two sheets of protective plastic, he began to read again, slowly translating the archaic Spanish.

Even now, with the ship in dire peril, Captain Ramos refuses to jettison any of the golden treasure that so destabilizes her. It is madness—the gold fever—in unholy alliance with his own hubris, which led him even to the folly of hammering a short golden shaft, sharpened into the semblance of a nail, into the foremast below the main deck, to bedazzle the crew and taunt the Ocean Fates. This two days ago, and having loaded the Arista's nethermost holds to bursting with the spoils of Montezuma's ravaged empire, pressing her waterline almost to the lower gunports, and seeing yet upon the shore, scattered here and there in great gleaming heaps, a thousand times the weight he had already commanded aboard, he was unable to set sail without taking on another forty barrels of golden chain, which he ordered secured about the lower gundeck. Each barrel contains a single chain, eighty rods in length yet not above the diameter of a man's finger, the links of which are wrought with such cunning artifice as to beguile and confound the senses.

It is these chains, not so much of gold as of Captain Ramos' greed, which now threaten to drag us to our doom. Not content with his gratuitous butchery of the Aztec peoples during his raiding sorties—in which I, as master of swords and arms, took a shameful part—he appears bent upon his own destruction, as well as the destruction of this noble vessel and her entire crew.

God save me, this I cannot permit.

Ben looked up as he finished the page, glancing first at Eugene McCluskey, the old oilfield diving supervisor with whom he'd worked on numerous offshore construction jobs over the years, and then at the slender lawyer in the dark suit who sat beside him— displaying the saturnine legal smile that says *I know something you don't.*

The lawyer, one Mr. Gomez, extracted another laminated manuscript page from a folder in his lap and passed it across the table to Ben. "There are a few more. Take your time."

Ben nodded, tipped the page to catch the best light in the restaurant's dim interior, and concentrated again on the elegant, spidery handwriting.

We have taken the ship. Captain Ramos and the few officers remaining loyal to him have barricaded themselves in the forecastle, cursing us for mutineers. This in the very heart of a tempest that threatens to tear our overburdened ship asunder. I have ordered the forty barrels of golden chain brought up to the main deck one at a time and cast into the sea. There is no alternative to this laborious method of lightening the Arista, for I dare not permit the gun ports to be opened, that the barrels might be expelled through them. We are too low in the water, and already the pumps, each manned by three stalwart men, cannot keep up with the invasion of the sea.

Ben looked up again as he finished the page. "Sounds like a real pleasure cruise," he commented.

"Doesn't it?" Gomez responded, trading laminated manuscripts with him. "Please read on, Mr. Gannon. It gets even more interesting."

"Sure." Ben let his eyes rove over the lawyer's face, examining it, before turning his attention to the new page.

Disaster. Even as we struggled to divest the ship of her extra weight, Captain Ramos, enraged at seeing his bounty of golden chain so discarded, charged from his barricaded sanctum as we labored to dispose of the final barrel, sword and dagger in hand, in the company of his officers. Attacking us directly, they seized the barrel and rolled it into their forepeak stronghold. A vicious skirmish ensued, during which three of my weary men and all five of the captain's compatriots were slain. What a grievous trial the Heavenly Father has set us that we should find ourselves killing each other at a time when every able hand is so desperately needed to save the Arista! But perchance, with Captain Ramos now restrained, we may yet complete the stabilization of the ship and, by the Grace of God, survive this hellish night.

Once more, Ben traded the page he'd just finished for a fresh one. "Whoever this guy is, or *was*," he said, "he's a cool hand."

The lawyer shrugged noncommittally. "The final manuscript fragment is signed, Mr. Gannon. I'll let you read on, from start to finish. Only one more page."

"Fair enough."

Our efforts have come to naught. As dawn breaks the storm continues unabated, the sky boiling with clouds as black as Satan's legions. We pray for Deliverance even as we strive to prevent the water in the lower holds from rising too rapidly. One pump has broken under the constant strain. Now we must keep the ship afloat using only the remaining pump and a double file of exhausted men who pass buckets from hand to hand as quickly as their flagging energy will allow. The mizzenmast has carried away, and we wallow helplessly through the mountainous waves, trailing warps in a poor attempt to keep the Arista's bow into the tempest.

The ship's carpenter reports that the bottom is sound; therefore, I cannot comprehend why so much water enters the hull. No matter. Enter it does. We must further lighten the ship if we are to survive. We will open the nether holds and cast the treasure of the Aztecs into the sea. Of what consequence are worldly riches to dead men?

Ben leaned back in his chair, rubbed his eyes, and took a sip of Sierra Nevada pale ale. "Light's a bit poor in here for reading this fancy penmanship," he said, "and this old-style language is straining my street Spanish. But it's a great story. Compelling."

"Yup," McCluskey said, nodding. It was the first sound he'd uttered in ten minutes.

"The guy wrote all this as it was happening?" Ben directed his query at Gomez. "Seems as if he'd have been a little too busy, don't you think?"

The lawyer made a pyramid of his long, graceful fingers and nodded at the ceiling. "A good observation, Mr. Gannon," he said, "but the archivist who prepared these selections from the diary explained to me that military leaders of this period had a tendency to document events virtually as they happened, as such records were often later used by tribunals to justify their actions. Even in the heat of battle, an officer might slip away for a few minutes—perhaps during a brief lull in the action—to jot down a few observations in his personal journal." He smiled his patronizing smile. "No audio or videotape, you see."

"Nixon should have been so lucky," Ben said. "Okay. Last page?"

"Here you are."

Upon hearing my order that the treasure holds be unsealed and their contents cast overboard, Captain Ramos, who had been permitted to join the pump detail, eluded the two men assigned to guard him and flung

himself upon me, raving as if possessed. His derange-
ment was such that I ordered him tied into one of the
ship's two boats, in anticipation of the likely event that
we shall have to abandon the Arista. He continues to
scream that I am responsible for all that plagues him:
the mutiny of his crew, the loss of his plundered treas-
ure, the storm itself. But perhaps his reason may yet
return should we find, in days hence, that we have
survived the tempest.

I go now to supervise the opening of the treasure
holds and the jettisoning of our priceless ballast. I pray
that this final act of expediency may suffice to preserve
the Arista and the brave souls aboard her.

The manuscript ended. Ben glanced up at Gomez.
"That's it?"

The lawyer gestured with his forefinger. "Turn it
over. It's the only page with writing on both sides."

Ben did so. The remaining script, hastily scrawled
and badly water-stained, covered approximately two-
thirds of the available parchment.

The Arista is lost. Upon opening the main treasure
hold, we were greeted by an explosion of seawater,
mingled with the bodies of three Aztec warriors, long
drowned. As my companions and I struggled up the
central ladder to the main deck, the water surging at

our heels, I recognized the Aztecs by their dress as members of the fierce and wild Jaguar warrior cult— brothers-in-arms of those who so brutally assailed us during our sorties into the interior of the New Land. I can only surmise that they were responsible for opening the ship's bottom to the sea, sacrificing their lives even as they denied us retention of our stolen riches. Their treachery may prove to be our doom as well as their own. Such are the strange and violent ways of these heathen people.

Ben paused on that last sentence. For the first time, he found himself losing empathy with the long-dead Spaniard who had penned these elegant, faded words more than four hundred years earlier. Undoubtedly, he had been a brave man, a natural leader, and unusually enlightened for his time. Certainly more so than Captain Ramos. But his perspective, through no fault of his own, was ultimately one-sided. Ben did not share his surprise at the actions of the natives who had somehow secreted themselves in the *Arista*'s treasure hold. They must have been proud men, members of a warrior elite—perhaps some type of Aztec Praetorian Guard—and unable to stand idly by as their great empire was systematically pillaged. A capacity for violence? Treachery? Pride? These traits should not have seemed strange to a sixteenth-century Spanish *conquistador*.

Ben resumed reading. The script was now very compact and unadorned, penned with a shaking hand.

We have taken to the boats. I make this final entry huddled beneath my cloak, as we toss upon dark waves that twist and writhe like sea serpents. The noble Arista is gone, swallowed up by the awful deep. Captain Ramos raves and babbles, alternately cursing me and imploring Heaven to send a thunderbolt to strike me dead. I direct that he remain tied to the main thwart lest, in his madness, he cause injury to himself or any of the surviving company.

By lightning flash, I have discerned that we are roughly in the center of a triangle delineated by three small islands, which rise sharply above the surrounding horizon. The nearest of these, toward which the tempest seems to be driving our frail craft, I estimate to be no more than half a league distant.

We will strive to make landfall there. I now make ready to seal this journal in a small oiled cask I have prepared, in hopes of preserving it against the moisture of the sea. This cask I will lash into the bow of our tiny vessel. Should we perish in the maelstrom, or be dashed to pieces attempting to cross the outer reef of the island, those of our countrymen who search for us in weeks and months hence may yet find this record of our passing, and know the fate of the noble Arista and her company.

May God, in His Infinite Grace, grant us strength to survive the fury of the sea.

Sebastian Rodrigo Nunoz
Master of Swords,
Spanish Imperial Warship Arista,
Set down this 17th Day of November, in the Year of Our Lord, 1539.

Ben let his eyes linger on the bold signature, feeling the spirit of Sebastian Rodrigo Nunoz pulse faintly across the centuries. The Spaniard had lived and breathed in a very different world, but his struggle against the sea was timeless. *We're not so different*, Ben thought, *you and I.*

He passed the manuscript page over to Gomez. "Whew. That's about as real as it gets. Did Nunoz and his men manage to land safely on the island?"

"Yes indeed," the lawyer replied. "Their descendants live there to this day."

"They never returned to Spain?"

Gomez shrugged. "They intermarried with Carib and Arawak Indians on that island and others nearby. Some died of various tropical diseases. A few were rescued several years later."

"And Nunoz?"

"Our archivist isn't quite sure. There's some indication that he was killed by his own men." The saturnine smile returned to Gomez's face.

"Huh." That didn't quite ring true, for some reason. Ben shifted in his chair and reached for his beer. In his forty-two years he had acquired a distaste of being smiled at by lawyers.

"So what do you think?" McCluskey asked, his tone casual. One thick finger drummed lightly on the tablecloth.

Ben drained his glass and set it down. "Well, I think it sounds interesting. I also think that four hundred years is a long time, and one thousand feet is a lot of water."

"One thousand, two hundred and seven, to be precise," Gomez said.

"A lot of water," Ben reiterated, trading smiles with him like two rapiers crossing. "And you haven't confirmed her exact location yet."

"But we have good preliminary sonar hits from a survey vessel," McCluskey countered. "We've got at least two irregularities in an otherwise flat bottom profile that are exactly the right size to be a sunken Spanish galleon, in the correct general area."

"And the fact that this is where the *Arista* sank is supported not only by this manuscript," Gomez added, "but by additional documentary evidence found in the archives of the Imperial Fleet in Madrid."

McCluskey leaned forward, his eyes bright in his seamed face. "She's *there*, Ben. Look. We weld a sat system to an ocean barge, throw an ROV unit on for good measure, and tow the thing down into the Caribbean with Boyd Matthews' tug. I already talked to him. He's up for it. Then we confirm the presence of the wreck using the ROV's video cameras, get a four-man team into saturation, and start making bell runs. We scoop up all the treasure we can get our hands on, until the ship either runs out of loot or we run out of enthusiasm."

Ben considered. "Who's footing the bill? The upfront money?"

"My client," Gomez said quickly, "a private investor of considerable means who has an interest in both profit and the preservation of valuable antiquities. All preliminary costs will be covered, in cash."

"A saturation diving system? A deepwater Remote Operated Vehicle? A barge big enough to hold them both, an oceangoing tug to tow it, and at least six or seven top commercial diving hands?" Ben paused. "That's a lot of cash—even before we leave the dock."

"It will not be a problem. There will be no delay in payment. I will see to it personally." The lawyer leaned forward, elbows on the table, hands clasped in front of him, the very image of sincerity. "Mr. Gannon. You are an offshore commercial diver of over twenty years' experience, with literally thousands of hours in saturation. You come highly recommended by Mr. McCluskey—his first choice as lead diver and assistant supervisor of this project." He smiled. "You are a professional, and as such expect to be properly paid. I—that is, my *client*—would not waste your time."

Ben looked at McCluskey, holding his old colleague's eye for several seconds. "Okay, Eugene. What's in it for me?"

McCluskey sat back and grinned. "Ten percent of everything we bring up. Same as me. The other guys get five percent each."

"Of the *value* of the recovered antiquities," the lawyer clarified hastily. "You will be paid in cash based on their worth—not given the artifacts themselves."

"How many other people in the crew?" Ben asked.

"So far, four," McCluskey said. "We need one more topside mixed-gas tech. Five in total, plus you and me. Boyd Matthews is taking a juicy flat rate for piloting the tug."

"Five percent times five," Ben mused, "plus twenty percent for you and me. That's forty-five percent." He looked at Gomez. "Pretty generous."

"Fifty-five percent of an almost unimaginable fortune in Aztec gold, Mr. Gannon," Gomez said smoothly, "is quite sufficient for my client. Without your participation and unique skills, there would be no hope of recovering any treasure at all. You will not take on this project without sufficient motivation. A fair percentage of the salvage value provides that."

Ben signaled to the waiter for another beer. "I'd like to talk to Eugene, here, a little more, if you don't mind. Think it over a bit. When do you need an answer?"

"Tomorrow would be fine," Gomez said. "I have a little flexibility as far as scheduling goes." He got to his feet, his black gabardine suit falling immaculately into place on his slender frame. "You can let Mr. McCluskey know your decision, and he in turn can inform me. The assembling of the crew is really his department. I just came along to help him sell the project to you. And please, as I mentioned earlier when we first met here: not a word to anyone. This kind of project tends to attract all kinds of meddlesome creatures—journalists, government officials, fortune hunters. We don't need any undue complications." Extending his hand, he smiled, and for once it almost appeared genuine. "Enjoy your beer, perhaps a light snack. The food at this restaurant really is quite excellent. It's on me."

Ben shook with him. "Thanks. I might try the gumbo. Nice to meet you."

"Likewise."

Gomez nodded to McCluskey and made his way across the dining room, gliding between the tables as if he had helium in his shoes. Ben watched him go.

"What is it about lawyers," he muttered, "that makes my skin crawl every time I get within ten feet of one?"

"It's something they're born with," McCluskey said, "and a prerequisite for law school." He waved a hand. "Never mind him. What about this deal? You in or out?"

Ben grinned and lifted his pale ale. "I'm half in."

"What the hell does that mean?"

"It means I still have a couple of questions."

"Such as?"

"What if we don't find anything? Do I just eat the three or four weeks it's gonna take to fool around down in the Caribbean with an ROV? I don't usually work for free, Gene. I mean, this is the high season. I could be out on an oil platform welding up risers at five hundred dollars a day. And even though there's not a lot of sat work going on in the oil patch right now, if a job came up, it'd be worth more like eight hundred a day to me."

McCluskey slapped a hand on the table. "Gotcha covered there. Gomez has five grand set aside for each man if we don't find anything in the first month, to compensate us for our time. That's not for diving, that's just for standing by topside and helping out with the ROV once in a while. And yes"—he raised a forefinger before Ben could ask—"it's here in New Orleans in an escrow account."

Ben's expression became less skeptical. He sipped his beer. "Who've you got for crew so far? Anybody I know? No, wait. Anybody I feel like trusting my life to?"

McCluskey settled back in his chair, making it creak. He smiled, looking halfway relaxed for the first time in an hour. "Gonna be a hard sell all the way, ain't you? Well, tell you what, partner: you just drink down the last of that legal eagle's bar tab, and we'll perambulate on down the street a ways to another establishment. Got a few of the boys waiting for me there. You can look 'em over yourself. *Fine* offshore oilfield stock."

Ben gave a snort of laughter and raised his glass. "Huh," he said. "I bet."

Chapter One

The bar was a ten-minute walk down Bourbon Street from the toney restaurant selected by Gomez. A chorus of voices reverberated through the open doors as they approached. Ben looked at his watch. Barely two in the afternoon. A bit early for the shipyard bubbas and college football players to be liquored up enough to start pounding the piss out of each other.

"Just to remind you," McCluskey said, "these boys haven't been told exactly what we're after. They're a good bunch, now, but you know what offshore hands are like once they get to drinkin'. If I told them they were goin' on a treasure hunt that might make 'em rich, they'd blab it all over New Orleans. Right now, all they know is that this is some kind of survey-and-salvage job." He winked. "Safer that way."

Ben glanced dubiously at his old colleague, and the two of them stepped through the doors into the little tavern's seedy interior. They paused near a dilapidated pool table, its chalky green cloth ripped by innumerable miscues, letting their eyes get accustomed to the dimness.

A little knot of patrons had collected at the far end of the long marble bar, encircling what appeared to be two gargantuan escapees from the World Wrestling

Federation—twins, by the look of them, both clad in coveralls and Peterbilt baseball hats, wispy blond hair sticking down around their ears like straw. One lounged back on a barstool, a beer in his hand. The other was on his feet, arms at his sides. Ben put the standing twin at six-seven or six-eight, well in excess of three hundred pounds.

Confronting the erect giant was a dark, swarthy, perfectly-proportioned midget, bouncing on his toes like a windup toy.

Ben blinked and looked again. It wasn't a midget, just a man who happened to be somewhere in the vicinity of five feet two inches tall. And he was fit, the muscles of a bodybuilder bulging against his white T-shirt. It was only the relative size of the two hulking redneck brothers that had made him appear even smaller than he actually was.

Whatever he lacked in stature, he made up for in feistiness, like a Yorkshire terrier yapping back a Great Dane.

"You owe me twenty doll*air*!" the musclebound little bantamweight was saying. "Remit, oaf, *immediatement!*" The accent, Ben noted, was not New Orleans Cajun, but Parisian French. Then recognition dawned and he smiled. *LeRenard.*

"Hell," the redneck grunted. He pronounced it *hail*. "Ah ain't payin' you doodly-squat for that arm-wrassle.

You cheated." He rubbed his massive upper arm. "Musta snuck yer other hand under the table, got leverage on me."

The Frenchman rolled his eyes. "Do you delay me further, *imbecile?* Pay what you owe!"

The sitting brother stirred on his barstool. "Dang. Ah think that little French poodle just insulted you, Vern."

Vern considered for a moment, a blank look on his face. "Think so, Earl?"

"Damn straight."

The redneck chewed his cud for a moment, slack-jawed, then arrived at a conclusion. "Well then, Ah guess Ah'll just have to open up a can o' whup-ass on him." He swung ponderously, his ham-like fist orbiting toward the Frenchman's head.

The bantamweight ducked easily and stepped in. Something snapped out from his shoulder in a blur.

Pop.

Vern's head rocked back on his shoulders, his nose stinging from its sudden encounter with the little Frenchman's knuckles.

"Aha, villain!" the pint-sized Schwarzenegger said. "You attack me? I must repulse you, no?"

Looking confused, Vern rubbed his nose, blinking.

"Waitin' on the whup-ass here, Vern," Earl said.

"Right, right," the big man muttered, and lunged at his opponent with all the agility of a lactating Holstein. The little Frenchman dodged under his grappling arms and hit him twice as he went by. *Pop. Pop.*

"So, clod," he declared. "Will you desist and pay? Or must I thrash you further?"

Vern grimaced and pressed a hand to the ear that was rapidly turning the same angry crimson as his nose. "Can't you stay still?" he complained. A ripple of laughter came from the watching men.

The Frenchman continued to bounce on his toes, rolling his fists in the air. "But of course I can, oaf. Are you brainless? What a question!"

"Then why don't you stay in one place, dang it?"

The little man stopped bouncing. "Because then you would hit me," he explained carefully.

"Ohhhh," Vern said.

The Frenchman rolled his eyes and began to float and feint again. *"Et maintenant*—you will calm yourself and remit the twenty, *n'est-ce pas?"*

"The hail Ah will," Vern rumbled, and started forward.

The bantamweight backpedaled. *"Sacré bleu!* The beast persists in its folly. *Eh bien!* Let the thrashing continue."

He bobbed just out of reach as Vern, looking very much like a human landslide, pursued him through the little ring of men and across the room, swiping at him with his massive arms. Ben and McCluskey glanced at each other as the combatants neared the opposite side of the pool table, stepping back in anticipation of the impact—and then the little Frenchman abruptly dropped from view.

A split second later, he back somersaulted out from beneath the table and sprang to his feet beside the two divers.

"Allô, Eugene!" he said, grinning. *"Et toi aussi,* Ben." He let out a little snort of laughter as Vern stumbled, lost his balance, and did a face plant on the torn green velvet of the pool table.

"Hey there, Pierre," Ben replied. "Long time no see." The corners of his mouth lifted in an amused smile. "Busy?"

"Not for long, *tabarnac!"* the little man assured him. "A few minutes more to dispatch this ox, and we will have a cognac or two, eh?"

"I've got a better idea," McCluskey said. "Why don't you and *Vern"*—he shot a look at the giant resting on his elbows on the tabletop—"bury the hatchet right now—since you're going to be working together for at least the next three weeks—and we'll *all* go have a drink?"

"Eh?" The Frenchman lowered his fists and ceased bouncing. "You know this brontosaurus?"

McCluskey grinned. "Pierre LeRenard, shake hands with one of the men you're going to be sharing a sat pot with. This is Vern Pickins. His brother Earl is sitting over there on that barstool."

"Non," LeRenard said, appalled. *"C'est ne pas possible!* I must be confined and pressurized with this simian person? The bone of his head will not fit through the main hatch of the saturation chamber."

Ben was unable to stifle a laugh. The little Frenchman, an old acquaintance from the North Sea, was a real card—a metric ton of physical energy and sardonic intelligence in a hundred and thirty-pound package.

He looked down at Vern. The big man was grinning gap-toothed at his pint-sized antagonist. "Won't be able to skedaddle away from me so easy in there, will yuh?" he declared.

LeRenard smiled in return. *"Attention, mon ami.* If necessary, I will perpetrate a batterment upon your brain case that will put you to sleep *tout de suite! Tu comprends?"*

"All right, all right," McCluskey interrupted, walking around the pool table with his arms outspread. "Playtime's over. Let's all sit down at this table over here and have us a serious chat. Okay? Or don't you guys want to make any money this season?" He gave LeRenard a mock glare as he ushered Vern across the barroom.

"I'll get a couple of pitchers," Ben said, chuckling.

"Ask that saucy *coquette* behind the bar for Pierre's bottle of cognac," LeRenard called, eyeing Vern as McCluskey herded them both toward a corner table. "I must fortify myself with something other than the pisswater draft you Americans drink." His gaze shifted to Earl, lumbering through the little ring of onlookers to rejoin his brother.

Ben smiled, nodded, and headed for the bar, pulling his wallet from the rear pocket of his jeans. The female bartender sauntered down to meet him, one hand on her hip, giving him the high-speed once over. *Not bad*, she thought. Six feet of hard muscle, arms and hands veined and scarred by heavy work. Skin burned a permanent brown by constant exposure to the sun, a commercial diver's tattoo on the right forearm. Long-ish auburn hair bleached by salt water, a few streaks of gray at the temples. Steady gray-green eyes with deep crow's feet radiating from their outer corners. An odd, lopsided smile—as if its owner was perpetually amused by the world around him. Clean work shirt, jeans, and boots. She ran a hand back through her bleached blond hair, arched her back a little so that her breasts pressed against her sleeveless black T-shirt, and gave him her best lazy smile.

"Can I getcha somethin', baby?" Her accent was pure East Texas trailer park.

Ben set a boot on the bar's brass foot rail and regarded her. The bartender was a Bourbon Street classic—thirty-two or thirty-three, with the slender body and too-large, clearly-fake breasts of an ex-stripper, topped by a plain, hard, unlovely face. Limp colorless hair in a shaggy pixie cut. Too much makeup, bags under her eyes, and puckered wrinkles around her mouth from sucking on cigarettes every waking hour. Lurid blue biker tattoos staining both arms from shoulder to wrist. The phrase "rode hard and hung up wet" came to mind. She looked fifty. A spent fifty.

Ben smiled and pointed at the Budweiser tap. "Two pitchers of Bud."

The woman cocked a hip and wrinkled her pug nose at him. "Say please."

He extracted a twenty from his wallet and dropped it on the scarred marble counter. "Please." Looking out into the street, he let his smile fade.

The bartender's face fell a little as she began to pull down the two pitchers of draft. But when she set the beer order in front of Ben, she tried again. Leaning forward so that the loose-necked T-shirt revealed her torso from collarbone to navel, she batted her mascara-caked eyes at him. "Izzere anything else you need, honey?" she drawled. "Anything at all?"

Ben was sure he could see the vulcanized seam of the silicone bag in her left breast through the skin. *Scary*. He smiled again. "Yeah, there is."

The woman brightened.

"Six draft cups." He pointed at the stack next to the taps. "And Pierre's bottle of cognac."

The bartender's puffy, painted face sagged in annoyance. She plucked a handful of plastic cups off the stack and banged them down next to the draft pitchers. A half-empty bottle of Courvoisier followed with an even louder bang. Then she inverted a small brandy snifter and clapped it over the bottle's cork. "Eight-fifty a jug for the beer," she snarled. "Seventeen bucks."

Ben nodded down at the twenty he'd dropped on bar top. "Keep it," he said, winking. Then he gathered up his order, turned, and made his way across the barroom.

"Eh, Ben," LeRenard cackled, grinning like a demonic imp, "that delicate angel behind the bar—I think you disappoint her, *mon ami!*"

Ben set the cognac in front of him. "I don't think so, Pierre. But if I did, I'll bet she gets over it before you can pull the cork out of that bottle." He smiled and glanced over his shoulder. "She'll be all right. She looks pretty tough to me."

"Ah, you must not talk about my next wife in such a way," LeRenard declared. "She does not know it yet, but tonight she will find herself in a condition of ecstatic swoon, courtesy of Pierre LeRenard!" He made a sweeping theatrical gesture with his right hand and puffed out his chest.

"Not if yer dick's as small as the rest of you," Vern muttered from across the table.

"Merde!" The little Frenchman half rose from his chair. "You have just signed your own death warrant, gorilla! On your feet, *tabarnac!* My sense of honor prevents me from thrashing a mental incompetent while he is seated!"

"Be mah pleasure—"

McCluskey slapped his open hand on the table. "Okay, *enough!* Pierre: you can thrash him later. Vern: just stay there and drink your beer. Jesus Christ, some of the best sat divers on either side of the Atlantic are sittin' right here, not a man younger than thirty-five, and you'd swear we were in a goddamn kindergarten! Now *shut up* for half a minute, willya?"

There was a brief silence.

"Ah never said a thing, Gene," Earl commented.

"He started it, Gene," Vern followed up, pointing across the table at LeRenard.

"A lie!" the Frenchman retorted. "You are a poor loser, you mastodon, you!"

McCluskey put his head in his hands.

"Guys," Ben said, pouring draft into plastic cups and pushing them around the table, "give it a rest. You're gonna make Gene develop a brain tumor." He raised his own cup. "Cheers. Let's talk a little business."

Earl and Vern looked at each other, shrugged, and hoisted their beers. LeRenard held out his small snifter of cognac.

"A votre santé."

"Here's mud in yer eye, froggy."

The little Frenchman stiffened, but let it go.

McCluskey drained half his beer in three chugs and turned to the Pickins brothers. "You guys know Ben Gannon?"

"Think Ah seen 'im around a few times," Earl said. "An' Ah definitely heard of him." He extended a hand the size of a dinner plate. "How you doin'? Ah'm Earl. This here's mah brother Vern."

Ben shook with both of them, smiling. "Earl and Vern. Got it. Ben Gannon." He looked from one to the other. "You both divers?"

"Nope," Vern said. "Ah do the underwater stuff. Earl here's all topside—gas tech, compressor mechanic, equipment riggin'—if it's dive support; you name it, he does it."

"We bin a team like that since we was runnin' our own two-man divin' company up in Tennessee when we was sixteen," Earl explained. "Had a small compressor in the bed of this old Ford pickup, one beat-up Navy surplus hardhat, and about eighty feet of hose. We used to git hired to clean the day-bree out of sluice gates and intakes on inland dams. Vern went down; Ah stayed up and made sure the air kept comin'. We just bin workin' that way ever since, him in the water and me up top, 'cept offshore and with better gear."

Ben nodded. "I've done some inland dam work. Dangerous. You can get sucked into an intake or a crack in a New York second, and you'll never get out. Too much head pressure."

Vern chewed his lip thoughtfully. "You sho' coulda might," he said. "Got a boot sucked off once. Didn't think about it much at the time."

"Probably just as well."

McCluskey straightened up in his seat suddenly, looking past Ben toward the entrance of the bar. "Ah, there he is." He glanced at his watch. "About time. Dammit, that sonofabitch is always late."

Ben turned in his seat as McCluskey waved. "Hey, boy! Over here!"

The mid-twentyish man coming through the main doorway was bracketed by a pair of giggling off-duty Bourbon Street strippers, both clad in tank tops, short shorts, and blocky high-heeled sandals. Young enough that the street hadn't yet taken its toll on their looks, they shimmied and pouted at the patrons in the bar, reveling in their ability to attract male attention. The inevitable groundswell of hooting and whistling arose. The girls remained pressed up against the young man, whose well-muscled arms were locked around their shoulders, as they all moved further into the room. Ben caught a glimpse of the bartender, who was leaning back against the glass-washing machine with a half-sad, half-knowing expression on her face. *Enjoy your looks while you've got 'em, little sisters,* it said. *They don't last long in your line of work.*

The young man paused by the pool table, gave each girl a long open-mouthed kiss and a fondle, and sent them tittering and wiggling out the door with slaps on their behinds. Then he moved on toward the divers, the dim light from the ceiling lamps playing over his chiseled features.

"Oh, Jesus," Ben muttered to McCluskey under his breath. "Not the Golden Guido."

"Give him a chance," the old supervisor hissed back. "He ain't near as arrogant as he was a few years ago, and I owe his daddy a favor. He needs to be on this project with us. I'll tell you all about it later."

Ben grimaced into his beer and took a long sip. "If you say so, Gene."

The young man stalked up to the table and struck a pose, spreading his arms wide. "Well, here I am,

29

Gene!" he announced, grinning broadly. "Now the party can start, eh?"

McCluskey's smile was slightly pained. "Gentlemen, this is our fourth sat diver: Chris Toricelli. His dad's Gus Toricelli of Toricelli Offshore Diving Services. I know you've all heard of *him*." There were nods around the table. In the small world of deepwater commercial diving, the senior Toricelli—like fellow pioneering divers Swede Momsen and Edwin Link— was a legend. "Chris, meet Pierre LeRenard, Vern and Earl Pickens. You already know Ben."

"LeRenard, Pickens, and Pickens," the young man recited, pointing at each in turn. "Easy enough. Hey, Gannon. Howya been?"

Ben nodded patiently. "Good, Chris." One of the things he found hardest to take about Christian Toricelli, along with his self-satisfied, rich-kid smirk, was his habit of referring to everyone by their last name, regardless of their age or experience . . . unless it was someone in authority, in which case he would presume an immediate familiarity and use only the person's given name. It was a way to ingratiate and condescend at the same time, and it always ground on Ben's nerves. Simply put, the kid was an arrogant, transparent kiss-ass. He got away with it because he was Gus Toricelli's son, could be charming and funny when it suited him, and had been blessed with absolutely striking good looks, of which he was quite vain.

Ben looked him over, standing at the end of the table and lifting the beer Vern had passed him to his lips. He wasn't more than twenty-five or twenty-six, but due to an early start in his father's company, already had a half-dozen offshore commercial diving seasons under his belt. And because he'd been the boss's son, he hadn't had to do the two years of hard grunt labor as a topside tender—lugging around hoses, welding cables, gas cylinders, compressors, and an infinite assortment of related equipment—that was *de rigueur* for most commercial divers in the Gulf of Mexico: the tough, dues-paying part of the career.

There was a crash and a breathless curse as some biker chick who'd just entered the bar with her boyfriend walked straight into a table, too absorbed in staring at Chris to watch where she was going. The boyfriend, a Mr. Clean type with a bald pate, black goatee, massive arms, and club colors adorning the back of his sleeveless denim jacket, demonstrated his annoyance by cuffing her sharply on the side of the head and yanking her along behind him, spitting and writhing, to the far end of the bar. Ben shook his head and sipped slowly at his beer. For as long as he'd known Chris Toricelli, women tended to act like befuddled hens whenever they laid eyes on him.

The kid looked like a combination of Brad Pitt and Fabio, complete with Hollywood-perfect tan, weight-room physique, and flowing blonde locks. His face was strong-featured yet boyish, his smile white-toothed and dazzling. Physically, there was little about him for most females not to like, and Chris knew it. He went through girlfriends and one-night stands like a sinus sufferer going through Kleenex.

McCluskey cleared his throat. "All right. Grab a chair, Chris. Let me lay a few things out for everyone. The deal's on. Like I told you all, this is a deep salvage job in the western Caribbean. We're mobing up an old SeaTrek saturation system and putting it on a four-point anchor barge. There's also gonna be a small ROV aboard, a launching system to deploy it, and the opera-tor's control van."

Earl groaned. "Those things are a pain in the ass. They're always breakin' down, snappin' their tethers, driftin' off somewhere. You spend half yer time fixin' 'em or tryin' to recover 'em when they eck-scape."

"Not this one," McCluskey said. "We're going with a new guy out of Houston, a real tech-head. Name's Gerald Posey. He used to work in Silicon Valley doing black projects for the Department of Defense. When he left DOD work, he formed a one-man company based around a new type of ROV he'd designed. Built it in his garage, believe it or not. We're gettin' him cheap because he wants to use this salvage job to prove to the oil companies that his machine can work deeper, faster, and more reliably than any of the older models."

"What's differ'nt about it?" Earl asked.

McCluskey went on. "Well, for one, it doesn't have a tether. No cable umbilical attachin' it to the surface."

"Nawww," Earl responded, incredulous.

Ben raised an eyebrow. "How does it send data back to the control van, Gene? How does it get power for lights, propulsion?

"Posey tells me it's all microwave controlled. Satellite frequency stuff. It's related to the same technology the DOD uses to guide missiles, smart bombs—that kind of thing. The servos and receivers are so reliable now that he can fly this ROV all through the water column with virtually no hardware failures. And batteries have gotten so sophisticated that it can power itself independently for nearly twelve hours. It has onboard video cameras, lights—the usual array of equipment. The images get beamed back up to the control van, just like satellite TV."

"Incroyable," Pierre said. "These machines—one day I think they do us out of a job, eh?"

McCluskey smiled. "Maybe some day, but not yet." He swallowed some beer. "Anyway, Gerald's gonna have his control van, ROV, and launching system trucked over from Houston tomorrow. All we need to do is find space on the barge for his equipment and weld it down."

"Gerald," Chris remarked. "I hate that name. Reminds me of a wimpy kid I used to beat up in grade school."

The childish remark hung in the air for several long seconds, until Ben picked up one of the draft pitchers and refilled his cup. "What about sat techs, Gene? You mentioned to me earlier that you were looking for one more."

"Yeah," McCluskey replied. "I can't really think of anyone else besides Earl who's available. A lot of the old hands have moved into front office work, and a good number have moved into ROV divisions. There just isn't that much decent sat work in the Gulf lately."

Ben thought for a moment. "Well, how about Sass?"

McCluskey brightened. "You think she'd do it?"

"I could ask her."

The old diving supervisor nodded. "Boy, that'd be great. I remember you got her hired on that six hundred-foot sat for Titan Diving out of Corpus Christi a few years back. She spent the whole summer lookin' at her old man through a little round window." He grinned. "Your gal sure learned the ropes, though. Turned into a great little sat tech, from what I heard."

"She can do the job, Gene," Ben said. "A few days to study up on the new tables and procedures, and get

34

familiarized with this old SeaTrek system, and she'll be ready to trade shifts with you and Earl in the gas shack. She's qualified, and has the job log to prove it."

"And Ben's lady would improve the scenery on board the barge, *n'est-ce pas?"* Pierre chimed in, winking at him. "Especially since part of the crew consists of knuckle-dragging Neanderthals." He shifted his gaze pointedly in Vern's direction.

"An' midgets," Vern grumbled. "Don't ferget midgets."

"How about this old SeaTrek sat system, Gene?" Ben asked quickly. "What model is it, and what year?"

"It's the old six-man flyaway design," McCluskey said. "The SeaTrek 1200. You know the one. It has the diving bell that rotates ninety degrees in its A-frame crane to lock onto the transfer lock of the sat pot. It was built in 1983."

"Ahhh," Ben groaned, rubbing his forehead. "That thing. The one they squashed down so it would fit into a C-130 cargo plane without taking up too much room."

"You got it."

"Christ, Gene," Ben said. "Living in that damn pot's like living in a sewer pipe, even with three other guys instead of five. Smallest, tightest quarters ever designed for sat work."

McCluskey shrugged. "The price was right. It was sittin' in the weeds in an equipment yard on the

Atchafalaya River down in Morgan City, rusting away. We bought it, had it reconditioned, and presto!"

"You bought an entire SeaTrek sat system?" Ben repeated. "How'd you afford it?"

"Gomez. He gave me a certified check to cover the purchase, no questions asked. And another one to pay for the reconditioning." McCluskey grinned. "You see? These people put their money where their mouth is. Okay, so it's not top-shelf, brand-new. But it's a good system and it'll do the job. Every through-hull was re-tapped and tested. Every fitting, hose, O-ring, and gauge was replaced. We even painted the pot and bell a real pretty international goddamned-orange. Okay?" McCluskey was getting wound up, his finger tapping on the tabletop.

Ben smiled at him. "Okay, Gene."

He watched as the old oilfield supervisor settled back and reached for his beer. McCluskey was doing a decent job of keeping his game face on, but it was apparent that just beneath the surface, he was fairly boiling with nervous excitement. And why not, Ben thought. After forty-plus years of offshore construction work, here was a chance for him to go out with one phenomenal career-capping payday. Hit the mother lode, win the lottery. Retire to the beaches of Aruba, as he always liked to say, and teach vacationing coeds in itty-bitty bikinis how to windsurf.

36

"So look," McCluskey said, wiping beer foam from his mouth with the back of his hand, "I need a final commitment from all you guys. Are you in? You need to guarantee me a minimum of four weeks on this barge, pullin' twenty-four hour days if I ask you to, in sat or working topside. What I'm guaranteeing you is five grand per man for your time, whether we locate the salvage target or not, and five percent—also per man—of the value of anything we recover. Decision time, boys."

"Can't you tell us a little more about what we're looking for, Gene?" Chris prodded.

"All I can tell you now is what I told you over the phone," McCluskey said stubbornly. "We're attempting to pinpoint the location of a small vessel that was lost in a storm while carrying export goods from Central America, and recover as much of the cargo as possible."

Chris grinned. "Sounds like a sunken drug boat," he said. "Fulla cocaine! Is that what it is, Gene?"

"No," McCluskey growled. He gave Chris a hard look, then turned to LeRenard. "Pierre?"

The little Frenchman tipped his brandy snifter. *"Mais certainement.* You have Pierre LeRenard for four weeks, more if need be."

"Thanks. Chris?"

"Why not?" The young man shook back his blonde curls and stretched his tanned arms over his head, causing the biker chick at the stand-up bar to choke on her gin fizz. "Sounds like a blast. What the fuck—at least I'll get some decent sun down there."

McCluskey smiled as if trying to swallow a thistle and nodded. "Appreciate it. Earl? Vern?"

The two giant brothers shrugged as one. "Sure, Gene, we're in," Vern said. "Cain't leave you stuck down in the lower Caribbean with only two-and-a-half divers." He grinned happily at Pierre, who stared daggers at him in return.

Finally, McCluskey turned to Ben. "Well, old buddy, how about it?" The genial expression he always cultivated looked slightly frozen. One fingertip vibrated on the side of his draft cup.

Ben looked at the faces around the table. Not the perfect crew, but then, there was no such thing. Personalities aside, every man knew his business, he was sure of that. LeRenard and Toricelli he'd worked with. The little Frenchman was a diving fiend, absolutely first-rate in the water, under any conditions. Chris was nearly as good, athletic and strong, if a little lacking in judgement and maturity. Kept in hand, he was quite reliable. And Vern, although he'd take up half the space in the cramped sat pot and bell, seemed steady and experienced, as did Earl. If they were good enough for Gene, they were good enough for him.

Here we go again.

Ben held out his hand. "Okay," he said. "Count me in. And I'll talk to Sass tonight."

Chapter Two

"The arrangements are complete," Gomez said, speaking toward the intercom telephone on top of the immense mahogany desk that was the centerpiece of his lavishly furnished office. He walked across the room, loosening his tie and removing his suit coat—charcoal-gray silk today—as he went. Draping it carefully over the back of a large leather armchair, he turned to the ornate teak-and-crystal service bar that stood along one wall beneath an original painting by Goya.

The voice that came out of the telephone speaker was soft and precise, with an almost musical lilt. In pitch and articulation, it occupied an indeterminate zone between male and female. "Good. McCluskey and his crew will be leaving New Orleans presently, I take it?"

Gomez took an ice cube from a cut-crystal bucket with a pair of silver tongs and placed it in a heavy rocks glass. "Probably within three days, if the equipment mobilization goes smoothly. Barring mechanical problems with the tug, there shouldn't be any delays." He poured two fingers of Cardhu single malt over the ice. "Gannon's common-law wife agreed at the last minute to join the crew as a saturation technician, completing the roster of necessary personnel. I got the word this morning."

"Gannon?" The lilting voice paused. "Ah, yes: the senior diver who signed on yesterday afternoon." Another pause. "His *wife* also works in the oilfield industry?"

Gomez strolled back across the expensive Turkish rug to his desk, savoring the scotch. "No. But apparently she's qualified to assist in the operation of a saturation diving unit. Gannon's had her out on several diving jobs as a topside freelancer over the years, McCluskey tells me. Her full-time occupation is running a small marina she inherited from her father over on the Panhandle of Florida. She and Gannon both live there."

"How fascinating." The voice sounded bored. "I imagine she's a real mountain woman, complete with a cleft palate and hair on the backs of her hands."

Gomez smiled over the rim of his glass, gazing out through the large picture window behind his desk at the opposite bank of the Mississippi River. Across from glitzy downtown New Orleans, the tough, hardscrabble waterfront of Algiers, with its aging warehouses and industrial dry-docks, glimmered gray-black and rusty in the midday sun. "I don't know about that, Alberto. I met Gannon face to face, and he didn't seem like the kind of man who'd have a female companion of that description."

"You never can tell about these blue-collar primitives," the voice went on, becoming petulant. "Ah, well: it's of no consequence. As long as the diving operation can be conducted successfully, we really don't care what they look like."

Sure you don't, the lawyer thought. But what he said aloud was: "I think you can rest assured the crew is capable."

"Just out of curiosity, what was the woman offered to join?"

Gomez rolled scotch around his tongue and swallowed. "Five percent of the appraised salvage value, the same as the other secondary crew members."

The laugh that came out of the speaker was short and sharp, very high-pitched. It startled the lawyer, as it always did. The sound wasn't quite canny. *"HAAH! That would make an even fifty percent we're giving away in total, wouldn't it?"*

Annoyed at having his composure shaken, Gomez took a few seconds to answer. "So they think."

Once again: *"HAAH!"*

The lawyer rubbed the back of his neck, where the hair was prickling, and stared across the lazily swirling surface of the Big Muddy. On the bow of a huge petroleum barge tied up alongside one of the industrial docks, a shower of blue sparks erupted as a welder struck an arc. Gomez swallowed a large mouthful of scotch. Strange how such a cold light could come from a heat source so intense that it liquefied steel . . .

"You're still there, aren't you, counselor?"

How had he gotten involved with these people? Oh, yes . . . *the money.* The money, the money . . .

He cleared his throat. "Of course, Alberto. I'm sorry. Go ahead."

The voice had regained its soft precision. "The receipts for the last quarter. You were given instructions regarding distribution of funds."

"I wish you wouldn't bring up these matters over the phone."

"Why not?"

The lawyer gritted his teeth. "Because of the risk of surveillance, as I've already explained to you. Electronic eyes and ears are everywhere these days."

"And we have explained to *you*, counselor, that we wished to be able to speak freely to our primary lawyer via telephone. Which is why we gave you a quarter of a million dollars to put a foolproof scrambler on this satcom line. That was the figure you quoted us, as I recall. I'm *sure* it wasn't inflated. Now: I was speaking of distribution of funds."

"Yes, yes." Gomez set his glass down on the desk. "Two-thirds has been dispersed through our shell corporations in Houston, Miami, and the Virgin Islands.

One third is in cash—three point four million. I'll be flying it down to you in the Beechcraft this weekend."

"I'll meet you at the property in Grand Cayman," the voice said. "We have a few things to discuss. A few accounting discrepancies, among others."

The freezing sensation began at the base of Gomez's skull and rapidly spread over the top of his head. "Discrepancies? I'm not aware of any."

"Odd." The voice was very soft now. "My sister and I are. No doubt they are the result of some small bookkeeping oversight. I'm sure you'll be able to explain it."

The freezing sensation was traveling down Gomez's spine. He picked up his empty glass and headed for the Cardhu bottle. "How is your sister?" he asked, barely managing not to stammer.

"Grizelda is . . . fine," the voice said. "Energetic and focused, as always." Once more, the sharp, neurotic chirp of a laugh burst out of the desk speaker, causing Gomez to bobble his scotch glass and drop it on the imported Turkish carpet. *"HAAH!* She's out taking a little exercise, the dear girl."

*****

The young man had been running for more than an hour, barefoot. Not quite seventeen, he was mature for his age: lithe and well-proportioned, with the smooth musculature of the newly adult male. Naked but for a pair of cheap athletic shorts, his coppery-brown skin was slick with sweat and peppered with fragments of jungle foliage. His face, high-cheekboned and rather pretty, revealed the strong Arawak bloodline common to peoples inhabiting the western rim of the Caribbean Sea. The shoulder-length hair that had been cut into a rough bang just above his brows was straight and jet-black, plastered to his forehead with sweat. Below the bang, his dark, darting eyes were bright with fear.

Razor-edged sawgrass slashed at his legs, drawing blood, as he fled along the cliff-top trail that followed the north coast of the little island. Two hundred feet below, on his right side, the rolling swells of the Caribbean churned against jagged rocks at the base of the precipice. Far off in the distance, across the whitecap-dotted expanse of indigo-blue water, two more islands sat on the horizon, dark lumps against the hazy sky. The one on the right was his home, the place where he had been born and dwelt his entire life.

The dense jungle that covered most of the island had opened into a large clearing at the highest section of the cliff, the trees beaten back from the edge by direct exposure to seasonal hurricane winds. The youth paused, gasping for air, at a small cairn of boulders about three-quarters of the way across the open space, the sawgrass around him undulating in the brisk sea breeze. Leaning on the rock, his entire body trembling uncontrollably, he stared back the way he had come.

The wind moaned over the top of the cliff, its pitch rising and falling. On the far side of the clearing, the heavy jungle foliage formed a dancing green wall—a moving mosaic of leaves, vines, and shadows. A line of drool fell from the young man's lower lip as he sucked in great racking draughts of air. Unmindful of it, he continued to scan the jungle with wild, desperate eyes.

He thought he heard a sound above the keening wind and rustling sawgrass—a deep giggle that seemed to carry over all natural noises. As if caught in a trance, he began to shake his head back and forth, his foam-flecked lips working wordlessly . . .

Suddenly, with a violent thrash, the foliage on the far side of the clearing parted. A tall figure burst into view; charging out of the jungle at a dead run, arms and legs pumping. Sunlight flashed off the wickedly-hooked blades of the long knives the runner was carrying, dagger-fashion, in either hand.

The youth screamed and flung himself away from the rock cairn and down the trail, stumbling in his panic. A hundred yards behind him, his pursuer—clad only in a black tank top, abbreviated track shorts, and white running shoes—let out another low, giggling laugh and began to close the distance.

The trail was descending steeply now. Sobbing with fear, the young man plunged into the jungle once more, broad leaves whipping across his face and chest. Behind him, the faint, rapid pounding of rubber soles on hard ground seemed to grow louder. The remaining adrenaline in his body surged, and for several minutes, he fairly flew down the increasingly rocky and treacherous grade.

The fishing cave. If only he could get there, he might be safe. It had been a family secret for generations, the place where his father and grandfather had come to fish when the reefs around their home island were unproductive. No one else knew about it—the entrance was too small, too well-concealed.

The trail had leveled off again, and he was running pell-mell along the very lip of a thirty-foot cliff that plunged into water of the deepest azure blue. Streamers of sizzling white foam laced the briny surface, twisting and whirling, as swell after swell rolled in to surge up the rock face. The wind moaned through the scattered boulders along the cliff-top—a hollow, lonely sound.

The marker rock! The young man halted once more beside a massive upright pillar of fossilized coral, leaning on it heavily, his legs nearly collapsing under him. His bare feet were two bloody lumps, cut to shreds during the mad scramble down the rocky trail from the upper clearing. Each breath he took went into his burning lungs with an audible screech. Head pounding, he tried to blink the stinging sweat out of his eyes, to get his bearings.

He had to move. He couldn't let her see where he had gone. She would be coming down the trail any moment now, those terrible twin knives—a metal fang strapped onto each hand—glinting in the sun.

Stepping around to the inland side of the coral pillar, he leaned back against the rough surface, his chest heaving. When he nestled the base of his skull into a small recess in the rock and looked straight ahead, the pointed tops of three large boulders, sitting in the jungle at varying distances, lined up with one another. Behind the furthermost boulder, on a steep, thickly-foliated slope, was a small slab of limestone, indistinguishable from other similar formations around it.

Carefully, the young man moved his head out of the depression in the coral pillar. This was the only way: you had to line up the boulders, then keep your eyes trained on the correct spot as you approached. Something about the landscape, some trick of terrain and geometry, made the slab that concealed the tiny cave entrance virtually impossible to find once you'd lost sight of it.

There was no more time to waste. He started forward, forcing himself to look at the tiny gray blotch of limestone and not back up the trail where—

A deep giggle sounded in his left ear, very close.

Before he could react, a whipcord-muscled arm, deeply bronzed, snaked around the coral pillar and slammed against his sternum. A knife blade, cold and hard, went across his windpipe, its point pricking the skin near his jugular vein. The breath went out of him in a despairing gasp, and he sagged back, paralyzed, against the rough stone.

She stepped out slowly from behind the pillar, keeping the knife across his throat at arm's length. Five feet ten inches of red-brown muscle, sharply defined and glistening with a light sheen of perspiration. A body more masculine than feminine—narrow-hipped and wide-shouldered. Long legs and arms laced with veins and muscle striations. A short, V-shaped torso, large breasts flattened under the black athletic tank top. Turtle-shell abdominals rippling down into the black runner's thong, the cut of which fully exposed tanned, muscular buttocks.

The young man's eyes fluttered. The face staring into his was broad and flat, with high cheekbones and a pug-like, slightly twisted nose. The lips below the nose were lush and full, the teeth behind them large, white, and protruding. Beneath plucked, arching brows, eyes like two pellets of black obsidian gaped at him with an alert, almost reptilian concentration. The thick, red-hennaed hair was crew cut, military style, with the exception of one-foot-long tendril—like a cat's tail—at the base of the neck.

The woman's mouth opened as she moved around in front of the young man, her nostrils flaring. Her tongue appeared, curled upward, and licked a light residue of white powder off her upper lip. Very slowly, she brought her free hand up to her face. The long, hook-bladed knife she wielded appeared to have a special grip—a combination of molded plastic, finger-less leather glove, and buckle-down straps that secured the weapon to her palm and made it impossible to drop.

Using her thumb, she slid back a tiny cover on the butt of the knife haft, revealing a shallow recess filled with white powder. Lifting it to her left nostril, she paused to grin, staring at the youth, and abruptly sniffed hard. A little explosion of white dust coated the rim of her nostril and part of her upper lip. Her eyes rolled up in her head as she held her breath, swallowing convulsively.

The young man watched her, horrified, feeling the knife blade across his Adam's apple tremble. The point dug into his skin, drawing blood. When he tried to lean away, the pressure instantly increased.

"Aaaghaaaghaaaaaagh," the woman said, grimacing and smacking her lips.

She straightened up, breathing hard, and fixed her eyes on his again. Very slowly, she backed away a step, still holding the knife at arm's length as it left the young man's throat. His knees sagged, but he managed to brace himself against the rock and stay upright.

The woman's eyes were wide, unnaturally so, and her nostrils flared in time to her rapid breathing. She looked like a lioness about to feed.

"What's the matter, Fernando?" she cooed in Spanish. "Don't you like me anymore? After all the fun we've had over the past two days?" She lowered the knife and carefully inserted the tip of the hooked blade into the top of the young man's athletic shorts, just below his navel.

He was crying now, soundlessly shaking his head, his saliva-flecked lips trembling.

The woman leaned in close to him, almost nose to nose. "That's too bad, pretty, pretty boy," she whispered, gently turning the flat of the blade against the smooth, tanned skin of his lower abdomen. "Grizelda likes *you.*"

She giggled once, deep in her throat, and ripped the knife downward.

*****

It was late in the afternoon when Gomez returned to his downtown New Orleans office. Once more, he headed straight for the Cardhu bottle, pouring a double and banging most of it back in one swallow. He topped the glass up, then crossed the room to the plush black-leather swivel chair behind his desk and sat down.

Rotating the chair so that it faced out the window, he gazed again across the river at Algiers. There was a full team of welders working on the docked petroleum barge now, six icy-hot pinpoints of light shedding incandescent showers of blue sparks against the lengthening shadows. The welders and their helpers moved about the deck of the great rusty vessel like a small troop of dirty, coverall-clad monkeys.

An honest day's work for an honest man's wage. Work to live and live to work. Build an entire life on the income of a blue-collar rod-burner. Gomez swallowed another mouthful of his expensive single-malt scotch. The poor fools.

That was no way to get rich.

It was only a way to live in perpetual debt to the large corporate interests that controlled—owned—America. The car companies. The mortgage companies. The insurance companies. The banks. The credit card companies. Not to mention the tax man. Economic indentured servitude, self-inflicted by choosing to live on a pay scale that was somehow always just *under* the amount needed not merely to survive, but get ahead.

If you wanted to drive a burgundy-and-gold, twelve-cylinder E-type Jaguar—like the one he had parked in the underground garage twenty-two floors beneath his river-view office; if you wanted to look down from the top of the ivory tower instead of up from the street at its tightly-closed, smoked-glass windows; if you wanted to sip imported single-malt scotch instead of guzzle warm Miller-fucking-Light by the keg in some rat-hole shipyard-district roadhouse—you had to take a few chances in life.

Which was why he'd jumped at the opportunity to launder Alberto and Grizelda Ramos's drug money for them, for an absolutely breathtaking fee. But not as breathtaking as the amount he'd managed to skim off their quarterly profits by bouncing money back and forth between the numerous shell corporations he'd set up in offshore locations from Panama to Grand Cayman to Bermuda to the Isle of Man.

And now Alberto and his lunatic sister suspected him. There wasn't a doubt in his mind. And once the Ramoses had decided you'd crossed them, you had a *serious* fucking security problem.

He swiveled the chair around to face the desk again and stared at the small metal suitcase he'd set down next to the door upon entering the office. Seven hundred and seventy-five thousand dollars. A quick skim of what *he'd* skimmed—and might have to very rapidly put back into the correct accounts, depending upon how the meeting with Alberto went in Grand

Cayman. One thing he was fairly sure of: they wouldn't whack him until they'd sorted out where all their money was—they needed him to tell them that.

He smiled at the suitcase over the rim of his glass. A little fast-getaway cash, if the shit really hit the fan. He could access the two million or so he had stashed in private accounts later, at his leisure. Not the fortune he'd recently embezzled from the Ramoses, but what the fuck—sometimes you had to know when to fold your hand, take what you'd already won, and walk away. If he dumped the majority of what he'd stolen back into their corporate accounts, then made himself scarce until they cooled off, it was unlikely that they'd go to the trouble of hunting him down. They might even think they'd misjudged him; scared him into hiding without justification.

Not that the Ramoses ever needed any.

He drained the scotch and set the glass down on the desktop. There was a little more packing to do before he made the trip to Grand Cayman. Rising from his chair, he walked over to the large Goya on the wall above the bar.

He flicked a catch behind the right edge of the gilt frame and pulled. The painting swung out on hinges, revealing a large circular wall safe. Rapidly, Gomez spun the lock dial, listening to the tumblers click. Then he manipulated the latch and pulled the thick steel door open.

The safe was stuffed full of currency, stacks of old bills in denominations of twenty, fifty, and one hundred. Street cash, direct from the dealers. The lawyer breathed in deeply. The heady aroma of paper money was cut by the faint tang of cocaine. Traces of the drug were visible on several of the bills.

Gomez began to remove the bundles from the safe and place them on the service bar, shaking his head. He'd been in a couple of coke dens in his time, the dealers weighing, cutting, and packaging the white powder on tables that were stacked high with cash. This while constantly sampling the merchandise and making a general mess of everything. No wonder the money they used to buy bulk product from the Ramoses always had that smell. It was amazing that most of them could manage to find the floor when they had to pass out, much less count grams and dollars.

It took Gomez five minutes to empty the safe, building a pile of grubby bills two feet high on the service bar. When he was done, he closed the steel door, swung the painting back into place, and stepped over to a mahogany armoire in the corner of the room. Opening it, he pulled out a second metal valise, twice the size of the one near the office entrance, and propped it open on the Turkish rug.

Pocket money for a pair of psychos, he thought, and began to layer the bundles of old cash inside the suitcase.

*****

The stiff Caribbean wind had subsided to a mere breeze by early evening, wafting the humid fragrance of salt water and tropical flowers across the swimming-pool terrace of the *hacienda*-style house. Built into the hillside that overlooked the island's best small lagoon, it provided a commanding view of the north and south coasts, as well as routinely spectacular sunsets. With the exception of a dock at the head of the lagoon, it and several outbuildings were the only manmade structures on the island.

Alberto Ramos stood near the knee-high rock wall that bordered the terrace, sipping a pink gin cocktail and taking in the last rays of the sun as it dropped below the western horizon; a shimmering copper fireball in a cool magenta sea. About thirty-five years of age, dark-haired and slender, his body had a round-shouldered softness to it that suggested a near-total lack of physical exertion. Clad only in a high-cut black bathing suit and short, zebra-striped pool kimono, he stood lazily—arms folded and swaybacked. Gut out and one hip cocked sideways. His face matched his physique: it was puffy, blandly handsome, with a permanent cast of fey dissipation.

He didn't turn as Grizelda Ramos emerged from the hibiscus bushes at the far end of the terrace and padded silently up behind him, sweaty and disheveled, breathing deeply. The twin knives were still strapped to her hands.

"Pooh," Alberto said, wrinkling his fine nose, "you smell like some sort of farm animal."

Grizelda didn't reply, merely stared over his shoulder at the last remaining sliver of setting sun.

"The pool is right at seventy-eight degrees," he went on. "The perfect temperature for a dip. I was just in myself." He turned and smiled. "Then we'll eat. I've made a parrotfish soufflé from some of the specimens you speared this morning."

"Mmmm." Grizelda's eyes remained fixed on the glowing horizon. "You made it, or Javier did?"

"Well, of course, I directed *him* to make it," Alberto said, looking put out. "You don't expect me to slop around in the kitchen like some kind of servant, do you?"

His sister's obsidian eyes flickered, then drew away from the sunset to fasten onto his. "No, I don't," she said softly, smiling. "You never get your hands dirty, do you, little brother?"

Alberto's gaze went up and down her, over the taut muscles of her arms, belly, and thighs, glistening with perspiration in the dying light. "No, big sister," he countered, returning her sardonic smile, "that's your department." He reached out a languid finger and brushed away one of the numerous flecks of blood that had spattered the right side of her face and neck.

Without comment, Grizelda began to unbuckle the straps that held the right-hand knife to her palm. The blades of both weapons were dark with half-dried gore. Working her hand free, she let the knife fall to the flagstones with a metallic clatter.

Alberto watched her, sipping his pink gin, as she tugged at the straps of the second knife, his eyes roving over the flexing muscles of her shoulders and biceps. He reached out again, gently, and touched her upper arm. The knife dropped free, joining its twin on the flagstones, and Grizelda regarded him with her flat, reptilian stare.

"Did you enjoy yourself?" Alberto inquired, stroking the slick, red-brown skin of her triceps.

"Mm-hmm," she grunted, deep in her throat. She crossed her arms over her chest and in one motion pulled off the black athletic tank top. Her heavy breasts wobbled free, round and high, punctuated by large, dark nipples.

58

Alberto sucked in his breath, stroking harder. "Are you tired?"

"Mm-hmm," she repeated, turning her back to him and facing the pool. Hooking her thumbs into the sides of her black running thong, she stripped it over her buttocks and down her long, muscular legs. "But I feel good," she said, stepping out of the tiny garment and leaving it crumpled on the flagstones.

Her brother gulped the last of his pink gin as she stalked toward the pool, erect and glistening, nude but for her white running shoes. There was a smear of blood—half a handprint—where her hip joined her left buttock. Alberto didn't give it a second thought as he moved after her, drinking in every curve, every rippling bulge, of her sculpted body.

Grizelda paused at the edge of the pool, bent down, and unlaced her shoes. Alberto halted, swallowing. She straightened up, toed them off her feet—then looked over her shoulder at him. Her lips twisted into something ugly resembling a smile.

Alberto smiled back, his eyes slightly glazed. "Do you think, later, we can—"

His sister let out a deep giggle, tensed her Amazon's body like a coiled spring, and launched herself into the pool in a perfect racing dive.

Chapter Three

"Careful, dammit, careful!" Ben yelled at the dockside crane operator, as the twenty-foot-long rack of helium gas cylinders plummeted toward the barge. The operator braked the lift cable just enough to prevent the heavy load from denting the steel deckplates as it slammed down with a resounding boom. Every one of the half-dozen other men working on the barge—chain-binding and welding down equipment—flinched visibly and glanced around to locate the source of the impact.

Tipping up his battered, sticker-covered hardhat, Ben glared across the ways at the crane cab, looking disgusted. The operator gave an unconcerned shrug and dug into his shirt pocket for a cigarette. *I'm in the union,* his body language said. *Bitch at me and see how much of your gear makes it off this dock today.*

Seizing a rung of the helium rack's corner ladder, Ben climbed up on top of the big tank bundle and disconnected its four lifting slings from the ball-and-hook of the crane cable. Looking again at the operator, he waved a finger over his head. The ball-and-hook accelerated skyward. A shadow passed over him as the crane boom swung around to the quay to pick up another load, and he felt a trickle of sweat run out from under his hardhat and into his right eyebrow. Barely nine in the morning and already the sun was hot. With the humidity unseasonably high, it was going to be a steamer of a day on the New Orleans industrial docks.

Gene McCluskey was waiting for him at the bottom of the rack ladder, looking very supervisory in a new yellow hardhat and clean khaki coveralls, a clipboard tucked under one arm. He grinned as Ben hit the deck and peeled off one of his rigging gloves, scowling.

"Crane operator's a little independent-minded, eh?" Gene commented.

Ben wiped sweat out from under his eyes with two fingers. "The usual shit. Union dockworker won't take direction from anybody." He smiled his lopsided smile. "He can break all the equipment he wants, tossing it around like that—but personally, I'm not interested in being teed up by three or four tons of steel that's moving too fast to be controlled properly."

Gene clapped him on the shoulder. "I'll go talk to him."

"You better hurry," Ben said, replacing his rigging glove, "he's going for another kamikaze lift right now."

As the project supervisor moved off toward the barge rail, Ben caught a glimpse of a familiar sky-blue pickup truck entering the security gate of the fenced-in parking lot at the far end of the dockyard. The expression of annoyance disappeared from his face and he glanced at his watch. She was a half-hour early, as usual.

A few minutes later, Sasha Wojeck walked out of the security shack and began to make her way across the hard-packed gravel of the yard, lugging two large waterproof duffel bags. Ben got as far as the top of the gangplank before seeing her intercepted by Pierre LeRenard, who made a little continental bow and relieved her of both items. The compact Frenchman lifted the heavy duffels up onto his shoulders as easily as if they had been filled with popcorn and proceeded toward the barge.

Ben smiled as he watched Sass approach, admiring for the millionth time the slim, athletic figure that wore jeans, boots, and faded plaid work shirts so well. She moved with a no-nonsense assurance that was nevertheless unconsciously feminine. Her long blonde hair was pulled back and pinned up, out of the way, a couple of stray tendrils falling to her collar from beneath her scarred blue hardhat. Catching sight of Ben at the top of the gangplank, she beamed and lifted a hand, her teeth white in her tanned face.

He returned the gesture, stepping aside as Pierre puffed up the gangplank, looking like a voyageur portaging his own bodyweight in furs. *"Mon dieu!"* the little man whispered under his breath. "Either I am older than I thought, or your *femme* has packed everything including the silverware into these miserable bags, *mon ami*."

"See what you get for showing off?" Ben said with a grin. "You wouldn't be trying to pick up my old lady, would you, Pierre?"

"Absolument," the Frenchman panted. "She is too good for the likes of you." He staggered off toward one of the cowled companionways that led to the barge's belowdecks living quarters.

Sass pulled off her mirrored sunglasses as she stepped down from the gangplank. Her eyes, set wide apart above sharp Slavic cheekbones, were a brilliant blue, creased at their corners with laugh lines. Just shy of forty, she looked ten years younger. She moved in close, one eyebrow raised, waiting. With a soft chuckle, Ben put a finger under her small, pointed chin and kissed her on the lips.

"Running off with Pierre, are you?" he muttered into her cheek.

Sass shrugged. "Mmm. Could be. If you fail to please me." She twirled her fingers in the hair at the nape of his neck, hugging him.

Discreetly, Ben gave her a soft bite on the earlobe. "Well, I'll try to stay on top of things," he whispered.

"Perhaps you two would like to rent a room somewhere," Gene called from the dock. He nodded, grinning. "Hi, Sass."

"Hi, Gene." She fluttered her fingers at him.

"You and Ben have your own quarters down below," the supervisor said. "Room Three. Follow LeRenard. There's only one hallway." He turned to wave his clipboard at the crane operator. "Okay, Ben. This guy's ready to lift again. One more gas rack and the ROV stuff, and we're done. He'll be cool this time; I straightened him out."

"What'd you do?" Ben laughed. "Threaten to kick the shit out of him?"

"No," Gene replied. "I gave him a fifty-dollar bill and told him there was another one waitin' for him if he finished the lifts like a sane person, watchin' your hand signals. I ain't got time to fuck around, here. I want to be off this dock and headin' out into the Gulf by one o'clock. 'Scuse my language, Sass."

Sass grinned. "Not a problem, Gene."

"You're a peach, kid. Okay, Ben, let's get it done."

"I'm there," Ben said, heading for the center of the deck. "Tell him to pick that other gas rack first. I want to put it on the opposite rail—balance out the load."

The supervisor looked over his shoulder as he walked away. "Okay."

"After I stow my gear in the quarters," Sass called, "I'm going to check out the sat system's command van. Get familiar with the plumbing."

Ben nodded, watching the second helium rack rise into the air from its spot on the quay, several tons of steel wobbling at the end of a slender thread of cable. "Good idea," he said. "Just keep looking up, in case this guy decides to start moving to the beat of his own drummer again."

Sass nodded, waved, and headed for the companionway.

It took Ben nearly five minutes, using hand signals, to coerce the crane operator into positioning and landing the second helium rack exactly where he wanted it. Somehow, he managed to get it done without inflicting any permanent damage to the barge. As he was releasing the lifting slings, he noticed Gene coming up the gangplank again, followed by a second man who walked with a substantial limp.

"Hey, Ben," Gene called. "I'd like you to meet somebody."

Ben climbed down off the rack and removed his sunglasses. The man behind Gene was short—only three or four inches taller than Pierre LeRenard—and rather weedy-looking, with a skinny, stoop-shouldered frame and narrow, pinched face. His complexion was anemic, the color of ash, as was his limp, thinning hair. A cigarette jutted from a mouth that resembled a horizontal rip under his nose. He was dressed completely in black, his hands jammed into the pockets of a threadbare pea coat that was buttoned to the neck. The only color to the man was his eyes; they were a vivid green, magnified by the thick lenses of his steel-rimmed glasses, and bright with intelligence.

"Ben," Gene said, "this is Gerald Posey, the ROV expert."

"Right, right." Ben extended his hand. "I remember. Nice to meet you, Ger."

"Gerald," the pallid man corrected him, his lips barely moving around his cigarette. A long piece of ash fell onto the front of his pea coat as he extracted his right hand from its pocket and dangled it near Ben's. Ben shook with him. It was like squeezing a handful of cold, overcooked spaghetti.

"Gerald," Ben said. "Sorry." He gestured at the flatbed truck that was parked on the quay near the bow of the barge. "That your stuff?"

Posey turned and looked. "Yep."

"We're gonna put it amidships, right? With the launching skid hanging partly over the port side?"

"Yep."

Ben cleared his throat. "Okay. How about the control van? Want me to set it down just behind the hydraulic davit on the skid?"

"Yep."

There was a pause as Ben regarded the ROV man. He actually looked cold, standing there with his pea coat collar turned up and his hands buried in his pockets. His cigarette was little more than a smoldering filter, still clamped in the corner of his mouth.

Smoke trickled out of Posey's nose as he exhaled. "Think I'll go to my room. I'm tired." He looked at Ben with his huge green eyes. "Try not to break anything."

Without another word, he limped off toward the companionway.

"Nice talking to you," Ben called after him, giving Gene a dry glance.

The little man appeared not to hear. Sass, just emerging from belowdecks, smiled at him as they passed. Her face fell slightly at Posey's indifferent, minimal response.

"Who was that?" she asked, on her way down the deck toward the saturation van. "Mr. Personality?"

"Yes," Ben replied.

Gene shrugged. "Our resident technical genius. He drove all night from Houston, shepherding his gear along I-10. He's a bit out of sorts."

"Looks like he's out of it, *period*," Sass declared. She stepped around a small rack of acetylene bottles. "I'll be on the stern, memorizing the sat hookups."

"See you later." Ben blew out a long breath and tipped back his hardhat. "Okay, Gene. Last thing to do is put Mr. Personality's ROV equipment in the right place and get it all welded down. Then we're good to go, am I right?"

"You are right," the old supervisor said. "Good to go, on the afternoon tide."

*****

Alberto Ramos sipped his fifth pink gin of the morning and gazed at his sister through a comfortable alcohol fog. Grizelda was slouched low in her favorite chair—a futuristic Swedish item that clashed horribly with the traditional Caribbean décor of the *hacienda*'s living room—her hands gripping the wooden armrests. Her bare feet were flat on the floor, her knees apart. She'd spent the entire morning lifting weights on the pool terrace, after which she'd showered, wrapped a red-and-black sarong around her hips, and slipped into a fresh black tank top. A headband of rich green silk contrasted vividly with her short, red-hennaed hair.

She was staring with her usual baleful intensity at two petri dishes that sat on top of the mahogany coffee table. Opposite her, the third person in the room—a pudgy Mexican with a toothbrush mustache and horn-rimmed glasses—was leafing through a folder of papers, periodically licking his thumb. Every so often he hmm-hmmed.

Alberto crossed his legs the other way and shifted position in the leather Lay-Z-Boy with a deep sigh. It was all such a bore—except for the possibility of recovering untold millions of dollars in gold from the bottom of the sea—but Grizelda was incorrigible, obsessed. She'd latched on to this family ancestry nonsense with her customary pathological single-mindedness, and there was little hope of dissuading her until she lost interest on her own. Alberto rolled pink gin around his tongue. It was dangerous to come between Grizelda and her fixations—even for him.

"Here they are," the chubby Mexican said. He laid two sheets of paper down next to the left-hand petri dish. "These are the comparisons for the hair samples." Two more sheets went down beside the right-hand dish. "And these are the skin comparisons." He looked up at Grizelda, blinking owlishly through his horn-rims. "As I mentioned, we only needed one good sample. DNA is DNA, whether it comes from hair, bone, skin, or any other part of the body."

"Two tests," Grizelda grunted, staring at him from under her arched eyebrows. "I want two tests."

The Mexican flushed and waved a fat-fingered hand. "But of course, Senorita Ramos," he said hurriedly. "It is good to be certain in matters of such impor—"

"Get on with it," Grizelda ordered, raising her voice a mere fraction. Her eyes had a black gleam in them that didn't look quite human.

"Yes, yes, at once." The chubby man cleared his throat. "First: the hair sample." He leaned over the table, pointing at the papers with a silver pen. "As you can see, there are multiple points of positive comparison—matches, if you will—in the DNA structure. The chance that these two people are *not* directly related is only one in twenty-two point four million, according to calculable scientific probability."

He looked up, smiling, locked eyes with Grizelda—and looked back down quickly, swallowing hard. "Second: the skin sample." He held up the right-hand petri dish. Inside it was a shriveled piece of brown material that resembled greasy tanned leather. "Identical DNA testing procedures, seeking additional points of comparison. Matches replicating those of the hair sample were obtained, along with numerous others. In this second test, using alternate samples from the same two individuals, the chance that they are not directly related is calculated to be only one in twenty-two point *nine* million."

The Mexican glanced from Alberto to Grizelda and back to Alberto again. "In other words, it is safe to say that all the DNA samples tested come from members of the same family. It is virtually guaranteed."

Grizelda was breathing hard, staring past the chubby man now, out the open doors to the terrace. Her face twisted, the muscles along her jaw working rapidly. There was a creaking sound as her powerful veined hands flexed on the wooden arms of the chair.

"Well," Alberto said fuzzily, "that settles that." He raised his stemmed glass in a mock toast, spilling pink gin on himself.

Abruptly, Grizelda thrust herself to her feet. The Scandinavian armchair skidded backwards across the terrazzo floor. In one furious motion, she swept a small bronze statuette of a marlin from the corner of the coffee table and hurled it toward the partially open terrace doors. The heavy figurine smashed through the one of the tinted panes in an explosion of shards and wood splinters.

Grizelda stood with her arms dangling by her sides, breathing hard and glowering at the ruined door. The chubby Mexican across the table had recoiled into his rattan settee, his arms around his head, cowering. He stared up at the hulking woman in mute shock, his eyes like saucers.

"Do you feel better now?" Alberto inquired. There was only a hint of sarcasm in his tone, but Grizelda's head snapped around instantly. Alberto blanched. Before he could move, his sister had taken two strides toward him and seized him by the throat. The gin glass smashed on the floor as she yanked him out of his armchair with one hand, kicked his legs out from under him, and slammed him onto the coffee table on his back. The Mexican floundered off the end of the settee trying to stay out of the way.

"What was that again, little brother?" Grizelda snarled, squeezing.

"Urghkkurgghh," was all Alberto could manage. His bare, soft legs thrashed feebly across the terrazzo.

"That's what I thought you said." She eased the pressure on his windpipe slightly.

Alberto took in a ragged, rattling breath. "You're *hurting* me!" he mewled, clawing at her fingers.

"Yes, I am," Grizelda said. "And do you know why?"

"Urghgh—no . . ."

She leaned down close. "Because I love you," she whispered, and kissed him hard on the mouth. The chewing and slurping went on for a full minute.

When she finally broke away and straightened up, leaving her brother sprawled like a half-stuffed scarecrow across the tabletop, the chubby Mexican was standing in a far corner of the room, his knees knocking.

Wiping her mouth on the back of her hand, Grizelda stepped around the Lay-Z-Boy and moved toward him, her bare feet padding panther-like on the cold stone.

She stopped barely six inches from the Mexican—who began to wilt like a dying weed—and squared herself to him; legs apart, fists balled at her sides. The ugly smile spread over her acromegalic face; her black eyes burned into his.

"I-I-I-I didn't m-mean to upset y—" he began.

Grizelda reached out with blinding speed and clapped a knobby-knuckled hand over his mouth. The index finger of her free hand came up in front of his gaping eyes. Very slowly, it waggled back and forth.

"Good work, Fuentes," she said. "Go have some lunch. Then get started on the blood samples."

She removed her hand from his mouth and turned away, leaving him to sag back against the wall in a near faint as she stalked out the damaged doors and onto the pool terrace.

Chapter Four

It was the start of a new weekend, and a fresh batch of tourists had begun to flood the Seven Mile Beach district just north of Georgetown, Grand Cayman. Shuttled in from Tampa and Miami by Cayman Airways, they came in all shapes and sizes: fat car-dealer types with perfect hair and decorative trophy wives; mid-western families lugging bulging suitcases and barking at the kids to stay close; young professional couples looking prosperous in Gucci casuals and Serengeti sunglasses. All passed through the lobbies and pool courtyards of the big Seven Mile Beach resort hotels with the same lemming-like single-mindedness of purpose: to have a seriously good time before their pricey long weekend in paradise was over. There was a kind of happy desperation on every face: hurry up and relax, dammit—the meter's running.

Sitting on a stool in the poolside tiki bar of the Treasure Reef Hotel, Jeremiah Sligo took a sip of his Mango-Bango rum punch and glanced at his watch. One thirty-five. That slick lawyer from New Orleans he was supposed to pick up at the airport—Gomez; he'd be touching down in just under an hour. Time enough to finish this drink and check out the new pale tourist titties that were bouncing around the pool. Several sets definitely bore closer inspection. Wouldn't want to cut it too fine and be late, though, not with fucking Alberto in town. The guy was nearly as temperamental as his wacked-out sister.

Sligo adjusted his Ray-Ban sunglasses on his beak of a nose and regarded himself in the little beer-promo mirror that hung on one of the back-bar's bamboo uprights. Yeah, pretty slick, he thought. He didn't really look fifty-two. Nah. Take twenty off that. Thirty-two. The temples weren't really that high, the long, dirty-blonde hair that was tied back into a ponytail not really all that thin and shot through with gray. The tanned Jimmy Buffet face wasn't *too* wrinkled and jowly; the small, glittering blue eyes, close-set on either side of the hawk nose, not too droopy-lidded and bloodshot. He grinned at himself. The teeth were still china-white, if a little long and crooked, against his deep, leathery tan. He'd come a long way from that shitty little Canadian logging town he'd been born in. A fucking modern-day Caribbean pirate, that's what he was. Career dope smuggler *extraordinaire* (temporarily recovering from a few setbacks and cash short, but sooner or later the worm always turned again). The real goddamn article. Yo-ho-ho and a kilo of blow. Or a bale of Jamaica's finest.

He patted his rum gut under the red, blue, and green floral shirt he wore. *That ain't no belly, girl—that's a gas tank for a sex machine.* That line always got them laughing, got them interested. A gram or two of coke later, back on the Ramoses' yacht (when they weren't aboard themselves) and, more often than not, he'd end up getting some of that tourist pussy. Never tell them it isn't your boat, though, that you're just the captain. Middle-class American broads want to fuck *owners,* not the hired help. Pumps up their own ditzoid egos.

A couple of sixteen-year-olds in K-Mart bikinis went wiggling and giggling by, followed by a pear-shaped retiree who must have weighed in at close to three hundred pounds. He plodded past the tiki bar like a gray-haired robot, dressed to kill in a cheap Panama hat, cataract-surgery shades, voluminous floral beach shorts that extended from just under his sagging pectorals to just above his pudding-pie knees, black dress socks, and laced brown oxford shoes. The drink he held in his hand looked more like a potted plant than a form of liquid refreshment, blossoms and foliage and swizzle sticks jutting out at all angles. Idly, Sligo glanced at the glossy drink menu propped up on the bar top. There it was. The *Rain Forest Orgy.* Six different kinds of booze and four fruit juices. Enough mashed-up papaya, mango, and pineapple to give you the trots for a week. Breakfast of champions.

Sligo looked at himself in the mirror again, his expression turning glum. He had to get out of here. Make something happen. Another month of sitting at the dock on the Ramoses' fifty-five-foot Cheoy Lee trawler—the *Cucaracha*—listening to the generators grumble away, with nowhere else to go other than these goddamn tourist bars, and he was going to be a prime candidate for disconnecting his own brain with a three-fifty-seven magnum.

He scared himself with that thought and chugged down a fruity mouthful of Mango-Bango. *Shit.* If only he hadn't lost his primo smuggling boat a couple of years back, trying to run those Arab terrorist-looking psychos from Cuba to that offshore drilling rig up in the Louisiana oil patch. Fucking boat had blown up in the middle of the night for some reason, and he'd nearly died of thirst and exposure floating around the Gulf of Mexico for a couple of weeks on a glorified inner tube, sharks circling and the whole bit. If he hadn't washed up on the north shore of Cuba again when he did, he'd have been mako bait for sure.[*] Sometimes life just wasn't fair.

If he could just get Alberto and that nutcase Grizelda to let him run a load of coke up to Galveston or Corpus Christi or Miami, for a decent percentage, he'd be able to buy his own vessel again and finance a

---

[*] See *CRASH DIVE*, Ben Gannon's first adventure.

few dozen bales of sensimilla out of Jamaica. Quit the Ramoses and get back into business as a one-man operation, self-employed. Being someone else's underpaid boat jockey was for the birds. Hell, the damn yacht hardly ever moved off the dock in Grand Cayman. In the past fourteen months since he'd met Alberto and landed the gig, he'd put out to sea exactly twice: both times a three-day hop over to the Ramoses' recently-acquired private island off the coast of Nicaragua or Belize or something—it was too far offshore to be certain what banana republic it belonged to—and back again. Fucking Alberto and his sister preferred to run that souped-up long-range cigarette boat they had when they wanted to get to the mainland or the Caymans. For all the use they got out of the Cheoy Lee, they might as well just turn it over to him—let him work it.

But nooooo. Assholes.

And now Grizelda had a bug up her chute about tracing some ancestor who'd filled a Spanish galleon full of Aztec treasure, set out for home, and promptly lost the whole kit and kaboodle in a storm, the moron. That was why she'd bought the island—she was sure that she and some of the native fishermen who lived in the little archipelago shared the same bloodline. Or something like that.

And damned if she hadn't found what looked like the wreck of the treasure ship, too, sitting in about twelve hundred feet of water midway between the archipelago's three islands. Now she was on a tear to salvage whatever golden goodies might be on it, track down the bloodlines of all the survivors of the—what was that galleon called? Oh, yeah—the *Arista*. Track down their bloodlines and, ultimately, satisfy some point of honor with respect to that idiot ancestor of hers who'd managed to deep-six his own ship.

Jesus. Talk about a loser. What kind of *dickhead* loses his own ship?

Sligo caught a glimpse of his face in the mirror just as the thought occurred to him that he himself had lost his own vessel less than two years ago. Well, hell—that was different. Fucking boat had gone and blown up on him. Not the same thing at all. He sucked down a slushy gulp of Mango-Bango.

Grizelda didn't talk much; mostly, she just lifted weights, shot steroids into her ass, and flew into violent rages at the drop of a hat. Scary broad. More like a female gorilla than a normal human woman. Alberto, now, he could be pretty bitchy, but at least you could shoot the breeze with the guy, if he was in the mood. Get some interesting information. Like the fact that he and his sister had hired a big-time commercial diving team to check out the *Arista*. Like the fact that there

79

might well be several *tons* of golden treasure still aboard her. Chains, goblets, plates, statues, lamps, and ceremonial swords. Bricks, bars, and coins. All of solid Aztec gold.

Man.

One or two decent-sized items like that and his money troubles would be *over.*

It was all only twelve hundred feet away. Four hundred yards. Less than a quarter mile. Sligo gazed out at the gleaming white beach behind the tiki bar. In the Georgetown direction, perched right at the high-tide line, was a blue-and-yellow-striped gazebo that rented out umbrellas and mattresses to the sun-hungry tourists. *That* was twelve hundred feet, from here to there. A fast Jamaican in track shoes could run it in forty seconds—hell, they did it on TV all the time. Twelve hundred feet was nothing.

Unless it was straight down to the bottom of the sea.

Dejected, Sligo was about to order another Mango-Bango when something caught his eye on the far side of the pool. A slender man in a yellow polo shirt and white chinos was pushing a two-wheeled loading cart past the rows of oily, prostrate tourists. On the cart was a contraption that reminded Sligo of the jet pack from 1960s Disneyland, its fiberglass cowl, the same emergency yellow as the man's polo shirt. Propped on top of it was a commercial diving helmet—a heavy-duty item also of yellow fiberglass, with fittings of stainless steel and brass.

The man wheeled the space-age gear around in front of the tiki bar and began to unload it at the edge of the pool. There was a small steel frame that held the backpack unit vertical, apparently for display, and another for the diving helmet. The last thing the man did before stepping into the shade of the tiki bar was to erect a small collapsible sign on a chrome pedestal.

"There," he said to the bartender and Sligo. "Let's see if I get any takers in this crop of *touristas.*"

Sligo looked at the sign. Damn, he really did have to face reality and buy a pair of prescription glasses. He pulled off his Ray-Bans and squinted hard. *TRY THE WORLD'S MOST ADVANCED REBREATHER!* the sign read. *THE DOA-9000 from KRONOS INDUSTRIES. DIVE INTO THE 21st CENTURY!*

Sligo digested that for a moment. Beside him, the man in the yellow shirt was patting beads of sweat from his forehead with a paper napkin and accepting a Sprite from the bartender. Sligo glanced over at him. The polo shirt was monogrammed with *KRONOS INDUSTRIES—DIVETECH DIVISION* on the right breast, and *BOB* on the left.

Deep in Sligo's brain, something began to wiggle.

He grinned at *BOB*. "Hiya!" he said. "How you doin'?"

BOB smiled back, still patting sweat from his forehead. "Not bad, not bad. Just not used to this heat yet. Ten days ago, I was still in Seattle. It was cold and rainy up there—has been all winter long."

"That sucks," Sligo said. "Believe me, I know. I was born in Canada."

BOB nodded. "The Great White North, *aayyy?*"

"Yeah. Colder 'n shit. I couldn't wait to get out of there." *Blah blah blah.* Every American, as soon as they heard you were from Canada—first thing they did was hit you with that fucking 'aayyy' thing . . . as if the entire population of Minnesota didn't use exactly the same expression. Sligo refocused. Get to the point before *BOB* here puts you into a coma. "So. What's this spacey-lookin' gadget?"

BOB sat back on a stool, folded his arms, and gazed proudly out at his hi-tech display. "Well, like the sign says: that's the DOA-9000. The most highly advanced, cutting-edge rebreather on the market today."

Sligo thought a moment. "D-O-A?"

"Deep Operations Apparatus." *BOB* was smiling like a proud poppa. "Series 9000 prototype—soon to be in full production. I'm down here to let people with a few bucks to spend try it out in the pool and on shallow beach dives, just to see how much of an improvement it is over old-fashioned SCUBA gear. Its applications are mostly military and industrial, but some folks in recrea-

82

tional diving like expensive toys and have deep pockets. Kronos sent me down here to start developing the recreational market—even though, at the price of this unit, it's never going to be very large."

"How much is the thing?" Sligo asked.

"It retails for forty-two thousand seven hundred and ninety dollars," *BOB* replied mildly, without batting an eye. "Out of reach of most sport divers."

That had to be the understatement of the year. "Holy Jesus," Sligo said. "You don't say?"

"Yeah, unfortunately I do." *BOB* looked sidelong at him. "You can buy introductory training and two demo dives in the pool and off the beach, with me, for a hundred and fifty U.S., if you'd like to give it a try."

"I'm thinkin' about it." Sligo nodded slowly. "Can I ask you a few more questions first?"

"Sure. I'm not exactly being swamped with takers right now."

"Cool. Lessee: how deep can you dive with this— this—"

"Rebreather," *BOB* filled in. "Operational limit is one thousand six hundred feet."

The number echoed in Sligo's head. "What?"

"One thousand six hundred feet. With proper surface support, of course. Supplemental power umbilical, hardwire communications, alternate breathing gas sources, open-to-closed circuit switching options . . ."

Sligo heard nothing as *BOB* blathered on. The DOA-9000 would let you dive sixteen hundred feet. Which was four hundred feet more than twelve hundred.

Whoa.

". . . Optimizing the rate of inert gas diffusion out of the bloodstream," *BOB* was saying.

"Yeah, yeah, right," Sligo interrupted. "Look, slick—I've been a SCUBA diver for twenty-five years. You pump compressed air into a bottle, carry it on your back, and suck out what you need until it's gone. Then you come up. Simple. These rebreathers now, I've been hearin' about 'em for a while. Seems like every Joe Diver-type is hot to try one out. How're they different from SCUBA gear, and what advantages do they have over regular tanks?"

"Well—" *BOB* began.

"Keep it simple," Sligo added.

"Okay. Simply put, the difference between the two is that with a rebreather, you use the same volume of inert gas over and over again, breathing it in a closed loop or circuit and replenishing the small amount of pure oxygen your body metabolizes in order to stay alive from a reservoir—a supply cylinder. The carbon dioxide you exhale into the loop is removed by a scrubber containing a soda canister—the CO_2 reacts with and is captured by the soda, so you don't poison yourself with your own exhalations.

"The advantages are: you don't have to carry huge amounts of compressed air around in big tanks, only to breath it once and then blow it out into the water—that's an *open*-circuit system, by the way. You don't have to breathe dry, cold air that chaps your throat and lungs; you breath warm, moist, recycled air that's had the CO_2 removed and the oxygen level bumped up. Because you're only carrying metabolic O_2 and a little more than a lung-sized amount of inert gas that you don't waste—you can stay down a *lot* longer . . . within the decompression tables, of course. You're not breathing out big bubbles of air all the time, so you don't make any noise and you don't scare any fish you might be trying to spear or photograph. If you happen to be a commando—a Navy SEAL, for example—you use a rebreather to sneak up on an enemy target because you can't be spotted from the surface—again: no bubbles." *BOB* smiled. "You see?"

Sligo's mind was reeling. "You—I—uh—what's *inert gas*?"

"Inert gas refers to the large component of a breathing medium that is not metabolized or used by the body upon inhalation. It's just non-reactive, inert volume—hence the name. You're a SCUBA diver; remember your theory? The breathing medium keeping us alive as we're standing here, for example, is air. And air, if you recall, is about twenty-two percent oxygen—which we metabolize or burn in our bodies' cells—and seventy-eight percent nitrogen—which we don't consume at all. It just goes in and out of us. So if we replace the oxygen in air that we burn, and scrub out the carbon dioxide we manufacture as a by-product, we can use the same nitrogen over and over again."

"Ohhh, I get it," Sligo said, nodding slowly. "You just have to put back in what your body uses up."

"And scrub out the by-products," *BOB* reminded him. "Yes."

"Huh." The smuggler stirred what was left of his Mango-Bango with a straw. "So: you can really dive sixteen hundred feet with this thing?"

BOB laughed. "Well, theoretically. You'd need to switch out the breathing medium to heliox or trimix first, or you'd be narked out of your skull before you were a third of the way there."

"Yeah, yeah," Sligo mused, "the nitrogen narcosis thing. Usin' these other gases solves that?"

"Pretty much," the tech replied. "Heliox is just helium and oxygen, used for mid-range deep diving, and trimix is for going *wayyy* down there, where you can develop HPNS."

"HPNS?"

"Correct. High Pressure Nervous Syndrome. It affects some people after about six hundred feet of depth. Muscle tremors, jitters, nervousness—that kind of thing. Trimix is heliox with a little bit of nitrogen dumped back in. The nitrogen has a sedative effect, like being just a *little* bit narked. Not enough to scramble your brains; just enough to calm you down."

"Yeah," Sligo said. "Calm is good."

"Definitely, when you're down there."

There was a pause as both men watched a voluptuously chunky twenty-year-old woman in a gold lamé thong bikini undulate past the tiki bar.

"Sweet Jesus," *BOB* breathed, patting his chest. "I think I'm getting HPNS right here. There oughtta be a law."

"Hey, enjoy it," Sligo told him. "If she didn't want to be stared at, she'd be wearin' a sack dress." He slurped down the last of his Mango-Bango. "You know, I think I'm gonna get you to give me a demo on this thing. It's pretty cool. I still can't believe a few valves and hoses and a couple of small tanks are worth forty grand, though—even if they *are* locked up inside a snazzy-lookin' fiberglass cover."

BOB patted sweat from his forehead with another paper napkin, gazing after the meaty brown buttocks as they swayed out onto the beach. "Well, most of that money's in the three computers in the control console.

That's the heart of the whole rebreather. The unit's completely automated. The control console senses how deep it is, keeps a digital record of the entire dive profile, and automatically adjusts the gas mix to give you a safe partial pressure of oxygen so you don't take an O_2 hit. Then, on the way up, it continuously adjusts percentages in the blend as you ascend to give you the optimum decompression mix. Helps you offgas more efficiently so you don't get the bends."

Sligo got about a quarter of that. Mostly the part about the unit being completely automated. *Perfect.* If it had its own brain and automatically took care of the diver it was strapped to, he didn't need to bother learning all the gory fucking details.

"What's an O_2 hit?" he asked, just because it sounded ominous.

BOB was still staring after the thong bikini. "A massive seizure, like an epileptic fit, caused by breathing in too high a partial pressure of oxygen in a gas mix. Get one underwater and you'll probably drown, because you can't help yourself. But the DOA-9000's mini-computers prevent that from occurring, because they keep the O_2 in the mix at the proper level, regardless of your depth."

Sligo grinned. This was too good. A godsend.

"Let me ask you something else," he started to say, and then the cellular phone clipped to his hip beeped twice.

Oh, shit. *Alberto.*

He flipped the phone open. "Hey," he said, glancing at his watch. *Shit, shit . . .*

"Sligo!" The effeminate voice came screeching out of the ear speaker several notches above its customary well-modulated level. *"I just got a call from Gomez at the airport! He's been waiting for half an hour, you incompetent asshole! You're late, so why aren't you fucking dead? Where the hell are you?"*

Sligo slid off the stool, holding the phone away from the side of his head, and waved a hand at *BOB.* "Hey," he said, as Alberto's tirade continued, "something's come up. But I'll be back for a lesson later. Save me a spot, okay? Sligo's the name."

"Sure," *BOB* shrugged. "Anytime. I'll be here."

"Far out," the smuggler declared, and began to jog around the pool toward the hotel lobby.

Chapter Five

The hard vibration of a diesel engine throttling up somewhere on the barge deck above shook the Spartan fixtures within the cramped stateroom. Blinking through his early-morning drowse, Ben reached out just in time to catch the small illuminated alarm clock as it walked off the edge of the night table on its nonskid rubber feet. Beside him on the narrow bunk, Sass stirred and groaned into her pillow.

"Th' hell's that?" she grouched, her voice thick with sleep.

Ben smiled into the darkness and rubbed his eyes. "Turning over a diesel topside, checking it. Maybe the engine on the main crane."

"Make them stop it," Sass sighed, pulling the covers over her head.

"Sure thing. Right away." Ben laughed and placed the alarm clock in the corner of the bunk next to his pillow, behind the fiddle where it couldn't fall to the deck. The diesel revved a little higher for a few more seconds, then died away to nothing in a long, descending growl. "There, Empress, how's that?"

"Uh-huh," Sass muttered.

Ben worked a hand between her upper arm and rib-cage and flexed his fingers. "Sorry, Your Highness. I didn't catch that?"

She tensed and twisted away from his hand with a little yelp. "I said: 'Begone, peasant, you're vexing me.'"

Ben rolled close and tickled her again, holding her against the mattress with his body weight. Laughing, she arched and clamped his hand between her arm and ribs, trying to immobilize it. "That does it, you're in trouble now, buddy. Off with your head!"

"Ouch," Ben said, nuzzling. "Which one?"

Sass squirmed. "Will someone *pleeeeeze* get this big ape *off* me?" She levered him back across the bunk. "Jesus. Can't a girl even wake up without being mauled?"

Ben gave her one last squeeze and rolled away, chuckling. "It's good for you, kiddo. Gets the blood flowing."

"Thanks a million."

Ben switched on the small bedside lamp mounted on the bulkhead just above the night table. The dim yellow light suffused the windowless room with a warm glow. Locating his watch, he held it up and squinted at its digital face. "Morning of the fourth day out of New Orleans," he said. "Seven-thirty."

Sass sneezed. "Excuse me. What is this, Sunday?"

91

"Yeah." Ben swung his legs to the deck and sat up. "We should be entering the Yucatan Channel some time this morning, if the tug's kept up its same speed."

Sass brightened. "Hey. Maybe we can stop in at Cancun. Have a turtle steak on Isla Mujeres."

"Not this trip," Ben replied. He smiled. "When this project's done, whether we hit pay dirt or not, we'll take the *Teresa Ann* for a cruise through the Mona Passage and back up this way. Chill out for a month and visit the islands. Visit Cancun."

"Sounds good." Sass frowned. "By the way, George Randall came by last week and did the bottom inspection we wanted. He gave her a clean bill of health—no rot, no soft spots, no shipworms. He says the *Teresa Ann* is the best-maintained fifty-foot wooden cruising sailboat he's ever seen."

"That's nice to hear," Ben said. "She's been good to us; I want to be good to her. Is she back in the water, by the way?"

"Not yet. I've got her chocked up on a cradle in the west corner of the marina yard. I'm having George touch up the bottom paint while we're away. He'll splash her with the TraveLift as soon as he's done so the seams and bilges don't dry out—move her back into her slip."

"Great." Ben scratched his tousled hair and got up. "You ready for a little breakfast? We can find out exactly where we are, then go run through some saturation procedures in the dive shack."

"Huh," Sass said. "So much for getting laid."

Ben looked at her. "Hell, you just told me to get off you."

She folded her hands behind her blonde head and gave him a languid smile. "Silly boy. After all these years, don't you know an invitation when you hear one?"

*****

The galley of the barge, like the staterooms, was a drab, utilitarian affair with a low ceiling, harsh fluorescent lights, and industrial vinyl tile underfoot. The cafeteria-style food preparation area ran along one wall, cordoned off by a stainless-steel-and-glass barricade of self-service hot tables. The remaining space was taken up by four long mess tables and several dozen chairs, all rendered in gray Formica and brushed aluminum.

Gene McCluskey and Chris Toricelli were sitting at one of the tables as Ben and Sass entered, chatting idly over their breakfasts. Two chairs away, Gerald Posey, apparently lost in thought, was staring into his scrambled eggs, a fork poised in one hand and a cigarette smoldering in the other. Sass fluttered her fingers at Gene and Chris, then grimaced as Posey speared a chunk of egg, popped it into his mouth, and immediately chased it with a lung full of smoke, chewing glumly.

"Good God," she whispered to Ben, as they each picked up a cafeteria tray. "Do you think he really likes the taste of that?"

Ben shrugged. "A man who smokes that much, everything's got to taste pretty much the same to him."

"Ugh," Sass said. "I can't imagine how he tolerates it."

"Habit, I guess. Hey, good morning, Chako. Just oatmeal for me. Skim milk and a little brown sugar."

The little Hispanic behind the hot tables grinned, wiping his hands on his white apron. "Still no *huevos*, boss? No h'aigs?"

Ben smiled and shook his head. "No thanks," he said, putting a hand over his heart. "I like 'em, but their cholesterol doesn't like me."

"It's hell to get old, ain't it, Ben?" Gene called over from the mess table.

"That's the truth," Ben replied, accepting a bowl of steaming gray mush from the cook. "Look at this crap I force myself to eat."

Sass patted his shoulder and looked at Chako. "I'll have your *huevos rancheros,* please. Three eggs, and lots of hot sauce. And throw a few strips of bacon on there while you're at it, okay?"

The cook grinned again and cracked his knuckles. "Good h'appetite, Senorita," he declared approvingly, and turned toward his grille.

Ben stared at his oatmeal. "You're doing that on purpose," he said.

"Hey," Sass replied, shrugging. "What can I tell you. Sometimes it doesn't suck to be a girl. My cholesterol's fine. Estrogen, you know?" She smiled happily at him.

Ben slapped the outside of her thigh as he moved toward the mess tables. "I've got two words for you, Slim," he said. "'Size sixteen.'"

He set his tray down next to Gene, across from Posey. "Gene, Chris. 'Morning, Gerald."

"Mmph," the ROV tech mumbled, exhaling smoke and bits of egg.

"Hey, Gannon," Chris said. He glanced over at Sass, then grinned at Ben. "Get jiggy with it last night?"

Ben gave him a withering look and seated himself. "No details, Chris." He turned to Gene. "How're you this morning, Mr. CMIC? Sleep okay?"

"Okay, I guess." Gene scratched his stubble and yawned. "Got a lot on my—"

"Chief Motherfucker In Charge," Chris guffawed. "That's you for sure, Gene. Chief goddamn Motherfucker In Charge."

"—mind," the old supervisor finished. He regarded Chris wearily as the kid shoveled grits into his mouth.

Ben fortified his patience with a spoonful of oatmeal. It wasn't bad—for oatmeal. "Where are we now, Gene?" he asked. "Thought I felt the seas change against the hull just before dawn."

"Good instincts," Gene said. "We started to make the turn around the western end of Cuba at about five a.m. We're in the Yucatan Channel now." He sipped his coffee. "Gotta stay well outside Cuban territorial waters, or Castro's gunboats might wanna try to haul us in, see if we've got anything they can use. Pain in the ass."

"Ah, they're not doing that too much anymore," Ben said. "Fidel's not going to live forever. Cuba's into good will and 'welcome, *Americano*' these days. Those people aren't stupid."

"You never know," Gene replied. "We'll give the place a wide berth. Who needs the hassle?"

Sass pulled back the chair beside Ben, set down her plate, and nodded all around. "Hi, guys."

"Hey, good-lookin'," Chris said, chewing grits. Ben winced inwardly. That was the other thing Chris Toricelli did. Just as all superiors were first names and all equals and inferiors were last names, all women were adjectives. Clunky, trite, patronizingly sexist adjectives: *good-lookin', beautiful, superfine, foxy*.

Sometimes the kid sounded like he'd been taking notes from bad 70s blaxploitation movies. It was painful to listen to.

Sass batted her eyes at him. "Good morning, Chris. Still trying too hard, I see." She smiled frostily and dug into the steaming mountain of eggs, salsa, and jack cheese on the plate in front of her. Ben and Gene exchanged wry grins. Sass Wojeck was the wrong female for Chris to run his lines on.

"Thought Sass and I would head on up to the sat shack after breakfast," Ben said. "Check the gas sensors, do a few panel drills, and run through the blowdown procedures again."

"Fine," Gene replied. "But can you take a few minutes to help Gerald rig the deployment crane on the ROV launch system to the ROV itself? He wants to lift the vehicle out of its cradle a few times while the weather's calm—check the crane hydraulics under a load. And mess around with the ROV's internal components some."

"Sure, no problem."

"AHA!" Posey barked suddenly, sitting bolt upright. "That's it!"

Ben coughed up the spoonful of oatmeal he'd partially inhaled. "Jesus Christ, Gerald. *What's* it?"

The ROV tech looked at him in exasperation, the fluorescent lights gleaming off the lenses of his steel-rimmed glasses. "The electromagnetic activators, don't you see? Their current power routings across the dihedral circuit boards are causing resistance overloads in the transmogrification chips! All I have to do is increase the amplitude of the rheostatic compression diodes and balance out the resultant slump decay! What was I thinking? An *infant* could have seen it!"

There was dead silence at the table.

"Yep," Posey went on, staring at the bulkhead. "That's what I need to do." He sucked on the last of his cigarette, stubbed it out in his scrambled eggs, and pushed back his chair. "Logarithmic calculation of slump decay profiles . . ." he muttered, rising and hurrying toward the galley door.

And then he was gone, the door banging shut behind him on its spring-loaded hinges.

Sass chewed thoughtfully on a strip of bacon. "It's nice to see someone so involved with his work," she commented. "Don't you think?"

"I think that guy needs his frontal lobes shocked," Chris said. "What a geek."

"Hey, belay that shit, kid." Gene fixed Chris with a hard stare. "Gerald's a science guy, that's what he does. And he's damn good at it. Have a little respect. I need him and his skills on this job as much as I need you, see? Maybe more."

Chris spread his hands. "Whoa, Gene, sorry. I take it back. No harm done. Just bustin' the guy's balls a little bit."

"Behind his back," Ben pointed out.

"So he doesn't know they're busted," Chris retorted. His perfect GI Joe chin stuck out defiantly. "What's the difference? His head's spinning with wires and circuits all day long. Ah, what the hell,"—he got up as Gene began to say something again—"I'll go give him a hand topside."

He ran his fingers back through his mane of blonde hair. "See you on deck, Gene. You too, Gannon." He made a pistol out of his thumb and forefinger, pointed it at Sass, and produced a chucking sound with his tongue. "Later, gorgeous."

"I'll never be as gorgeous as you, Adonis," Sass remarked. "Ask the man in the mirror."

Chris laughed because, basically, he agreed with her, and exited the galley, flexing his sun-bronzed arms behind his head as he went.

Ben swallowed his last spoonful of oatmeal and sighed. "The Golden goddamned Guido. Gene, wasn't there *anyone* else you could have picked to go into sat on this job? If I have to listen to his shit for another four weeks, I may have to kill myself."

"Or him," Sass interjected.

The old supervisor smiled, looking a bit pained around the eyes. "I know what you mean," he said. "Chris is a handful. Still has a lot to learn about people, but he's better than he used to be."

"Not much," Ben observed. He stirred a teaspoon of sugar into his black coffee. "Seriously—there are a couple of other guys you could have gotten, especially for a potential payday like this."

Gene shook his head. "It had to be Chris, Ben."

"Why?"

"Because." Gene looked at him. "Gus Toricelli's got cancer."

"Gus?" Ben set his coffee mug back down on the table. "I didn't know that." He glanced at Sass. "We just saw him—what?—four months ago at a diving contractors' convention in Houston. He looked a little thin and tired, but basically healthy. He was still running Toricelli Offshore at the time."

"Not now," Gene said. "He's in the cancer ward of Pierpoint Tertiary Care Hospital over in Atlanta. Doin' poorly, too."

"Old Gus," Sass murmured, shaking her head. "What kind of cancer?"

"Liver." Gene clamped his lips together momentarily and stared down at his empty plate. "Aggressive in nature, his oncologist says." The supervisor looked back up with a short, bitter laugh. "He's always makin' cheery statements like that. You should see this guy. Looks about twelve years old, a Long Island blueblood straight out of some fancy Eastern medical school. Uses words I can't even pronounce."

"What's the prognosis?" Ben asked.

"Shitty. Right now, Gus has a fifty-fifty chance of makin' it through the next six months, all of it on chemotherapy. If the disease or the cure don't kill him, he's lookin' at a five-year survival rate of sixty percent."

"Jesus," Ben muttered. He stirred his coffee listlessly, his appetite gone. "How's Allie taking it?" Allie was Gus's wife of thirty years, and Chris Toricelli's mother.

"Damn hard," Gene said. "But you ain't heard the worst part."

Sass raised her eyebrows. "There's a *worse* part?"

"Oh, yeah." Gene put his face in his hands and rubbed his eyes. "Aaggh. I need to take a sleepin' pill tonight. Here's the bitch of it all: Gus has to stay in that hospital under treatment to even have a coin's-toss chance of pullin' through this thing. You know what that costs. Well, eight months ago he lost his health insurance."

Ben straightened. "But his company carries—"

"Toricelli Offshore is a small-group insurance buyer," Gene went on. "Eight months ago, the insurer that

Gus had contracted with to provide medical coverage for himself and his twenty employees arbitrarily pulled out on him. The *fifth* insurer in three years. There's no money to be made providin' health insurance to small companies or self-employed people in America anymore. So they bailed—left Gus and his people hangin'."

"Fucking insurance companies," Ben growled. "Forty percent of the working people in the country can't afford basic health care for their families, and those bastards keep tightening the noose."

"And the government lets them do it," Sass added.

"They *own* the government," Gene said. "As long as they can buy congressmen and senators, there aren't goin' to be any laws made that interfere with their profits. Too many powerful people makin' too much money." He took a sip of coffee. "There are only two ways to be able to afford to go see a doctor in the good ol' USA anymore. One: work like a robot for some monster big-brother corporation for a shitty salary and barely-adequate benefits—'cause lord knows the insurance companies will always sell *them* group-health policies—or two: be born filthy, stinking, George-goddamn-Bush Junior *rich* so you can buy all the health care you need no matter how much it costs." Gene gazed into his coffee mug. "The rest of us—like Sass, you, me, and Gus Toricelli—we can all go die on a street corner somewhere, I guess, if we have the nerve to get sick."

The galley was quiet for a long moment. Finally, Sass cleared her throat and tried on a thin smile. "Not mad, are you, Gene?" she asked softly.

"Hell, yeah, I'm mad," the old supervisor grumbled. "Gus Toricelli's three years younger than me. And he's one of my oldest friends."

"How about Medicare?" Ben asked.

"No way. Gus is only fifty-nine. Gotta be sixty-five to qualify." Another short, bitter laugh escaped Gene's lips. "He'd be long dead before they'd give him a dime of the thousands of dollars he paid into FICA over his working life."

Sass leaned forward on her elbows. "What happens to him without any kind of health insurance?"

Gene looked at her. "When he and Allie can't write any more checks to the hospital, they send him home to die. Get a payin' customer in their cancer ward." The color had drained from the old supervisor's face. *"'Next.'"*

"His company?" Ben asked. "Everything he's built over forty years?"

"Toricelli Offshore's already filed for bankruptcy. His and Allie's life's savings are almost gone."

Ben raised his coffee to his lips. "So that's why you took Chris on."

"Right. I know he's an arrogant young goofball, but I owe it to Gus. Chris's share of the salvage, if we find anything substantial, could go a long way toward keepin' Gus in that hospital. Maybe even buy him enough time and treatment to beat this thing."

"Long odds," Ben observed ruefully.

Gene looked at him. "What am I gonna do? Give up on Gus Toricelli?"

"Not hardly."

"You got that right. Not hardly."

They finished their coffees in silence, listening to the deep groaning creaks that echoed through the barge's steel hull as it flexed over the ocean under tow. Behind the row of hot tables, the little cook, Chako, was washing up, clanging his pots around in a large stainless steel sink.

Finally, Ben pushed back his chair and stood up. "Okay, Gene," he said. "For Gus's sake, and for yours, I can put up with Chris." He smiled at Sass. "How about you?"

She brushed a strand of blonde hair out of her face. "Hey, I can handle anything he throws at me. And even if he does act like a conceited jerk, he's still *real* easy on a girl's eyes. No problem."

"Thanks," Gene said.

"Don't mention it." Ben put a hand on Sass's shoulder and squeezed. "Okay. Let's go see what our guy Gerald's up to."

Chapter Six

"The corpse is gone, Senorita Ramos," the lead bodyguard said, peering up at her from beneath his cheap straw hat. He was squatting at the base of the coral pillar, his cut-down shotgun across one knee. "It lay here for at least two days—see how flattened the grass is in this one spot? And how much blood?" He shook his head. "But when we came yesterday to dispose of it, as you ordered, we found nothing."

Grizelda Ramos stared at the ground, nostrils flaring, her hands balled into fists at her sides. A slight twitch developed in the right cheek muscle of the bodyguard's dark, narrow face. His eyes dropped to the heavy German hiking boots she was wearing, and rather than stay within easy stomping distance, he rose to his feet and walked toward the edge of the cliff. Thirty feet below, the sea, calmer now than it had been for the past several days, swelled and subsided rhythmically against the vertical rock.

"Perhaps, Senorita," the guard suggested, "he was not yet dead. He tried to crawl away in the dark and fell over the cliff."

Grizelda continued to stare at the flattened grass. "No, that is not possible."

"Forgive me, but you're certain he could not have moved even a short distance?"

The obsidian eyes flickered up and locked onto the guard's. "He was in no condition," Grizelda snapped. "Didn't you yourself just mention the amount of blood on the ground? There must be six quarts here, idiot. He bled out quickly, even without taking a death blow."

"Again, forgive me, Senorita," the guard said, standing his ground and demonstrating a certain amount of innate courage, if rather questionable judgement, "but perhaps once you've had your sport with these—uh—companions, you might dispatch them more conclusively . . . say with a knife thrust to the heart."

For a second or two, the musclebound woman looked as if she would erupt like a live volcano. Then her acromegalic face relaxed slightly. "Kill them outright?" she snarled. "What fun is that?"

The lead guard fell silent as she stalked around the flattened, bloodstained grass again, muttering under her breath. After a moment, one of the other two bodyguards stepped forward.

"Your pardon, Senorita Ramos," he said, dipping his head, "but there is a possible explanation for the body's disappearance."

Grizelda spun and fixed her gaze on him. "Oh, yes? What?"

Nervously, the man's eyes shifted left and right. "Hogs."

"What?"

"Hogs," the guard repeated. "Feral pigs. There is a small population of them on the island. They may have dragged the body off."

"Pigs?" Grizelda's facial muscles flexed. "Pigs don't eat people."

The man swept off his straw hat and looked earnest. "Oh, but they do, Senorita. Not live people, not usually, but all pigs will scavenge dead bodies. Especially big farm boars or wild pigs. In my hometown in central Mexico, when I was a boy, there was an old farmer named Jorge. Jorge was known to have a very bad heart, but every morning he would get up and go feed his two old boar pigs in their pen. He called them Pancho and Villa, ha-ha."

Grizelda's eyes were like black ice, her face expressionless.

The chuckle died on the guard's lips. "Yes, well— anyway, he would stand on the split rails of their pen, lean over, and dump them their slops. Every morning. Then, one day—no Jorge. Ah, his neighbors said. The old man has finally died. So they went into his little house to find him, but he was not inside, not in his bed. We all looked outside—all around his little plot of land, but found nothing. This was very strange, because he never went anywhere, ever.

"And then someone looked in the pig pen. There were Jorge's old army shoes—with his feet still inside them. There was almost nothing else left; a few scraps of cloth, some blood and bits of flesh mixed into the mud—that was all. And we knew what must have happened: the old man's heart had given out while he was balancing on the split rails, slopping his hogs, and he had fallen into the pen. Pancho and Villa had promptly eaten him—bones and all—leaving only his feet and the old army shoes. Someone whispered that they smelled so bad even the hogs wouldn't touch them, since Jorge never took them off, even to sleep."

Muted guffaws came from the other two guards, and even Grizelda's brooding expression lightened. The storytelling bodyguard went on:

"So you see, Senorita, pigs *do* eat people—wild pigs even more so than farm pigs. And look here." He walked a few feet toward the undergrowth and pointed at the ground. "Here are some drag marks. And some broken twigs on these bushes." He smiled triumphantly. "*That* is what has happened to the body, Senorita Ramos. The feral pigs have dragged it off into the jungle to eat it."

"Hmm." Grizelda's eyes followed the faint drag marks. "Will there be anything left when they are done?"

The guard shook his head emphatically. "The hogs will leave nothing, Senorita. They will devour it completely. Even the bloody clothing. Even the shoes—if they do not smell as bad as old Jorge's." All three guards laughed, sensing that Grizelda was now marginally more relaxed.

"He had no shoes," she said, "and since the pigs are disposing of him, we have no reason to keep searching and sweating in the heat of the day." She grinned suddenly, and the effect was like that of an upright wolverine licking its chops. "Back to the house. You will all have a sangria with me on the pool terrace."

*****

The boy continued to watch from the concealed opening of the fishing cave as the henna-haired woman and her three gun-toting male companions moved away from the marker rock and off into the underbrush. Not quite thirteen, and rather slight, it had taken him the better part of two hours to drag his brother's slashed body through the jungle and up the slope to the cave entrance. It had been a difficult, ugly task. Strangely enough, he had never once felt the urge to cry, although he had loved his older brother Fernando with all his heart. He brushed his long black hair out of his eyes and watched, keeping absolutely still, until the trailing gunman disappeared down the narrow cliff-top path.

He crept back from the opening and carefully descended deeper into the cave, clambering down a steep incline of jagged coral rock. It was very damp, relatively cool, and dim, but a kind of pale phosphorescence emanated from the slimy moss that lined the cave walls, providing a minimal amount of light. The void in the rock narrowed rapidly, like an elongated funnel, over the course of thirty feet, finally shrinking to a sloping passageway less than a yard wide.

The boy slipped through, emerging into a large, dome-like cavern some sixty feet in diameter, twenty-five in height. The cavern had no floor; in its place was a wide, circular pool of seawater, glowing blue with filtered sunlight and darkening with depth, the surface of which heaved ponderously up . . . then down . . . within the confines of its rock basin. Tendrils of salt foam sizzled on the water, the sound very loud in the grotto's resonant emptiness. With each upheaval, the internal atmospheric pressure increased—the newly compressed air whistling out through unseen cracks and crevices—until the surface of the pool receded again and returned the cavern's pressure to normal.

The boy climbed down to one of the lower ledges, mindful not to catch his ragged cutoff shorts or battered rope sandals—his only apparel—on any of the numerous spurs of sharp rock. Squatting at the very lip of the ledge, he clasped his arms around his shins and looked down into the darkly luminescent blue water as it surged up the coralline walls of the basin. Small tropical reef fish of every description teemed just beneath the surface. Further down—from five to twenty feet, perhaps—thick schools of snapper, parrotfish, and sea perch hung along the basin's vertical contours. Below them, barely visible in the shadowy depths, larger shapes moved . . . big grouper, nurse sharks, and even barrel-sized jewfish, their mouths wide enough to swallow a goat.

This was the fishing cave, the secret place known only to members of his family. It had always been that way, for generations. The place that always had enough fish to feed everyone in the village, and always would—as long as its location was *kept* secret. For, the boy remembered his father telling him, men being men, if any but a scant few knew of the fishing cave, the greedy ones among them would seek it out, take *all* the fish—whether they needed them or not—and the bountiful, dependable resource would be lost.

It had taken him the better part of a week to work up enough courage to come looking for Fernando. Nearly a month had passed since his older brother had accepted the rich woman's offer of one thousand U.S. dollars for ten days of construction work at her new house on Isla Tequesta—the local name for what he always thought of as Fishing Cave Island. When he had not returned, the fearful whispers had begun. The new woman was evil, the elders said. A *narcotista*.

This in spite of the fact that she had sent her own personal physician to test everyone in the village for diseases such as smallpox—taking swabs from the inner cheek—and administer donated oral vaccine. Her charitable duty to her less fortunate neighbors, the physician had told them. But still the negative rumors persisted.

The fishwives were the most adamant. Did you see the way she looked at Fernando? they hissed. How hungry her eyes were? She'd practically drooled over him. And Fernando, too handsome for his own good, too young to know the folly of vanity, had been flattered—and hungry for the money, which was far more than he could make in a year.

And there had been the troubling issue of the village's little hillside chapel and sepulchre. Even before the new woman had come, someone had entered the old shrine and desecrated it, breaking open both coral-rock sarcophagi and removing the remains within. Stealing the old inscription tablets. Sacrilege, the elders said. Nothing good could come of it.

There had been no talk of reporting the disappearance or vandalism, or of trying to get help from any kind of policing authority. For all practical purposes, as far as the people of the village were concerned, there was none. Their isolation made them a world unto themselves.

On no less than three separate occasions during the boy's thirteen years of life, by his recollection, a flat gray gunboat had pulled up to the village dock and disgorged an official in a military uniform and peaked cap. This official had informed the elders that their tiny island group was now part of the sovereign nation of such-and-such, that they were now fortunate enough to be under the protection of this-or-that government, and henceforth would be expected to conduct themselves as responsible, loyal citizens of the aforementioned such-and-such.

Then the official had re-boarded his gunboat and sped off over the horizon to the west, never to be seen again. Life continued, as always, and after a while a new official would appear to recite the same litany—except that he wore a different uniform and peaked cap, and spoke of a different sovereign nation and government. Then, he too would go away. This had been happening since time immemorial, the elders said.

However, it made little difference to those living in the village just what faraway government claimed them as citizens. The fish were still biting.

And they were accustomed to solving their own problems. So, early one morning, the boy had slipped into his small outrigger canoe, hoisted its patchwork canvas sail, and crossed the intervening seven miles of deep water between his home island and Isla Tequesta on the dawn breeze. He had hidden the canoe in a stream inlet near the fishing cave, climbed the low cliffs, and began the search for his brother. Since he had decided to work his way from the marker rock toward the rich woman's house, it had not taken long to find him. Or what was left of him.

The boy looked over at the bloody bundle of palm fronds lying against the wall at the far end of the ledge. He had bound them around Fernando's slashed body with vines he had ripped down from the trees. It was the best shroud he could manage. The flat rocks he had lashed to the bundle would carry his brother down. And hold him down . . . long enough.

He unfolded his arms, stood up, and walked slowly over to the body. Through the thin layer of palm fronds he could see the word that had been carved, with deep, savage strokes, into Fernando's chest: RAMOS. He bent down, grasped his brother under the shoulders, and pulled him to the brink of the ledge.

The light-shot blue water was receding, on the out-flow of a swell. The boy squatted beside his brother, thinking. Remembering.

The lonely whistling moan of air squeezing out through cracks in the rock began again as the next swell pushed the pool's surface upward. When the surge reached its highest point, the boy tipped the palm-frond bundle off the ledge. It hit the water with a gentle splash and plummeted downward, sheathed in bubbles, into the flickering blue shadows.

The boy watched silently until his brother could no longer be seen. It took a while, for the waters of the fishing cave were very clear. Then he blinked hard, his eyes suddenly hot and stinging.

"Go back to the fishes, Fernando," he whispered.

Chapter Seven

"Did I or did I not," Alberto said, grimacing in distaste, "*specifically* tell you to stock the onboard bar with Bombay Sapphire gin? Not this revolting North American hooch. Where was it concocted—New Jersey?"

"Uh—I dunno," Sligo mumbled, slicing limes in the *Cucaracha*'s galley. He glanced out into the luxurious teak-and-green-velour interior of the Cheoy Lee's main salon, where Alberto and the lawyer, Gomez, were reclining in a pair of plush, bolted-down armchairs. "I thought you asked for this stuff." Gomez was smirking at him, the shyster prick. Probably a Jew. No, wait . . . a Jew named Gomez? Well, maybe—

"Once again, Jeremiah," Alberto went on in that liquid, irritatingly superior tone of voice, "once again you demonstrate to me that you *cannot—follow—directions.* And you wonder why Grizelda and I hesitate to forward you an entire boatload of product to take up to the U.S. mainland. *HAAH!*" At the sound of the sharp, chirping laugh Sligo cut his finger and Gomez flinched upward three inches in his chair.

"I wish you wouldn't—" the lawyer started to say. Alberto's eyes fixed on his, narrowing.

"—concern yourself so much about the disposition of your funds," Gomez finished hurriedly. "They're quite safe." He swallowed and glared at Sligo. "What's keeping you with my drink?"

The smuggler's eyes were tearing with the pain of the lime juice irrigating his sliced digit. *Fuck you; you want blood garnish in your strawberry daiquiri—that's okay by me.* "Comin', comin'," he grumbled. He hit the switch on the Mixmaster and whirled the fruit, rum, and ice it contained into a vortex of red slush.

When it was sufficiently masticated, he popped the blender off its base, inverted it, and poured the frozen glop into a large hurricane glass. Then he decorated the drink with a bloodstained slice of lime and walked it over to Gomez. "Here y'go," he said, forcing a grin. *Choke on it, asshole.*

He turned to Alberto. "I need to get up on the bridge. Check our course and make sure the autopilot's workin' properly."

"Absolutely," Alberto replied. "Let's not bump into the wrong island and sink ourselves." He waved a limp hand. "Away with you, 'Captain.'"

Sligo smiled weakly, turned, and exited the salon through its port-side door. Gomez watched him through the watertight windows as he made his way forward along the rail, mounted the ladder leading up to the yacht's flybridge, and climbed out of sight.

The lawyer cleared his throat. "A real piece of down-island boat trash, that man. You're quite right not to trust him, Alberto."

"I believe the technical term is 'scumbag'," Alberto said. "But he has his uses." He smiled over his pink gin. "As do you."

The vaguely insulting association made the lawyer's bowels squirm. "Ah—heh, heh—well, that's true, that's true . . ."

Alberto sipped. "I appreciate you flying down the cash," he said.

"Don't mention it. Glad to do it."

"But we still have that small problem I spoke of over the phone to discuss." The fey man sank back in his chair, stretching his soft legs out in front of him. "Relax. We'll have plenty of time to chat about it as we're running across to the island during the next couple of days."

Gomez sat up in his chair. "What?"

"You heard me."

The lawyer paled and took a big gulp of his daiquiri. "Now? But I thought we were just going to take an afternoon cruise around Grand Cayman."

"That was the old plan," Alberto said. "I've changed my mind."

"But—but," Gomez protested, "I've got to get back to New Orleans, dammit. This is my second day out of town. I've got clients . . . appointments . . . obligations…"

Alberto waved a finger. "My friend, you have only *one* obligation that matters, and that is to my sister and me." His expression was pleasant. "It's time we ironed out a few bookkeeping irregularities, that's all. Had a . . . policy meeting."

He stretched his legs again. "Enjoy your daiquiri. Enjoy the view."

"My plane . . ."

"Your plane will be fine where it is. The airport has good security."

Realizing the futility of arguing with his employer, Gomez fell silent and buried his nose in his daiquiri.

"Ahhh," Alberto sighed, gazing out the window at the sparkling blue waters of the Caribbean. "This is a nice change. The cigarette boat is fast but uncomfortable. The crossing from our island to Grand Cayman the other day was an absolute trial. This is a much more genteel way of traveling, don't you think?"

Gomez replied that yes, he thought it was—and tried *not* to think about the seven hundred thousand-plus dollars of skimmed U.S. currency sitting relatively unprotected beneath the pilot's seat of his tarmac-parked Beechcraft.

*****

Back at the Treasure Reef Resort, *BOB* the Kronos technician could still hardly believe his luck. The guy he'd met the previous afternoon at the tiki bar—Sleego or Sluggo or something like that—had returned that same evening, friendly as hell. He'd been after a lesson on the DOA-9000, but it had been too late. The shadows had been lengthening as the tourists milled around the pool, shifting modes from naked-and-baking to soused-and-boogying. Sloggo had nevertheless helped him dismantle his display and cart the rebreather back to its nighttime home in a locked utility room next to the hotel's main trash dumpster. Nice guy.

But it had gotten much, much better. The chunky little middleweight in the gold lamé thong bikini—the one who'd nearly made him cream his polyester Sans-A-Belt slacks when she'd pulsated past the tiki bar earlier in the day—had been perched on a stool in the lobby bar when he and Slaggo had strolled in for a drink, looking pouty and unattached. She'd changed into a white minidress of some clingy, nearly transparent material that somehow made her look more naked, more voluptuously fleshy, than even her thong bikini had. With her dark Latin hair and skin tones ripened by the tropical sun, she'd looked *seriously* hot.

As they'd taken stools next to her at the bar, he himself had been able to do little more than concentrate on not drooling openly down the front of his mono-grammed company shirt. But Sluggo had approached her without hesitation. The guy was some kind of chat wizard or something, because he'd had her laughing and flashing coy glances in less than two minutes. Then he'd pressed something into her hand and whis-pered in her ear, at which point she'd hopped off her barstool and made a fast pilgrimage to the ladies' room. When she'd returned, sniffling a bit, she'd been a regular spark plug of affectionate flirtation, with plenty of rubbing and bumping and wide-eyed giggling.

Slaggo, God bless him, had gradually diverted her attentions away from himself and onto *him*. It hadn't seemed to bother the girl—one Consuela Jones, vaca-tioning church secretary from Scranton, Pennsylvania—who was apparently content to babble nonstop to whichever one of them was closest, all the while gyrating spectacularly atop her barstool.

During one of her rare pauses for breath and a gulp of her *Rain Forest Orgy*, Sleego had leaned in close, slipped a small vial of white powder into his hand, and whispered in his ear:

"On me, pal. Give her a little toot once every half hour—no more—and by midnight she'll be bangin' your pecker off." He'd smiled and backed away. "I'll get with ya for a rebreather lesson in a day or two."

And then he'd vanished. But Consuela—*thank you, God, thank you*—had remained at the bar, as bright-eyed and attentive as ever. Throughout the rest of the evening, she'd gotten edgy every twenty minutes or so, sucking her teeth, sniffing and swallowing, looking expectant; but a fingernail-sized bump from the cocaine vial always put her right again. The mating ritual had continued until one forty-five a.m., at which time—as Sligo had predicted—a rocking and reeling Consuela Jones had led him up to her economy-class hotel room and proceeded to bang his pecker off.

Well . . . not quite *off*. But it had been a near thing, by cracky, with lots of howling and moaning and invoking of The Lord's name and bouncing off the walls and furniture. When she'd finally finished with him, the room had resembled a combat zone.

He'd been so sore and hung over when he'd awoken to the insistent buzz of his watch alarm that he'd practically cried. But after crawling to the bathroom and having a good vomit followed by a cold shower, he'd felt much better—comparatively speaking. Consuela Jones, sprawled on the bed snoring at the ceiling, fat and sticky, hadn't looked nearly as appealing as she had the previous night. But his workout with her had been fun, if physically costly, and being a sentimental sort, he'd even given her a kiss on the toe before creeping out into the hallway. Not that he was going to marry her or anything.

Now the late-morning sun was searing into his eyes and turning the inside of his skull into a pressure cooker as he stumbled across the hotel's service parking lot toward the big trash dumpster. Reaching the door of the utility room where the DOA-9000 was stored, he paused to lean on the wall as a wave of nausea passed over him. He could not afford the luxury of retching in some corner all morning, however; he had an important promotional clinic on the rebreather scheduled for eleven a.m. out beside the pool. Steeling himself, he dug into his pocket for his keys.

Shit. Where were those keys?

Don't tell me I left them up in that fat hosebag's hotel room.

Another sickening attack of shakes and chills seized him, and he sagged back against the corner of the dumpster. *Oh God, if you'll just get me through this, I swear I'll never, ever take another drink or fornicate again as long as I live . . . it's because she was a church secretary, isn't it?* As he waited for the episode to pass, he noticed one of the janitors wheeling a cleaning cart toward the main kitchen service entrance.

"Hey! Simon!" The effort of shouting made his head throb. "C'mere a minute, will you?"

The janitor paused, then left his cart and came ambling across the parking lot, his keys jangling on their chain. As he drew near, his toffee-colored Caymanian face broke into a wide grin.

"Eh, mon!" he declared. "You look like you party too hearty las' night, mon! Catch de cocktail influenza, ha-ha!"

BOB smiled bravely. "Ohhh, yeah." He pointed at the door. "Simon. I've misplaced my keys and I have to get my rebreather out of here. I've got about ten minutes to set up for that big talk I'm giving out by the pool. Could you open the door for me?"

The janitor chuckled. "You look like de walkin' dead dis mornin', mon. One voodoo zombie! I hope 'twas worth it." He picked through his keys. "Jus' cool, mon. I get you inside in a jiffy."

Simon inserted a master key, twisted, and let the heavy steel door swing open. "Dere you go, mon," he said, still chuckling. "Easy now. Have some rum 'n' orange squash at de tiki bar—set you right, mon! Hair a de dog dat bitcha, ha-ha!"

"Thanks," *BOB* replied, wishing the janitor would stop talking now and go away. Simon did, and *BOB* took a moment to re-swallow something sour that had burbled up from his queasy stomach before stepping into the doorway of the utility room.

He stood there for quite a long time, blinking. Then it came. The panic seemed to start deep in his intestines and spread rapidly through every alcohol-tortured organ in his body. He blinked some more, which didn't change things in the slightest.

No.

It had to be a nightmare . . . a horrible, waking nightmare . . .

The DOA-9000 was gone.

*****

One of the really *bitchen* things about working for Alberto and Grizelda Ramos, Sligo had discovered right away, was that they kept him pretty readily supplied with small amounts of cocaine for his own personal use. High-grade Peruvian flake for the most part—the good stuff. Not so much that he'd be tempted to sell any for his own profit; just enough for his own nose and in-house party favors. The Ramoses and most of their associates indulged in a toot now and then, and when they were entertaining aboard the *Cucaracha* Sligo's role was that of boat captain, gofer, cigarette lighter, bartender, and *maitre d' cocaine.*

He popped the lid off the plastic film canister he kept under the seat cushion of the flybridge helm chair and dipped up a nostril-load of powder with the tiny gold spoon he wore on a chain around his neck. Inhaling the hit, he did the same with the other nostril and sat back behind the steering wheel, snuffling and smacking his lips. *Aaahhhhhhh.*

Handling that doofus *BOB* had been so easy it was pitiful. He'd been so blue balled by the chubby slut in the white dress that he hadn't noticed Sligo's palm the small set of keys he'd left on the bartop. A little gift of coke to make sure that the Kronos tech and his new flame stayed in love for the rest of the evening, and he'd been outta there, hightailing it for the rebreather storage room. It had taken less than five minutes to load the DOA-9000, along with its manuals, accessories, and extra gas bottles, into the little sport-utility vehicle that the Ramoses kept on Grand Cayman for local use.

Sligo braced himself as the motor yacht heaved gently over the wake of a passing freighter, which was the only other vessel visible on the sea's calm, cobalt-blue surface. He twisted in the helm chair and glanced astern. Grand Cayman Island had dropped below the eastern horizon, taking with it the law, *BOB*, and sweaty church secretaries from Scranton, Pennsylvania.

He faced forward again, settling himself, and checked the heading on the autopilot. Perfect. Two-five-oh, straight as an arrow. The DOA-9000 was secreted away in the topside dinghy locker, ready and waiting. The manuals were under the bunk in his cabin; he'd have a look at them later, just for shits and giggles.

When the time was right, when this commercial diving crew he'd been hearing about had found the treasure ship for sure, when Alberto and Grizelda had the *Cucaracha* out on site so they could eyeball the salvage—*splash*. Over the side . . . a quick shot down to the bottom with this Buck Rogers rebreather . . . grab all the golden swag he could lay his hands on, and beat feet back to the surface. Simple. Hey—the thing had three of its own electronic brains.

Sligo giggled to himself, coke-happy and tickled pink.

How hard could it be, right?

Chapter Eight

"I think we need to tighten up on that starboard stern anchor just a little more," Ben said, pointing at the GPS screen with a pencil. A schematic representation of the barge and its four-anchor spread was superimposed in glowing green lines over a central red circle labeled TARGET. The floating rectangle was slightly off-center, its orientation to the red circle changing every few seconds as small shifts in the barge's position were picked up by the Global Positioning System's orbiting satellites and relayed to the onboard unit. "Let's crank in another twenty feet and see how she settles."

"Sounds good to me," Gene agreed. "If we don't drag any of the other hooks, that oughtta do it. No real current out here to speak of." He raised a handheld VHF transmitter to his mouth. "Earl. C'mon up on the starboard stern winch twenty feet."

"Roger that."

Through the salt-stained window of the barge control bridge, Ben could see the big man, clad in brown Carhart overalls, denim shirt, work boots, and yellow hardhat, wave once and pull a lever on the massive anchor winch mounted on the corner of the deck. Its huge drum spun slowly, reeling in a section of grease-coated three-inch cable, then halted. Earl set the hydraulic brake and tipped his head toward the transmitter sticking out of his breast pocket.

"That there's about twenty feet, Gene." His disembodied drawl crackled through handheld's small speaker.

"Good. Sit tight. We'll see if that does it." Gene looked over Ben's shoulder at the GPS. "We movin'?"

Ben adjusted the contrast of the display. Slowly, the flickering green rectangle migrated into the exact center of the screen, directly over the red target indicator. It did not drift again. After fifteen seconds, the green lines thickened and the word LOCK began to flash repeatedly at the bottom of the monitor.

Ben looked at Gene. "Good enough?"

"I'd say so."

Flexing his fingers, Ben typed a code into the GPS's keyboard and hit Enter. The LOCK indication disappeared and, in its place, a narrow sidebar scrolled down the right side of the screen, displaying a wealth of navigational data: latitude and longitude, Greenwich Mean Time, local time, water depth, and the like.

Ben hit one more key and straightened up, rubbing the small of his back. "There. The position's locked in and the alarm's set. If a hook drags or a winch slips and we drift more than fifteen feet off location, this baby'll start buzzing us. And the alarm's tapped into the barge intercom system, so we can't ignore it." He grinned.

"Great, great," Gene said. He shook his head. "This stuff still amazes an old pipe-flanger like me. Modern technology sure makes things a lot easier out here, don't it?"

"When it's not malfunctioning and fouling everything up," Ben commented. "Sometimes simpler is better."

"No doubt about that, son." Gene looked out the opposite set of bridge windows. "Well, if you're satisfied we're stable, I'm gonna cut loose the tug. Weather's supposed to be good for the next week, and Boyd wants to run her over to Costa Rica for a low-dollar bottom job—get her cleaned up and have a few plates rewelded for next to nothin'. Compared to U.S. dry dock rates, anyway. He's takin' Chako, too, so we're all cookin' if we want to eat anything that ain't cold out of a can."

"Let him go," Ben said. "We're holding position."

He crossed the cramped interior of the bridge—little more than a metal box with windows, welded to the barge's stern—and stopped in front of the single most important piece of equipment on board: the topside coffee maker. As Gene conversed with Boyd Matthews, the tugboat captain, Ben filled a paper cup with thick

black java and took a long swallow. Its mellow bitter-
ness revived him somewhat. It had been a long night.

They'd arrived on location at one a.m. and spent the
next seven hours setting the barge's four huge anchors,
running out thousands of feet of heavy cable as a warm
tropical drizzle slicked the deck. The sparse clouds had
scudded away to the west with the coming of dawn, and
the wind had dropped to less than five knots. Off in the
distance, three islands had become visible—two to the
south and one to the north.

Those would be the islands mentioned in Nunoz's
manuscript, Ben thought, gazing out the bridge window
at the closest of the three—the one to the north, perhaps
four miles distant. Perhaps less. It didn't look inhabit-
ed. But supposedly, according to what Gomez had told
Gene, it was owned by the moneybags who had paid for
the entire salvage—and who would be putting in an
appearance via private yacht soon after the on-site
operations had commenced.

Ben chewed his coffee. That part wasn't so good.
People who paid for commercial diving services rarely
helped their own cause when they inserted themselves
into the work environment. He'd seen it time and time
again in the oilfield. One too many chiefs in charge of
the Indians. Result: indecision, confusion, wasted time.

But what were you gonna do? He who pays the
piper calls the tune. Maybe the guy would turn out to be

okay... know when to keep his mouth shut and stay the hell out of the way.

The door opened just as Matthew's tugboat began to pull away from the barge's starboard side, her deckhands pulling in her cast-off bow and stern lines. The roar of the tug's big diesel engines filled the bridge as Sass entered, shaking her hair free of her hardhat. Gene put a hand over one ear as he continued to speak into his VHF unit.

"What's it like to work indoors?" Sass asked, picking up a coffee cup. Her cheeks were slightly windburned from five days at sea, the rest of her face deeply tanned.

"Pretty good when it's raining," Ben replied. He smiled. "You tired?"

"A little. Coffee'll wake me up."

Gene came around the chart table and set his VHF unit down in its recharger. "Okay, that's it. The tug's gone until next week, maybe eight or nine days. We're stuck here 'til then, hurricanes or no hurricanes." He grinned at Sass.

"Don't even joke about that," she said moodily.

"Relax," Ben put in. "These days, we find out about 'em by weatherfax when they're still coming off Africa. Lots of time for Matthews to come back and tow us out of the way."

"Sez you," Sass replied. "I'd rather they didn't happen at all when I'm out here."

Ben nudged Gene. "Stop scaring the female. She'll get angry."

Sass stirred a packet of sugar into her coffee and grinned. "I take after the Hulk, Gene," she said. "You wouldn't like me when I'm angry."

Gene laughed. "Mrs. Hulk."

"That's me." Sass winked good-naturedly and toasted him with her coffee cup.

Ben yawned and cracked his knuckles. "So now—I guess we have a look-see, huh?"

"Right," Gene said. "We're anchored over the only likely anomaly in this area. Next thing is to splash Posey's ROV and get some video of whatever's down there." He paused. "It has to be the *Arista*. The position corresponds perfectly to the details given in Nunoz's log."

Ben nodded slowly. "Back in the restaurant that first day, didn't you mention you'd found two anomalies that could be the wreck?"

"Oh, yeah," Gene replied. "You know what that other one was? Turned out the Navy had records on it. It's a Venezuelan pocket freighter that was sunk by a U-boat during World War Two. Hit bottom only about four hundred yards from what we figure must be the *Arista*."

"No kidding?" Sass's eyebrows went up.

"Nope. Just west of her."

"I didn't know those Nazi subs were hunting as far down as the southwestern Caribbean," she said. "I know they got into the Gulf of Mexico . . . torpedoed ships off New Orleans and in the Straits of Florida. My dad used to tell me about it. Sometimes the tourists could see the tankers burning right off Miami Beach."

"That's right." Gene nodded. "And they got down here, too. There was a lot of oil comin' out of Venezuela at the time—Lake Maracaibo, you know? And it was all headed overseas in tankers to fuel up British and American bombers. So the Germans sank as many of 'em as they could. Got quite a few, too."

"But not enough," Ben said, "fortunately for us."

"Right."

"She's a freighter, not a tanker. Did the records say what she was carrying?"

"As a matter of fact, they did." Gene poured himself a cup of coffee. "The manifest showed that she had a cargo of aircraft cable—spools and spools of it. It was made of some early kind of stainless steel, apparently."

"How about that," Ben said. "Interesting." He looked out the forward bridge window. "Well—we ready? Gerald's going to need a few hands."

Gene gestured his coffee cup. "Lead on. Let's do it to it."

They exited the bridge and began to make their way toward the ROV area on the port side, skirting the compressors, winches, hose trees, and gas cylinder racks that cluttered the work deck. The rest of the dive crew had already gathered around the launching skid, looking bleary-eyed and damp from handling anchor winches in the rain all night. But as yet, Ben was glad to observe; no one appeared to have lost his sense of humor.

Vern pulled a crumpled packet of Redman chewing tobacco from the pocket of his sleeveless plaid shirt, dug into it, and inserted a fist-sized wad of brown leaf into his cheek. He put the packet away, the muscles of his huge arms bulging, and grinned at Pierre, who was standing on the opposite side of the launching skid.

"Sacré bleu!" the little Frenchman exclaimed. "Could you be any more disgusting, you overgrown peasant, you? What a habit!"

Vern continued to grin, chewing, his right cheek swollen like an abscess. Then he pursed his lips and abruptly sent a dark brown stream of saliva across the entire width of the skid. It splatted onto the deck at Pierre's feet. The Frenchman leaped backward, cursing.

"Jump, froggy," Vern called, chuckling around his chew.

Pierre grinned in return. "You see, *mon ami?* You prove my point, *n'est ce pas?* The *savoir faire* of a Neanderthal. And by the way, you still owe me twenty doll*air!"*

"Don't hold yer breath waitin' for it."

A ripple of laughter went through the collected crew, and then Chris spoke up: "What's the deal, Gene? We gonna launch this thing or what?" He slapped a hand on the tarpaulin-covered ROV. "Where's Mr. Personality?"

As if by way of reply, the door to the ROV shack swung open and Gerald Posey emerged—muttering to himself, as usual. "Signal deterioration," he grumbled. "Erosion of optimal wave amplitude due to fluctuations in water density . . . salinity . . . thermoclines . . . suspended biological materials . . ."

He looked up suddenly, as if surprised to see everyone standing around. "Well?" He gestured at the ROV, scowling around generally. "That cover has to come off before it can go in the water."

The sudden impulse to squash Mr. Posey like the bug he resembled passed through each member of the dive crew simultaneously—without anyone acting on it. Instead, Pierre, Vern, Earl, and Chris stepped up on the launching skid and began to peel back the vehicle's tarpaulin.

Posey hovered around, fluttering his hands. "Careful! *Careful!"* Ash flew from the cigarette stub he had clamped in the corner of his mouth.

"You ain't helpin'," Vern growled, not quite under his breath.

The ROV tech ignored him. "Roll the cover up and stow it in that locker over there," he ordered, pointing a bony finger. "Watch you don't tear it."

"Hey," Chris said, gathering in the thick plastic, "when you ask so nice, how can we refuse?"

Posey ignored him as well. "Stand clear of the davit crane," he went on. "Those hydraulic rams are going active in a minute."

Vern muttered something inaudible as the four crewmen finished stripping the tarpaulin off the ROV. The unit hung in its skid supports, its flat black surface bedewed with condensation, looking not so much like a benign robot sub as some kind of weapon.

Unlike most ROVs, which were boxy, ungainly contraptions festooned with thrusters and manipulator arms, Posey's vehicle resembled a thick, nine-foot-long torpedo. A pair of stubby, swept-back wings, each one inset with a small directional thruster, protruded from the unit's midpoint, and an arrangement of four stabilizer fins ringed its aft end. There was no drive propeller at the stern extremity, merely an opening resembling that of a rocket exhaust.

The foremost section of the ROV consisted of an expanded nose cone—an instrument blister—that was adorned with sensor ports, camera eyes, and a variety of small, nearly seamless cover plates and doors. A similar, even more streamlined blister was mounted between the wings on the unit's dorsal surface. On top of this was a lock-and-release mechanism of diabolical complexity, which attached the ROV to its lifting cable.

"That davit crane don't have no controls," Vern observed.

Ben, who'd helped Posey test the davit hydraulics during the passage through the Yucatan Channel, opened his mouth to speak. But before he could say anything, the ROV tech whipped out a device resembling a large television remote from the pocket of his pea coat. He held it up and glared at Vern through his steel-rimmed glasses.

"Davit and basic ROV drive and thruster controls," he said. "For deployment and surface maneuvering outside the control shack. Waterproof, too—in case it rains." He smiled thinly and pushed a button.

There was a hum of hydraulics and the crane's small boom moved upward, picking the ROV out of its supports. It wobbled slightly on the end of its cable, but the design of the lock-and-release mechanism kept it from rotating out of position above the launching skid. Posey manipulated a small lever on the remote control and the boom swung slowly sideways, taking the ROV outboard until it was suspended over the clear, indigo-blue water off the barge's port side.

Earl moved up beside Posey. "Where's the pro-pelluh at?" he inquired.

"There isn't one," Posey said, making minute adjustments to the crane's position. "Just some angled blades in the wing thrusters. Anyone can see that."

"Just askin'," Earl pressed on, determined to take a friendly interest. "Ah ain't never come across no ROV like that before. What makes it go, if'n there ain't no pro-pelluh?"

"Internal turbines," the tech replied. The perpetually cranky, preoccupied look on his face moderated somewhat. "Water goes in that scoop-vent under the hull, see? The turbines compress it slightly, create a pressure differential, and shoot it out the back."

"Sounds like an underwater jet engine," Ben said, joining the discussion.

Posey nodded, looking almost pleased that someone had shown evidence of half a brain. "Basically, that's what it is."

"Makes sense," Earl mused. "No prop to get tangled up, for one thang."

Again, Posey nodded appreciatively. "Yep. And it's faster and more power-efficient, too."

"How 'bout close-in manueverin'?" Earl asked. "Hoverin'?"

"The turbine flow gets redirected out through six small lateral nozzles," the ROV tech explained, "which I can control individually. And I have the two directional thrusters in the wings."

Earl smiled and crossed his big arms, towering over Posey like a friendly giant. "How 'bout that," he said.

The tech hit a switch and the two wing thrusters began to spin. Then he thumbed another button and the crane cable began to spool out, lowering the ROV toward the water. As the vehicle touched the gently heaving surface, the thruster blades threw up twin geysers of white foam, accompanied by the throaty whine of cavitation. The commotion ceased rapidly as the ROV sank through the swells.

Posey continued the descent for about twenty feet, then braked the load. A smattering of air bubbles and salt foam hissed on the water's surface around the vertical cable. Below, the sleek ROV had become a fluctuating dark shape, silhouetted against the blue void. As Ben watched, a school of small silver jacks flashed past the cable and into the shadow of the barge.

"Why'd you start the thrusters *before* you splashed the ROV?" he asked Posey. "Just to make sure they were working?"

"No," the tech said. "Without the thrusters running in an upward orientation, pushing *down*, the unit won't descend once it's lowered into the water. It's positively buoyant—it floats."

Ben considered for a moment. "Then how do you get it down to the work site? Remote onboard ballasting? If it doesn't sink—"

"One of my innovations," Posey declared, "is that the unit can't be lost if there is a power failure. Unlike a standard ROV, which can be reeled back up to the surface on its umbilical in the event of a malfunction, my vehicle is not physically attached to the support vessel. Therefore, I cannot have it sinking to the bottom—however deep that may be—if it loses propulsion. It must float back to the surface, where I can track and recover it using its independently powered locator beacon.

"To answer your question: it does not sink down—it *flies* down. You may have noted the cross-section of the pectoral wing; it is the exact inverse of an aircraft wing. At speed, instead of generating upward lift, it generates *downward* lift, or pull. I pilot it toward the bottom in a descending spiral. Then, when it reaches the work site, I switch to directional nozzles and wing thrusters to hold the unit at depth and perform close-in maneuvers."

"Cool," Chris proclaimed, having drifted over to listen in.

Posey examined him briefly through his steel rims before continuing. "One of the side benefits of relying upon upward thrust to keep the unit from floating, rather than downward thrust to keep it from sinking, is that when working close to the sea floor—which is most of the time—there is no ventrally-directed turbulence to stir up bottom sediments and interfere with visibility."

He paused, came perilously close to cracking a smile, and raised a hand toward the door of the ROV shack. "Shall we fly, gentlemen?"

Chapter Nine

"Is it a match?"

Grizelda Ramos was sitting erect on the end of a poolside weight bench, doing alternating arm curls with a pair of forty-five-pound dumbbells. She was staring straight ahead, her jaw set, not looking directly at Fuentes—or the pudgy geneticist would never have risked running his eyes up and down her sweaty, glistening body. He couldn't help himself, though; she was clad only in running shoes, workout thong, halter top, and headband. *Spectacular*, he thought. *Stupendous. A veritable Amazon . . .*

"Fuentes. I asked you a question." The weights had not stopped moving, but now her coal-black eyes were fixed on his.

"Senorita, I beg your pardon, I was going over a few . . . figures in my—my mind, and—"

Grizelda set the weights down with a bang. "You were going over *my* figure in your mind," she grunted. As the geneticist fumbled for a reply, she plucked a towel from the chair beside her and wiped the sweat off her face. "Now tell me: is it a match?"

Hurriedly, Fuentes stepped around in front of her, brandishing a sheaf of papers. "Yes, Senorita. The blood is a match. Statistically, the chances that the two people in question are not related is only one in thirty-six point six mil—"

The musclebound woman held up her hand. "Spare me the numbers." She drew a long breath and let it out slowly. "So that bloodline is direct . . . as is mine."

"Yes, Senorita," Fuentes said, his head bobbing. "DNA science confirms it."

Grizelda bent down and picked up the dumbbells again. Straightening her spine into a strict exercise posture, she began another set of curls, her face a mask of concentration. With every repetition, a little burst of breath escaped her lips: *chuff . . . chuff . . . chuff . . .*

Fuentes stood in silence, looking uncomfortable, as the big woman heaved the weights up and down. After a minute or so, she dropped the heavy dumbbells, picked up a lighter pair, and began lifting more rapidly.

"Exactly why did you poison your wife, Fuentes?" Grizelda asked, her tone matter-of-fact. The weights pumped up and down steadily.

The chubby man's face twitched. "Uh—as I have always claimed, Senorita, that was an accident . . . an unfortunate misunder—"

His voice trailed off as Grizelda's black eyes bored into his.

"Ahhh—she was a vile woman, Senorita Ramos, with no respect for my role as a husband. She deceived me, married me because of my family's social position and the money attached to my research work. She carried on numerous affairs behind my back, ridiculed me, made me a laughing stock, even as I supported her." Fuentes' lower lip trembled, his soft, bespectacled face turning a deep red. "So I taught her that Dr. José Rodolfo Fuentes is no one to trifle with." He nodded, a sick smile twisting his lips. "Yes, I did. I taught that bitch. She's sorry now."

"She's *dead* now," Grizelda clarified. She dropped the small dumbbells and began to shake out her biceps. "How did you do it?"

Fuentes continued to smile, as if relishing the memory. "Strychnine, Senorita Ramos. Coyote poison, in her peppered bean casserole. She never tasted it until it was too late. It took her nearly half an hour to die, rolling around on the dining room floor, holding her stomach and screaming."

"And what did you do?"

Fuentes blinked happily. "I watched her."

Grizelda mopped her face with the towel, regarding the little scientist without expression. "But the authorities found you out."

Fuentes' smile faded. "Yes. One of her lovers became suspicious and called the police. I fled, but they searched the house and found her body where I had hidden it—in the septic tank. The freshly dug earth caught their attention." He shook his head. "A shame.

It would have taken only a few months for the aerobic bacteria to digest her completely and eliminate all evidence of foul play."

Grizelda stood up, flexing her legs. Though she was only half a head taller, she all but dwarfed the bookish scientist. "So—if I had not found you and hired you to come here and do this research for me, you would probably be rotting in some Mexican prison right now. Instead, you are starting a new life in Panama tomorrow with a quarter million U.S. dollars in cash and my thanks."

"As per our agreement, Senorita Ramos," Fuentes said. "I am most grateful for the opportunity—"

Grizelda walked past him a few steps, faced the pool, then bent down straight-legged and touched her toes. Fuentes gulped hard, staring. His entire abdomen seemed to lurch.

Grizelda straightened up languidly, her red-brown curves gleaming in the midday sun. "I know you're grateful, Fuentes," she said, her back to him. He could not tear his eyes away from her hard, naked buttocks. "But you've earned what you're going to get."

She turned and smiled at him, and even on her coarse, heavy-boned face it was a winning smile—or so it seemed to Fuentes. His mind reeled.

"Go to your room, José," Grizelda said, using his given name for the first time ever. "When I have

147

finished taking my exercise, we will continue our discussion there."

Without waiting for a reply, she began to jog around the pool toward the terrace steps that led down into the jungle, leaving Fuentes to stare after her, agog and mute.

*****

The boy was less than a quarter mile from the house, working his way cautiously along the narrow path, when he became aware of the fast-approaching sound of running feet. The jungle on either side of him was virtually impenetrable, thick with brambles, but just a couple of yards ahead stood an ancient, gnarled mahogany tree. The boy stepped up on a root, jumped, caught one of the lower branches, and hauled himself up into the concealing foliage.

He held his breath, lying along the thick limb with leaves ticking his nose. The faint pounding and crackling of dead twigs grew steadily louder. And then, she was there—the red-haired woman, directly beneath him, her odd little ponytail bouncing on top of her powerful shoulders.

All at once she slowed, drew back, and halted. The boy's heart skipped a beat. Stepping over beside the tree, she put a hand on the trunk and began to stretch her calves, breathing heavily. From above she looked huge, a streamlined mass of coppery muscle.

The stretching went on for several minutes. The boy's arms and legs began to cramp from the effort of hugging the tree limb; it was becoming difficult to remain motionless. He flexed his thigh—and dislodged a piece of loose bark.

At that instant, the woman stepped back out onto the trail. The little chunk of bark fell past her left shoulder, missing it by an inch, and dropped into the leaf litter without a sound. She bent down and touched her toes as the boy willed his aching body to remain still.

Then she straightened up and fished around in her halter top with one hand. Extracting a short brass tube about the size of a cartridge casing, she twisted off one end and raised it to her face. There was a loud sniffing sound. And another.

The woman let her head loll back on her shoulders, her face turning directly upward. The boy's blood froze in his veins. But her eyes were closed, her heavy lips peeled back in a grimace. A light coating of white dust rimmed her nostrils.

"Gaaaghhaaaghaaaghhhh," she croaked, the sound wet and nasal. Her fists were balled so tightly they were shaking, the muscles of her arms and shoulders taut as cable. The boy watched transfixed. It was as if one of the old demons of legend had come to life—

something part human, part animal. She would open her eyes now, look straight up into his . . .

"Acchh!" With the harsh exclamation, the woman's head jerked down. She snorted once, spat, and wiped her nose on the back of her hand. The little tube she replaced in her halter top. Then she moved off down the trail, broke quickly into a loping run, and disappeared.

The boy listened until he could no longer hear her feet pounding along the hard path. Then, shaking, he slid off the limb, hung at arm's length, and dropped to the ground. Somewhere off in the treetops, a parrot screeched, insects buzzed through patches of sunlight, but there were no sounds to indicate that anything human might be nearby. Quietly, he resumed making his way up the trail.

The house was visible now—a sprawling two-story affair constructed atop one of the island's largest central hills. The boy swallowed, steeled himself, and continued to creep forward. The wood and stones from all the shacks in his village would not have built one quarter of such a mansion.

He stopped under the huge leaf of an elephant-ear plant, squatted back on his heels, and studied the place from a distance of about two hundred yards. There was a big terrace with a pool, surrounded by a low wall. The wall continued on down from the terrace level for another fifteen or twenty feet, becoming part of the vertical rock outcropping that formed the back of the property. There were several detached buildings, like small cottages, that were connected to the house by their extended roofs, which created open breezeways. And there was a glass shed—a greenhouse—sitting at one end of the terrace. As the boy looked on, a pudgy man in a white lab coat scurried out of the back of the main house, around the pool, and entered the shed.

A moment later, two other men strolled into view through one of the breezeways and began to walk slowly along the terrace wall, talking. Both were smoking cigarettes, and both had shotguns slung over their shoulders. Frequently, one or the other would cast an eye over the surrounding terrain, as if out of habit. *Guards*, the boy thought, and was careful to remain very still beneath the elephant-ear.

He shivered suddenly, although it was far from cold, and hugged his knees. A hollow, aching feeling swelled in his chest, and he knew he was afraid. But that was all right. He closed his eyes, concentrating, and willed the sensation away. It was all right to be afraid. Everyone was afraid sometimes.

It was not all right to be paralyzed. His father had once told him as much: to be afraid and let it paralyze you was to be a coward. A brave man was afraid—

sometimes terribly afraid—but did what he had to do anyway. That was the only difference.

The boy smiled to himself as he huddled beneath the elephant-ear, remembering. He'd asked a question: were there any men who did brave things and were never afraid? Yes, his father had replied, they were called *fools*.

Sometimes he missed his father. And his mother. One lost in a storm outside the reef. The other dead of some terrible coughing sickness. And now the older brother he had relied upon was gone, too. He was the only one left.

The only one who could get justice for Fernando.

The boy waited until the guards turned to watch the white-coated man emerge from the glass shed, then darted out from under the elephant-ear and began to work his way closer to the foot of the terrace wall.

*****

Fuentes' mind was in a whirl. The Ramos woman was actually going to favor him with . . . an intimate visit! She'd removed all doubt out by the pool, hadn't she? And he'd thought she was only interested in his DNA analysis skills. What a delicious, unbelievable turn of events! This kind of thing *never* happened to him.

He slipped into his bedroom—top of the main stairs, first door to the right—and took a moment to gaze out the open window. This end of the house was built on the lip of a steep, rocky slope that fell away from the concrete foundation for a full sixty feet before terminating in dense hillside jungle. It was like being seven stories up instead of two, and the view—like all views from the house—was magnificent, encompassing the entire eastern end of the island.

Fuentes drew in a deep breath—the air was like perfume—and turned to look at his reflection in the full-length mirror on the door of the walk-in closet. A chubby, stoop-shouldered little man in a white lab coat looked back at him, toothbrush mustache twitching beneath a red-veined drinker's nose. The eyes that flanked the nose were glittery and close-set. They had a furtive quality, like a ferret's.

But what Fuentes saw was a debonair academic: an elegant Man of Science. He patted his lank black hair over his noticeable bald spot. There. The very picture of Andalusian gentility and refinement. No wonder the Ramos woman wanted him. Come to think of it, considering the figure he cut, it was amazing that she had been able to restrain herself for this long.

He was feeling positively lusty. In quick succession, he stripped off his lab coat, shirt and tie, correctional shoes (bad arches), and pinstriped suit pants.

Turning sideways to the mirror, he sucked in his flabby gut and flexed his biceps—and was fairly certain he saw the pallid flesh of his upper arm move slightly.

He smiled at his reflection. Grizelda Ramos was about to meet her sexual match in Dr. José Rodolfo Fuentes, or his name wasn't . . . wasn't . . . er . . .

His smile faltered as his train of thought sabotaged itself. Well, anyway—*he* knew what he meant.

He turned the other way, pulled in his belly again, and made another muscle.

Olé!

*****

It took the boy the better part of an hour to retreat back into the jungle a safe distance, then work his way around to the foot of the terrace wall beneath the greenhouse. The terrain was treacherous: steeply sloped, pocked with sinkholes and gullies, and over-grown with strangler vines, scrub palms, and thorn bushes. But negotiating it was the only way to ap-proach the house—the guards were apparently quite content to spend the rest of the afternoon lounging on the section of wall that overlooked the lone footpath.

Crouching low in the dense brush, his cheek pressed up against the rough stone, the boy examined the twenty feet of wall above him. It was constructed of quarried coral blocks, about three feet long by two high, which had been mortared together in such a way that the seams were wide and decorative. He tested his grip on the closest horizontal edge. The seam was deep enough to accommodate the first two joints of his fingers—easy to hold on to.

The terrace wall was not straight, but followed the contours of the hillside. The guards were at one end, talking and smoking. He was at the other, out of sight behind the first curve. Taking a deep breath, he reached up for the seam above his head—and stopped before lowering his hand.

The three-inch scorpion scuttled away beneath his fingers, its stinging tail poised above its armored body. The boy exhaled slowly, watching it. When the tiny predator had passed, he took hold of the first edge, got a toe into a lower seam, and began to climb.

He was eight feet up, his arms and legs shaking with the effort, when he realized that he was now visible to anyone coming up or down the path that led to the terrace steps. But it was too late to worry about that now. Gritting his teeth, he continued to climb toward the greenhouse, the roof of which he could just see behind the wall's capstone.

"Hoy, Senorita Ramos!" The sound of the guard's voice sent a thrill of panic through him. He jerked his head around, looking over his shoulder. Off in the

jungle, along the thread of trail, he could make out the bobbing head and bouncing ponytail of the red-haired woman as she jogged toward the house.

If he dropped into the brush, the guards would certainly hear him. If he stayed where he was, the woman would spot him instantly as she came around the last bend in the trail.

Climb.

He reached up for the next horizontal edge—and found nothing. Where there should have been a seam, his scrabbling fingers encountered only a rough, flat surface, flush with the surrounding rock. Frantically, he stood on his toes and stretched up as far as he could, trying to see. The seam was completely full of mortar, trowelled off smooth. There was not even enough of an edge to hang a fingernail on.

He shot a look back over his shoulder. The red head and bouncing ponytail were less than a minute from the open bend in the trail.

Forgetting about scorpions, the boy probed with his hand in the closest vertical seam, searching for something—anything—to grasp. This gap had not been filled flush with mortar, but the sides of the stone blocks were featureless, devoid of holds. In desperation, the boy scanned the remaining twelve feet of wall. It was the same all the way to the top: horizontal seams mortared flush; vertical seams open, but providing nothing in the way of purchase.

He was about to give up, jump back down into the brush, and take his chances fleeing into the jungle when his right toe slipped. The breath came out of him in a rush as he dropped with sickening suddenness.

The hand with which he had been probing the vertical seam turned sideways, clenching into a fist out of reflex—and wedged itself between the two adjacent blocks like a stopper. The boy hung splayed on the wall, supported by only his jammed fist.

It took him a second or two to realize what had happened. Here was something he hadn't thought of . . . but now, here also was a way up. Keeping his fist clenched, straight-armed, he leaned back and got the balls of his feet against the wall's rough surface. Friction on the soles of his battered sandals made his feet stick, and he managed to shuffle them upward a few inches.

He didn't bother looking over his shoulder to see where the red-haired woman was. It was a race now; either she would see him or she wouldn't. With his free hand, he reached above his secure fist, inserted it into the seam, and jammed it. Again, the technique worked, allowing him to take all his weight on one arm. He shuffled upward, careful not to let his feet slip, and repeated the motion.

The guard called out again, and this time the woman replied, her hoarse, deep voice resounding off the terrace wall. Sweat stung the boy's eyes as he powered his way up the second-to-last vertical seam, sticking hand jam after hand jam . . .

"Hey!" the woman yelled. *"What are you doing, there?"*

His heart sank. She'd seen him.

"I said, what are you doing there, eh?"

There was no alternative but keep climbing, then try to run for it.

The woman continued to shout angrily. "You think I don't have eyes, perhaps, Miguel? I can tell when you are smoking *basouko* and not regular cigarettes on guard duty! *Bastard!* Unreliable bodyguards I don't need!"

"Por favor, Senorita Ramos, I . . ." The guard launched into a groveling, imaginative denial of her accusation that the boy was too occupied to appreciate—because with his last reserves of strength, arm tendons screaming and hands scraped bloody, he was muscling up the final three feet of wall, clambering over the capstone, and collapsing unseen in a heap behind a row of garbage cans at the rear of the terrace greenhouse.

Chapter Ten

The interior of the ROV shack was dark and cramped, packed wall-to-wall with electronic panels, display screens, exposed circuit boards, and wiring. The single air-conditioning unit mounted in the roof did little more than re-circulate the same hot, smoke-laden air, all the while leaking drops of condensation on whoever happened to be standing beneath it. In spite of the discomfort, the entire dive crew had crowded inside to form a tight semi-circle behind the ROV pilot's chair—a synthetic leather and aluminum contraption that looked like a cross between a space shuttle seat and an inquisitor's torture rack.

Said contraption contained Gerald Posey, who was staring with intense concentration at the five-screen video display before him. The flickering, full-color monitors occupied the most central position on an intricate control console that was built partially around the pilot's chair, putting every switch, button, and dial within easy reach. The screen array was such that the single large monitor was surrounded by four smaller ones.

Posey's right arm rested on a padded support, at the end of which was a pistol-grip joystick. This he clutched firmly in his right hand, continually adjusting its angle while depressing various triggers and buttons with his thumb and forefinger. His left hand roamed over the rest of the console; punching keys, hitting switches, and turning dials in response to the various instruments' visual and aural feedback.

Sass, squashed between Ben and the colossal Earl, did her best to stifle a fit of coughing. The atmosphere in the shack was nearly intolerable. Posey, true to form, was generating smoke like a Birmingham steel foundry, his ubiquitous cigarette rooted in the corner of his mouth. Despite the toxic onslaught, everyone remained hunched behind the pilot's chair, eyes glued to the center screen.

"Lemme get this straight," Vern rumbled. "That there middle tee-vee's the nose camera?"

Posey's left arm snapped out. "Nose camera, mobile," he recited, pointing at the main monitor. His bony index finger shifted to the other four screens in rapid succession, moving clockwise. "Dorsal camera, fixed. Caudal camera, fixed. Starboard camera, fixed. Port camera, fixed. All wide-angle, all twenty-to-one zoom, all fields overlapping. The only blind spot is dead astern." He puffed smoke. "My fish has five eyes that see three hundred and sixty degrees in all spatial planes, simultaneously." The ROV tech glanced over his shoulder at Vern, the console lights reflecting off the lenses of his steel-rimmed glasses. "Did you get that?"

"Hail, yeah," Vern said. "The thang sees real good."

"Precisely." Posey turned back toward the screen.

"Looks to be 'bout as bright and cheery down there at twelve hundred feet as it usually is," Gene drawled, his voice low.

Ben nodded, concentrating on the monitor. "'Bout as."

The picture on the main video screen was of a flat gray plain of sediment, eerily illuminated for a distance of about ten feet by the ROV's forward lights. The surrounding water was absolutely black, and out of the blackness whirled a storm of suspended particles, rushing past the camera lens as the vehicle flew forward. Every so often some bottom-dwelling creature— a flatfish, an eel, or a crab—would bolt to the side, kicking up a spurt of sediment, as the oncoming lights startled it.

"Don't see a damn thing yet," Chris muttered, tapping his finger on the chair's headrest.

Posey aborted the tapping with a sour look over his shoulder. "*Thank* you for not doing that." He pointed at the position reading in the lower corner of the screen. "We're running down the exact line of latitude now. About another three hundred fee—"

He stopped in mid-sentence as the fluke of what was clearly an old-style grappling anchor rushed into view and off the bottom of the screen. A chorus of exclamations and admonitions filled the ROV shack.

"Hey, slow down!"

"See that?"

"Whoa! Dang!"

"Alors, you go too fast, *mon ami!"*

Posey ignored the comments and continued to fly forward, manipulating buttons on the head of the joystick. Gradually, the ROV's forward movement slowed to a crawl. Slight irregularities in the bottom sediment became increasingly well defined; a greater number of small animals became visible.

"We're there," Ben said, watching the position numbers tick up in the corner of the screen. "Ought to be seeing something right about—"

All of a sudden, the flat bottom began to bank like a snowdrift. Several large chunks of what looked like rotten wood came into view, sticking up at odd angles out of the abyssal plain like crooked headstones in a sunken graveyard. Posey grimaced slightly and inched back on the joystick as the chunks slipped out of view at the bottom of the screen.

As the ROV coasted to a halt and began to hover, a huge black mass loomed up dead ahead, poorly defined at the outermost limit of the forward lights. Posey's fingers darted over the thruster buttons, holding the robot sub in position. A round of low cheers filled the stale air.

"Yee-haw! That's it!"

"Dang, that's purty. Anybody see any gold layin' around?"

"Not yet. Be patient."

"If there's any dang gold down there, the first piece has ol' Vern's name on it."

"*Zut!* Then you would be able to pay the twenty dol*lair* you owe me, behemoth."

"Quiet, froggy. Don't rattle muh walnuts right now."

Gene leaned over Posey's shoulder. "How close can you get, Gerald?" he asked.

"Pretty close," the tech replied, manipulating the joystick. "I'm just stabilizing the unit right now, seeing if there's any current I have to deal with . . . doesn't seem to be much." He exhaled a long stream of smoke at the screen. "I'll do a slow hover over the entire structure as a preliminary survey. My caudal camera is interfaced with an onboard computer program that will map the site from a known point, then consolidate all the digital video imagery and linear distance data into a three-dimensional graphic that we can utilize as an analysis tool."

"What?" Vern said.

"The ROV can draw us a map of the wreck," Ben explained, "as it's making its first pass. Help us figure out where we are when we're down there working out of the bell."

"That'd be good," the big man conceded.

"You got that right," Chris cut in. "That's one seriously broke-down pile of wood, there." He pointed over Posey's shoulder at the screen. "Looks like sediment's drifted all through it."

"I don't think so," Gene said. "The hull is still basically intact. If it had collapsed, it would have been completely covered over by now, and we'd never have gotten a profile on it usin' sonar. The echo reading would have been totally flat." He glanced at Chris. "The sediment's just banked up against it, see? Most of the structure is well above the mud line. There's gonna be some muck inside, but not so much that the hull can't be cut open and penetrated."

The center screen was now showing yard after yard of parallel planking and supporting timbers, the black wood encrusted with a thin layer of deepwater growth that resembled lichen. In the harsh glare of the video lights, the encrustation revealed a wealth of colors: vibrant reds, pale yellows, royal purples. Here and there, the delicate appendages of deep-sea anemones and tube worms waved and fluttered in the slight current.

"This looks like the bow," Sass said, as Posey piloted the ROV expertly around what appeared to be one end of the structure. "See where the planking is pegged into the stem?" She grinned, totally absorbed. "Isn't it amazing we can still see that after four hundred years? And that the hull's still holding its shape? You'd think it would have collapsed by now."

"Built to last," Ben said. "And maybe the oxygen levels down here are low enough to inhibit the rotting process—I've seen that before. She—whoa!"

A long cylindrical object loomed out of the darkness at the upper edge of the screen. Posey dipped the joystick forward, and the ROV dropped toward the bottom. A little puff of sediment billowed up in the lower half of the main monitor. The caudal monitor went black.

The tech sat back and lit a fresh cigarette off the butt of the old one. "I've set her down on the seabed," he announced. "The caudal camera's in the mud; that's why it's blacked out." He pointed at the upper left-hand monitor. "The dorsal camera points straight up. See what it's looking at?"

Ben examined the image on the small screen. "I'd say that was a spar. Maybe part of a mast." He nodded. "Yeah, that's right. The manuscript I read said that the *Arista*'s masts had been carried away in a storm. This section was probably dragging alongside, still attached to the foredeck by a tangle of rigging." He fell silent for a moment. "They'd have been trying like blazes to cut it away, before it made the ship wallow and sink."

"Looks like it didn't work," Chris observed.

Posey activated the thrusters again, and the ROV lifted off the bottom. It resumed its slow forward hover, the overhead spar moving out of the dorsal camera's field of view. The caudal camera screen brightened again, showing the sea floor passing slowly beneath the vehicle.

"By the way," Posey said, "I just flew this ROV directly under an overhead obstruction. Try *that* with a unit that has to tow a tethering umbilical."

Ben cleared his throat, which was sore from inhaling Posey's smoke. "I'd like to ask you something. I thought the jet-propulsion intake was on the underside of the ROV. How can you set it down in the mud and still keep the engine and thrusters operating?"

The tech smiled around his cigarette. "That's a good question. The answer is that I switched to the alternate intake before I let the vehicle come into contact with the sediment. It's the small, vented opening on the dorsal side of the hull just aft of the secondary blister. You asked me about it a few days ago when we were testing the crane hydraulics, remember?"

"I think so," Ben said. "Lots to remember about your sub, Gerald."

"It's somewhat complex, I grant you."

Gene scratched his stubble, eyeing the main monitor. "You know," he mused, "as structurally intact and high off bottom as this wreckage is, you'd think it'd be longer."

"Mmm." Ben nodded. "I see what you mean. The thing's sitting upright, on its keel, with only a slight list to starboard. This is the bow and forward section. If the aft section has collapsed, there should at least be a low-profile debris field, the remains of the keel and ribs—something. Like I said, the rotting process seems slow down here. If the bow's in this good a condition, the rest of the ship should be as well."

"Certainment," Pierre put in. "But when we approached the first time, I am sure I recognized the reinforcement timbers of a foremast step—and this was at the aftermost part of the wreckage. Something is not right, *par tonnerre."*

"How the hail would you know what a mast step on a Spanish galleon looks like?" Vern grumbled.

The little Frenchman inflated his chest. "Because, you human orca, you, I have done three salvages off the coast of Portugal on ships very similar to this, and, in so doing, took the time to examine the old design blueprints. *Tu comprends?"*

Vern looked a little nonplussed. "Don't be braggin' on it."

167

The encrusted timbers began to slide across the screen diagonally as Posey maneuvered the ROV through another turn. After another ten seconds of flying, the wreckage gave way to a broad bank of sediment, and the tech put the vehicle into a motionless hover.

"We're back at ground zero," he announced. "This is where we started."

Gene leaned in. "Really outstanding, Gerald. The video, the handling—everything. Now, how quick can we get a look at that map graphic you were talkin' about?"

Posey executed six rapid strokes on the small keyboard under his left hand. The display on the main monitor split; the right half retaining the picture from the ROV's nose camera, the left flashing up a detailed, full-color virtual image of the entire wreck *in situ*, complete with seabed contours and black, abyssal background.

"Cool," Chris proclaimed.

Seven heads crowded in closer above Posey's chair. The tech's left hand pattered on the keyboard again, and the perspective of the image changed, pulling up and back. The point of view moved over the top of the wreck, rotated a hundred and eighty degrees, and dropped down the opposite side.

"Let's try this," Posey said, and hit another combination of keys. Instantly, the image of the wreck converted from a semi-realistic computer painting to a transparent line drawing—a virtual blueprint. Both external and internal features were rendered in exacting detail.

"How does it do that?" Ben asked. "Draw the interior, I mean. The camera can't see inside."

Posey turned and flashed a rare smile. "That's one of my innovations," he declared. "When I wrote this computer program, I incorporated a historical database containing all the fundamental structural elements of nautical architecture, from triremes to hydrofoils. Once a wreck has been located and mapped, the program analyzes the design features of the outside, then extrapolates from that analysis what is most likely to be supporting them on the *inside*. What you're seeing is a representation of the best guess the computer can make, based on all the data."

"Ingenious," Sass commented, shaking her head. Posey nodded.

"Watch this," he said, typing a fresh sequence into the keyboard. The line drawing of the wreck lifted off the virtual seabed, did a slow horizontal rotation through three hundred and sixty degrees, then settled back down on its footprint.

The ROV tech hit one more key and the line drawing was instantly replaced by the previous, more realistic image. He sat back in his chair, exhaling smoke, without further comment.

Gene spoke first: "Well, I guess we can all pretty much figure out what we're lookin' at, eh?"

There was silence in the ROV shack. Then Earl cleared his throat. "This here doohickey o' Gerald's makes it purty dang clear to me," he said.

"Me too," Vern echoed.

Gene looked over at Ben. "What do you think?"

The smile that came back his way was rueful. "I think," Ben said, "that we're looking at half a ship."

"That's what I'd say," Chris chimed in. "Maybe even a third."

"Tabarnac! It is as I feared," Pierre said. "She has broken in two just behind the foremast, the poor lady."

"At least two," Vern grunted. "Maybe more. We don't know."

There was another long silence. Carefully, Posey began to back the ROV away from the wreck, keeping the nose camera trained on a large chunk of timber that extended out over the sediment bank. A strange, eel-like deepwater fish, about a foot long, undulated past the lens as the wreck faded out of range of the video lights.

"Well, which half is it?" Sass asked finally, giving voice to what everyone was thinking. "The half containing the treasure? Part of the treasure? Or the half that held the dirty laundry?"

"Spaniards don't do laundry," Pierre muttered. "No one does who lives south of France. Trust me on this."

Gene gave a snort of laughter. "You're a card, LeRenard." He clapped his hands. "All right. We've got half a ship, and no idea where the other half is. It might have shattered as it fell through the water column, for all we know. Spread itself so thin that no one'll ever find it. *So*—we work with what we've got. We want to find out if there's any gold on that wreck, and there's only one way to do it."

He stepped over to the door of the ROV shack and opened it, letting in a flood of eye-burning sunlight. "Ben, Chris, Pierre, Vern—get ready to press down in the sat pot. Let's go deep-sea divin', heroes."

Chapter Eleven

The saturation system consisted of an on-deck pressure chamber—a horizontal steel cylinder seven feet in diameter by eighteen long, in which the divers would eat and sleep between bell runs; the diving bell itself—a steel sphere six feet in diameter that could be mated to and detached from the outboard end of the on-deck chamber; and a hydraulically-operated A-frame handling system that would lift the bell outboard, lower it to the bottom, and recover it when the run was completed. The bell was a roll-over design: mating it to the end of the on-deck chamber required that it be lowered into a supporting wheeled trestle, rotated ninety degrees so that its tubular entry/exit trunk was oriented horizontally and trundled forward on a short rail system until the trunk and chamber flanges could be locked together. All operations would be controlled from the sat shack—a fiberglass van with large, tinted windows that was mounted on an elevated I-beam framework at the inboard end of the main chamber, overlooking the bell-launching area.

Sass passed Ben a stack of towels as he squatted in the chamber's outer lock, his hip blocking open the massive circular hatch to prevent it from swinging on its precision hinge with the slight motion of the barge.

She sat on the lip of the hatchway—the larger of the two, one at either end, that provided access to the "sat pot"—and held the heavy steel door as Ben moved to the entrance of the inner lock and handed the towels on to Vern. As always, despite her long familiarity with it, there was something vaguely frightening about watching him prepare to be sealed inside a giant steel can and pressurized to a degree that was totally unnatural for humans—in a breathing environment of weird gases, no less. Even from the open entrance, the interior of the chamber felt dim and close . . . *very* confining. A little chill of claustrophobia flickered through her, and she wondered for the hundred-thousandth time how Ben was able to stand it. On one deep job for the U.S. Navy, working in the Indian Ocean off Diego Garcia, he'd lived in saturation with seven other men, in a pot not much bigger than this, for fifty-six days.

She thought back to their reunion. His only comment had been "Good paycheck." His only concerns, in order of importance: a hot shower, a cold beer, and a decent hamburger . . . and two solid days with her—the shades drawn and the phone off the hook.

She smiled, remembering. *Nice.*

"Okay, that's it." Ben turned around in the restricted space of the outer lock and sat back on his haunches. Behind him, through the second hatchway, Sass could see Pierre, Chris, and Vern all busily stowing clothing and equipment in and around the two pairs of cots that were hung on either side of the inner lock, one above the other. There was precious little room to move.

Sass took Ben's hand. "Vern looks like he needs a whole sat pot to himself," she said, keeping her voice low.

"Yeah, he's a big one." Ben grinned, squeezing her fingers. "But he knows the drill. He'll be good at sharing space, managing his size in there." He whistled lightly through his teeth. "Tight fit in that small bell, though. Gonna have to pair him up with LeRenard, I guess."

"You don't think they'll murder each other on their first run?"

"Nah. They like each other; they'd just never admit it. Anyway, the only time they have to be in the bell together is when they're riding up and down. On bottom, one guy's outside working for half the run while the other tends his hose. Then they switch."

Sass puffed her cheeks. "Still going with the six-hour bell runs?"

"Yeah."

She shook her head and smiled. "That's brutal. You're going to be exhausted."

"Ah, it's not bad. Six hours on, six hours off to lie on a cot and sack out. You can get by on that for a week or so. Potentially, it's twelve hours of sleep a day."

"Not including rinsing off, changing, eating, chewing the fat about the job, and using the head. And that's *if* you can make yourself fall asleep."

"Believe me," Ben reassured her, "after a six-hour bell run, three of it dressed in and humping around on bottom, none of us are going to have any trouble falling asleep."

"I hope not." She looked into his eyes fondly. "I have to say it, you know."

He ran his forefinger along the line of her jaw to her chin. "I know."

"Please be careful. Don't do anything heroic down there. All the gold in the Spanish fleet isn't worth my losing you."

Ben smiled. "Funny. That's how I feel about you. What a coincidence, huh?"

She kissed him. "Get in your tin can, hero. Try not to stub your toe."

"With you, Gene, and Earl running the sat up here, what can go wrong?" He ducked back into the lock, pushed the hatch into alignment, and grinned. "See you, kiddo."

There was a gentle clang as the heavy steel door shut on its O-ring seal, and he was gone. Sass ran her finger around the edge of the hatch, checking that the O-ring had not been displaced, then pushed the TALK button on the small communications unit clipped to the collar of her denim shirt. "Ready to try for a seal at the main hatch, Gene," she said, "if the guys inside are."

"Roger that," came the supervisor's voice. "They're ready. Stand by. I'm gonna put pressure to the pot. We'll blow down to twenty-two feet with 80/20 heliox, like we planned, and then do a complete life support system checkout. Everything goes nice and slow and steady, y'all."

"Roger," Sass replied.

"Roguh that." Earl's deep voice resonated out of her comm unit. "Ready to check for leaks up at the bell-matin' flange."

"Here comes the pressure."

There was a hiss of gas, and the entire sat pot seemed to ring with a soft, metallic note.

"Two feet," Gene said, calling off the blowdown depths. "Three . . ."

Sass set a hand on the inward-swinging hatch and pushed hard. It didn't budge. She did the math in her head, quickly, just for practice. At an internal atmospheric pressure equivalent to three feet of seawater, every square inch of the hatch's surface was being pushed shut by one point three pounds of outward force. The hatch was a disk forty-eight inches in diameter . . . pi times the square of the radius equals total surface area . . . about eighteen hundred square inches, times one point three . . . about twenty-three hundred pounds.

The hatch was being held shut, at only three feet of equivalent depth, by well over a ton of internal pressure.

She smiled. Her one hundred and thirty-five pounds wasn't going to move it much. At twelve hundred feet, the pressure on every square inch of the inside of the sat pot would be . . . somewhere around . . . five hundred and thirty pounds. *On every square inch.* The hatch alone would be withstanding a total pressure of nine hundred and fifty *thousand* pounds. Four hundred and seventy-five *tons.* No wonder the chamber and bell were made of five-inch-thick steel.

It was these mind-boggling numbers that always troubled her, though she knew the physics theory by heart. Every square inch of the surface area of Ben's body, at depth, would be subjected to that five hundred and thirty pounds of pressure, including the linings of his lungs, respiratory tract, sinuses, and ears. That he would not be crushed to jelly or immobilized by this tremendous force was due to a simple fact of physics: a fluid cannot be compressed. And Ben's body, like that of every other human, was composed almost entirely of fluid. In addition, it contained no gas-filled spaces or voids that were not connected in some way to the outside of the body. All would equalize as the blow-down progressed. The lungs would vent through the trachea; the sinuses at the back of the throat; the ears through the Eustachian tube; the intestines, should internal gas be present . . . well . . .

God help a diver whose dentist had inadvertently trapped a bubble of air in a gold filling, and who then attempted to go under pressure. Ben had several stories of having to hold down and administer emergency tranquilizers to a fellow diver who'd suddenly gone insane in saturation when a tooth had blown. "It's one reason I floss regularly," he'd told Sass, flashing his wry grin.

"Twenty-two feet, all stop," Gene reported. The hissing ceased.

Sass pulled a small plastic squirt-bottle of soap solution from the back pocket of her jeans, and proceeded to wet down the hatch's seal, looking for telltale bubbles. There were none.

"Leak test completed on the main hatch, Gene," she said into her comm unit. "Tight as a drum."

"Roger that, Sass. Earl?"

"Just gettin' a good looksee here," Earl grunted. "Nossuh. Not a bubble. No leaks."

"Good work. All right, I want every fitting on this sat system sprayed and leak tested again while I'm establishin' the correct gas percentages in the pot. Clear?"

"Roger that," Sass replied, moving around to the side of the chamber and the mass of valves and plumbing that decorated it.

"Roguh," Earl rumbled. "Doin' it now."

"Thank you. See you both in the shack when you're done."

*****

Inside the pot, Ben and Chris were lying on the two upper cots, comfortably clad in gray sweats. Between them, Vern and Pierre were completing the organization of their lower cots, trying to give each other room. Vern's head continually skimmed the uppermost curve of the chamber.

"Dang, you take up a lotta space, froggy," he grumbled. "You sure you done this before?"

Pierre squeezed past the big man, sat down on his bunk, and looked up at Ben with an incredulous Gallic shrug. "*I* take up a lot of space? *Moi? Mon dieu*, you make a joke, yes? I saw one time in the North Sea, for sure, an *elephant seal* that did not possess your bulbosity! And you have the nerve to insinuate, cretin, that *I* am not entitled to my fair share of room in this glorified soup can? *Quelle impertinence*, I say!"

"'Bulbosity'?" Chris muttered

"Ah ain't *insinuatin'*," Vern growled, "whatever that means. Ah'm *tellin'* you."

"Incroyable!" The Frenchman swung his legs up onto his bunk, kicking Vern in the process, and lay back with his hands behind his head. "I give you notice, my Brobdingnagian friend: do not force me to chastise you in here. The various pieces I detach from you— particularly your head—will not fit out through the door of the medical lock, and we will all have to endure the presence of your putrefying carcass for the duration of the job." He waved a sly finger at the eighteen-inch hatch of the small side-mounted air lock that was used to transfer food, medical supplies, and personal items in to the divers.

"Y'all believe the noise this little feller makes?" Vern declared to Ben and Chris, sitting down on his cot. "Like listenin' to a June bug in a bottle."

"Sapristi!" Pierre went on, in full continental paroxysm. "And another thing, monster—you will pay me the twenty dol*lair* you owe for your pitiful showing during our combat of arms, eh? *Mon dieu*, look at the puny muscles on you, you semi-human caricature, you . . ."

"Ah wouldn't pay you that twenty bucks if'n Jeezus Christ hisself ordered me to do it. Rather burn in hail . . ."

Ben rolled over on his side, chuckling at the stress-relieving rhubarb going on beneath him, and pillowed his head on his upper arm. What made the exchange really funny was that the helium gas they were all breathing made the two jousting divers sound like a pair of hyperactive Donald Ducks. Hilarious.

Reaching up, he re-coiled a fallen loop of hose around the emergency oral-nasal mask hanging over his cot, then closed his eyes. The chamber was filled with little hisses and spurts as Gene continued to optimize the gas percentages. He closed his eyes and yawned, clearing his ears, as the pressure within the pot varied slightly.

Pretty soon, Gene's voice would come over the intercom, informing them that the internal atmosphere was stable, and the blowdown would begin. Then they would press down for the next fifteen hours or so, at rates varying from twenty-five feet to one foot per minute.

Ben yawned again, glad he'd brought a paperback to read. This was the trudge part of being a sat diver. Twelve hundred feet of compression was a long, slow ride.

*****

"Sass," Gene said, setting his sixth cup of coffee down on the sat shack console, "have a look at that third oxygen sensor, would you? I think it's out of sync with the other two."

"Sure." Sass stopped jotting down gas, humidity, and temperature readings in the operations log and spun her office chair on its casters, facing the sensor panel. As she did, the door to the sat shack opened, a billow of heat invaded the air-conditioned interior, and Gerald Posey stepped inside, looking half-frozen with his hands jammed into the pockets of his pea coat. Gene nodded to him briefly, then continued monitoring the blowdown rate, looking at a rack of pressure/depth gauges mounted next to a chronometer. It had been several hours since the main hatch on the sat pot had clanged shut, and the internal pressure of the chamber was now reading the equivalent of five hundred and seventy-two feet of seawater.

"You're right, Gene," Sass said. "It's off about three one-hundredths. I'll recalibrate it, and if it doesn't stabilize, I'll yank it and install another one."

"Good, thanks." Gene looked up at Posey as the ROV tech leaned back against the wall. "Have a seat, Gerald."

"That's all right," Posey said, with a quick, tight smile. "I'd rather stand. I've been sitting in that pilot's seat all afternoon." He glanced at Sass. "Sore, uh—"

She raised an eyebrow in his direction as she fiddled with the calibration knobs of the oxygen sensor. "Sore ass?"

Posey smiled again and nodded, a slight flush on his cheeks. "Exactly." He shifted his dead, half-smoked cigarette to the opposite corner of his mouth.

"You want a light for that, Gerald?" Sass asked. "You can smoke in here if you like."

The tech looked at his feet through his steel-rimmed glasses. "Well, I just thought, since none of you smoke, and this isn't my control shack . . ." He pulled his Zippo from his pocket and flicked it. "But thanks." He fired up the cigarette and inhaled, looking intensely relieved.

The setting sun had just begun to dip into the western sea, a molten orange ball sinking into a shimmering expanse of purple and blue. For several minutes, Posey gazed through the shack's large observation windows at the fiery seascape, then shifted his attention to the foreground where Earl, standing beside the bell, was installing an additional wire-rope clamp on the main lifting cable. As he watched, the barge's night-lights—banks of halogen lamps mounted on twin towers amidships, port and starboard—came on, flooding the work deck with a bright, artificial illumination. Thin gusts of blue smoke from the growling topside generators, compressors, and Environmental Control Units puffed through the evening air.

Gene leaned toward a small microphone on a desk stand. "How you boys feelin' in there?" he asked casually.

Ben's voice came back over the helium descrambler radio mounted in the console next to Gene's station, throaty and distorted, but intelligible. "Just fine. Maybe a touch humid. The atmosphere's thick enough in here as it is."

"Roger that. I'll tweak the ECU's a bit, pull some of that moisture out." Gene smiled. "Heavy puffin', huh?"

"Yeah. Dense. We're all adapting pretty well, though."

"Okay. Shout if you need anything." The old supervisor settled back in his chair.

Posey stirred against the wall. "They having trouble breathing?"

"Uh-uh." Gene glanced up. "Not the way you mean. The atmosphere they're inhalin' right now is denser than what's around us—much more compressed. But the helium's a lighter gas, too, than nitrogen, so that kind of offsets it. But you still feel like you're moving a godawful heap of molecules in and out of your lungs with every breath. A kind of . . . *heavy* sensation."

The ROV tech grimaced around his fresh cigarette. "Sounds like you'd feel smothered all the time."

"Nah. You get that suffocating sensation if you don't have enough oxygen. There's plenty of that in there. We maintain the PPO_2 in the pot at right around point three-five atmospheres." Gene grinned. "Keeps the boys happy."

"'PPO_2?'" Posey's brow furrowed. "Not my area. My sub doesn't have to breathe."

"Partial Pressure of Oxygen," Sass volunteered, still adjusting the malfunctioning sensor. "It's what this unit I'm fixing over here measures. Let us know exactly how much oxygen the guys are getting, no matter what equivalent depth they're at in the chamber."

Posey eyed the semi-dismantled electronic housing, his appetite for technical information whetted. "I guess you can't let it get too low, eh?"

"Or too high. That's just as bad."

"Really? Oxygen is bad for you?"

Sass smiled at him. "At too high a concentration— too high a *partial pressure*—it becomes toxic. It can kill you."

"It's called Central Nervous System Oxygen Toxicity," Gene rejoined. "To us old dogs it's an O_2 hit. You go into convulsions, shake like an epileptic, puke all over yourself—"

"It's not a good thing," Sass finished up.

"Huh." Posey drew on his cigarette. "You've probably guessed by now that I like to know the numbers. How do you calculate what percentages are safe?"

Sass pushed a strand of blonde hair out of her eyes. "Easy. The air we breathe on the surface is roughly seventy-eight percent nitrogen, twenty-two percent oxygen. At sea level, we say we're under one atmosphere of pressure. Of that one atmosphere, the pressure exerted by oxygen is the same as its percentage in the gas mix: twenty-two. Or point two-two ATA— which is shorthand for "Atmospheres Absolute."

"Let's say you lower an open-bottom diving bell down to a depth of thirty-three feet. The air trapped inside will now be under a pressure of *two* atmospheres, because every thirty-three feet of seawater is equivalent to another entire atmosphere of sea-level air pressure. The air volume in the bell also shrinks by half, since it's being squashed under twice the pressure. The bell floods halfway, in other words. The molecules of oxygen and nitrogen become more densely packed—the same number in half the space.

"So if a diver takes in a lung-full of air from that bell, he gets twice as many oxygen molecules in that one breath at thirty-three feet as he would on the surface. The percentage of oxygen in the compressed air is the same, twenty-two, but the partial pressure has doubled. It is now point four-four: twenty-two percent times the number of Atmospheres Absolute—one for the weight of the atmosphere at sea level, plus another for the thirty-three feet of seawater. See?"

Posey nodded slowly. "I remember this. It's called Dalton's Law."

"Right." Sass smiled. "Basic physics. Now in your case, you must use Boyle's and Charles' Law for calculating the relative buoyancy of your ROV, right?"

"Right." Posey looked at her, impressed. "Exactly. I use the combination of those two laws for my buoyancy, displacement, and payload calculations. It's called—"

"The General Gas Law," Sass filled in. "Fundamental diving theory. Anyway, to finish what I was saying about oxygen partial pressures: for every thirty-three feet of depth, you have to add another atmosphere to the total ATA, which you then multiply by the percentage of oxygen in the mix to get the partial pressure." She pointed at the depth gauges near Genc's gas-mixing rack. "The sat pot's at nearly six hundred feet now. Six hundred divided by thirty-three feet gives you the number of atmospheres: call it eighteen. Those are Atmospheres *Ambient*—atmospheres of pressure exerted by seawater. You have to add one more to account for the pressure of air at sea level, which makes nineteen Atmospheres *Absolute.*

"Now you can do your calculations. Twenty-two percent times nineteen equals four point one-eight ATA. And that would be the partial pressure of oxygen in air at six hundred feet—four point one-eight Atmospheres Absolute.

"And that would mean some seriously screwed-up divers," Gene said. "Because the safe limit for exposure to higher PPO_2 is about one point five. Varies a bit with the individual, but not by much."

"So that's why we reduce the oxygen percentage in the sat pot to about nine-tenths of one percent at twelve hundred feet," Sass continued. "Any more, and the divers would start having oxygen toxicity problems." She grinned at Gene. "In the bell, when they're doing their runs, we bump it up a little higher, though; to a PPO_2 of around one. Puts a little more zip in their work, so to speak. They can tolerate that exposure as long as they're able to go back into a lower PPO_2 in the on-deck chamber when they trade shifts."

Posey ran his eyes over Sass's face, as if reappraising her. "You really know your stuff," he said, a new respect in his voice. "I didn't think it was quite this complicated. I mean, I've worked a variety of ROV's on offshore platforms in the Gulf of Mexico, and the divers I've run into almost always seem to be a bunch of ignorant meat—" He bit off what he was saying with a sudden look at Gene.

The old supervisor lifted his coffee cup to his mouth and chuckled. "Meat-what? Meat*heads?* Meat*balls?* *Dead* meat?" He shook his head good-naturedly. "You don't have to look like you just crapped on the altar, Gerald—you're right. I've met all of the above in my workin' life. Just so happens that along with the meatpies, drunks, and deadbeats in commercial divin', there are a few good people too. And we've got a whole crew of 'em out here."

"No offense," Posey said hastily. "I've just met too many of the other kind, I guess."

"None taken," Gene assured him.

The tech opened the door and flicked his cigarette butt out onto the deck. When he closed it again, Sass was already installing a replacement oxygen sensor in the wall panel. He watched her for a moment, bemused. She glanced over at him, caught his eye, smiled, and kept working.

"Whatcha thinkin', Gerald?" she inquired.

The ROV tech reddened slightly. "To be honest, I was just thinking . . . well . . . that I'd formed an unfair opinion of you. I mean . . . I know Gene, and I expected a certain degree of competence from everyone, I guess . . . but I thought that you . . . er . . ."

"You thought I was just this dumb blonde bimbo who got to come along for the ride because she was the lead diver's main squeeze, right?"

Posey gulped. "Ah—I wasn't going to put it quite like that." He fished vigorously for a cigarette. "But . . . yes."

Sass finished making the last connection to the new sensor and locked it into place. Then she spun the calibration knob, set it, and turned to face Posey, once again brushing random strands of blonde hair from her eyes. Her expression was no-nonsense, yet friendly and sincere.

"Look how wrong you can be," she said.

Chapter Twelve

"That crazy bitch," the bodyguard complained to his comrade, as they patrolled past the rear of the glass shed. "How can she say I'm unreliable on guard duty when there is absolutely nothing to guard against? I'll smoke all the *basouko* I want to—so fuck her!" This was Miguel, the terrace sentry who'd been berated by Grizelda for his choice of cigarettes as she'd finished her midday run through the jungle.

The other guard chortled and fanned a few mosquitoes away from his face with his battered straw hat. "So brave, Miguel. I tell you: keep your voice down or you'll end up providing the bitch-*jefe* another hunt for her entertainment—with *yourself* as the quarry. You wouldn't be so *macho* then, eh?" He cackled deep in his throat.

"I wouldn't let her flush me through the jungle like those other fools," Miguel declared. "I'd stand and fight. One good-sized branch for a club—"

"You talk through your asshole, my friend: all bad wind. You've seen her prepare for a hunt—the hand-knives, the coke-and-meth stimulants, the rage she works herself into. And all that training she does." The guard laughed. "She'd carve you into *fajita* strips in thirty seconds."

"Think what you like, but I say . . ." The two sentries moved off toward the far side of the terrace, away from the glass shed, smoking and continuing their low-toned conversation. The boy let them get a good ten paces past the front of the little building before rising cautiously to his feet. He nearly fell right back down again; both of his legs were nerveless, asleep. He had been lying in amongst the garbage cans at the rear of the shed for more than six hours, watching the henna-haired woman and her armed associates come, go, and otherwise occupy the pool terrace until well after dusk. There had been no opportunity to make a move, either to investigate or escape.

Two questions burned in his brain: why had Fernando been killed, and exactly who had done it? The answers were somewhere in this house, of that he was certain. And, frightened though he was, he was not going to leave until he had found them.

And avenged his brother.

Silly, perhaps—he was still only a boy of thirteen. But if not him, then who?

Who more *fitting?*

He swallowed hard, steeling himself. The task was his, and that was that.

Keeping to the shadows on the outer side of the shed, in the little space between the side of the building and the low terrace wall, the boy padded forward, feeling his way along. The two sentries were on the far side of the pool, still talking animatedly, smoke from their cigarettes drifting around their heads in the soft glare of the mansion's exterior lights.

He was at the front corner of the shed now, just barely concealed within the shadows. The door to the glass building was a mere two steps away, but they were steps into the direct illumination from the house. He glanced up at the windows overlooking the pool; at the French doors—one of which was damaged—that led out onto the terrace from the ground floor. He could see no one.

Only the two guards. He glanced at the flagstones around his feet. Along the base of the terrace wall were several small chunks of rock—chips left over from the fitting of the capstone. He stooped down and selected one about the size of an avocado seed. It felt good in his hand, just the right heft.

He waited until Miguel tipped back his head and let out a raucous laugh—then threw the stone as high and hard as he could. It arced above the lights, over the heads of the two guards, past the opposite end of the house, and dropped into the trees somewhere beyond the far curve of the terrace wall. A second after it disappeared, a satisfactorily loud clatter reverberated through the night air.

The two guards leaped as if stung, spun around, and ran to the wall, yanking their shotguns from their shoulders. One of them switched on a large, handheld spotlight that had been clipped to his belt and began to pan the beam across the darkened trees.

Without a sound, the boy slipped around to the shed's front door while their backs were turned, opened it, stepped inside, and pulled it closed behind him. His heart pounding, he watched them through the dusty glass as he quietly worked the latch closed.

They hadn't seen him, and in a few minutes, they turned away from the wall, shrugging and shaking their heads. The boy crouched low behind a table, aware that his movements might be spotted through the shed's translucent walls, but again the guards halted at the far end of the pool and resumed their conversation.

He turned and looked down the length of the shed's interior. It was about thirty feet long and ten wide. Metal cabinets lined both walls, waist-high, and a long counter—a four-foot by twelve-foot rectangle of what looked like polished stone—occupied the central floor space. A sharp, chemical smell permeated the air.

The boy crept forward through the jagged shadows, ducking pools of light that gleamed in through the glass from the house. The tops of the cabinets at the far end of the shed were cluttered with scientific equipment— test tubes, funnels, beakers, siphons, and an assortment of complicated-looking electronic instruments. What such things were used for was beyond his knowledge—he'd seen pictures of laboratories before, in one or two of the few books to be found in his village, but that was all.

There were several large items on the central counter. One was a six-foot-long bag made of heavy black plastic, with a large zipper running along its entire length. The zipper was closed. Beside the bag was a round metal canister, about eighteen inches high by twelve in diameter, with a series of stainless steel clips around its bottom edge. On the opposite side of the bag was a narrow, three-foot-long item wrapped in soft cloth.

The boy glanced around, unsure of what to do. Something told him that the objects on the slab were important, but he could not imagine why. And then he saw the rubbings.

There were two of them, mounted on cardboard backings and propped up next to a microscope on the work counter that spanned that entire end wall of the shed. The boy looked closer, his eyes wide. There was no mistaking them. They had been made from the sepulchre tablets that had adorned the old coral-rock sarcophagi in the chapel of his own village—before the tablets had been destroyed by unknown vandals.

Unknown no longer.

He licked his lips and looked again at the three items on the countertop. The old sarcophagi had been broken open, their contents stolen. Over there were the rubbings. And here—here were . . .

What?

He reached out, trying to still the trembling of his hand. A force seemed to emanate from the three objects—something that could not be described . . . a cold heat . . . a repellent magnetism . . . a lifeless breath from the grave . . .

The boy blinked, shook his head, and refocused. No. There was nothing. Nothing but the dark imaginings of his own mind. Flexing his fingers, he took hold of the zipper and in one swift motion pulled it open.

The halves of the bag separated, and a withered hand dropped onto the slab, the white bone of fingertips protruding through what remained of a covering of thin, age-darkened skin. From the back of the hand, through the wrist, and up the exposed half of the forearm, dried tendons stood out in bold relief under the parchment-like epidermis.

The boy drew back with a sharp gasp, reacting not just to the sudden appearance of the hand but also to the powerful smell of chemicals. When the shock had passed, he leaned forward, grasped the edge of the opening between his thumb and forefinger, and gently pulled the bag open a bit further. There was an entire body inside—a very old body, strangely preserved.

The muscles had deteriorated to almost nothing, so that the corpse was little more than a skeleton covered by a shroud of stretched, desiccated skin. The abdomen was completely sunken, the upper torso a bony, hollow cage of ribs. Above the collarbone, the neck was a twisted wrinkle of hide. Most of the head was covered by the upper part of the bag, but the boy was startled to see the remnants of a dark, wispy beard clinging to a lantern jaw beneath a grimacing, tooth-studded mouth.

Until recently, this man had rested in one of the chapel sarcophagi; he was sure of it. Who he had been exactly, the boy did not know. There was an old oral fable about the origins of the strange little shrine, one that had been told in his village for centuries. But most of the hard facts about the twin crypts, and of the chapel itself, had been lost in time.

Very carefully, he closed the bag, pulling the zipper up toward the head of the corpse until it locked. The smell of preservative chemicals was almost overpowering, and he turned away to wipe his tearing eyes and stifle a sneeze. In doing so, he caught a glimpse of a man's silhouette approaching the shed door.

His heart racing, he dropped into a crouch and moved around behind the very end of the central counter. The latch rattled as the door opened, and there was a shuffling of feet on the flagstone floor. The boy glanced around. There were any number of cabinets that might have hidden him, but it was too late now.

A heavy footfall began. The man was walking toward the rear of the shed. Desperate, the boy shot a quick look around one corner of the counter. Nothing. The intruder had to be on the opposite side. Moving with all possible stealth, the boy slipped around the corner and crept forward a couple of yards, hugging the cabinetry and holding his breath.

The man coughed, a deep, rattling sound, and came to a halt as he reached the end of the counter. There was a metallic clunk, as if the barrel of a shotgun had come into contact with the edge of the slab, followed by a scraping sound and a grunt of effort. The boy caught a pungent whiff of tobacco and body odor, and then the man was walking back the way he had come.

Almost overcome with relief, he scuttled back around the end of the counter. There was a muffled curse as the man struggled to open the door—while holding something heavy, from the sound of it—and then a glassy bang as it swung to and latched itself. The boy chanced a look over the top of the slab in time to see the man's silhouette lurch past the pool in the direction of the house.

Cautiously, he rose to his feet. The first thing he noticed was that the round canister was gone. *That* was what the unwelcome visitor had been after. The other two items remained undisturbed.

His gaze fell upon the narrow, cloth-covered object. He reached out and touched it. The material felt soft under his fingers, like cotton batting, and infused with some kind of light oil. The item it concealed was long, thin, and hard. After only a moment's hesitation, he began to peel back the layers of cloth, one at a time, to expose what lay within.

It was a sword. A very old sword, bearing the stains of age and corrosion, but nonetheless in remarkably good condition. The blade was three feet long and just over an inch wide for most of its length, double-edged and tapering to a sharp point. Near the hilt it bore a considerable amount of fancy scrollwork, partially obscured by some kind of black residue. There were a number of chips in both edges, but otherwise the weapon was quite serviceable. In addition to a crossguard, the hilt was equipped with an oblong metal cage, thin and ornate, that almost completely enclosed the handgrip. A ball of what appeared to be brass or bronze, carved into the shape of a lion's head, adorned its butt end.

On impulse, the boy lifted the sword out of the folds of cloth and slipped his right hand around the grip. It felt lighter than it actually was, which he realized was due to its perfect balance. It seemed to float in front of him like a natural extension of his arm.

He was suddenly seized by an overwhelming sense of *deja-vu*. He had never so much as touched a sword of any kind before, and yet this antique weapon felt as familiar in his hand as his favorite fishing spear. It was as if he had stepped back into another place and time—a reality that he had known well, forgotten, and now, in a rush, remembered.

The sword was his—if not by right, then by virtue of possession. The thought occurred to him that it had probably shared a sarcophagus with the man whose remains now lay in the black plastic bag . . . in which case he had a far more legitimate claim to it, as a village son, than did the red-haired woman or any of her thugs.

And he had discovered enough for one night. He was tired, stiff, and hungry. He would return to the fishing cave to rest, eat one of the coconuts he had stored in a niche above the great pool, and consider what to do next. The sword would go with him. For some reason, in a matter of only a few minutes, leaving it behind had become as unthinkable as discarding one of his own arms or legs.

He examined it again in the partial light that filtered through the glass panes from the house. The scrollwork on the blade just forward of the cross-guard really was beautiful, despite its coating of black grime. On a whim, he laid the sword down on the slab, gathered a corner of the wrapping cloth, and scrubbed hard at the etching for the better part of a minute.

He turned the sword in the light. The middle part of the stain had been rubbed away, revealing the letters "FRN" inscribed in a flowing, illuminative style. The letters were surrounded with much filigree and intricate detail, only part of which he could make out.

"FRN," the boy whispered aloud, looking over at the black plastic bag. "Is that you?"

He placed the sword back on the oiled cloth, bundled it up, and tucked it under his arm. There was a short length of cord dangling from a nearby rafter. This he pulled down and tied around the bundle at either end. Slinging it over his shoulder like a rifle, he made his way up to the front door. The two guards were sitting in chairs at the far end of the terrace, facing out toward the moonlit Caribbean.

Forty seconds later, the boy was working his way down the vertical cracks in the terrace wall, jamming one fist after the other and placing his feet carefully to control his descent. In less than a minute, he reached the ground, mercifully having been spared any encounters with night-crawling scorpions. He paused for a moment, listening, and then disappeared silently into the dense, black jungle.

*****

Grizelda Ramos sat in her Swedish armchair in the ground floor study, wearing only a short blue-satin robe and black Doc Martens combat boots. She was staring at the cylindrical canister one of her bodyguards had retrieved from the greenhouse and set up on a small wooden pedestal beneath a recessed ceiling light. In her lap, and on the table beside her, were numerous pages of yellowed manuscript, laminated in plastic.

As if in some kind of trance, she glowered at the canister with her obsidian eyes half closed, her face twisted into an ugly scowl. A muscle twitched repeatedly at the corner of her mouth. The wooden arms of the chair creaked in protest as she flexed her powerful hands around them.

Slowly, she dropped her gaze to the manuscript page lying atop the half-dozen in her lap. She stared for a moment, then began to read, her dead black eyes tracking back and forth over the spidery, handwritten words.

The situation with regard to Captain Ramos and his men has become intolerable. In the five long months since all souls who survived the sinking of the Arista were cast ashore on this tiny island, he has schemed to create division within the crew, despite my entreaties that, for the mutual good—nay, for survival—our differences should be set aside. Alas, he has succeeded in convincing the weaker spirits among us to join him, tempting them with promises of monetary reward upon rescue, and terrifying them with reminders of the awful fate that awaits unrepentant mutineers.

Upon this island (and, we have since learned, upon those two neighboring) there are Indians—a naked race of primitive aspect and pagan spirituality. Though Godless, they have proven to be our salvation, for without their knowledge of medicinal herbs, roots, and balms, and their skill at gathering food from sea and land, we would all surely have perished during the first month of our enforced tenure. As it was, only three of the most gravely injured gave up the Breath of Life; the rest of us were nursed back to health and strength by these strange, gentle people, who came and went amongst us in our little camp like dusky, unclad angels. To thank them, and to ensure that their heathen souls will not, in their ignorance of Father, Son, and Holy Ghost, be damned to Hell's Fires for all Eternity, we have endeavored to convert them to the Mother Church, that they might know the Everlasting Love of Jesus Christ Our Lord.

It is disconcerting when they laugh at our attempts to tell them of the Gospel in sign language and mime. Like children, they are frivolous in their spirituality, seemingly content to pass their days in hunting, fishing, gathering, and play. But, with continued instruction, both patient and firm, we hold dear the expectation that they will yet learn to tremble before the Awesome Majesty of the One True God, and come to know His Love.

Captain Ramos and his men entertain no such self-less notions, though they owe their survival to these natives. Having retired into a picket of their own, on the far side of the island, they have taken a half-dozen of the most comely Indian girls and women as camp slaves, to be used as their vile appetites dictate.

Grizelda's mouth curved into an unconscious smile as she set the two uppermost pages aside on the end table. Her tongue appeared between her heavy lips, licked them slowly, and retracted. Then she continued reading.

In a state of distress and confusion pitiful to look upon, the elders of the island's native inhabitants pleaded with me, in sign language and the few words we share, to intercede on their behalf and entreat Captain Ramos to return their daughters and wives to them. Such was their misery that I acquiesced, and proceeded to the stockade on the northern shore under a white flag—but in the company of two armed companions.

Alas, Captain Ramos, speaking from the gate of his stout picket enclosure, rebuffed my solicitations, damned me for a traitorous dog who would surely feel the headsman's ax if I did not feel his blade in my heart first, and ordered my two comrades to abandon me and join him. Being steadfast, they refused, unmoving, which drove Captain Ramos into yet another rage. Screaming that he would wreak vengeance upon all those who chose my company and that of filthy, naked heathens in preference to his, he seized one of the slave girls—a comely child of not more than twelve—and ran her through the chest with his sword. We could only watch in horror as she sagged off his blade to the ground, bleeding out her precious life, and expired. In order that Captain Ramos should not murder any more of his Indian captives for our benefit, and seeing that further attempts at parley were useless, we retired into the jungle in some haste.

That very night, Captain Ramos and his band attacked our beach camp, falling upon us under the waning light of a quarter moon. They did not take us by surprise, however. I had foreseen such an attempt and posted not only perimeter sentries, but Indian spotters hidden in the jungle itself, along all possible approaches. The scant warning they gave was sufficient for those of us sleeping to rouse ourselves and seize our weap-ons.

The engagement was savage and brief. We repelled Captain Ramos and his intruders in short order, but at considerable cost. Of my thirteen loyal companions, one was slain, and two others mortally wounded. Despite the best efforts of our native friends, they are unlikely to survive through the coming day.

And so, here we sit, bleeding and disheartened, as the dawn approaches. I have made my decision. We will take to the small outrigger canoes and abandon this island to Captain Ramos. Across an intervening league of ocean lie the other two islands of this lost archipelago. Perhaps there, with the help of our pagan brethren, we will find sanctuary from Captain Ramos' madness, and, at long last, peace.

Grizelda gazed down at the last page for a long moment, then opened her knees and let it fall to the floor. Her jaw muscles worked continuously; little beads of sweat glistened on her forehead and upper lip. From deep in her throat, there came a low rumbling sound.

Very deliberately, she raised her right foot and brought the Doc Martens boot down on top of the manuscript. Her hands wrung a new spate of agonized creaking from the wooden arms of her chair.

Once again, she lifted her reptilian eyes to stare at the canister sitting on the pedestal across the room. For a long time—an unnaturally long time—she did not move.

She did not even blink.

Chapter Thirteen

"What's the exact water depth under the barge again?" Gene asked, watching the sat system's blow-down gauges.

"One thousand two hundred and seven feet," Sass informed him. She eyed the readout on the bottom sounder for a few more seconds. "Bouncing between six and seven."

"That's us heaving slightly in a one-foot swell." The old supervisor grinned at her. "The ocean's never really still, even when it looks it."

Sass smiled back. "I guess. Pretty accurate instrument, too, to pick up one foot of variation in twelve hundred."

"Yeah." Gene rested his hands on the needle valves controlling the last stages of the blowdown. "I'm gonna stop them at eleven ninety-five. That'll put the bell twelve feet off bottom when the hatch pops. Even if we get a six-foot sea, we should still be able to work without planting the clump weight in the mud every time we dip into a trough."

"Got it," Sass said. "Or maybe it'll just stay dead calm."

"Yeah, maybe. That'd be nice. Okay, now . . ."

Gene touched a button on the deck communications radio. "Earl. You still awake out there, son?"

"Sho' nuff," came the deep-voiced response.

"Good. Bell ready to go?"

"Yep. Hot water suits is in there, soda canisters for the CO_2 scrubbers, extra onboard metabolic O_2, dive hats, emergency BIBS masks, Broco burnin' gear and rods with one cylinder of cuttin' oxygen on board, phosphorus torches, pryin' tools, lights . . . oh, yeah— and drinkin' water, hot tea, and a couple of ham sandwiches."

Gene grinned at Sass. "The caps loose on those jugs of water and tea?"

Earl's reply sounded affably peeved. "Ah bin doin' this for a while, boss. Ain't nothing in that there bell gonna crush or implode when you pressure it up."

"I didn't think so," Gene chuckled. "Okay. If the bell's mated to the transfer lock, I'm gonna blow it down to pot depth and adjust the gas mix."

"Roguh. How deep you got the fellas stored?"

"Eleven ninety-five."

"Roguh that. Dang, that's deep, ain't it? Well, whatevuh—better them than me." The big man's resonant guffaw rumbled out of the speaker. "Y'all can start the blowdown any time."

"Stand by." Gene leaned over to the sat system mike and cleared his throat. "Ben. You still hear me okay?"

"Got you loud and clear." Sass winced slightly at the sound of Ben's voice. It was nasal, high, and garbled almost beyond intelligibility, despite being filtered through the helium descrambler radio.

"I'm pressuring up the bell. When you get a hatch, I'm gonna want the first team in there pretty quick. Let's use this good weather while it lasts." Gene paused to sip cold coffee. "You guys pair up yet?"

"Yeah," Ben replied. "Pierre and Vern, Chris and me."

"Who's got the first bell run?"

"Chris and me."

"Lucky you. You're the first ones to get your hands on all that treasure layin' around down there . . . you know—just waitin' to be picked up."

Even distorted by helium, Ben's tone was dry. "Yeah, right. That's what it looked like on the ROV camera. Piles of it, just *layin'* there."

"Think positive," Sass chided him, leaning over Gene's shoulder.

"Always," came the reply.

Gene reached out and grasped the handle of a large quarter-turn ball valve on the gas panel. "Blowin' down the bell," he announced, speaking into the sat mike and the on-deck radio simultaneously. He threw the handle over and the familiar hiss of rushing gas joined the other ambient sounds in the control shack—

the hum of electronic monitors, the slight buzz of the failing ballast in one of the overhead florescent lights, the soft perking of the coffee machine, the muted roar of the generators and compressors on the deck outside.

*****

Ben propped himself up on one elbow and looked across the narrow chamber at Chris, who was lying prone on his cot with his arms folded across his chest, trying to whistle. "That doesn't work under pressure," he said.

The younger diver kept pursing his lips and blowing. "Yeah, Gannon, I know. Just seeing how it feels." He looked at Ben and shrugged. "I did manage to whistle in a decompression chamber once, though."

"Mm." Ben raised an eyebrow. "How deep were you? Bet it wasn't more than one atmosphere."

"Four feet," Chris admitted. "On the way out of a Sur-D O$_2$ run. Whistled the first line of 'Jingle Bells.'"

"Did you tell yore mama about it?" Vern growled from the cot beneath Ben's. "She musta bin real proud."

Chris rolled over and glared down at the big man. "You're not talkin' trash about my mama, are you, Pickens?"

"Ohhh-*kay*," Ben said, swinging his legs off his cot and dropping down between the two divers. "Time to go to work. Chris: you and I have the first bell run. You ready to earn your pay?"

"Sure. I'm there."

"Good. Get your butt up out of that rack and give me a hand in the bell transfer lock. When the hatch pops we're going in and running a checklist on the onboard life support systems. Then, if everything's okay"—Ben clapped a hand on the younger man's shoulder—"we're locking off and heading down into the briny blue."

"Six hours of fun 'n' adventure," Vern remarked. "Don't be noddin' off down there, kid—especially when you're tendin' hose for half the doo-ration."

"Don't worry about me," Chris told him. "I've got it covered."

"Sure you do, kid." With a grin, the big man settled his head back on his pillow and covered his eyes with a massive forearm.

Chris followed Ben through the open hatch in the chamber's subdividing wall into the bell transfer lock. "What's with the Elephant Man back there?" he complained, his voice slightly less cocksure than usual.

Ben hunched down at the bell-trunk hatch and looked back over his shoulder. "He's an old sat rat," he said. "He's just busting your balls a little bit." The wry, lopsided smile began to play across his face. "You know about busting balls, don't you, Chris?"

"He's about to piss me off," the younger man said petulantly.

Ben continued to smile. "It's good for you," he said. "Builds character. 'Smatter? Can't take it?"

"There's nothin' I can't take."

Ben turned back toward the hatch. "Attaboy. That's what I like to hear."

He tipped his head back and spoke in the direction of the intercom speaker mounted high on the lock's curving wall. "Gene. How close are we to popping the hatch?"

"Bell's pressured to eleven ninety-two," the supervisor reported. "Three more feet."

"Roger that." Ben hung his head and waited, one hand on the hatch handle. Another fifteen seconds crept by . . . and then there was a sudden sucking *pop* and the heavy steel disk swung inward on its hinges, revealing the interior of a three-foot-diameter, three-foot-long tube. Beyond it was a cramped-looking spherical compartment, dimly lit by a single pressure-resistant light and jammed to apparent capacity with rubber suits, umbilical hoses, helmets, and emergency oral/nasal masks.

"Got a hatch, Gene," Ben said. He twisted sideways and slid headfirst into the cylindrical trunk of the diving bell. "Home sweet home."

"Man, that's crowded in there," Chris commented, looking past Ben at the crush of equipment. "Sure woulda been nice if Gene had found a bigger goddamn bell."

Ben squatted on his haunches, leaned back against one of the hose coils, and began checking switches and valves. "Yeah, well, this is what we've got to do the job with. This is an old bell-bounce system, not a full-blown, live-under-pressure-for-a-month saturation habitat. You know: you're supposed to blow down in it, do some kind of emergency repair for a few hours—two or three bell runs, tops—and then bleed back to the surface. Short-term stuff. But we're gonna run a real multi-day sat in it, even if it is a little cramped." He grinned at the younger diver. "Hey, it is what it is. You knew the system was small when you signed on, so quit whining."

"Screw you, I ain't whining," Chris said. "The bitch is just tight, that's all."

"Good. Now crawl on in here partway and help me run down these life-support checks. And remember: I could put you in here with Vern. Then you'd really be hard up for elbow room."

"What's the problem in there?" Gene's gravelly voice crackled through the bell speaker.

Ben laughed. "No problem, Gene. We were just debating the fact that nothing in life is ever perfect."

"Tell me about it," the old supervisor growled. "If it was, you'd be on bottom right now and that bell would already be half full of gold."

*****

"What are you looking at, José?"

The hiss of Grizelda's hot breath on his ear nearly made Fuentes jump out of his skin. *"Haaghh!* God— you startled me, Senorita Ramos!" He put a hand on the sash of his open bedroom window, gulping and steadying himself.

Grizelda stood with her arms crossed and her weight on one leg, hip cocked out, watching him impassively. Her large breasts swelled out of her blue-satin robe practically under the geneticist's nose. The lower hem of the garment barely reached the tops of her muscular thighs. Fuentes' eyes glazed over, went on autopilot, and began to rake up and down her body from collarbone to kneecaps.

"José," Grizelda said.

Absorbed, the little scientist didn't answer.

"José," she said again.

215

"Mmmurrghmmphff."

"Fuentes!"

The geneticist snapped to as if released from hypnosis.

"Yes, Griz—Senorita Ramos?"

"I asked you what you were looking at." Grizelda stepped in closer, her substantial endowments jiggling atop her folded arms and threatening to spill out of her robe completely. She regarded him down the bridge of her nose, unsmiling, her flat black eyes half-closed.

Fuentes smoothed his oily hair across his forehead and tried to reestablish the aura of sensual confidence he had been working on since midday. Unfortunately, he found it heavy going, standing there under his supposed paramour's reptilian gaze clad only in black dress socks and boxer shorts patterned with furious-looking little cartoon bulls.

"Er . . . I was . . . watching that—that ship out there," he stammered. "The lights, about halfway between the islands . . . they don't seem to be moving."

"Mm," Grizelda said, looking past him and out the open window. "Nor should they. That isn't a ship, it's a barge loaded with diving equipment. And it's working for me."

Fuentes squinted out into the darkness. "They're here already? You actually went ahead with the salvage plan?"

"Mm."

"So much . . . well—the *possibility* of so much gold." The little scientist chewed his lip. "If there is even a fraction of what was indicated in the manuscript, it would be a fabulous . . .stupendous . . . incredible . . ."

A shadow of impatience flickered across Grizelda's face as the pedantic string of adjectives trailed off. "An incredible find," she finished. "Oh, it's down there, and it's *mine*. I can feel it." She reached out and grasped Fuentes' pudgy shoulder, turning him to face her. "Do you know what else I can feel, José?"

He shook his head, mouth open, mooning up at her like a drugged puppy.

"An incredible natural attraction between you and me." She came in close, pushed her nipples into his chest, and grazed a lacquered talon along his chin. "Don't tell me you don't feel it too."

"I—feel something, Senorita Ramos."

She ran the fingernail up to the corner of his mouth. "Gri-*zel*-da," she cooed.

"Yes . . . yes! Grizelda!"

"Why don't you come over here," Grizelda instructed, pulling him along by the shoulder, "and get on the bed."

"Yes . . . why don't I do that," Fuentes panted.

217

He clambered up on the big double-poster and faced her, kneeling, like a lap dog angling for a biscuit. Grizelda curled her lip into a half-smile, and in one motion shucked the short robe off her shoulders. It fell to the floor around her Doc Martens. The expression in her eyes never changed.

Fuentes nearly collapsed. Trembling, he goggled at the statuesque red-brown body, naked and gleaming in the soft light of the bedside lamp, all muscles, hips, buttocks, and looming breasts like some Frazetta fantasy illustration.

"Oh, my *God*," he croaked.

"He isn't here, José," Grizelda whispered. "No interruptions. Now, take off your little bulls."

She moved forward, putting one knee up on the mattress. From the back of her throat, there came a deep, muted giggle.

Chapter Fourteen

"All right," Gene announced, his voice booming out of the barge's on-deck P.A. speakers, "go ahead and vent the bell trunk."

Outside, standing by the controls of the bell-launching A-frame, both Sass and Earl turned and sent a thumbs-up toward the sat shack's observation window. The hand signals and loudspeakers were necessary during the separation/launch procedure; the roar of the diesel-powered hydraulic unit that provided pressure to the crane's rams and main lifting spool made their individual communications radios useless.

Earl stepped forward, gripped the handle of a heavy ball valve on the bell's cylindrical trunk, and threw it open. There was a sharp blast of gas. Almost immediately, he closed the valve again, then looked up at Gene in the sat shack.

"Bell hatch has a good seal," the supervisor reported. "It's holding pressure." There was a pause, and Sass could see him talking into the deck chamber descrambler radio. Then his voice boomed through the P.A. speakers again: "Sat pot hatch also has a good seal. Vent the trunk all the way."

Earl nodded, gave him the thumbs-up again, and twisted the handle. The scream of escaping trimix lasted about fifteen seconds. Then he shut off the valve and actuated the hydraulic clamps that locked the bell trunk's flange to the end of the deck chamber. With a clanking of steel on steel, they broke loose and retracted.

Earl looked over his shoulder at Sass and nodded. She pulled a lever on the launching-system control panel and trundled the bell on its wheeled trestle back a couple of feet from the chamber's mating surface. Through one of the four tiny Lexan viewports in the bell's upper hemisphere, she could see Ben grinning at her, looking much like a mole in a very small hole.

A random billow of diesel exhaust wafted across her face, momentarily poisoning the night air and bringing tears to her eyes. She blinked them away, coughed, and blew Ben a quick kiss. The grin in the small port widened in response.

"Okay," Gene said, "they're all set for rotation. Whenever you're ready, Sass."

She gave the sat shack window the requisite thumbs-up and trundled the bell outboard another two feet to the end of the short track. Then, with Earl standing by and holding a long pinch bar that could be deployed if something began to bind or hang up, Sass eased back on the lever that engaged the lifting spool. Slowly, the huge drum began to turn, taking up the small amount of slack in the bell cable. As it came tight, the bell, still lying on its side in the trestle, began to rotate on its two laterally-mounted support pins, the trunk swinging from the horizontal toward the vertical. Vaguely, through the viewports, she could see Ben and Chris shifting positions as their cramped little world turned ninety degrees.

A gravelly chuckle came over the P.A. "Ben says now he knows what a hamster runnin' in a wheel feels like—'cept hamsters don't have hoses and rubber gear drapin' all over them while they're tryin' to move."

Sass smiled, and as the bell went completely vertical, she picked it out of the trestle and braked the spool. The big metal sphere hung just below the main pulley of the A-frame crane, suspended by its thick lifting cable, swinging very slightly in response to the barely perceptible motion of the barge.

Earl came back to join her. "Good handlin'," he called into her ear. "Lower the bell outboard, an' Ah'll feed an' clip the umbilical. Okay?"

Sass nodded. "Roger that, big guy."

"Outstandin'." Earl smiled and hurried over to the side of the barge, where another huge, eight-foot-diameter spool was positioned, the drum of which was loaded with an apparently endless length of bundled four-strand hose and electrical cable. This thick main umbilical had been plumbed into the top of the bell and would provide surface communications, replacement breathing gases, and primary electrical power during the dive. Every six feet, a large stainless steel D-ring had been lashed to the hose bundle with whipping cord. Hung on a rack beside the spool were hundreds of twelve-inch loops of light chain, each one fitted with a snap-shackle.

Sass pushed another lever and the A-frame began to rock forward, the bell dangling like a giant Christmas ornament between the two stout uprights. Earl walked beside it, tending the slack in the umbilical hose and eyeballing the deployment. There was a momentary pause as he attached the two chains of the clump weight—a two by two by four-foot concrete ingot that hung below the bell and stabilized it at depth—to their padeyes on the bell's lower hull. Then slowly, steadily, the entire apparatus continued outboard, picking up the clump, until the A-frame's hydraulic rams reached their maximum extension. With a metallic *clunk*, they locked. The bell swayed gently, suspended about fifteen feet above the black water, its bright orange paint job gleaming in the harsh radiance of the flood-lights.

Earl heaved the umbilical up on his shoulder, stepped to the rail of the barge, and placed the bight between the opposing rubber wheels of a large hydrau-lically-powered pulley that was shackled to a davit next to the spool. Then he put a hand on the spool controls and looked over at Sass.

She nodded and pushed a short lever on her own control panel. The bell began to descend, its support cable uncoiling from the massive drum at the rear of the launching system. There was a sizzling of salt foam and a belching of trapped air as the big sphere touched the surface of the water, wobbled, and sank through it. An eerie greenish glow lit up the night sea as Ben switched on the bell's four external "snoopers"—pressure-proof deepwater lights with bulbs so hot they would burn out in thirty seconds if turned on when not submerged.

Sass lowered the bell to a depth of about twenty feet and braked the spool. Then she raised the A-frame so that the cable tracked back in toward the side of the barge, stopping when it was less than a foot from the rail. Earl swung the umbilical davit around, moving the supporting pulley up beside the bell cable, then grabbed an armful of chain loops off the rack. Stepping to the very edge of the deck, he reached out one-handed and threw a loop so that the light chain wrapped around the vertical cable three times. Then he threaded it through itself, cinching it so it couldn't slip, and clipped its snap-shackle to a D-ring on the umbilical.

Sass began to lower the bell again. With considerable speed and dexterity, Earl paid out a corresponding amount of umbilical hose—using the spool's handheld cable-remote—and simultaneously threw chain, cinched the loops down, and clipped them to the rapidly passing D-rings. It was frenetic work, even at the bell's relatively slow rate of descent, but the big man handled it without any apparent effort. There was never a missed throw or clip, never a moment when the umbilical fouled or lagged behind the main cable. Sass smiled to herself. It was like watching a ballet.

"Everything goin' smooth out there?" Gene inquired. Sass turned to see him standing at the sat shack window, headphones on, a mug of coffee in one hand. She sent him the thumbs-up.

Gene bent down over the P.A. mike. "Good. They're just comin' up on three hundred feet. Gettin' cold, Ben says. I'm going to activate the hot water line, send some flow down to the radiant heaters in the bell."

Sass nodded and cast a glance at the hot water machine on the opposite side of the launching area—a four-by-eight-foot stainless steel box that sucked up seawater through an overboard intake, heated it to one hundred and eighty degrees Fahrenheit, and pumped it down to the bell through one of the umbilical's hose components. In addition to warming the bell's interior via two liquid radiators, the hot water would be plumbed into the divers' suits to offset both the heat-depleting effects of breathing a helium-based gas mix and the chill of immersion associated with performing excursions at great depth.

Briefly, she wondered what the ambient temperature on bottom—so different from that of the warm, inviting surface water—would be. Posey's ROV had taken constant temperature readings on its dive, but she'd failed to note them, so intent had been her concentration on the scenes captured by the video cameras. She watched as Earl threw his last chain, cinched it, and stepped quickly over to the rack to grab another handful before the next D-ring dropped past.

There was a crackle of static, and Gene's voice resonated out of the P.A. speakers once more: "Five hundred and seventy-five feet, people. Ben says they just passed through their fourth thermocline. Water temp outside the bell is now fifty-six degrees."

*****

"Man, I thought this was the Caribbean," Chris said, a momentary shiver seizing him. "It's cold enough to freeze the balls off a brass bull in here."

"It's worse out there," Ben replied. He held out a navy-blue wool knit cap. "Here, put this on. I'll dial us up some more heat." Reaching up over his head, he opened a valve in the tubing that provided hot water flow to the bell's two wall-radiators. "Don't lean back on 'em. They're going to get pretty warm."

"I know, I know."

Another of Chris's more appealing twenty-something traits, Ben thought. There was nothing he didn't know. He toyed briefly with the notion of letting him get his ass singed just to improve his character.

"Who's going out first?" Chris asked, tugging the watch cap down over his ears.

Ben looked at him and smiled. "Me. Try to think warm thoughts while you're tending my hose."

The younger diver patted the grillwork of the heater nearest him. "This damn thing's barely lukewarm. Think they oughta turn the hot water machine up some?"

"Nah." Ben shook his head, eyeing a gauge. He reached out and adjusted the makeup O_2 slightly. "I set it at one-eighty. By the time it travels through twelve hundred feet of hose it'll have cooled down to around one-ten or one-twenty. We'll use some bottom sea-water to mix it down to seventy-five or so for the suits. We don't want to get parboiled or develop heat stroke out there."

"Seventy-five degrees is damn cold," Chris argued.

Ben shot him a look. "Not if you're working hard."

He rose up into a half-crouch and peered out one of the viewports, the glaring light from the external snooper making him squint. Six inches from his nose, on the other side of five inches of Lexan, a small, tadpole-like fish with feathery red gills, no bigger than a man's index finger, undulated across the visual field. Beyond it there was nothing: clear water salted with tiny suspended particles, fading to dead black outside the limits of the bell's artificial illumination.

"Whaddya see?" Chris asked.

"Water," Ben replied. "Other than that, not a damn thing."

"No mermaids?"

"Not here. They were all at three hundred feet."

Chris grinned. "Shit. You shoulda told me. I'd have floated 'em out my address."

Ben checked the gas sensors. "Yeah, I saw how starved you are for female companionship back in New Orleans."

Chris looked pleased. "Hey, call it a gift, Gannon."

"Okay," Ben said. "It's a gift." He nudged his dive helmet with the toe of his sneaker. "Why don't you hook my hat up to that number one dive hose. I'm going to start getting dressed in. We'll be on bottom in a few minutes, and we don't want to waste any time once we're down there."

"Okay." Chris picked up the heavy helmet and fumbled for a wrench in the tool bag. "Think we'll be pretty close to the wreck?"

"Think so. GPS put the barge right over top of it, and there doesn't seem to be any current to blow us off a vertical line of descent. It ought to be right there."

"What if it ain't?"

Ben looked at him patiently. "Then we'll have to reposition the barge and try again. We've only got a hundred feet of excursion dive hose."

"That'd be a bummer. Waste of a bell run."

"Mm-hmm." Ben began to peel off his sweatshirt. "Got that hat hooked up yet?"

"Yeah, yeah. I'm right on it, Gannon."

Ben appraised the back of the younger diver's head as he bent over the helmet, wrench in hand. Sooner or later, someone or something was going to flog some of the attitude out of Chris Toricelli. He just hoped, for the kid's sake, that the lesson wouldn't turn out to be crippling or fatal. That he'd seen too many times. And Gus and Allie didn't need a permanently damaged or dead son along with all their other problems.

Gene's voice came over the bell speaker, interrupting his train of thought. "Eight hundred feet, boys, with all systems looking A-okay. You're gettin' there."

*****

.

Gold. Piles of it, in all shapes and sizes. Shiny doubloons spilling out of rotting wooden chests. Bars the size of construction bricks, stacked and gleaming a rich yellow-orange like blocks of solidified flame. Chains and necklaces of every description draped across antlers of coral and dangling from broken, waterlogged ship's timbers. Fantastic implements and works of art, each one worth a fortune all by itself: scepters, ceremonial axes and cleavers, spears, swords, thick Aztec calendar wheels, fertility statues, and more—all fashioned from warm, burnished, glowing *gold*. Tropical fish, like tiny Technicolor jewels, darting here and there through the dappled sunlight illuminating the fabulous undersea treasure trove.

A massive golden headdress, in the shape of a giant crab, advancing through the mounds of bullion. Schools of blue chromis, yellow tang, and red cardinal-fish parting like living curtains. A voluptuous female figure making its way across the pristine white sand of the sea floor, drawing nearer. The naked body—bodacious in the extreme—strangely familiar. A magnum of imported French champagne in one hand, two glasses in the other. High-floating breasts the size of basketballs, nipples like the pink rubber caps of baby bottles. Stomach, waist, and hips like the curves of a vintage Rolls Royce. Tanned, slender limbs seemingly of buffed bronze, decorated with tattoos of barbed wire, motorcycle parts, and cartoon figures in various erotic positions.

Beneath the headdress, sparkling blue eyes, rimmed with kohl and glitter, set in the face of a depraved cherub. Pouting lips like bruised strawberries. A cascading mane of frosted blonde hair drifting around the perfect shoulders and neck. So *familiar*. The ideal woman . . .

Trixie Hendrix! Miss February, 2002 from *Hawgs & Ta-Ta's Magazine*! And now she was pouring the champagne—standing there stripped and shimmying, ready and willing, in the midst of *all . . . that . . . gold . .* .

BLAAAAAAAAAAAT!

Sligo shrieked, jack-knifed out of the captain's chair, and executed a perfect bellyflop onto the teak deck of the *Cucaracha*'s flybridge, cracking his head against the helm console cabinet in the process. The giant air horn went off again, the earsplitting blast sustaining even longer the second time:

BLAAAAAAAAAAAAAAAAAAAAAAAAAT!

The smuggler jerked into a fetal position, covering his ears, the last shreds of his delicious dream blowing away like feathers in a hurricane. A strangled howl burst from his lips as his tympanic membranes vibrated to the limits of their design tolerance.

After a miniature eternity, the sound died away. Sligo clawed his way up the captain's chair to his knees and stared around wildly.

The pale gray bow of the onrushing freighter looked approximately the size of the Empire State Building against the starlit evening sky—an Empire State Building that was a mere fifty yards shy of crushing the *Cucaracha* like an expensive fiberglass egg.

"AAAGH!" Sligo screamed, throwing himself at the wheel and wrenching it to starboard—without disengaging the autopilot. The little connecting cog broke off and went spinning across the deck.

The *basso profundo* thrumming of the cargo ship's huge engines hammered the air around the smuggler's head, rattling his eyeballs in their sockets. The towering expanse of gray steel loomed over the yacht like the blade of a giant plow, blotting out every star.

"AAAAAAGGHH!" Sligo screamed again, because there wasn't much else to do. The wheel was already hard over, and he had the helpless cowering down pat.

It was too late. They were going to hit. Sligo made a command decision and acted.

"AAAAAAAAAGGGHHH!" he screamed once more, and flailed backward, covering his face with his hands.

The freighter's tremendous bow wave, aided by Sligo's barely-initiated turn to starboard, picked the *Cucaracha* up and dusted it aside like a chunk of cork. The vibration of the massive engines shook the yacht from stem to stern as the port side of the ship steamroll-ered past with barely three feet to spare.

And then it was over. The *Cucaracha* tossed and veered in the freighter's wake, her own engines grinding away as they continued to drive her into a tight starboard turn. Weak and trembling, Sligo rolled over onto his stomach and gazed after the departing vessel. *Ivanovich*, the name on the well-lit transom read, beneath its Cyrillic equivalent. And below that, in smaller letters, *Murmansk.*

Moving with cautious precision, Sligo crawled to the rail of the flybridge, leaned out far enough to hit the water cleanly, and threw up. When he'd finished, he made his way back to the captain's chair, sat down, and put the boat back on her proper heading.

A Russian freighter, most likely loaded down with Cuban cigars and citrus. Or on her way to *get* loaded. On autopilot, traveling at full speed, with one vodka-pickled watch officer on duty to blast the horn at anything that got in the way. No matter *what*, they never slowed down or altered course. Ever.

Sligo settled back in the chair and tried to calm his shattered nerves. How Alberto and that asshole lawyer hadn't woken up, he couldn't figure. Oh, yeah—they were self-sedated on multiple cocktails, a few lines of coke, and a calming bedtime hit of Thorazine. A mix guaranteed to knock the legs out from under a charging rhino. Thank Christ. They wouldn't be animate for eight hours yet.

He turned and looked one more time at the Russian freighter, disappearing rapidly into the night far astern. Sour bile clogged his throat. He hacked, spat the results over the port rail, and gazed in disgust at the little cog lying beside the deck trim of the port console locker. *Fuck.* Autopilot broken. Now he was going to have to steer manually the rest of the way to the island.

Goddamn commie bastards. Still cluttering up the planet. Kennedy should've nuked 'em back in '62, the chowder-sucking wimp.

They'd just ruined a damn fine dream.

Chapter Fifteen

Fuentes didn't think he was ever going to walk again, so mangled did his pudgy body feel. Sex with Grizelda Ramos had been akin to wrestling with a four-hundred-pound female orangutan, and he hadn't come close to winning a single fall. He couldn't recall one other time in his life when he'd been put into a choke hold and forcibly bent backwards into the equivalent of a human horseshoe. The uneven contest had gone on for what seemed like hours, with Grizelda roaring and him squealing for mercy, until he'd nearly blacked out from spinal trauma and lack of oxygen. And all the while, terrible, nutcracker-like assaults had been perpetrated repeatedly upon his genitalia.

It had been too horrible. The woman was an absolute brute. Thank God she hadn't actually torn any parts off him.

He lay on the disheveled mattress as if crucified, dripping with sweat, his severely overtaxed heart trying to beat its way out through his breastbone. She was prowling around at the foot of the bed, now . . . *oh, God—don't let her start on me again* . . .

"Fuentes," Grizelda said, her deep voice as ominous to his ears as the rumble of an earthquake, "make sure you take a shower. You smell like a pig."

She closed the short blue-satin robe over her prodigious breasts and knotted the sash. Fuentes' glazed eyes followed her as she strode across the moonlit room to the open window, halted, and stared outward—across the darkened ridgelines, over the black waters of the Caribbean, to the pinprick cluster of lights far offshore.

Despite his physical ruination, the geneticist again found himself swallowing hard at the sight of her. In the pale lunar wash, she looked like some kind of neoclassical goddess—a musclebound Artemis carved in white marble. Except for the bizarre punk-ponytail haircut. That didn't fit.

"Do you know what is wrong with you, Fuentes?" Grizelda growled, without looking at him.

"Uhh—yes, Griz—Senorita Ramos." The pudgy little scientist struggled up onto his elbows. "I believe it was the next-to-last position, when you twisted me over your leg and inserted your thumb—"

"No, idiot." She turned and gave him her basilisk stare. "In *general*. Do you know what is wrong with you?"

Fuentes had the presence of mind to realize that the question was rhetorical. "Ah—no, Senorita Ramos."

"You are unfit," Grizelda said, curling her lip. "Too soft. A flaccid lump of black body hair and adipose tissue."

"Er—"

"But I like you."

The haggard man brightened.

Grizelda turned and resumed gazing out the window. "Tomorrow, my brother will return to this island aboard one of our other yachts. He and I will take several bodyguards and go out to the diving barge to inspect the progress of the salvage work. You will stay here." A deep giggle suddenly escaped her throat. "To recover."

Fuentes swallowed again. "Recover?"

"Yes. Recover. We can't have you leaving for Panama in your weakened state, can we? You might catch a bug."

"But, Senorita Ramos," Fuentes protested, "I am perfectly fine. You have just . . . tired me out."

"Nonsense. You're overstrained. You will stay here and rest until I return. And then—once we are sure you're up to it—you and your money depart for . . . a new life."

She jerked her head around and showed her teeth in a slit of a smile. For the third time in five minutes, Fuentes swallowed hard. It was like being grinned at by an upright crocodile.

"As you wish, Senorita Ramos," he said in a hoarse voice and sagged back onto the bed.

Grizelda crossed her arms beneath her breasts and continued to stare out at the little cluster of lights. "Yes," she said under her breath. "As I wish."

*****

The bell lurched slightly, like an elevator halting at a given floor. Outside the viewports, the suspended particles in the seawater stopped moving upward and began to drift at random through the glare of the external lights.

"We're all stop up here." Gene's voice sounded very tinny through the little speaker. "Got you at eleven hundred and ninety feet."

Ben shifted awkwardly in his dacron-and-rubber hot-water suit. "Roger that, Gene. Eleven ninety."

"How you guys doin'?"

"Happy as a pair of clams."

"I bet." There was a brief pause. "All right. You ready to try poppin' her open?"

Ben bent down and gripped the handle of the inward-opening hatch in the floor of the bell. "Watch your feet, Chris," he said. "Okay, Gene. Bring her on down the rest of the way."

"Roger. Comin' down slow."

There was another lurch and the particles outside the viewports began to move upward again. Chris slid around beside Ben and also took hold of the hatch handle.

Ben eyed the external depth gauge. "Eleven ninety-three, eleven ninety-four, eleven ninety-five." He nodded to Chris. "Pull."

The two divers heaved. The hatch didn't budge.

"Drop us a touch further, Gene," Ben said toward the speaker.

"Roger that." The bell jolted once more. "How-zat?"

"Pull," Ben told Chris again.

They both lifted. This time they were rewarded with a sucking sound and a slopping of cold water as the hatch broke its seal at the top of the bell trunk and swung upward.

"Got it, Gene," Ben reported, as they locked the heavy steel door back in the upright position. "That last six inches equalized us." He looked again at the bell's external depth gauge. "I've got us at eleven hundred and ninety-five—and a half—feet."

"Calibration's a bit off on your gauge," Gene said. "I've got you at ninety-five on the money. Same with internal bell pressure."

"Close enough for government work," Ben replied. "Okay, we're here. I'm gonna blow some of the water out of this trunk and then go take a little stroll."

"Roger that," the old supervisor said. "Standing by."

Ben reached up and grabbed one of the gas-blowdown valves. "Watch your ears," he said to Chris, and opened it.

There was a *whoosh* of additional helium and the seawater that had been lapping over the top edge of the bell trunk began to recede. When it had dropped about eighteen inches down the steel tube, Ben shut the valve and checked the PPO_2.

"The trunk's partially dewatered," he relayed, for Gene's benefit. "I'll be in my dive hat in just a few."

"Roger that."

Chris lifted the heavy fiberglass-and-stainless-steel shell over Ben's head, then carefully lowered it. Ben worked the cushioned internal liner down over his ears until the dive helmet was seated on the crown of his head and its bottom edge was touching the frame of the fiberglass-and-neoprene yoke he wore around his neck. He fitted his mouth and nose into the oral/nasal mask and made sure he could see out through the thick Lexan faceplate properly. Then he pressed the camming mechanism of the yoke up over the hat's bottom O-ring and closed it, locking the entire assembly onto his head.

"How do you hear me?" he asked.

Chris leaned over and depressed the TALK lever of the bell's wall-mounted descrambler radio. "Loud and clear. First time in hours you ain't sounded *too* much like Donald Duck."

"Same at my end." He paused before continuing: "How's the feed to the surface, Gene? You got me too?"

"Roger that. Loud and clear."

"Good. Okay, then . . ."

Ben reached over and twisted the valves on the hot water mixing panel. He felt a spurt of warmth at the base of his spine, on top of both shoulders, and then the balmy, liquid sensation spread over his entire body. He checked the fitting at his waist where the narrow hot-water supply hose—an integral part of his dive umbili-cal—was plumbed into his suit, next to the shackle on his dive harness that secured the umbilical itself.

The last thing he did was attach the quick-disconnect whip from the bailout bottle he wore on his back—his emergency breathing supply in case the flow of gas through his dive umbilical failed—to the auxilia-ry input valve on the side block of his helmet. Then he pulled on his neoprene gloves, gave Chris the thumbs-up, and maneuvered to a sitting position on the lip of the bell trunk, his booted feet dangling into the black water.

"Leaving the bell," he said, and swung down into the trunk's narrow confines. There was a splash, an upwelling of bubbles, and he was gone.

He dropped through the three-foot tube cleanly and emerged below the bell, surrounded by the cage-like framework that held the external on-board gas supplies. His feet came to rest on the bell's clump weight, dangling from its supporting chains five feet below the bottom of the trunk. A couple of yards of dive umbilical coiled down beside him as Chris fed out some working slack.

"All stop on the diver, Chris," Ben said. "That's good on my hose. Let me have a look around before I go anywhere."

"Roger," came the reply. "All stop on your dive hose."

Crouching down, Ben took hold of the two chains and let himself sink to a sitting position on the clump weight. Despite the insulating warmth of the hot-water suit, he could still feel the extreme chill of the deep ocean; on his wrists, around his neck, near his ankles— anywhere the suit rubber was thin. Condensation was already beginning to form on the inside of his faceplate. He reached up, twisted the freeflow knob on his hat's sideblock, and cleared the fog away with a blast of gas from the internal diffuser bar mounted just above the faceplate's upper edge.

Shutting the freeflow down, perched on top of the clump weight, he looked out at the nearly quarter-mile-deep world surrounding him. It was like sitting on a swing in outer space—empty blackness ahead, below, all around. No stars. Just tiny particles, some of them alive, drifting through the limited glow of the bell's viewport snoopers.

"Switch on the down beams, Chris," Ben instructed.

A beat passed, and then two large lights mounted on either side of the bell trunk came on, bracketing Ben with twin shafts of brilliant white illumination. Eight feet below him, the sea floor suddenly appeared—a ghostly gray plain of talcum-like sediment, stretching off into the vacant darkness. With the exception of a couple of small sea whips and one blind crab, there was nothing to be seen.

Ben turned on his hat light. The narrow beam probed through the perpetual gloom as he swiveled his head, but revealed only more particles and a lone jellyfish with a mantle two feet in diameter and gossamer tentacles several yards long, pumping its languid way past the bell about ten feet higher in the water column.

"Gene," Ben said, "I can't see anything but clean ocean bottom. Can you give me a bearing to try?"

"Hang on," the supervisor replied. "Let me check the GPS."

Ben blew bubbles, waiting, and watched the jellyfish drift through the black void like a living parachute. Every so often, a linear pattern of bioluminescence would flash along its periphery, like the moving border of a neon sign.

"Assuming the bell's hanging straight down," Gene said, "a bearing of zero-eight-zero degrees oughta take you right to it. Shouldn't be more than twenty-five or thirty feet, I reckon."

"Got it," Ben said. "Eighty degrees. Lemme give it a try."

He held his wrist compass up in front of his face-plate and leveled it. "Huh. Two-fifty. I'm facing the wrong way."

It took him a couple of seconds to reverse his position on the clump weight. "Okay," he reported. "Zero-eight-zero, dead ahead." He looked out along the illuminated seabed. "Still pretty barren, but I think I see a chunk of wood at the limit of the bell lights. I'm gonna walk that way, see what I run into."

"Roger that," Gene acknowledged.

"Chris?"

"Go ahead, Gannon," came the cocksure reply. "I'll feed ya all the hose you want."

"Glad to hear it," Ben said. "All right. I'm jumping off the clump weight. Hope I don't sink up to my neck—it looks pretty soft down there."

He hoisted himself up, let go of the supporting chains, and drifted down toward the seabed. A small flatfish darted out of the way as his boots touched the sediment, and immediately a gray cloud billowed up around him, obscuring his vision. He felt his legs penetrate knee-deep, the cold mud sucking as if to pull him in all the way.

"On bottom," he said, holding still while the cloud of silt dissipated.

"One thousand two hundred and seven feet," Gene responded. "That your deepest?"

"I've logged one bounce to fourteen hundred off Buenos Aires," Ben replied. "Nine years ago. Other than that, this is the winner."

"What'd you do?" Chris chimed in.

Ben began to move forward, laboriously extracting one leg after the other from the sucking ooze. "Turned a valve," he said. "Then got back in the bell and left."

"Tough assignment."

"Gravy money. Makes up for all those other days I've spent jetting down pipeline in ten feet of muddy water in the Louisiana swamps."

"For no depth pay," Gene interjected.

Ben laughed. "For no depth pay. You got that right."

He was beginning to move beyond the small circular field of illumination cast by the bell lights when his boot hit something buried in the mud and he stopped. Bending over, he dug down with one hand until his gloved fingers came into contact with a rounded object about the size of a large coconut. Working it free of the ooze, he held it up in front of his faceplate.

"Found our first artifact," he said, scraping at the mud that clung to it. "I'm trying to clean it up a bit . . ."

"Solid gold, right?" Chris interrupted.

"'Fraid not." Ben turned the object over in the beam of his hat light. It was an oval disk of heavy black wood, about three inches thick and a foot long. A trio of holes, laid out in a triangle, had been bored through its center, and a semi-circular channel had been gouged in its outer edge. Even through his gloves, Ben could feel the wear marks where coarse rope had once chafed against it.

"Solid wood," he said. "Heavy, too. Probably lignum vitae. It's an old deadeye."

Gene grunted. "Pretty much what you'd expect to find around the wreck of a sixteenth-century sailing vessel."

"Yep."

"What's a deadeye?" Chris blurted.

Ben set the artifact down in the mud next to his ploughed trail of footprints. "It's a type of block that was used to tune a ship's standing rigging. You'd reeve a line through it, haul like hell, and tension up a shroud or stay."

"I don't get it," the younger diver replied.

"You will," Ben told him. "I'll bring it back to the bell when I'm done—show you how it works."

"It was before your time, Chris," Gene said. "Back in the days of wooden ships and iron men." Ben could practically hear the grin.

"Oh, great," Chris grumbled. "Now you're gonna pull this old-timer crap on me. 'You shoulda been there in the good ol' days, kid.' Back when men were men and sheep were nervous."

Ben laughed. "Not a chance. We weren't there either. It was long before our time, too—wasn't it, Gene?"

"Yeah," the old supervisor said. "Commercial divers came later, under their own special category: wooden men with iron heads."

This time Chris laughed too. "'Wooden men with iron heads,'" he repeated. "I like that. I do believe I resemble that remark."

"Use it all you want," Gene told him.

Ben pulled some more slack in his umbilical hose and climbed over a large timber that was blocking his way. The dark wood was almost entirely hidden by a crusty, lichen-like growth of yellow and beige, mottled with random patches of violet. Beside him, a sea whip fluttered its fan of thin fingers in the slight turbulence caused by his passing.

"Here's this big chunk of wood I saw from the bell," Ben said. "Doesn't look like a rib. Maybe part of a deck truss or something." He scraped at a bright orange stain in the middle of a purplish encrustation. It turned to powder under his fingertips. "It has what's left of an iron spike buried in it. Oxidized into a pile of rust."

"An old block and a rusty nail," Chris grumbled. "When are you gonna find something valuable?"

"Gimme a break. I haven't even laid eyes on the ship yet."

Ben checked his compass, re-oriented himself to eighty degrees, and panned around with his hat light. The blackness ahead of him was absolute, as cold and alien as the dark side of the moon. As he plodded forward again through the soft muck, his world shrank to a small pool of light wavering on the sea floor. His faceplate was accumulating fog again, and he could feel the intense chill on the other side of the thin Lexan pane against his exposed cheekbones. He glanced at the tiny thermometer attached to the wrist strap of his compass: fifty-four degrees Fahrenheit.

Nippy.

He kept moving, as much for the comforting sensation of generating his own body heat as for locating the wreck.

And then, all of a sudden, it was there. A looming black mass of twisted timbers and shattered planking, collapsed curves and distorted angles, still—by some unaccountable miracle—holding its shape after four hundred and fifty-plus years on the bottom. Ben halted, tipped his head back, and let his hat light play over the structure. The general outline of a wide-beamed ship's forward section was clearly discernable, its bow jutting up into the watery void at a slight starboard angle. All around it, half-buried in banks of gray-white sediment, were large sections of broken timber. Sea whips and the ubiquitous deepwater encrustation covered the wreck's visible surfaces. What Ben surmised was a bowsprit had broken at its junction with the bow and sagged into the bottom, angling up against the wreck like a fallen broomstick.

"The ROV gave us some good pictures," Ben said slowly, "but you've gotta be standing where I'm standing to get the overall effect."

"You found it?" Gene and Chris said simultaneously.

Ben nodded without being aware of it, his hat light bobbing up and down. "That's a roger."

There was complete silence for several seconds.

"How's she look?" Gene asked quietly.

Ben thought about it for a moment, standing there in the frigid darkness, gazing at the remains of the Spanish Imperial Warship *Arista*. Listening to her echoes.

"Dignified," he said at last. "Old and dignified."

Gene cleared his throat. "Yeah. I know what you mean."

Ben turned and looked back the way he had come. Just above his horizontal line of sight, perhaps forty feet away, the bell hovered in a faint corona of its own illumination, its supporting cable and umbilical invisible. It looked like a tiny lone satellite in an empty black sky, and just about as distant.

He turned back toward the wreck. Two things were gospel true when working in the deep ocean. First: it was a cold, dark, inhospitable, and often dangerous place. Second: there was absolutely no point in dwelling on it.

"Slack the diver," he said, pulling on his umbilical. "I'm gonna see if I can get a look inside."

Chapter Sixteen

Ben labored up the sediment bank, plowing along hip-deep in a cloud of muck, until he reached the *Arista*'s side. Here the bottom was firmer, scoured and compacted by occasional currents, and he was able to stand upright with his boots sinking only ankle deep. Up close, in the glare of his hat light, the wreck's growth-encrusted timbers revealed their undersea colors like a great abstract wall mural. He reached out and gently pressed his palm against the waterlogged wood—the first human hand to touch the *Arista* since 1539.

"She's even beamier than I realized," he said. "And built like a brick shithouse." He removed his harness knife from its sheath and slid the five-inch blade into an open seam. "These external timbers are pretty substantial." He angled his head so that his hat light shone into the gap. "From what I can see, they're nearly a foot thicker than the length of my knife blade . . . maybe fifteen, sixteen inches."

"Holy jeez," Chris declared. "The thing's a regular log cabin."

Ben pulled his knife back out of the seam. "A wooden bunker, more likely. It must have taken most of an entire forest to build one of these ships."

"I remember readin' something about that," Gene said. "Time was, in England back in the old days, ship-building trees were considered a military asset. You could be hanged or have your head lopped off for cuttin' down an oak tree without permission."

"No shit?" Chris's tone was incredulous. "For choppin' down a *tree?* That's the Brits for you. Wired wayyy too tight."

"Don't be too quick to knock the British," Ben said, moving along the side of the wreck. "Back in the nineteenth century, us Americans were pretty picky about our timber, too. You know all that naval oak that grows around Pensacola? We used it to build the knees and elbows in our warships. If you cut any of it down, Congress said it was okay to throw you into a military dungeon for the rest of your life."

"Bummer," Chris said.

"Yeah. Quite."

Ben stepped over a long, cylindrical object, lying half-buried in the seabed, that resembled a section of fifteen-inch pipeline. He bent down and wiped off the thin coating of sediment that covered its uppermost curve, expecting to see a spar of some kind. But the exposed surface was unlike that of waterlogged wood; too devoid of irregularities. On a hunch, Ben pulled the small chipping hammer he carried from his weight belt, picked a spot, and swung.

There was a metallic *clunk*. Bits of black-oxide crust and white calcification erupted from the point of impact. A greenish patch the size of a penny appeared.

Ben tapped several more times. Then he brushed away the debris and centered his hat light on the cleaned area. In the middle of the green spot, now enlarged to the size of a poker chip, the hammer's wedge-shaped tip had cut several deep gouges. These gleamed with a dull, yellow-brown hue.

"Huh," Ben said. "I just found a bronze cannon."

There was a static click as Gene depressed the TALK button on the topside descrambler radio. "How big?"

Rapidly, Ben swept the sediment off the cannon from end to end. "More than two body lengths. Maybe fourteen feet. Over a foot in diameter at the muzzle, two-and-a-half at the breech."

"That's a big one," Gene said. "It'd look good on my lawn back in Houston."

"I didn't think ships carried guns this size back then," Ben remarked. "This is a monster."

"Maybe it wasn't shipboard armament. Maybe they were transporting it to set up in some kind of land battery. A coastal fort in the New World, you know? Something to terrorize the native people with—make them keep their distance while the *conquistadors* loaded their ships with pilfered loot."

"That's as good an explanation as any," Ben said. He stepped over the cannon. "Okay. I'm at the aft section of the ship, where she broke in two. Give me a minute or so to scope it out and see if there's any way I can get inside without having the whole thing collapse on me."

"That would be bad," Chris put in.

"Very bad," Ben agreed.

His faceplate was fogging again, and he cleared it with a blast of freeflow. Despite the hot-water suit, the cold was beginning to penetrate now—in the joints of his fingers, his knees, his ankles. He considered asking Chris to alter the hot/cold ratio slightly at the bell's mixing tank, but thought better of it. Changing the temperature was a touchy business, and he'd been scalded before by bursts of near-boiling water when some tender had gotten too frisky with the blending valves.

The *Arista*'s uppermost deck had partially collapsed at the point where her hull had sheared in two. A log jam of shattered timbers blocked all but two possible interior access routes; both were dark, cramped gaps less than three feet wide by three high, partly filled in by low drifts of sediment.

"The good news is it looks like I can get inside without having to disturb any of the timbers," Ben radioed. "The bad news is I'm gonna have to dig and crawl."

Gene's reply was immediate: "Don't get in there where something can shift and fall on you, Ben. Take it slow and easy. If we have to, we can always cut our way in and put up shoring as we go."

"I'll be careful," Ben said. "These beams look stable. I'll try to get my head and shoulders inside and flash my light around, see what the deal is."

"Ben." For the first time, Sass's voice came over the comm line. "You be *real* careful, okay? You don't know what might be ready to cave in down there."

"Instructions direct from the boss herself," Gene said. "No accidents."

"Got it," Ben replied.

"And watch your exhaust bubbles," the supervisor added.

"Roger that," Ben replied again. "Thanks for reminding me." It was good advice: even the exhalation bubbles rising from his hat could disturb unstable overhead structures and cause them to come crashing down.

A movement in the darkness to his left caught his eye. He swiveled his head quickly, training his hat light in that direction, past the far side of the wreck, and thought he saw something dark and mottled disappear into the gloom. Something very large.

Huh.

Probably just a trick of the shadows.

He dropped to his knees and began to scoop arm-loads of sediment out of the larger of the two gaps. His light faded and flickered as clouds of gray silt boiled up around him, obscuring his vision. But he was accustomed to working by feel and continued to dig until he had another foot of clearance from the mud line to the opening's upper crossbeam.

Sitting back on his haunches, breathing hard, he waited for the sediment cloud to clear. "I've got room to crawl in now," he panted. "'Bout a yard square." He put his hands on the heavy timbers framing the gap and pushed, gently at first, then harder. "The wood's as solid as rock right here. I think I'm okay to look inside."

"Be careful," Sass radioed again, because she had to.

"You know it."

Ben took one last look back at the bell—still hanging out in the black distance like an illuminated metal moon—then sank onto his belly and began to squirm forward into the opening: head up, shoulders hunched, forearms under his chest. His dive hose dragged at its harness shackle on his right side, and he reached back to tug on it.

"Slack the diver six feet," he instructed.

"Roger," Chris said immediately. "Slackin' the diver."

The pressure on Ben's harness eased and he continued to inch into the gap, trying not to stir up any more sediment than necessary. Lying prone on the bottom compressed the front of his suit, preventing the usual hot-water circulation around his chest, stomach, and upper thighs. The chill of the mud began to seep into his muscles through the flattened rubber, the sensation comparable to that of lying full-length in the snow, clad only in shorts and a T-shirt.

There was a two-foot-thick timber wedged diagonally across the entrance, partially barring the way. Already inside up to his waist, Ben decided to chance putting a little weight on the massive beam and dragged himself slowly up on top of it. He could feel the edges of the access hole against his ankles.

Propping himself up on his elbows, he raised his head and waited for the silt cloud generated by his movements to clear. Gradually, the sediments settled, and the illuminated brown haze on the other side of his faceplate gave way to an impression of depth and space. Foot by foot, the interior of the wreck revealed itself in the darting glare of his hat light.

It was a semi-collapsed wooden cavern approximately twenty feet across, thirty long, and fifteen high. A middle deck had been crushed downward, partly filling the inside of the hull with broken timbers. To Ben's right, a barely-intact transverse bulkhead—probably separating the forecastle quarters from the forepeak storage, he thought—had been sprung like an old picket fence, its thick planking twisted and fractured.

The supporting framework of the foremast step, its huge vertical beams clearly visible, rose to his left. Within the framework was what remained of the foremast itself, a round wooden column nearly two feet in diameter. Only the after third of the hull's bilge and keel was buried under a layer of sediment; the remainder was exposed due to the slight upward inclination of the wreck from mast step to bow.

"I can see the belowdecks section of the foremast," Ben reported. "Plain as day. Looks like it was stepped on the keel and reinforced with a truss framework." He paused. "I don't remember any part of the mast sticking up when we videoed with the ROV, do you? It must have broken off flush with the upper deck."

"Probably," Gene replied. "Can you see anything else?"

"Sure. Water, more water, and broken wood everywhere."

"A wise guy. Think you can get around inside?"

Ben cleared his throat, which was becoming parched from breathing in the cold, arid trimix gas. "I'd say yes. There's plenty of room to move, and every-thing looks stable. Not too much sediment covering the bilge, either, so I can probably dig down and see if anything interesting has settled into the lowest part of the hull."

"See any gold?" Chris blurted.

"Not yet," Ben replied. "Not even a lost filling."

"Shit."

"Be patient. I just got in here. Slack the diver."

"Roger. Slackin' you."

Ben dragged himself the rest of the way over the fallen beam, planted his feet in the soft sediment, and cautiously stood up. Pulling in another twenty feet of hose, he laid the loose coils in the mud and took a few tentative steps forward, peering around.

There was something different about the interior of the wreck, as compared to being out on the sea floor. It took him a few seconds to realize what it was: with the exception of the small amount of silt he'd stirred up with his movements, the water inside the hull was absolutely clear—almost as if it had been distilled. Outside, there was a constant rain of drifting particles—an abyssal snowfall—that caught, diffused, and reflect-ed the artificial light from his hat. It had the effect of making even relatively good visibility seem limited and hazy. Inside, however, the water was shielded from the falling precipitate by the upper deck, and remained as pellucid as gin. As a result, everything in the wreck's interior—every timber, every splinter, every shadow—was unnaturally sharp and well defined, like a hyper-real painting.

Ben moved forward, circling the foremast and its supporting structure, and began to pick his way past the collapsed remnants of the middle deck, taking care not to kick up any excess silt. He soon emerged on the opposite side of the debris pile, and was able to get a close look at the *Arista*'s forward port quarter. If anything, it was better preserved and less inundated with sediment than the starboard side.

"It might be a good idea to run a cable and a clamp-on snooper bracket in here," Ben said. "Throw a little more light on the subject."

"The viz bad?" Gene asked.

"Hell, no. Just the opposite. It's like walking around in one of those freshwater springs in Florida—clear as a baby's conscience. I keep expecting to see a manatee swim by."

"Or maybe one'a them Weeki-Wachee mermaid babes," Chris suggested.

"Yeah, that'd be nice."

"What was that again?" Sass said sharply.

Ben laughed. "Nothing. Nothing at all. Just shooting the breeze."

"That's what I thought. Remember: I'm sitting right beside your gas-supply valves."

"I'll remember."

He proceeded toward the forepeak bulkhead, the glare from his hat light playing over the hull's strakes and ribs—some damaged, most intact—and creating a moving collage of shapes and shadows amongst the scattered debris. There seemed to be an absolute dearth of life in the wreck's interior: not so much as a crab or eel to be seen. Ben knew from long experience that the floor of the deep ocean didn't exactly teem with fish like a coral reef, but there was usually some kind of animate movement to catch the eye. In here—nothing. It was damned spooky.

He stepped carefully through a tangle of shattered planking and put a hand on the forward bulkhead. "In the movies, right about now is usually when the monster octopus makes his entrance," he said. "Oughta be a tentacle showing up any second, wanting to shake hands with me."

"If it does, you can just saw it off with your handy-dandy deep-sea diver knife," Gene said. "Or just stab the critter between the eyes and kill it. Just like in the movies."

"Dick Dauntless, Deep-Sea Diver," Chris added, snickering. "Our hero."

Ben put his faceplate up close to the twisted bulk-head, trying to see into the forepeak. "Yeah," he said, "that's me. Danger is my biz-ness." Maintaining up a running banter was one way divers warded off a creep-ing sense of isolation during extended dives at great depth. And it kept everyone relaxed, in contact. "There's a little gap here. I—"

His words were cut short as the umbilical clipped to his harness suddenly snapped tight and yanked him off his feet. Arms flailing, he was smashed sideways into the central debris pile and wedged there amongst the broken timbers. The strain on the umbilical increased rapidly, until he was sure his harness was going to rip right through his body. He clawed at the wood, trying desperately to get some leverage . . .

And then, as quickly as it had commenced, the pres-sure abated. Ben sagged onto his haunches, breathing hard. After a few seconds, he pulled in about ten feet of slack and draped it over a nearby beam.

"What the hell was that all about, Chris?" he de-manded.

"What?"

"You just yanked me off my feet and dragged me into a pile of junk, is what." Ben got to his feet, his voice raw with exasperation. "Did I ask you to come up on my slack?"

"Whaddya mean?" Chris retorted defiantly. "You started haulin' hose outta here all of a sudden, so I gave you what you wanted. What's the problem?"

"My problem is your bullshit. You nearly pulled me through the side of the ship." The sudden violent upending had effectively wiped out Ben's reserves of patience. "Don't do it again."

"What?"

"You heard me." Ben looked around and began to make his way toward the after section of the wreck. "Slack the diver. I'm going to probe in the sediment near the mast step. Maybe there'll be something along the keel."

"Roger, roger," Chris said, sounding both baffled and resigned. "Slackin' you."

Regaining his composure, Ben picked his way over to the stump of the foremast and took a telescoping steel probe from a vinyl sheath taped lengthwise along the first three feet of his dive umbilical. He extended it to its full six-foot length, steadied himself with a hand on the support framework, and stabbed the narrow shaft down into the sediment. It penetrated less than a yard before stopping with a *thunk* on something solid.

Ben extracted the probe and repeated the procedure, each time encountering an unyielding surface at slightly less than three feet. Little tendrils of silt curled up like smoke from the cluster of half-inch holes he'd punched in the sediment. *Thunk. Thunk. Thunk.*

"I'm hitting the keel around the mast step," he said. "Always at about three feet. At least, I figure it must be the keel. Pretty uniform."

"Roger that," Gene returned. "Well, you're able to probe right down to the bottom of the hull, anyway. That's better than having to move all kinda trash just to take a look."

"True," Ben grunted, stabbing the probe again. *Thunk.* "The smashed wood's all piled up in the center." *Thunk.* "Makes it easier to—"

Clank.

Ben stopped talking. On the opposite side of the mast, the probe had hit something metallic after penetrating only a few inches.

"Ben?" Gene asked. "Ben? You still got me, buddy?"

Slowly, Ben withdrew the probe, positioned it four inches to the right of the first hole, and shoved it down again. *Clank.*

"Yeah, Gene," he said. "I'm still here. Sorry."

"Thought we lost a comm wire there, for a moment."

Ben probed again, four inches in the opposite direction. *Clank.*

"Negative. Comms are fine. I've got something here down by the mast step. Something metallic."

"How big?"

Rapidly, Ben stabbed around the first three holes in a widening radius. "Mmm—feels like about . . . two feet wide by three long . . . maybe two-and-a-half high."

"If it's a treasure chest I'm gonna faint dead away," Chris said.

Ben smiled inside his dive hat. "We'll see." Collapsing the probe and reinserting it in its vinyl sheath, he knelt down and began to dig.

It didn't take long to uncover the blackened wooden box that lay in the bilge, wedged up against the base of the foremast. The box was heavily reinforced with wide metal straps over most of its surface. A couple of exploratory taps of the chipping hammer confirmed that the metal, like that of the cannon, was bronze.

"You're not going to believe this," Ben said, "but I just found a chest."

"You're kidding," Gene came back.

"Nope. It's an old chest, bound with bronze strapping. Swear to God."

"I'm fainting dead away," Chris declared.

"Think you can move it?" Gene's voice shook slightly as he asked the question.

"Dunno. I'll try. It might fall apart. Or maybe it's too heavy. Hang on a minute."

Ben bent down examined the one end of the box. A couple of bronze fittings that looked as if they might have been clamps for a leather handle were affixed to one of the horizontal reinforcement straps, but the leather—if indeed that had been the handle material—had long since rotted away. Shifting position, Ben dug down beside the chest until he was able to work his fingers under its bottom corner. He blew out a long breath, tensed his muscles, and heaved.

The end of the box lifted off the bottom in a bloom of sediment. It was heavy, but not so much so that the weight was unmanageable. Carefully, he rotated it a few degrees and let it rest at an angle on the edge of its own hole.

"Well, it didn't fall apart," he reported. "And I can pick it up. It's damn heavy, though."

"Heavy enough to be full of gold?" Chris inquired immediately.

Ben cleared his parched throat. "I don't know about that. If it was full of gold, I'm pretty sure I wouldn't be able to lift it. Like I said, this chest's about two feet wide by three long."

"Maybe it's half full," Chris persisted.

"Could be." Ben replied. "Let's find out. I think I can get it back to the bell."

"Got that small lift bag?" Gene asked.

"Yep."

Ben pulled a small roll of fabric from the pouch dangling off his harness and shook it open. His hat light revealed a two-foot-long by one-foot-wide tubular Dacron sack, bright yellow, with several lengths of nylon webbing stitched around its mouth. Attached to each webbing end was a heavy stainless-steel clip.

Bending down again, Ben worked the webbing straps under the chest one at a time, cinched them tight, and hooked their clips onto D-rings sewn around the bag's mouth. When he had satisfied himself that the bag was secured less than six inches from the box lid, he sat back on his haunches and grasped the free-floating end of a small-diameter hose that was married into his umbilical.

"Chris," he said. "Give me some gas to my pneu-mo."

"Roger that. Comin' atcha."

A burst of bubbles erupted from the end of the hose in Ben's hand. Primarily used as an extremely accurate form of depth gauge, the pneumofathometer line had secondary applications as well. It could function as an emergency source of breathing gas, for one, or as a means of inflating a lift bag. Grasping the top end of the bag and holding it up vertically, Ben pushed the bubbling hose-end up into its mouth. Immediately, the tubular yellow sack began to fill out, pulling against the straps that secured it to the chest.

Ben continued to fill the lift bag with one hand while pulling up on the webbing with the other. "I'm not going to get enough lift out of this one bag to float the chest," he said, "but I should get enough positive buoyancy that it won't be too hard to carry." Trimix gas began to belch out of the lift bag's mouth, and he removed the hose. "Okay, the bag's fully inflated. Shut off my pneumo, Chris."

"Roger that." The jet of bubbles died away.

Ben grabbed the webbing in both hands, bent his legs, and heaved. The chest came free of the mud easily, its dead weight reduced by the upward pull of the lift bag. He was able to carry it against his thigh with only one hand. Planting his feet carefully, and ensuring that the top of the bag did not hang up in any overhead obstructions, he made his way back toward the entrance gap.

When he reached it, he slumped to his knees, panting, and let the chest sink down onto the sediment. "Come up on my slack," he said, pulling his excess umbilical free of the debris pile. It slid rapidly out through the gap as Chris retrieved it, until he felt a yank at his hip. "All stop."

"All stop on you," the younger diver repeated.

"Okay," Ben said. "Now I've got to get this thing out through this hole." He dragged the chest under the diagonal crossbeam that obstructed the entrance, and then heaved, shoved, and kicked it halfway through the gap. Then he let some of the gas out of the lift bag using its small plastic bleed valve, pulled it down enough to clear the upper edge of the entrance, and pushed it through.

Lying on his right side, he got his dive hat up next to the chest so that he could just see the mouth of the bag through the drifting haze of kicked-up sediment. He fished for his pneumo once again, managed to stretch out his left arm far enough to get the end of thin hose directly under the half-deflated bladder, and spoke into his oral/nasal mike:

"Chris. Shoot some gas to my pneumo again."

The hose bucked slightly in his hand as gas erupted from its end and began to refill the bag. In less than a minute, it was fully topped up. "Okay," Ben said. "Shut it down."

"Roger. Shuttin' down the pneumo."

Ben put his shoulder against the chest, lifted and heaved, and slid it the rest of the way through the entrance gap. Then he crawled out of the wreck himself, stood up, and stretched to his full height.

"Aggh," he groaned. "Lying in cold mud can give you arthritis."

Gene laughed. "Like I told you: it's hell to get old."

"What now?" Chris broke in.

Ben looked at the chest sitting on the gray mud beside him. "Well, how about this: I haul the box back to the bell, you rig the come-a-long hoist to that padeye over your head, and we pick it up through the access trunk. Then we can set it down near the scrubber, pry open the lid, and see what's inside."

"Gonna be pretty crowded in that there bell with you two guys and a three-by-two-foot chest," Gene commented.

"I'll swing down that grating that locks between the two external gas racks," Ben said. "Set it back outside and tie it down after we take a look, bring it up that way."

"Cool as hell," Chris enthused. "I wanna see that gold."

"Okay," Gene said. "If you think you can do it. Your call."

Ben coughed to clear his dry throat. "No sweat. It's as good as done."

He started to bend down and take hold of the webbing—then paused in mid-stoop. Slowly, he straightened up, looking past the bobbing yellow tube of the lift bag, peering into the darkness with the thin beam of his hat light.

Once again, out of the corner of his eye, he thought—was almost *certain*—he'd caught a glimpse of

John McKinna

an immense shape, faint and mottled, disappearing into the shadows at the very edge of visibility.

Chapter Seventeen

"All right, come up on it."

Ben felt the lifting cable tighten in response to his command as Chris pumped the handle of the come-a-long and picked the chest off the sea floor directly beneath the bell. As it ratcheted steadily upward, he reached up and unscrewed the bleed valve on the lift bag. Gas belched out, and the long yellow tube rapidly wilted and collapsed.

"Lift bag's deflated."

"Roger that." Chris was panting as he worked the small manual hoist.

As the chest rose to the level of his faceplate, Ben turned and looked back along the seabed at the trail of churned footprints and drag marks indicating his path of return from the *Arista*. The humpback to the bell had been strenuous but uneventful, with only one quick pause to pick up the deadeye he'd left beside his incoming tracks. He could feel the weight of it pulling down on his harness, hanging in the mesh bag at his side.

"All stop, Chris. It's about to bind on the bottom of the clump weight. Let me hop up there and guide it past."

"Roger."

Ben climbed his own dive hose hand over hand until he was level with the clump weight, got a leg over it, and pushed the come-a-long cable and its load outboard. "Okay. Come on up again."

Gradually, four inches at a time, the chest ratcheted up into the mouth of the bell's access trunk, completely filling the yard-wide steel tube.

"Hey, cool," Chris said, puffing. "It just fits through."

"Just barely," Ben agreed, guiding the chest with a hand on its underside. "A few more cranks, Chris, and you'll have it."

"Doin' it, Gannon, doin' it."

The chest inched its way upward until at last it hung suspended inside the bell just above the trunk's upper edge. Ben pushed sideways on it from below, Chris leaned on the support cable from above, and together they maneuvered it off to one side. Chris reversed the cam on the come-a-long with a flick of his thumb, then cranked the chest downward until it rested partly on the floor grating and partly on the trunk lip.

"I'm coming in," Ben radioed.

He surfaced in the trunk, grabbed an overhead handle welded to the side of the bell, and hoisted himself past the dripping chest, barely squeezing by. Sitting on the floor grating, his legs dangling into the water, he popped the locking cam on his dive hat and lifted it off his head.

"Aaaggh," he said, wiping his face and spitting. "That's long enough in this head-vice for one shift." He twisted around and hung the heavy helmet by its bronze top handle on a protruding steel peg near his left shoulder.

Chris was already fumbling with the chest's locking mechanism, which had corroded into a shapeless black mass of deteriorated metal. Pieces of white, green, and red crust flaked off it with every touch of his scrabbling fingers.

"Bastard," he cursed under his breath. "Fuckin' thing's fused into a glob."

Ben watched him for a moment, then removed his chipping hammer from its harness lanyard and held it out. "Here. Why don't you just knock that mess off so we can pry the lid open."

Chris took the tool. "Might have to beat what's left of the hinges off, too."

Ben shrugged. "Why not? If they're nothing but lumps of oxidation, they're just in the way. Nothing to preserve."

The younger diver grinned, shielded his eyes, and swung the hammer. At the mild impact, the corroded lock shattered in a spray of fragments and dropped into the water, leaving in its place a chewed-looking area of punky black wood.

"Huh," Ben said. "That was easy. Can you open it?"

Chris jammed the sharp end of chipping hammer's head into the seam between lid and box and pried downward. There was a wet, sucking *pop* and the lid came free. Changing position slightly, Chris got his fingers into the gap and heaved upward. A crunching sound filled the bell's interior as the remains of the rear hinges gave way, and the lid dropped back against the housing of the CO_2 scrubber.

"Son of a bitch," Chris swore, panting.

Ben leaned forward. The inside of the chest was half filled by a lumpy reddish-brown mass that resembled a chunk of wet sandstone. Here and there, the remnants of wooden handles protruded from the conglomeration, and a few telltale shapes were still discernible within it.

Ben let himself sag back against the wall of the bell. "Tools," he said. "Iron and steel tools rusted together into a single chunk of oxidized metal. Look, you can still see the shape of a planing ax there. And a hammer, and a draw knife." He chuckled, shaking his head. "We found the carpenter's chest."

Chris stared in disappointment. "Shit. No gold?"

"I seriously doubt it, unless he was a very rich carpenter."

The younger diver spat. *"Bastard."*

"What'd you say was in there?" Gene's voice echoed in the metal sphere.

Ben coughed and cleared his throat. "Just old rusty tools, I'm afraid, Gene. I found the ship's carpenter's tool chest."

"Oh, yeah?" There was a pause. "Son of a bitch."

Ben smiled. "Chris just said that."

"Anything in there of any value?" Gene asked.

"Hang on a minute." Ben gestured to Chris. "See if you can break up that lump with the chipping hammer, okay? On the outside chance there might be something halfway interesting rusted into the middle of it."

"There ain't nothin' in here, Gannon."

"Just *do* it, will you?" Ben suppressed a surge of irritation. "And don't give me a hard time about it."

"Okay, okay."

Chris pounded on the chunk of rust for nearly a minute, chips and shards flying everywhere, before sitting back on his haunches again. "There. She's all broken up." He tossed the hammer down on the floor grating in disgust.

Ben leaned forward and looked inside. The chest now contained a coarse, reddish-brown rubble, studded with pieces of waterlogged wood. There was nothing of interest to be seen.

"It's a bust, Gene," Ben said. "There isn't even a nail in here. Unless you're in the museum business, and heavily into restoration, it's just junk."

"We ain't," the supervisor replied through the intercom speaker. "Toss it."

"Roger that." Ben pulled his legs out of the trunk, got up on his haunches, and nodded to Chris. "Unhook it. We're dumping the thing."

"Good riddance," Chris said, tugging on the come-a-long cable, "all that haulin' for nothing. Pain in the ass piece of shit."

The cable hook came free, and Ben rapidly unwound the lift bag straps. "Ready?" he cued Chris. "One, two, *three*."

Together, they tipped the chest forward and let it drop into the access trunk. There was a bang, a splash, and it was gone, leaving a gush of bubbles simmering on the water's surface. A second after it disappeared, Ben and Chris felt a mild jolt as the heavy box caromed off the bell's clump weight on its way to the seabed.

"Piece of shit," Chris muttered again.

Ben began to strip off his hot-water suit, tugging his arms free of the bulky garment one at a time. "Well," he said, "you've got a chance to do better than me. Get dressed in, buddy—you're up next."

"You know," Sass said, pouring coffee into a mug in the sat shack, "I don't think most marine archaeologists would approve of us just discarding an old artifact like that chest. They'd say it has historical significance." She gave a wry smile. "Not very politically correct, Gene."

The old supervisor looked across the shack at her. "Excuse me, Sass, but *fuck* politically correct. We're after gold. It's a rotted-out old wooden box and we've put it back down on the ocean floor where it was—close enough, anyway."

She shrugged and took her seat near the gas rack again. "Fine by me, boss."

Gerald Posey, who'd been leaning against the wall and smoking, stirred slightly. "I've been thinking," he announced.

Gene and Sass exchanged a quick glance that posed the unsaid question, "what elsc is new?" and waited for him to elaborate.

"I've got a new kind of electrical impulse detector on my ROV. Something I've been working on for a while. It's similar to a magnetometer, but it can find non-ferrous metals as well as iron and steel." The tech smiled around his cigarette and blinked through his steel-rimmed glasses. "Like gold, for instance."

"Go on," Gene said.

"Well, Ben's been inside the wreck, probed around, and really hasn't found much. I've been looking at the design profiles for this type of ship in my computer files, and there's very little indication that the crew would have used the forward section to store treasure. There isn't any hold space to speak of, for one thing, and for another, putting so much heavy ballast that far forward would have made the ship plow under sail—made her too bow-heavy."

"What are you gettin' at?" Gene asked.

Posey sighed, blowing out a long stream of smoke. "I don't think there's any treasure inside that wreck. The holds would have been farther aft, in her amidships section—where she broke in two—and her stern. If there is any gold to be found here, I'd say that it might be strewn along the bottom immediately behind this hull section."

Gene was silent for a moment. "That's not very encouraging, Gerald," he said.

The tech shrugged. "I'm just giving you my honest opinion. Frankly, I think there's an excellent chance that when the *Arista* broke up in that storm, she split right at her lower holds and scattered treasure all over the ocean floor as she sank. We don't know where the stern section is, and even if we did, there might not be any more gold in it than we're finding in the bow."

"You're really bursting our bubble here," Sass said. "So what's your idea with the ROV?"

"I thought I'd launch again," Posey replied, "and fly some passes just above the seabed behind the wreck. The detector in my fish's nose cone sends out a burst of electricity every two seconds, which travels down into the mud and temporarily energizes any conductive metal it hits. Then the detector's internal sensors profile the electrical shadow of whatever's buried there and give me an image on my topside screen.

"We could find out very quickly if there's anything worth digging for behind the wreck . . . or if we're just spinning our wheels here."

Gene sipped coffee, looked at Sass, and back at Posey. Then he set his mug down and lifted an eyebrow.

"Hell, yes," he said. "Might as well check out all the possibilities, eh? Splash your gadget and let's see what it can find."

Posey smiled, drew on his cigarette, and pushed himself off the wall.

"But bear in mind that we're nowhere near done with the inside of this wreck," Gene told him. "We're not givin' up until we've searched every nook and cranny of the interior . . . so keep your ROV clear of the bell, the divers, and their hoses. They've got first priority down there."

"Will do," Posey said, and exited the sat shack.

*****

"Okay," Ben said, pulling a heavy gray sweatshirt down over his tousled head, "remember—you want to probe around the mast step first, where the silt's the deepest. Check every four inches, working toward the port side. If we do it systematically, we won't be repeating each other's work when we switch divers. Take your time, watch your hose doesn't get fouled, and keep an eye on what's happening overhead." He smiled slowly at Chris, who was sitting on the edge of the access trunk in his hot-water suit, his dive hat resting in the crook of one elbow. "We don't want anything caving in on you."

"Appreciate the pep talk, Gannon," the younger diver responded. "You're a regular mother hen."

"Buk-buk-buh*caw*," Ben told him. "Down here, you better believe it." Being good-humored was ultimately less stressful than allowing himself to become annoyed. The kid would be out of the bell in thirty seconds anyway.

He helped Chris don his heavy dive hat and steadied it while the neck-cam was locked in place. Then he flipped several coils of dive umbilical off the hanging peg and clapped a hand on the young man's shoulder.

"Ready when you are," he said, speaking toward the bell's dive radio.

In response, Chris threw a thumbs-up and pushed off into the trunk. There was a splash that drenched one side of the bell's interior, and he disappeared into the bubbling pool of black water, his hose trailing rapidly after him.

"On the clump weight." His voice rang sharp and hollow out of the bell radio's speaker. "Pushin' off. On bottom, walkin' toward the wreck along your old footprints."

Ben flipped a few more coils of hose off the peg and fed slack to him. "Your light working okay?"

"Yeah, yeah."

Ben smiled to himself. "See the wreck yet?"

"Just abou—*Holy Jesus!*" At Chris's sudden outburst, the umbilical stopped paying out through the access trunk.

"What's the matter?" Ben waited, the dive hose slack in his hand.

When Chris's voice came back, it contained a noticeable tremor. "There's something out here, man. Something big. When I looked up to find the wreck, for a second or two, it was like there was a goddamn *wall* moving by in front of me—maybe fifteen feet ahead." There was a pause as the young diver swallowed. "I couldn't tell what it was . . . and I can't see it now . . . *at all.*"

Chapter Eighteen

Sligo couldn't sleep. He'd managed to re-install the little cog that linked the *Cucaracha*'s wheel to the autopilot, so he didn't have to steer manually, but the coke he'd been sampling since the near-disastrous encounter with the Russian freighter had put him on a bit of a jag. As an experienced consumer of high-grade blow, he was usually able to prevent any tooth-wiggling and/or skin-crawling side effects by limiting his intake to the small periodic bumps needed to keep a nice high going.

But not tonight. He put his jitters down to residual nervous trauma caused by nearly being squashed to a pulp, courtesy of the *Ivanovich*. Or maybe there was something wrong with the coke. Maybe Alberto had been passing him second-rate product with a weird cut in it—sour milk sugar or rat poison or some shit. Maybe the guy was trying to do away with him—hell, the interpersonal vibe had been pretty poor over the past day or two. Or maybe it was just the close call with the commie . . . Jesus, *jeeeeezus*—was his heart beating too fast? Was he getting short of breath? Was he—

Whoa.

Let's find something to focus on, here—before me, myself, and I go completely batshit.

The DOA-9000! There was still an hour before dawn, and half a day's travel left to the island—plenty of time to sort out that fancy-ass diving rig and look through some of the accessory equipment bags he'd stolen along with it. Get that puppy hooked up and ready to go! Alberto and his sleazy lawyer would sleep until noon . . . plenty of time to stow the rig back in the dinghy locker where they wouldn't see it.

Cool beans.

Sligo went aft to where the yacht's small Boston Whaler was strapped down in its cradle on the flydeck, stepped past the launching davit, and popped the latch on the big white fiberglass locker. It opened like a top-loading household freezer, the lid swinging up and back. Inside lay the gleaming Buck Rodgers assortment of underwater equipment that comprised the DOA-9000.

It took up most of the space in the locker. In order to make room for the main unit—plus its accessory duffel bags and half-dozen four-foot-long gas-charging cylinders—Sligo had taken out all the *Cucaracha*'s lifejackets, along with several large coils of expensive rope, and thrown them into the dock dumpster back in Grand Cayman. What the hell. If the boat sank, they could hang onto seat cushions.

He opened the nearest duffel bag and pulled out the contents. It was some kind of full-body suit, made of tough, flexible, plasticized fabric in brilliant Kronos Industries yellow, with gasket-like black rubber cuffs at the wrists and a similarly designed collar. The inside was lined with something that felt like thick terrycloth. A bit more digging around produced matching boots and gloves, with Velcro straps that secured them to the suit.

Outstanding. The suit collar sealed to the dive helmet's neck dam; that was obvious. Sligo giggled aloud, pleased with himself. The design was pretty much self-explanatory. Hell, this shit wasn't hard to figure out at all.

What was that idiot's name? *BOB*. Just like on his goofy company shirt. What had he said? Something about using a breathing gas called—uh—*trimix* when diving deep. And here was a charging cylinder marked—*tah-dahh!*—TRIMIX.

Too easy.

All there was to do was go down to his quarters, get the manuals he'd swiped, and read up on how to fill the rebreather's reservoirs with the right gas. The metabolic oxygen was already in place, clamped up under the yellow cowling in its little green tank. Flip through the manuals, brush up on this and that, and he was ready to go.

He'd even thought of taking a lift bag with him. Hey, he wasn't stupid. Gold was heavy. The little salvage barge moored behind the *Cucaracha* in the Cayman marina had had a couple of six-footers spread out on the deck, drying in the sun, complete with attached inflation cylinders. It had been child's play to snatch one of them, roll it up, and stow it in the dinghy beneath the rain-cover.

Sligo took a look at the *Cucaracha*'s heading, just to make sure that the autopilot was still working properly. It was, the yacht thrumming its way westward, straight and true, over the calm, starlight-dappled night sea.

YEAH, baby!

He turned and made his way toward the port stairs, heading for his quarters. Just before descending, he paused to take another bump from the little vial of cocaine he kept in his pocket.

Ahhhhhh.

Gold. Scattered all over the floor of the sea like pop cans along a freeway.

It was so close, he could practically *taste* it.

*****

Chris panned around slowly with his hat light. The low drifts of sediment gleamed a pale gray as the narrow beam passed over them, revealing nothing, then faded back into shadow. The black ocean was devoid of movement; not so much as a minnow or jellyfish lurked within range of the light.

He blinked a droplet of nervous sweat out of his eye and took a deep breath. "All right, Gannon," he said, "I can't see anything anymore. I'm heading for the wreck. Whatever's swimming around out here, if it wants me, it's gonna have to dig my ass out of the *Arista*."

"That's the spirit." Ben's voice crackled through the hat's ear-speakers. "I thought I caught a glimpse of something circling me when I was out there, too . . . but I wasn't sure." He paused. "Maybe it isn't one big critter, but a bunch of little ones. A school of fish, swimming close together."

"You think?"

"I've been fooled by it before," Ben said. "Poor light, a tight ball of fish all moving in the same direction. Looks like one giant animal when you can't see well."

"I like that idea," Chris replied, puffing as he struggled up the mud embankment toward the side of the wreck. "Yeah. A bunch of little guys . . ."

"By the way," Gene put in, "it's not the ROV you're seein'. Gerald hasn't even submerged it yet. He won't be flying passes near you guys for another forty minutes. Besides," he added, "it has lights all over it. You'll recognize it right away."

"Just great," Chris muttered. "Never mind the big whatsit that might be swimmin' around down here—I might get blindsided by Mr. Wizard's private submarine."

He halted at the crest of the little drift, knee-deep in sediment, and straightened up, aiming the illuminating beam of his hat light at the wall of encrusted wood before him. "Holy shit. Look at this thing."

"Yeah," Ben said. "Impressive, isn't she?"

"That's a fact. And like you said, still holding together real well. How long's she been down again?"

"Nearly five hundred years."

"Freakin' amazing." The younger diver sounded genuinely astonished. "I can't believe she hasn't rotted apart."

"I know. Deep-sea physics and chemistry working in her favor, I guess."

Chris turned and looked back toward the bell, hanging out in empty black space just above his horizontal line of vision. "You look about a million miles away," he said.

"The bell?"

"Yeah."

Ben chuckled. "Less than fifty feet, bud, judging by how much hose you've got out."

"Like a little ball of light in a big . . . black . . . nothing."

Time for the kid to refocus, Ben thought. "How's your water temp, Chris? Comfortable?"

"Huh? Oh—yeah. Just fine. A little warm, even."

"Want it dialed down?"

"Naw. I'm good."

Ben cleared his throat. "Okay. So, you're going inside now, right?"

Chris was still standing on the sediment bank, gazing back at the bell. "Yeah, yeah. Roger that. I'm just gonna—"

His voice broke off suddenly.

Without warning, right in front of his eyes, the illuminated bell had just disappeared.

"Chris?"

The young diver felt a freezing sensation travel up the back of his neck. "Very funny, Gannon. How about you turn the lights back on now, huh?"

"What?" Ben's answer was immediate, puzzled. "I didn't turn off any lights."

"Gene," Chris asked, his voice tight, "is that ROV down here yet?"

"Not even close," the supervisor radioed. "I told you: forty minutes."

Chris stared out through his faceplate at the dead blackness, fresh sweat trickling down over his brows from beneath his hat liner.

Then, like the moon bypassing the face of the sun in the final moments of a solar eclipse, a huge shape, far enough back to be out of range of his hat light, moved past the bell, revealing it again.

"What the fuck—" Chris muttered under his breath.

That was as far as he got. With tremendous force, his dive umbilical suddenly snapped taut, yanking him sideways off his feet. The motion was so violent that one of his boots stripped free and remained buried in the sediment bank. He hurtled through the dark water, parallel to the bottom, at the end of his dive hose, bent nearly double like a rag doll.

In the bell, Ben was struck in the face by a dozen loops of umbilical that suddenly peeled off their hanging peg and smoked out through the access trunk. Taken completely by surprise, he fell back against the CO_2 scrubber, flailing for balance.

"Chris!" he shouted, groping for the thrashing hose. *"Chris!"*

"What the hell's going on down there?" Gene demanded.

Ben barely heard him. Ignoring the pain in his shoulder blade where the sharp edge of the scrubber housing had gouged him, he seized the fast-disappearing umbilical and attempted to brake it with all his strength. It was like trying to stop a runaway train. The rough hose-bundle ripped the calluses from the pads of his fingers and palms without slowing in the slightest.

In the confusion and pitch-darkness, tumbling in a whirl of exhaust bubbles, Chris never saw the heavy timber coming. He hit it sideways, shoulder-first, at an odd angle. His right arm folded along his rib cage, and in that instant his wrist broke with a sickening crack that he didn't so much hear as feel. A scream of pain burst from his lips.

"Jesus H. Christ, Ben!" Gene's voice reverberated through the communications system. *"What the goddamn hell's happening?"*

Ben squeezed the escaping umbilical until blood dripped from his fingers. The effort was futile. Desperately, he glanced up at the hanging peg: three coils left. When those went, the hose fittings—the hot water, the pneumofathometer, the communications cable, and the breathing gas—would take the strain directly, break off where they were plumbed into the bell connections, and that would be *it* for Chris Toricelli.

One coil left.

With a last-ditch effort, Ben threw the remaining bight of hose around the hinge of the trunk hatch and leaned into it as if jamming a line on a cleat. The umbilical slipped once—then bound tight. The entire bell tipped five . . . ten . . . fifteen degrees as the force on the other end of the hose pulled it sideways. Water slanted up the access trunk and began to pour onto the floor grating.

Ben was sure the umbilical components were going to tear apart when the pressure suddenly slackened . . . then disappeared entirely. In response, the bell swung back to the proper vertical orientation, the black water in the trunk leveling again.

Outside, some one hundred and fifty feet away, Chris was lying flat on his back in the cold mud, clutching his broken wrist to his chest and groaning, blinded by the sediment cloud that enveloped him and rendered his hat light useless.

"Chris!" he heard Ben Gannon's voice say, from what seemed like a great distance. *"CHRIS!"* There was a tug at his waist, and the shackle that secured his dive umbilical to his harness D-ring took a strain again—though with only a fraction of the force he'd just experienced. He felt himself being dragged along the bottom, a few feet at a time, his own name echoing repeatedly in his ears. *"CHRIS!"*

His brain foggy with shock, he somehow managed to scramble to his feet—he was aware that one foot felt more exposed than the other, encased in the sock of the hot-water suit but without a supporting boot sole beneath it—and begin to stumble in the direction of the hose pull. His wrist was a throbbing ball of pain, and he was having trouble catching his breath, as if his lungs were lined with glue. The sound of his own gasping was shrill in his ears . . . his head was spinning, aching . . .

"CHRIS!" Ben bellowed. *"VENTILATE YOUR HAT! YOU'VE GOT TOO MUCH CO₂ BUILT UP IN THERE! I REPEAT: VENTILATE! YOU'RE OVERBREATHING YOUR HAT! I CAN HEAR IT!"*

Somehow, the meaning of the shouted words penetrated the dizzying pain in his skull. Letting go of his damaged wrist, Chris reached up with his good hand, grasped the freeflow knob on his hat's side-block, and twisted it as he reeled along the seabed, following the pull of his retracting umbilical. A cool blast of breathing gas immediately hit his face, clearing his hat of the excess carbon dioxide generated by his panicked breathing. The ache behind his eyes began to subside, as did the terrible, suffocating sensation of oxygen debt and CO_2 poisoning.

"Ga . . . Gannon . . ." he started to say.

Something hit him from behind like a Mack truck, hyper-extending his spine around his bailout bottle and driving him forward into the darkness. It carried him for several seconds—he could see the glow of the bell's lights directly in front of him—then plowed him face-first into the mud. A monstrous, fluctuating weight pressed him into the seabed for what seemed like a minor eternity, crushing the breath from his lungs—

And then it was gone.

He struggled to his hands and knees, gasping, barely conscious, feeling the tug of the umbilical at his waist again, and looked up—

Directly into a bulbous, protruding eye the size of a small bowling ball.

He could see the flash of his hat light, the reflected image of the hat itself, in the gigantic black pupil . . .

And then the eye disappeared, and a great mottled wall rushed at him. There was another bone-jarring impact, and everything went black.

*****

Ben heaved on the umbilical with all the strength he had left, his hands slippery with blood and brine. All around him in the bell, Chris's hose was piled in messy loops—there was no time to coil it back on its peg. Yet another backbreaking pull . . . and suddenly the top of the younger diver's hat broke the surface in the access trunk.

Seizing the top handle of the hat with one hand, and the shoulder strap of Chris's harness with the other, Ben hoisted him bodily up through the hatch and deposited him, streaming water, on the bell's floor grating. Panting with effort, he dragged the semi-conscious diver's legs and feet inside, made sure they were clear, and slammed the hatch shut.

"Gene!" he shouted. "Pick up the bell! Chris ran into trouble outside and got hurt! Pick us up to the surface!"

"Roger that," came Gene's terse reply. The bell lurched and started upward. There was a slight sucking sound as the pressure differential automatically sealed the hatch. "How bad is it?" the supervisor asked.

"Checking now," Ben informed him. He popped the cam on Chris's hat and gently lifted it free, supporting his head with a hand behind his neck. The young diver's face was deathly pale and his eyes were closed, but he was breathing and his facial muscles were twitching—like a deep sleeper struggling to awaken from a bad dream.

Ben got two fingers inside the collar of the hot-water suit and tugged, taking the pressure off his trachea and making it easier for him to breathe. "He's coming around," he reported. "So far, he just looks like he got his bell rung pretty good. I don't know if anything else is wrong with him yet."

"You're passing nine hundred and fifty feet right now," Gene said. "Sass and Earl are picking you up as quickly as they can."

"Roger. Hang on, he's opening his eyes."

Chris blinked several times and tried to focus on Ben's face. "Wha—" he mumbled. "What—where—" He began to struggle weakly.

Ben kept a hand behind his neck. "You're back in the bell, kid. Just take it easy."

Disoriented, Chris put out his right arm and tried to push himself up into a sitting position. Immediately, he let out an anguished howl and collapsed onto his back, grimacing with pain and clutching his right wrist to his chest. Even through the bulky rubber of the hot-water suit, Ben could see the swelling and misaligned bone.

He waited until Chris had calmed down a bit, then put a reassuring hand on his shoulder. "Anything else hurt besides the wrist?" he asked.

Breathing hard and gritting his teeth, but finally back in reality, Chris shook his head. "Naw. But the bastard hurts—bad enough—all by itself."

"Try to relax. We'll get you out of that gear when we're back in the sat pot." Ben looked up at the depth meter. "Only eight hundred feet to go. Stay cool."

Chapter Nineteen

"Wake up, idiot! We're there."

A ray of newly risen sun lasered through the stern window blinds of the *Cucaracha*'s main salon and into Sligo's right eye. Groaning, he rolled off the settee where he'd been napping since four in the morning and got himself vertical. Alberto, wearing only a black thong bathing suit and what looked like a pink plastic shower cap, was rummaging around in the galley refrigerator. He came up with a quart of orange juice, waved it at the smuggler, and set a hand on one cocked hip.

"Oh, so you aren't dead? Pity. Listen, Jeremiah: we're about three miles from running aground on our own island. Since you're ostensibly the captain of this vessel, I thought you might like to know that. Perhaps you'd care to go up to the bridge and avert disaster, hmm?"

Sligo blinked, burped. God, his mouth tasted awful. And his cranium was on fire. Must have been that half-fifth of bourbon he'd chugged down at about three-thirty in an attempt to offset the coke jag and get some shuteye. Bad move, in retrospect.

"What the hell have you got on your head?" he asked Alberto, too groggy to be his usual obsequious self.

The soft, nearly naked man pursed his lips in annoyance and patted the crinkly plastic cap encasing his hair. *"Chez Mustique Placenta and Aloe-Vera Gel*, you cretin. I'm *conditioning."* He banged the orange juice down on the countertop and began to search the cabinets for a glass.

Sligo stared at him for a moment, taking in the translucent cap with its unctuous contents, the marble-sack bathing suit, and the slender, spongy-looking physique. It was a sight to chill the blood if ever he'd seen one. The smuggler swallowed bile and looked away. Jesus Christ. What a fag.

A fag who was also his employer, at least for the next few days. Sligo considered asking for a shot of orange juice, but thought better of it. "Lemme go up and check our position," he said, his voice as raw as fresh beef liver dragged over broken glass.

Alberto smirked at him. "Why don't you do that?"

Prick. Sligo grinned lamely and went out the portside doors to the flybridge stairs. The sun was already hot on the back of his neck, even though it was barely nine o'clock. He trudged up the last few steps and slouched over to the wheel. Dead ahead on the bow, at least five miles distant, was the Ramoses' private island, a mist-shrouded green mass rising out of a calm, sparkling blue sea. That dickhead Alberto. They weren't even close to hitting it. The sonofabitch had just wanted to wake him up.

There was supposed to be a big commercial diving barge of some kind anchored about three miles south of the island. Sligo squinted into the hazy blue distance, but could see nothing. Rubbing his bloodshot eyes, he took a pair of binoculars from a compartment beside the wheel. The damn barge had better be out here some-where . . . it was marking the location of *his* gold.

It took him a minute or so of scanning slowly across the horizon to pick it out against the shimmering water. A rusty-black, industrial-looking thing, its deck crammed high with white, green, and orange-painted equipment. It was too far away to make out any real detail, but that was it—no doubt about it.

Sligo licked his dry lips, the pain in his head sud-denly forgotten. The gold. It was there, under the barge, twelve hundred feet down . . . no distance at all . . . a fast Jamaican in track shoes could run it in forty seconds . . . they did it on television all the time . . .

"Do you mind?" Alberto's whiny voice was practi-cally in his ear. Sligo flinched, startled, his daydream disintegrating. "I want to use the radio to call my sister."

Resisting the impulse to pound Alberto to the deck
with his bare fists, the smuggler twisted out a smile and
stepped aside. "The diving barge is over there," he
said, trying to sound helpful.

"Thank you, Jeremiah," the thong-clad man replied,
his tone dripping sarcasm.

Once I bail out of this gig, Sligo promised himself,
there's no way in hell I'm ever letting a fucking weirdo
like Alberto Ramos get a foot on my neck again—not
ever. That's for damn sure.

He turned and walked back toward the dinghy, leaving Alberto to fiddle with the VHF—punching buttons
and muttering curses as he tried to find the correct
channel. A little breeze picked up momentarily, darkening the sapphire-blue water off the *Cucaracha*'s port
side with a transient cat's-paw. The cool draft felt good
on his aching forehead, and he leaned against the
dinghy locker to take in the passing seascape and try to
forget how sick he was.

"Ramos to Ramos," he heard Alberto say. There
was a burst of static, followed by a male voice replying.
Sligo glanced up at the steering station. Alberto listened impatiently, then cocked his hip and set his free
hand on it. "Well, find her then, Sanchez! I want to
talk to my sister, *comprende?* Chop-chop! I'm waiting
on channel six-eight."

Sligo looked back out at the southern horizon. At least he wasn't special. Alberto, apparently, was being an absolute bastard to everyone who worked for him.

He squinted toward the southwest and was just able to pick out the diving barge—a black speck caught between sea and sky—with his naked eye. A little tingle of glee coursed through him, despite his hangover and aggravation. Beneath his very buns, in this dinghy locker, was the means by which he was going to escape his dead-end employment, finance a new boat, and get back into the game as a freelance smuggler. Footloose and fancy-free, with major bucks lining his pockets— back on top where he belonged.

YEAH, baby!

A scraping sound caught his attention, and he swiveled his head in time to see the lawyer, Gomez, drag himself up the last step of the stern flybridge ladder. At the sight of him, Sligo grinned. It was a beautiful thing. Gone was the smooth-talking, well-tailored attorney who had flown into Grand Cayman on his own private plane. In his place was a haggard, pale wretch with strawberry-red daiquiri stains on his expensive green polo shirt (the one with that fucking pretentious pony-boy emblem on the breast, something Sligo abhorred), flyaway hair, and eyes like two piss-holes in the snow. Clearly, this was not a man who was up to the physical demands of partying Caribbean-style, with unlimited quantities of 151 rum, ninety-percent-pure blow, and various sedative pharmaceuticals. Sligo chuckled happily. If there'd been a couple of Jamaican hookers aboard—real hard-case gals straight from Trench-town—Gomez would probably have died of a heart attack during the night. Too bad they were short in the poon-tang department on this trip.

"So," Sligo said, beaming. "How are ya?"

"Fuck you," the lawyer replied under his breath. "Do *not* talk to me." He moved past Sligo with the obvious intent of joining Alberto at the steering station.

"I wouldn't bug him just now," the smuggler said. "He's trying to get hold of Grizelda, and he's kinda cranky."

The information was sufficient to stop Gomez in mid-stride, a fact which Sligo noted with considerable satisfaction. Even this country-club shyster was tiptoe-ing around Alberto this morning. Sligo ruminated. Maybe they'd had a lover's quarrel. It would hardly come as a surprise to find out they were actually butt buddies. Both looked the part, and in the smuggler's experience, there wasn't a lawyer on the planet who wouldn't bend over for the right amount of money.

Gomez leaned against the flybridge rail, looking like a man who'd recently drunk a quart of weed killer. Sligo tried engaging him again, just to break his balls a little more: "Long night, huh?"

The lawyer stared at him, started to say something, then hunched over the rail and threw up noisily.

"Lean out, dammit, lean out!" Sligo exclaimed. Fuck if he was going to clean up someone else's mess on the lower walkway.

When Gomez was done, he remained collapsed over the rail, gasping for air. Up at the steering station, Alberto was engaged in rapid conversation with his sister. Sligo couldn't quite get the gist of it—something to do with scheduling . . . the island's remaining speedboat and the *Cucaracha* rendezvousing at the diving barge. Whenever Grizelda and Alberto talked, it was always half-Spanish, half-English, and completely antagonistic. With all their bickering, it was a minor miracle that they were able to keep their drug operation functioning.

Gomez dragged himself up on his elbows. "What the fuck are those things?" he mumbled thickly, pointing down at the water with a shaking finger.

Sligo eased his weight off the dinghy locker and sauntered over to the rail. "What things?"

Gomez fluttered his hand. "Those things there . . . those . . . those balloon things."

Sligo shaded his eyes with his palm, squinting downward. Every twenty feet or so, floating on the water's surface, was an oblong, translucent bladder about the size of a football, bluish-purple in the sunlight, with a sail-like ridge running across its top and a dense cluster of dark blue tentacles hanging beneath it. Some of the finer filaments stretched off into the depths for more than thirty feet.

"Portuguese Man O' War," Sligo announced. "Quite a few of 'em. Big ones, too."

Gomez gaped. *"Those* are Portuguese Man O' War? But they—they're gigantic!"

"Yeah. Nasty fuckers."

The lawyer pulled back from the rail, looking even paler. "I hate those things."

"What are we looking at, gentlemen?" Alberto's liquid whine gave them both a start, as always. He'd padded up from behind without making a sound.

Sligo pointed down. "Portuguese Man O' War. Seems like this part of the ocean's full of 'em. Converging wind and current, most likely."

"I got stung by one of those once," Gomez said, "when I was on vacation in Miami. Right off South Beach. I swam into it and the tentacles brushed my neck. It was only the size of a golf ball, but I blew up like an overstuffed sausage casing and stopped breathing. They had to rush me to the hospital, put me on a ventilation machine and shoot me full of antihistamines." He gulped, sweat running down his pallid brow. "I'm allergic, like some people are to bee stings.

Even a single Man O' War sting would probably kill me."

Alberto looked fascinated. "My goodness. Did it hurt?"

"It felt like someone had laid a red-hot welding rod across my neck. It was horrible."

"How awful," Alberto said, smiling.

Gomez peered up at him, his expression corpse-like. "Thank you."

"You're quite welcome. Now then." He turned to Sligo. "We will head directly for the diving barge. My sister is coming out on the small speedboat, and we will meet her there. It's time to see what these so-called big-time professional divers have been up to out here for the past forty-eight hours—at our expense." He licked his lips. "Perhaps they have a ton or two of gold on board already, eh? We need to keep an eye on them, you know. People have a way of getting greedy."

He let his gaze linger on Gomez, who seemed to squirm without actually moving, and moved off toward the port stairs. Sligo just looked at the deck and tried not to grin.

You don't know the half of it, nancy-boy.

*****

Grizelda was seated on a weight bench doing curls with fifty-pound dumbbells when Fuentes arrived out on the terrace, escorted by two bodyguards. The little geneticist was still half-asleep; his body black-and-blue from the sexual pummeling it had absorbed the night before. He blinked dazedly in the bright morning sunshine, taking in the Amazonian image of Grizelda Ramos—all red-brown muscularity and pulchritude; wearing black combat boots, matching camouflage running thong and jog-bra, and Rising Sun kamikaze headband; systematically pumping the heavy weights like an automaton. Her jaw was clenched and her black eyes stared straight ahead with ferocious concentration. Every square inch of her exposed skin glistened with sweat.

"You sleep too late, Fuentes," she said, without breaking the rhythm of her lifting. "Ingrained laziness is one reason why you are so disgustingly unfit." Her biceps bulged into vein-laced miniature mountains at the apex contraction of each curl.

"Er . . . yes, Griz—Senorita Ramos."

"I am going to help you with that this morning." She dropped the dumbbells to the mat with a heavy thump and began shaking out her arms.

"Oh, good . . . ah . . . help me with what?"

Grizelda turned and fixed him with her basilisk stare. "Your lack of fitness. You are going to exercise today." The bodyguards standing around in a loose circle glanced at each other and chuckled.

Fuentes swallowed. "I am?"

"Yes."

The little scientist looked at the weights that lay around the training area. The thought of actually having to lift them was extremely distasteful, but if such a masochistic act made *La Ramos* more kindly disposed toward him—then what the hell, as the Americans liked to say. Who knew what motivated women, anyway . . . particularly this one.

"All right," Fuentes said, forcing a smile. "I'm ready. What do you want me to do first?"

Grizelda motioned to one of her bodyguards, who stepped forward and held out a small nylon backpack. She took it from him, set it on the mat between her feet, and unzipped its top. It was crammed with stacks of American bills—twenties, fifties, and hundreds.

"I want you to put your money on your back and cinch the straps up properly," she said. "So they don't slip when you run."

Fuentes blinked at her, confused. "This is mine? My payment?"

Grizelda nodded. "In full. Two hundred and fifty thousand dollars in U.S. currency, in various convenient denominations."

One of the bodyguards leaned down, closed the backpack, and lifted it up for Fuentes to don. Still not sure of what was happening, the geneticist slipped his pudgy arms awkwardly through the shoulder straps. "I—*owww!* Be careful, you numskull, you're bending my elbow the wrong way!" The bodyguard growled an apology and proceeded to tighten the shoulder straps and waist belt, securing the backpack in place.

Fuentes stood there in the hot sun, sweating through the armpits of his white T-shirt, his slack gut poking out above the baggy, cartoon-bull boxer shorts he'd pulled on after being rousted out of bed by Grizelda's body-guards. A pair of cheap slip on water shoes completed his ensemble. The money pack was rather heavy, the straps cutting into his soft shoulders, and he began to feel vaguely ridiculous.

"What now?" he asked.

Grizelda grinned, showing her teeth. "Now you run," she said.

"Run? I don't underst—"

"Come close to me, Fuentes." She beckoned, her wolfish grin softening into what was, for her, a sweet smile.

He stooped over. "Um—yes?"

"Closer, José. Close enough to whisper."

The little geneticist shuffled forward a couple of steps and bent low, turning his ear toward her lips. "Yes?"

With one rapid movement, Grizelda seized the greasy hair on the side of his head and whipped up her other hand, which had been hanging down by her thigh. The hooked blade of one of her killing knives flashed in the sunlight, and Fuentes let out a strangled scream. He staggered backward into the arms of the bodyguards, clutching the side of his head, his eyes bulging in horror.

Grizelda let the ear she had just sliced off flop back and forth between her thumb and forefinger, slippery and bright red with blood. Fuentes continued to shriek, tightly restrained and kept on his feet by two body-guards. Blood was running down the side of his fat neck and staining his white T-shirt collar.

Grizelda rose to her feet, holding a small plastic container. She poured some of the contents, a white powder, into her palm, and nodded again to the body-guards. One of them pried Fuentes' hand away from the side of his head, exposing the bloody patch where his ear had so recently been attached. Grizelda reached out and slapped the powder onto the wound in a little white puff, which set off fresh howls from the stricken geneticist.

Stepping back for a moment, she dumped some more powder into her palm and examined him with complete lack of emotion. "Fuentes," she said.

The howling and shrieking did not diminish.

"Fuentes," she repeated.

More energetic vocalizing.

She sucked her teeth impatiently. "All right, enough," she barked. "Hold his head still, Sanchez."

The burly bodyguard clamped a forearm across Fuentes' brows, immobilizing him. Grizelda stepped forward, jammed her cupped palm up against the struggling man's nostrils, and held it there. "Inhale," she instructed.

Fuentes had little choice. It was either inhale or asphyxiate. With much snuffling and choking, he inhaled.

"Again," Grizelda ordered.

Another wheezing inspiration accompanied by an explosion of white dust.

"Let him go," Grizelda said, stepping back beside the weight bench.

Fuentes reeled but kept his feet, sagging off to one side on quivering legs, his face screwed up in shock and plastered with a sticky combination of sweat and cocaine. He had stopped screaming.

"Listen to me," Grizelda said, buckling the straps on her left-hand knife. "The Boston Whaler is down at the lagoon dock. Both outboard engines have been serviced, and the fuel tanks are full. There is extra oil on board. The bow locker contains enough drinking water and canned food to last one person a week. The compass is accurate, and there is a chart of the western Caribbean in the center console locker. There is even a course and heading drawn on it between this island and Panama." She paused. "Stop whimpering, little man. The cocaine has taken away nearly all the pain."

She flexed her left arm and the hooked blade flashed through the air. With a grunt, she re-examined the straps that held it to her palm. "The keys are in the ignition locks. If you can reach the boat and pull away before I catch up to you, you and your quarter-million dollars are free to go." She stared up at him suddenly, her black eyes terrifyingly wide. "If I catch you . . ."

She shrugged, leaving the threat hanging in the air. "I will give you a fifteen-minute head start. Even an unfit man can make the dock from here in less than half an hour. Sanchez." The bodyguard lifted his wrist and pushed a button on his watch, grinning.

Fuentes stared at him in horror. "But . . . Griz—Senorita Ramos . . ." he stammered, "I—we—"

Casually, Grizelda began buckling the right-hand knife onto her wrist. "Fourteen minutes and forty-five seconds, Fuentes."

"But—I—"

"If you are still here at the thirty-second mark, I will take the other ear."

The geneticist turned whiter than the coke powder plastered to his jowls, stumbled backward, and turned and ran awkwardly across the terrace toward the stairs that led down into the steaming midmorning jungle.

John McKinna

Chapter Twenty

The boy had been prowling around the little lagoon since dawn, carefully avoiding the lone guard who had appeared just after sunrise. The shotgun-toting man had emerged from the narrow jeep track that led, in an interminable series of switchbacks, up to the hilltop house, and made his way onto the long, narrow wooden dock that extended out into the deeper waters of the cove. He'd boarded the small twin-engine speedboat that was tied up to the end pilings and spent five minutes or so tinkering with something in one of the aft compartments. Then he'd shouldered his shotgun and departed, hiking back up the jeep track the way he had come.

The boy had kept himself well concealed in the thick jungle foliage that surrounded the lagoon, uncertain if there were any more of the red-haired woman's henchmen nearby. He had slept badly back at the fishing cave, tormented by nightmares of fear and self-doubt. Even so, his fatigued body had managed to get four or five hours of crucial rest, and, upon emerging from the cave's mouth with the sky lightening to the east, he had decided to scout around the *narcotista*'s property some more while he tried to sort out his thoughts.

Now, squatting on his haunches atop a six-foot-high boulder of coral rock at the edge of the lagoon, hidden from view by the broad leaves of a low banana tree, he gazed out across the glassy, emerald-green water at the dock and speedboat. He was tempted by the thought of swimming over and inspecting the craft—it was only a hundred yards away—but quickly decided that doing so would leave him too exposed. There was no point to it, anyway; he wasn't interested in stealing the boat. He was able to leave the island any time he wished using his sailing canoe. He drew in a long breath and slowly let it out. His dilemma wasn't about leaving, at any rate. It was about staying. And doing what had to be done to avenge his brother.

The other thing that kept him from slipping into the limpid water was that he had noticed the dark, sinuous shapes of several resident sharks undulating lazily around the lagoon's perimeter. Normally this would not have been of any particular concern, but one was quite large, and as it had come ghosting by the foot of the rock, the boy had immediately recognized it by its faint body stripes, scythe-like tail, and massive, squared-off head as a tiger. It was nearly fourteen feet long—an animal to be avoided.

A smaller shark—a lemon, this one—patrolled in close to the rock, broke the surface briefly to inspect a floating leaf, its back flashing yellow-brown in the morning sun, and cruised unhurriedly away. The boy watched it go, thinking.

It was no small thing to kill a person. Even if they deserved it. Even if you were . . . were . . . *almost completely* sure they had been responsible for the murder of your own brother. Fernando was dead. He thought he had overhead the conversation between the red-haired woman and her henchmen correctly, the day they had searched for his body outside the fishing cave. It was she who had killed him; mutilated him in such horrific fashion.

Or was it? He wasn't quite sure. Perhaps it had been one of her men. If you were going to take someone's life to avenge a murder, you wanted to be sure you had the right person.

The lemon shark was circling back under the floating leaf. The boy tossed a pebble at it. *Plunk.* The shark did not react, did not change the rhythm of its swimming.

If only he could be certain. Or perhaps he was just a coward. Perhaps he was merely inventing an excuse, creating an imaginary doubt, which would allow him to back out of what he had to do. It would be easier just to stay out of sight until dark, get quietly into his canoe, and sail back across the strait to his home island. Forget about the red-haired woman and her gunmen. Much easier.

Forget about Fernando.

The lemon shark's dorsal fin broke the surface again, directly below the rock. This time, the boy snapped his arm forward and launched a chip of coral downward at high speed. The stone hit the animal just in front of its exposed fin and bounced two feet in the air. The shark took off like a wriggling torpedo, fleeing for the deeper water in the center of the lagoon.

The boy stared at it until it disappeared from view, his jaw set. He wasn't going anywhere. And he wasn't forgetting about Fernando.

But you couldn't just kill someone because you *suspected* they had committed a terrible crime. You had to be sure.

*****

Fuentes burst clumsily through yet another tangle of thorny vines, wheezing like an overworked steam engine, his filthy T-shirt in tatters and his skin raked bloody. Wild-eyed, he glared around the encroaching jungle, searching for the path of least resistance. Beneath his flabby pectorals, his coke-stoked heart was skittering like a snare-drum paradiddle.

Immediately upon stumbling off the terrace stairs and down the footpath that led to the jeep track, he'd floundered off the trail and become hopelessly lost in the thick undergrowth. Weeping and cursing, he'd crashed through the vegetation in a blind frenzy as the precious seconds of his head start ticked away. Then, quite unexpectedly, he'd helped his own cause by blundering off the edge of a hidden ravine and sliding down a nearly-vertical trough filled with dead leaves and mud—screaming like a banshee—for over five hundred feet. By incredible good fortune, the trough had regurgitated him out onto one of the lower stretches of the jeep track, at least a quarter-mile from the house.

Tarred and feathered by muck and detritus, cut and bruised over ninety percent of his body, Fuentes had nonetheless been cognizant of the fact that he'd almost certainly gained at least six or seven minutes on his pursuer, and that she was unlikely to be aware of it. The lagoon had been clearly visible, only a half-dozen switchbacks farther down the hill. A thrill of elation had surged through him—and then he'd looked back up toward the house.

Between the trees, far above him on one of the highest switchbacks, he'd caught sight of a small, red-brown figure running full-tilt down the jeep track, arms and legs pumping. Sunlight glinted off the hooked blades projecting from its hands.

Fuentes had turned and fled off the side of the jeep track again, choosing to crash downward through the brush to the next stretch rather than follow the switchback all the way around. It was a straight line to the lagoon dock, his scientist's mind reasoned, and therefore shorter.

A woodsman's mind—the tool of preference considering his immediate situation—would have told him that it might be shorter, but not necessarily faster. Now, at every step, vines and brambles ripped at him, impeding his progress, lacerating his flesh, and eliciting yelps of pain. Which way to go? He saw a hole of daylight in the dense tangle of green and plunged for it, gasping.

His toe caught under a root and he pancaked face down on the next stretch of jeep track, his money pack riding up onto his head. Shrugging it back into place, he rolled onto his side, stared back up through the trees—and let out an involuntary shriek. Grizelda was charging like a female bull along the fourth stretch up, knives flashing and hennaed ponytail fluttering behind her. She'd eaten up five switchbacks in the time it had taken him to bushwack down one.

No more bushwacking. Staggering to his feet, Fuentes fled down the jeep track as fast as his doughy legs would carry him. The lagoon dock was close now. He could see it through the trees to his right, the Boston Whaler—his means of escape—sitting on its lines beside the end pilings.

The sight energized his collapsing quadriceps. He could still make it.

Slavering at the mouth, he negotiated the last turn, crossed the little strip of coral sand between tree line and water's edge, and pounded out onto the dock.

He was going to make it!

A small flock of sacred ibis that had been loitering at the end of the dock picking sea-roaches off the pilings, took to the air as he approached. Wobbling, he half-fell into the Whaler, clawed his way forward, and cast off the forward dock line. Then he flailed aft and did the same at the stern. As the rope left his fingers, he glanced up in time to see Grizelda dashing down the last stretch of jeep track before the beach, her musclebound form flitting along behind the foliage.

She was too late! He stepped toward the center console as the twenty-two-foot boat rocked under his weight and bumped the pilings. The keys were in the twin ignition locks, small orange floats dangling from their tiny chains. The gearshifts were in neutral, ready to go (he knew that much about outboards—they wouldn't start unless the drives were disengaged).

He gripped the keys and looked back down the dock again. Grizelda was sprinting across the beach, her shoes churning sand, carving the air with her twin knives. But again—no doubt about it—she was *too late.*

Fuentes could not resist. All the pent-up frustration of dealing with Grizelda and her brother—the moods, the tantrums, the psychotic episodes—burst out of him, unleashed by the certain knowledge that he was home free.

"You insane bitch!" he screamed, laughing. *"You've lost! I've beaten you! José Fuentes has beaten you at your own game! You BITCH!"*

He turned the keys.

And nothing happened.

"No!" he shrieked.

He turned them again, nearly breaking them off in the ignition locks.

Nothing.

Frantically, he jiggled the gearshifts—they were set firmly in neutral—and cranked the keys over. And again, and again.

Grizelda strolled up alongside the Whaler as Fuentes collapsed over the back of the console seat, sobbing hysterically. With athletic ease, she jumped the three-foot water gap between dock and boat, landing just in front of the two big outboards. The craft rocked slightly as she bent down and opened one of the aft compartments, reached inside, and pulled something up into view.

"José," she said softly.

Slowly, the beaten man's bloody head came up, his expression vacant.

"You should always check the battery cables on your boat." She wiggled the thick red wire with its heavy lug. "They have a way of coming loose." The killing knife on that hand caught a ray of sunlight as she lowered the wire back into the compartment, sending a bright flash into Fuentes' eyes. His lids fluttered, trance-like.

Grizelda shut the compartment hatch, stalked forward to the console, and turned the keys, one at a time. In quick succession, the big outboards growled into life, spitting cooling-water and blue smoke. She watched the tachometers for a moment, tapping a knife tip on each of the glass covers . . . and then her odd, masculine giggle rose above the muttering of the engines.

"You would be at the outer reef right now, Fuentes," she said, turning, "if you had just—"

Letting out a howl, Fuentes slashed at her head with the short, heavy gaff he had seized from the stern rod-rack. Grizelda saw it out of the corner of her eye in time to duck, but the point of its big hook caught in the center of her left shoulder muscle. She twisted, snarling in pain. The violent motion ripped the gaff from the scientist's hands. With an incoherent scream, he flung himself at her, clawing for her eyes.

Grizelda met him with open arms, allowing the two of them to collide sternum-to-sternum. Fuentes' momentum barely rocked her on her feet. The hooked knives, held far out to either side, turned toward his torso.

Grizelda snapped her arms inward, grunting, and the twin blades buried themselves between Fuentes' second and third ribs on either side of his body. The geneticist made a sound like *"heeeeeeeeeeeeee!"* and stiffened, his eyes bulging . . . staring into hers.

"But I beat you," he choked out. *"I beat . . .you . . ."*

Grizelda giggled into his contorted face. "What's the matter, José?" she whispered. "Don't you like me anymore?"

She smiled, her lips curling beneath her mad gaze. Then, keeping him impaled, quivering, on her left-hand knife, she wrenched the other free, cocked her massive arm behind her head, and drove the blade eight inches through his right eye.

*****

The boy thought he was going to be sick. The scene across the lagoon had become reminiscent of a pig-slaughter. After stabbing the chubby man several times aboard the boat, the red-haired woman had flopped him over her shoulder—she'd plucked out the short gaff hook that had been hanging from it—and stepped up onto the dock. Then she had let him slip to the planks, his feet still kicking, and dropped to her knees, straddling him.

Now, in a homicidal frenzy, she was dismantling him with her knives, the blades rising and falling, ripping and tearing, while she shrieked and bellowed and gnashed and writhed, bathed in blood. Near the shore end of the dock, the boy noticed, several of her bodyguards had gathered. They stayed on the sand, close to the jeep track, watching in silence.

The boy cowered beneath the banana leaves, on the verge of shock. This was what must have happened to Fernando. To his own brother. He closed his eyes and drove the horrible image from his mind.

When he opened them again, the man on the dock was in several pieces. Blood was dripping in sticky streams through the walkway planking and into the water, and in the shaded area between the pilings, triangular dorsal fins were knifing back and forth. There was a leg, hacked off at the hip, lying near the speedboat's stern mooring cleat, and an arm, sawn through at the shoulder, dangling from the edge of the dock. As the boy watched, the madwoman slashed, ripped the corpse's head loose, kissed it on the lips, and flung it down the wooden walkway. It bowled off the end of the dock and hit the water with a splash. Instantly, there was an eruption of foam, accompanied by a cluster of wildly jockeying fins.

The red-haired woman—completely red, at this point—got to her feet, panting like a bullock, and began to kick the body parts off the walkway. When all that remained was the torso—a hideous, half-gutted lump of bloody meat and viscera—she knelt back down, got her forearms under it, and heaved it off the dock like a bale of rotten chum.

The water around it exploded with shark activity as she turned and walked away, her nearly-naked body— arms, chest, back, buttocks, legs—covered in blood. She paused to swing a small, gore-stained backpack up onto her shoulder, then strode on. She was actually strutting, the boy noticed; her shoulders back, chin up, moving on the balls of her feet. Like an athlete after a successful contest. His eyes traveled back to the feeding frenzy alongside the dock. The big tiger was there now, his blunt head half out of the water, thrashing his great crescent-shaped tail as he engulfed his share of the feast.

The boy furrowed his brows, listening. He could hear something coming across the water, a deep, heavy sound that traveled above—or perhaps under—all other noises. It was the red-haired woman. She was gig-gling.

He heard her instructions to her bodyguards as she swaggered past them on her way back up the jeep track to the house: "Hose that mess off the dock. We're going out to the barge within the hour."

Chapter Twenty-One

The *Cucaracha* was less than three hundred yards off the stern of the barge, still cruising toward it at about nine knots, when Sligo, at the flybridge wheel, noticed a stocky, gray-haired man in khaki coveralls run back to the aft rail and begin waving them off. He was being quite forceful about it, as if irritated. Throttling down, the smuggler squinted at him through his polarized sunglasses. It looked as if he had something in one hand . . . something small and dark . . . a radio . . .

Oh! The radio! Sligo reached up and switched it on. It was already tuned to the international hailing channel, 16. He rarely cruised offshore with the VHF on unless he specifically wanted to call someone or check a weather broadcast. Why listen to other people's noise? Might even receive a mayday call, which he'd feel vaguely guilty about ignoring for maybe two, three minutes. Who needed that kind of aggravation?

"Coo-coo-*ratcha* callin' big ugly barge," he drawled into the hand mike.

"Channel ten," came the terse reply.

Sligo reached up and punched the radio's selector button until the digital display showed one-zero.

"Coo-coo-*ratcha*," he repeated.

The voice that growled out of the VHF's speaker was not friendly. "Goddamn it, what the hell do you think you're doing, runnin' up on a commercial divin' operation at that speed without a radio watch? Shear off! Don't you see our damn flags and day shapes? We've got divers and equipment in the water over here!"

Sligo was taken aback. "Hey," he said, "ease up, Bligh. I'm your employer." Which wasn't technically correct, but the guy on the other end of Channel 10 didn't know that.

"I don't care if you're the Archbishop comin' to bless the fleet," the voice informed him. "Get that toy boat out of my divin' zone, call back when you're holdin' position at a proper safe distance, and I'll instruct you on how to approach."

Whoa. A hardass. Sligo spun the wheel to port and scowled across the water at the man on the barge—it was safe; they were too far apart to distinguish facial expressions. Obviously, some cranky old oilfield despot with diesel fuel in his veins and "By the Book" tattooed across his forehead. Guys like that were such a fucking bore.

He steadied the *Cucaracha* on a southerly heading, away from the diving barge, and mopped the slimy sweat from his neck with a small towel. Damn, he was relapsing a bit, here. Return of the Beastly Hangover.

Might have to do a little bump from the coke vial just to—

"Where are we going, Jeremiah?"

As usual, the abrupt intrusion of Alberto's liquid whine—right in his ear—gave Sligo a nasty jolt. *Bastard!* He jerked around to see his bikini-clad boss standing less than two feet behind him. He'd drifted silently up the port-side stairs and across the flybridge like some kind of faggy ghost—there wasn't a doubt in Sligo's mind—just so he could give him the heebie-jeebies when he finally opened his mouth.

The smuggler mopped his face, wincing as a hot pain seared behind his eyes. "Motoring south a ways. The guy on the barge ordered me to back off and call him before coming in. He was a real jerk about it, too," he added, hoping that it might cause trouble for the prick who'd just chewed him out.

No such luck. *"HAAH!"* Alberto barked. That sudden, nerve-twisting laugh. "Then I think you'd better do as he says, since he's a professional and you are a mere incompetent." He turned and began walking back toward the stairs. "Call me on the intercom when we get near the barge again. I'll be in the main salon. I do believe it's time for a pink gin."

Sligo ground his teeth silently, watching him amble across the deck.

Just wait, you greasy faggot. You'll get yours.

328

*****

A half hour later, Gene stood in the doorway of the sat shack, watching the Cheoy Lee trawler approach the barge again—on the side opposite the diving bell and ROV launching systems. He could see only three people aboard: a man on the lower aft deck in a blue polo shirt and black pleated trousers that he recognized as Gomez, the lawyer; an aging-hippie type with long, dirty-blonde hair, a deep tan, and a druggy demeanor up on the flybridge wheel; and a third man, slender and apparently naked, standing on the yacht's foredeck with a foot propped on top of the anchor winch.

Gene shook his head. Bizarre. The naked guy looked as if he was wearing some kind of ladies' shower cap. Pink, yet. Well, undoubtedly Gomez would explain everything.

As Earl strode over to the far side of the barge to take the yacht's lines, Gene turned and looked at Sass, who was sitting in front of the gas rack wearing a set of headphones. She smiled, tapping her pencil on the clipboard across her knees, and pulled one of the phones off an ear.

"The client finally showed up, huh?" she asked.

"Looks like it," Gene said. He watched as the naked man with the pink shower cap on his head tossed

Earl the bow line and sauntered aft along the starboard rail. Actually, he wasn't completely naked; he was wearing the kind of butt-floss black thong that you usually only saw on an eighteen-year-old female stripper. Gene shook his head again. Men had definitely changed since the Korean War, when he and a couple hundred other scared American teenagers had charged their way through snow and machine-gun fire up Pork Chop Hill.

"How's Chris doin'?" he inquired. The young diver was coming out of sat. After transferring from the diving bell to the main lock of the sat pot, he'd been thoroughly examined by Ben and Pierre; both certified Emergency Medical Technicians. Diagnosis: a broken wrist, a few bruises, and a bad scare. The wrist had been splinted and some mild pain and sedative medications administered. Chris had then been moved to the single bunk in the sat system's outer lock, to be decompressed to the surface on a slow bleed. His treasure hunt, at least as a saturation diver, was over.

Sass clicked the TALK button on the descrambler radio. "So how you doing in there, Chris?" she asked.

"Just great," came the disembodied reply. "I'm beaten black and blue, my wrist's busted, and I didn't even get to see the inside of the wreck, much less find any gold."

"I meant, how are you feeling, decompression-wise?"

"Oh, hey, never better. Of course, with these pain shots in me, I could be bent like a pretzel and never know it."

"Any neurological symptoms?" Sass pursued. "Numbness, tingling?"

"Only when I think of you, hot mama."

Oh, that 70's blaxploitation slang. Sass grinned at Gene and pressed the TALK button. "Down, boy. Let's not forget I'm old enough to be your—well . . . older sister."

Chris sighed.

Gene glanced out at the yacht again. The druggy-looking captain was trying to get some big plastic bumpers deployed along the Cheoy Lee's starboard side, and making a real clusterfuck out of it. It was kind of entertaining, watching him flounder around in a spaghetti-like tangle of badly coiled lines. This was certainly the clown who had cruised up on top of the dive operation without first establishing radio contact and advising of his intent.

"Gene," Chris said.

The old supervisor stepped inside the doorway and leaned down to his descrambler. "Yeah."

"LeRenard and Pickins still doing their bell run?"

"That's a roger."

"Who's inside the wreck?"

"Pierre. Vern took the first divin' excursion. Had a little trouble squeezin' through the gap Ben cleared, but he made it. He checked the entire starboard-side keel area with a probe and that hand-held metal detector. No gold. Pierre's checkin' out the port side the same way. Nothin' so far."

"Goddamn." There was a pause. "And neither of 'em saw whatever it was that hit me?"

"Nope."

Chris was quiet for a long moment. "I can't figure that, Gene," he said finally. "That thing was big, and it was on me the minute I got near the wreck. Yanked me around like a cat playin' with a ball of yarn. I can't believe they haven't even *seen* it."

"Well," Gene said, "we came up on the anchors and moved the barge north another twenty-five feet. Pierre and Vern say that's put the bell within twenty feet of the wreck on bottom. Maybe with the shorter travel distance, whatever it is don't have time to line up on a diver any more before he makes it into the hull."

"Goddamn," Chris said again. Another long pause. "Gene. You believe me, don't you? About this big sonofabitch that hit me, I mean. I didn't just go down there and get hurt doin' something stupid."

"Of course I believe you, kid. You didn't even get inside the wreck. There wasn't time." Sass smiled faintly as she heard Gene trying to soften his usual gruff tone of voice. "You're beat to shit, there's a big chew mark in the middle of the dive umbilical you were using, and Ben is pretty sure he saw something sizeable swimming around durin' his dive. Not to mention he had his hands ripped raw tryin' to hold your hose while something stripped it out of the bell. You couldn't have done that." He shrugged, forgetting that Chris couldn't see him. "Don't worry about it. You did fine."

Chris sighed again. "Still can't figure why LeRenard and Pickins haven't spotted anything . . ."

The discussion drifted to an end. Gene put a set of headphones on, sat down at his station, and switched to the primary dive radio. "Vern," he said.

"Yeah, boss."

"What's goin' on down there? You guys are runnin' up on six hours of bottom time now."

"Well, mah little buddy Pee-yair is still out yonder in the wreck. Want me tuh cross-link the radios again so you can talk to 'im?"

"Yeah, go ahead."

There was a clicking noise, a burst of static, and Vern's deep voice rumbled through Gene's headphones again: "Hey, froggy. Gene's comin' on, son. He wants an update."

"Rogere, hippo. I am here."

Sass laughed, eyeing an oxygen sensor. "You'd swear they were brothers, the way they dig at each other," she remarked.

"That you would," Gene said. He pressed the TALK button. "This is Gene, Pierre. The client who's payin' for this dog-and-pony show just pulled up in his yacht. Why don't you give me a rundown of where we're at, so I have something to tell him?"

"Rogere, d'accord," the Frenchman replied. "I have just completed the probing and detector sweeps of the port side. I regret to say that there is nothing beneath the sediment, *mon ami*, but the keel and bottom of the hull. There are no cracks or holes through which treasure could have fallen—only solid wood. The sediment is not deep, and I have probed every inch. Nothing but wood. I register nothing of consequence on the hand-held metal detector, either. Only the occasional remnant of an iron spike, embedded in the hull strakes."

Gene cleared his throat. "Well . . . that's disappointing," he said.

"Oui," Pierre went on. *"C'est vrai."* There was a brief roar of exhaust as he cracked his freeflow on and off. "Condensation," he muttered. *"Il fait froid*—it is cold down here."

"Quit bitchin', froggy," Vern cut in.

334

"Quoi? What?" The little Frenchman's voice went up in pitch several half-tones. "Was I speaking to you, orca? *Non*, I was conversing with Gene—which I will attempt to continue doing in spite of your boorish interruption."

"Well, what's your opinion, Pierre?" Gene's voice had a sober quality to it that took the spice out of the usual back-and-forth bantering.

"I think," Pierre said, "that there is no bulk treasure here, *mon ami*. Not within this hull, at any rate. It is intact, and anything it contained would still be inside. There is no sediment further forward, and I can see clearly that there is nothing there. A small space exists behind this collapsed forward bulkhead, but it is a forepeak—a small bow triangle that would have held ropes and perhaps grappling hooks and sounding leads. *Certainment*, it is not large enough to hold any substantial amount of treasure, and I doubt if it holds any at all."

Before Gene could comment, Pierre continued: "But, that said, I have found something for you, *mon ami*. It is not much, but it is something. And I must tell you: it took twenty minutes of hard work with my knife and crowbar to get it free, *tabarnac!"*

Gene gave a hollow chuckle that failed to conceal his disappointment. "What is it, another deadeye like the one Ben found?"

"Non," Pierre replied. "Something more interesting than that."

"Okay, so you're gonna keep me in suspense," Gene said patiently. "You obviously think it's interestin'. Why are you so sure it's gonna be interestin' to *me?"*

"Because," Pierre told him, "it is made of solid gold."

Chapter Twenty-Two

Gene was relieved to see that the bikini-wearing man from the yacht had removed the pink plastic cap from his head and donned shirt, shorts, and sandals before crossing over to the diving barge. He and Gomez were the only two who'd disembarked; the antiquated hippie with the ratty hair had remained aboard the—what was it?—the *Cucaracha*. Gene had a little trouble understanding that one. Who would name their yacht after what was arguably the Earth's most despised insect?

Earl and Sass were both on deck beside the sat system's launching skid, preparing to pick up Pierre and Vern, rotate the bell, and lock it onto the sat pot. Posey was still ensconced in his ROV shack, running search patterns with his submersible over a wide area of sea bottom behind the wreck. He'd been at it for nearly seven hours. Gene sighed and rubbed his eyes. With any luck, he'd locate something. God knew, the forward hull section had been a complete letdown, except for the small item Pierre had found—whatever it was. The little Frenchman was being a pisser about giving out details until the bell was topside.

As he watched the big metal sphere break the surface and sway awash at the end of its lifting cable,

Gomez and the other man—Gene now thought of him as Pinkcap—started across the deck toward him. Both had that look of distaste, as they picked their way past winches, compressors, and cable spools, that was characteristic of men who never, ever, *for any reason*, handled greasy machinery or tools. There was a mincing quality to their movements, as if they were afraid some of that blue-collar grime might leap off the equipment and contaminate their Fifth Avenue sports-wear.

Gomez put his blandly agreeable lawyer face on as he approached and extended a manicured hand. "Nice to see you again, Mr. McCluskey. Quite a change from New Orleans, isn't it?" He nodded around at the sea and sky.

Gene took the hand and shook it. Same irritating, wet-noodle grip on the guy. He squeezed until he felt Gomez's knuckles crack in his palm. The patronizing expression on the lawyer's face crumbled slightly. Gene let go and smiled.

"Likewise, Mr. Gomez." He turned to Pinkcap, waiting.

"This is the man you're working for, Mr. McCluskey," Gomez said, rubbing his hand and re-composing his visage. "Alberto Ramos. He and his sister Grizelda, whom you'll meet shortly, make up the family business team that is financing this operation."

He glanced at Alberto. "They operate one of Central America's most successful and respectable venture-capital enterprises."

"Is there such a thing?" Gene asked, extending his hand again.

Alberto shook with him, an amused look on his face. "A venture-capital enterprise?"

"No, one that's successful *and* respectable."

Alberto laughed. "Ah, I see. You're a cynic, Mr. McCluskey. Well, I agree with you: it *is* hard to be both of those things at the same time."

"Forty years of workin' for Big Oil tells me it's damn near impossible."

All three of them laughed, but Gene thought Gomez looked a little edgy. Well, that was his problem—stock in trade of the profession he'd chosen. It was a lawyer's job to have elevated blood pressure around a wealthy client.

Pinkcap—*Alberto*—turned and regarded the activity around the sat system's A-frame. Sass and Earl had recovered the bell inboard and were just executing the rotation procedure. The bell trunk swung up ninety degrees to the horizontal and steadied. Then Sass trundled it in so that the trunk and sat pot flanges mated, and Earl was able to lock the two pressurized units together.

"Excuse me for a moment," Gene said, stepping back from the sat shack doorway. "I have to watch that we don't lose pressure in the system when the trunk gets flooded with breathing gas."

Alberto's clever eyes roved over the bell and sat pot. "Of course. So . . . let me see: the diving bell and the big chamber are at the same high internal pressure . . . ah!—I understand. In order for the two to reconnect, you must put an equivalent amount of pressure into the—*trunk*, is it?—so that the opposing hatches will open. And that will take extra air or gas."

Gene glanced up from his gauges at him. "Gas, in this case. Trimix. And you're right about everything you said. Pretty good. You're a quick study, if you've never done this type of divin' before."

Alberto fluttered a hand in mock horror. "Good heavens, no. Not for me, I'm afraid."

"Mm." Gene noted the effeminate gesture with a dry look. "I'll make up any pressure drops caused by the bell-mating procedure with these valves." He touched the gas rack in front of him. "Shouldn't be much adjustment needed, though. Small volume in that trunk."

"How fascinating," Alberto said. "An absolute science, diving deep into inner space. Are all the divers in there right now?"

Gene nodded without looking away from his gauges. "Yeah. Two in the bell, one in the pot. And a fourth guy who just broke his wrist a few hours ago. He's in the forward lock of the deck chamber, on a slow bleed up to the surface. His treasure divin' is done for this trip."

"Already you've hurt someone? What happened?"

Gene cracked a valve slightly, continuing to eye the gauges, before answering. "He was on the bottom and ran into something alive and big. It decided it didn't like him and knocked him around a little bit before his partner could haul him back into the bell."

Gomez spoke up: "Was it Gannon?"

"No, our youngest guy. Ben was the one who hauled him back into the bell."

"Good heavens," Alberto said again. "That must have been terrifying."

Gene shrugged. "Goes with the territory in this job. A little rougher in this case than we usually deal with, but commercial divers are always findin' themselves nose-to-nose with weird ocean critters—most often when we're tryin' to concentrate on a difficult task. That's usually when they show up to bother you."

"Does it happen often?" Alberto asked.

"Nah. Very rarely." The old supervisor shrugged. "This just happened to be one of those times."

"What was it that attacked your diver?" Gomez asked, his voice thin.

"We don't know. We didn't get a good look at it. Maybe one of those sluggish deep-water sharks—a six-gill or something. They can get pretty big, bump into you."

The lawyer whitened under his sun lamp tan at the thought. "I can't believe you people actually opt to do this on a regular basis," he said. "For a living."

"Beats sittin' in an office six days a week," Gene replied, looking at him pointedly. "And it's one thing a poor man who can't afford a college education can get into when he's young—eighteen, nineteen, say—and be makin' fifty to a hundred thousand a year by the time he's twenty-five, if the oilfields are boomin' and there's enough deep work to go around." He grinned. "It ain't a clean-fingernail job, though."

"Yes, I noticed that," Alberto remarked, glancing around at the oily diesel compressors and generators with pursed lips.

"Got hatches on both the bell and the wet lock, Gene." Ben's voice crackled out of the descrambler radio. "Pierre and Vern are coming out now."

"Roger that," Gene returned. "We're gonna hold to the new plan, right? See what Posey's got to tell us about what's buried in the sediment behind the wreck. Then, if there's anything worth investigatin', go to a three-man rotation with you guys takin' turns doublin' up. Four-hour rest between all runs, so the guy pullin' the consecutive twelve hours on bottom don't get worn out."

"Sounds good to me," Ben said. "Let us know if you want us to dive again after you talk to Gerald, and we'll get on it. Vern'll go with me on the next bell run. He says he's not tired."

"That is because," Pierre broke in, "*I* did all the work on the last run. My partner, the redneck ox, was *fait a dormir*—gone to sleep—in the bell. *Sacré bleu,* my back is fatigued from the labor of carrying him all day."

"Don't believe the little froggy," Vern yelled in the background. "He's just croakin'."

"All right, all right." Gene grinned in spite of himself. "Pierre. When am I gonna get to see what you found in the wreck?"

"Immédiatement, mon ami," the Frenchman replied. "I am putting it in the medical lock right now."

Alberto brightened. "They found something?" he asked Gene.

"Yeah. Not very big, apparently, but it's made of gold. Let's go see what it is."

Gene flipped the radio onto P.A. and stepped outside the sat shack. As he moved past the other two men, Alberto shaded his eyes with one hand and pointed with

343

the other, limp-wristed. "That must be my sister coming out," he declared.

Gene followed the finger. Against the hazy green backdrop of the island to the north, the pale dot of a speedboat hull was growing steadily larger, twin bow waves creaming off to either side as it approached.

"That's your private island?" he asked Alberto.

The slender man nodded. "Our little sanctuary from the pressures of business and the woes of the world."

Gomez smiled to himself. Obviously, it wouldn't do to explain that on a private island it was also easier to defend yourself against assassination attempts by rival drug lords you'd double-crossed; that the ongoing question of which Central American government had sovereignty over the archipelago made it difficult for the DEA to organize effective investigations of your affairs; and that owning your own piece of real estate in the middle of the Caribbean Sea pretty much made you a law unto yourself while you were on it and surrounded by heavily armed sycophants.

Gene walked down the short flight of metal steps to the side of the main deck chamber, followed by Alberto and Gomez, and halted in front of the medical lock—a small tubular extrusion with a heavy hatch on its end. From inside the big chamber, there came the clanking sound of an inner hatch being dogged shut, and then Pierre's voice resounded over the P.A. speakers: *"Eh bien.* Depressurize and open the med lock whenever you are ready."

Gene reached up and twisted a valve. Instantly, there was a high-pitched rush of escaping gas and the valve's body turned white with frost.

"Why does it do that?" Alberto shouted over the noise.

"Extreme heat loss in the metal as the gas escapes," Gene called back. "Before they found the right alloys, flash freezin' a valve like that could make it shatter."

The screaming noise gradually died away to nothing as the pressure bled off. The frost on the valve quickly turned to water droplets in the direct sunlight. Gene undogged the hatch and pulled it open. There was a puff of water vapor. Slowly, he reached into the cold white fog wreathing out of the lock, grasped something, and withdrew his hand.

It was a metal rod ten inches long by three-quarters of an inch in diameter—about the size of a large carriage bolt. One end had been crudely sharpened to a spike-like point. The other was flat and slightly mushroomed, as if it had been struck repeatedly with a hammer. It was yellow in color, with the silvery, slightly greenish cast of very pure, and very real, gold.

Gene whistled between his teeth. "Whew. That's a pretty sight." He hefted the spike in his hand. "Heavy, too."

Alberto reached for it, then stopped himself. "May I?"

"Sure, 'course you can." Gene passed it to him.

The effeminate man's dark eyes flickered over the spike as he rolled in his fingers. "Astonishing," he murmured absently. "My sister was right."

"Speaking of whom," Gomez said, "she's here."

The three of them looked up in time to see Grizelda leap off the rail of the Boston Whaler as it nosed in alongside the barge. Her Doc Martens combat boots thudded onto the steel deck and, without hesitating, she began to make her way toward them, moving with her characteristic loose-limbed, panther-like stride.

Gene found himself doing a double take. And he'd thought Pinkcap-slash-Alberto had been an eyeful. His sister—apparently the spawn of Mr. Universe and a female mountain gorilla—was attired in skin-tight black bicycling shorts that came to mid-thigh, a blue-and-white-striped athletic bra, and an orange headband covered in strange, rune-like black symbols. Business partners? The two of them looked more like refugees from the Mardi Gras parade, late-night weirdo edition.

He was struck by the deadness of the woman's gaze as she approached. He'd seen tiger sharks with more warmth in their eyes. And the muscles . . . like a walking steroid.

Jesus. She was a freakish piece of work.

She halted in front of Alberto, unsmiling, staring down at the golden rod in his hand. Then she fixed her black eyes on Gene.

"My sister, Grizelda," Alberto mewled, his tone suddenly fawning. "Grizelda, this is Mr. McCluskey, the diving supervisor I told you about."

"Mm-hmm," the musclebound woman said, nodding. She shook Gene's hand briefly. From her grip, he deduced that she had more strength in her little finger than her brother or Gomez did in their entire bodies—no doubt in complement to her scintillating personality.

She took the golden rod from Alberto without asking him and held it up in the sunlight, inspecting it and frowning. "There's more?" she asked simply.

"We're not sure," Gene said. "Our ROV expert, Gerald Posey, is completing a detailed metal-detection survey of the bottom around the wreck right now, using his robot sub."

"Where did this come from?" Grizelda kept examining the rod as she spoke, talking out of the side of her mouth at Gene without looking at him.

"Let's find out," the old supervisor replied, his hackles rising in response to her arrogant demeanor. He picked a hand mike off a descrambler radio mounted in a waterproof box on the side of the chamber and disabled the P.A. interface with the flick of a switch. "Pierre, this is Gene. You got me on this radio?"

"Rogere," came the immediate reply. "I hear you fine."

Gene glanced at Grizelda, Alberto, and Gomez, who were crowding in close. "The client is out here. We'd all like to know where you found this gold spike."

"Mais certainement," Pierre said. "I found it inside the wreck. It was stuck in the remaining section of foremast, about eight feet above my head. I was looking up at the mast's support timbers and my light glinted off something, so I climbed up to see what it was. This *clou d'or*—this nail of gold—had been hammered into the mast for over half its length. I dug it out with my knife and crowbar."

"Thanks, Pierre," Gene said. "Stand by." He released the TALK button and turned to face Grizelda. "That," he told her, indicating the gold bar in her hand, "is the only item of gold in the wreck's interior. We've probed the silt that covers the keel and found nothing. The bottom of the hull is intact, so we know if there was any treasure still in her when she hit the seabed, it would still be there. There simply isn't any."

"How do you account for this single golden spike?" Grizelda demanded. She was scowling, her brows working up and down.

Gene shook his head. "Maybe the guys have a theory." He pushed the TALK button. "Pierre. You have any explanation as to why this spike was where it was?

I mean, the Spanish didn't build galleons out of wood and gold nails."

"Ben and I were just talking about that," the Frenchman said. "I'll let him tell you what he told me."

There was a buzz of static, and then Ben's voice came on: "Hey, Gene."

"Hey."

"I was wondering, the same as you, why someone would hammer a ten-inch gold spike into a ship's foremast. Then I remembered the manuscript Mr. Gomez showed me back in that restaurant in New Orleans. The first passage I read described how the captain of the *Arista*—Ramos, I think his name was—hammered a golden rod into the foremast to impress his crew and . . . uh . . . *taunt* the sea gods, I guess. Maybe he was acting on that old sailor's superstition about sticking a knife in the mast to conjure up brisk winds." Ben paused to chuckle. "He sure got more than he bargained for. He conjured up what must have been a hurricane, from the description in the manuscript."

Gene looked startled and glanced quickly at Grizelda and Alberto. "Ramos," he repeated. His gaze lingered on Grizelda's impassive face. "How 'bout that."

"Anyway," Ben went on, "I think that explains why this one golden spike was embedded in the foremast.

Just a fluke. There's nothing else inside the hull—no cargo of Aztec treasure, at any rate."

The muscles in Grizelda's face were working ever more energetically as she listened, twisting the golden rod in her hands. "Then where is it?" she blurted at Gene.

The old supervisor's expression hardened. His dislike of Grizelda Ramos had been immediate and was deepening by the second. And, after weeks of hard organizational work, lack of sleep, and stress, he was just plain tired. "Well, lady," he said, "if the ROV's metal detector doesn't turn up anything in the sediment near the wreck, we're gonna have to conclude that either it spilled out all over the ocean floor as the ship broke up, or it's still in the stern half of the hull—which we haven't found." He took a distinct pleasure in delivering the punch line: "If it ain't buried in the muck just aft of the wreck, it more'n likely got scattered so far and wide that a squadron of ROV's and magnetometers might take a year to locate a single piece like the one you're holdin' in your hand—and *that* would still have to be dug out of god-knows-how-much mud."

Grizelda just stared at him, her black eyes as dead as spent coals. As Gene turned toward Alberto, Sass walked by the far end of the sat pot, coiling a length of rope. Instantly, Grizelda's attention riveted on her— taking in the yellow hardhat, the sleeveless red-and-white plaid work shirt with the tails tied across the flat brown navel, the cutoff denim shorts, leather gloves, and steel-toed work boots. Taking in the lithe, tanned legs and arms, the sun-streaked blonde hair tucked up under the hardhat, and the sharp, high-cheekboned face behind the polarized safety glasses.

"Then we'd better have a chat with Mr. Posey," Alberto was saying, "and see what he's found with his miraculous submersible."

"Fine. He's over here in his control van," Gene replied. To Grizelda: "Are you comin', lady?"

Her black eyes snapped around onto his as Sass disappeared behind a generator.

"Yes," she said.

Chapter Twenty-Three

Shit! He's back already!

Sligo slammed the lid of the dinghy locker shut as Alberto's head appeared in the port flybridge stairwell. The skinny bastard was so light on his feet that you couldn't hear him coming. He didn't trudge up stairs like normal people; he did a minuet up them. The smuggler spun around hurriedly and sat back on the closed lid that concealed his stolen high-tech diving gear, folding his arms.

"Hey, boss," he said, with a skulking grin.

Alberto patted his oily hair as he approached and eyed him suspiciously. "Why do I so often get the feeling that you're up to something, Jeremiah?" he remarked. Then a blasé sigh: "Because you would be, I suppose—if you had the nerve and I gave you half the chance."

Sligo's grin faltered only slightly. "Er—takin' a trip?" he asked, gesturing.

Alberto was holding one of those expensive, soft-leather fanny packs that were the sporty urban male's substitute for a woman's purse. He buckled it around his waist and adjusted the pouch so that it rode on his left hip. "Yes, in fact," he replied. "When Grizelda and I have finished reviewing the diving team's progress, she, I, and Gomez will take the small speedboat back to the island. We have some business to attend to with him. You will remain out here with the *Cucaracha*, to monitor the work and provide a civilized day base for us when we return. God knows I'm not about to spend any more time than necessary aboard that greasy scow. The yacht stays here for the time being—and make sure you keep the air conditioning running."

Sligo nearly leaped for joy. *Perfect.* He was going to be left alone—free to slip into the water, drop down to the wreck, and scoop up some of the golden goodies. It should be simple to avoid the other divers if he timed it right, and it wasn't like he needed much—just a million bucks' worth or so, that's all. Ride the lift bag back to the surface, hide the swag in the *Cucaracha*'s sewage tank (nobody, especially not Alberto, ever looked in there), and bide his time until he hit Grand Cayman again and could safely offload his loot and make a discreet exit from the Ramoses' employ.

It was all lining up for him like a string of pearls. The worm had finally turned.

"I'm on the job, chief," he called after Alberto as the slender man disappeared down the port stairwell. "Don't worry 'bout a thing!" He grinned and snapped his fingers, finishing the famous Bob Marley song in his head:

'Cause every little t'ing . . . gonna be all right . . .

*****

"You're sure about this, Gerald?" Gene was looking over Posey's shoulder in the darkened ROV shack, intent on the graphic images popping up one after the other on the main computer screen. Behind him, silent and impassive as a golem, was Grizelda.

"Unfortunately, yes," the tech replied, shifting in his pilot's chair and tapping away on the keyboard in front of him. "What you're seeing is a graphic summary of the metal detection scans around the *Arista*. You'll note that with the exception of a few tiny hits in conjunction with large wooden beams—I read them as remnants of corroded iron nails—there is no metal of any kind within a two-hundred-yard radius of the wreck.

"I concentrated especially on the area just aft of the hull section. Nothing but nails. This survey is accurate, Gene, and penetrates the sediment right down to the bedrock—more than forty feet below the mud-line." Posey swiveled in his chair and faced the supervisor, the LED lights from the battery of electronic panels around him reflecting off his glasses. "I'm sorry, but there's absolutely nothing of any significant size made of gold or silver—or any other metal, for that matter— buried around this wreck."

Gene let out a long sigh. "All right, Gerald. Your fish back on the surface?"

Posey nodded. "Yep. Floating alongside on its davit tether."

"Good. Stand by." He looked at Grizelda. "Can I talk to you outside?"

The musclebound woman grunted and moved after him as he opened the door of the ROV van, letting out the usual cloud of cigarette smoke. He stepped out into the sunlight, donning his sunglasses, just as Gomez and Alberto arrived from the opposite side of the barge. Gene sucked his teeth and spat onto the deck. They were all here . . . just as well. He'd only have to give them the bad news—and their lousy options—once.

Alberto's face twitched as he approached, glancing back and forth between Gene and Grizelda, who was standing behind the diving supervisor. "My sister doesn't appear to be happy," he said, and looked nervous about it.

"Well," Gene responded, "I can't say as I blame her. I'm not real cheerful myself, right about now."

"Why is that?"

The old supervisor chewed the inside of his cheek before answering. "Because there's no gold in that there wreck. And none around it."

Alberto's eyebrows went up. "None? What about that golden spike your diver found?"

"Well, there's that. But like Ben said, it's a fluke. It's just one small piece and it's only there because the captain hammered it into the foremast. The rest of the treasure—who knows? When we were down here a few months ago doin' the initial survey, we ran sonar all over the bottom of the strait between these three islands. We found only two anomalies: this wreck and the wreck of a cargo vessel that was torpedoed by a U-boat durin' World War Two.

"We've checked what's left of the *Arista* and found nothing. Because there are no other anomalies in the ocean bottom anywhere near it—with the exception of that cargo vessel—I have to conclude, like I told you earlier, that the rest of the hull broke up as she sank, and the treasure she was carryin' got scattered to hell and beyond—all over the goddamn sea floor." Gene's weariness and disappointment were simmering to the surface. "So unless you feel like payin' for a comprehensive, foot-by-foot metal detection survey of the entire strait between your island and those other two, usin' our ROV—which could take months if not *years*—I think you've got, in that one golden spike, all of the *Arista*'s treasure you're going to get."

Gene folded his arms and looked through his sunglasses at Alberto and Gomez. He did not turn around to look at Grizelda.

"That is not the news we wanted to hear," Alberto said slowly.

"Me neither," Gene said. "But there it is."

They stood there in silence for nearly a minute, Gene stone-faced and gazing at the deck, Alberto chewing his lip and glaring at the old supervisor in agitation. Gomez shuffled his feet carefully and looked off toward the horizon, his hands in his pockets.

"You were hired to find the treasure of my ancestor."

At the sound of Grizelda's rasping voice, Gene turned, facing her squarely. "I didn't know the captain of the *Arista* was your ancestor. I didn't know your last name was Ramos, the same as his—Gomez never told me. But it wasn't relevant. I was hired to run a dive job. We made an educated guess that there was likely to be treasure in that wreck. We were wrong. Now, like I said before, there's probably quite a bit of it scattered along the bottom of the strait—remember, they were pitchin' barrels of golden chain over the side for hours before the ship actually sank—and maybe even a big pile or two buried in the mud. But we'd have to go lookin' for it. The forward section of the hull just hasn't panned out."

Grizelda glowered at him, her fists balled by her sides. "You told us that the preliminary survey was promising. You told us that with the supporting docu-

357

mentary evidence we had, the wreck was likely to contain my ancestor's treasure."

"It was." Gene shrugged. "Very likely. It just didn't pan out. That happens sometimes."

"We have spent a lot of money," Grizelda observed, her black eyes like slits, "financing this expedition—on your recommendation. And now there are no results."

Gene's already-worn patience began to shred. "Lady, I gave you the survey information that was available. You had some of your own from the Spanish naval records in Madrid. I put two and two together and came up with four. Look: maybe I didn't make it clear enough that every salvage job or treasure hunt is basically a crap shoot. There ain't any guarantees. Maybe I oversold the project to you a little bit—maybe I *wanted* there to be a fortune in gold sittin' in that old hull, but I was tryin' to be optimistic. Let you hear what you wanted to hear." Gene's voice faltered, and for a second or two he looked very old, very tired, and very desperate. "Give *all* of us a shot at a real prize. Give *myself* a real payoff, for once in my life."

Grizelda was literally trembling with suppressed anger, her facial muscles working and her eyes staring. All at once she stepped forward and cracked Gene across the cheekbone with her open hand. The blow had the force of a welterweight's jab and took the old supervisor completely off guard. He reeled sideways, bewildered, and caught himself against the side of the ROV shack. Then he got mad.

Seeing red, he cursed and grabbed at Grizelda's arm. She twisted away, and as he lurched after her, all his frustration boiling over into fury, there were two quick reports: **POP! POP!**

Gene McCluskey staggered, looked around in confusion, took two more steps, and fell face down on the steel deck. There were two small black perforations in the light gray material of his coveralls, directly between his shoulder blades. Behind his prostrate body, Alberto was still sighting down the barrel of the compact .32 caliber Beretta automatic he'd whipped out of his fanny pack.

Gomez's face was the color of ash. Knees knocking, he stared over at Alberto, incredulous. "Wha— what did you just *do?*" he croaked.

The slender man's face was twitching furiously. He licked his lips. "Nobody puts a hand on my sister," he shrilled, "unless she invites them to." He looked back at Gomez and grinned, his eyes wild. *"HAAH!"*

As the high-pitched shriek of laughter stung his ears, the lawyer stared down in horror at Eugene McCluskey's body. The light gray material covering the dead man's back was dark and wet now, soaked with blood, and a sticky pool was beginning to spread across the deck beneath him. Gomez gagged suddenly, nearly overcome by a surge of emotion—not of empathy for the murdered supervisor, but of revulsion that an act so visceral and . . . *messy* . . . could have taken place in his presence.

Grizelda was standing over McCluskey now, feet spread apart, arms at her sides, fists balled, staring down at him with a look of black hatred on her face. Very deliberately, she drew back her Doc Martens boot and kicked him in the side of the head. The corpse shook with the impact. Then, hearing the pounding of footsteps behind her, she whirled. The five armed guards who had accompanied her out from the island in the Boston Whaler were dashing up the deck as a group, dodging around cable spools and machinery skids.

"Oh, my god!"

At the sound of Sass's shocked exclamation, Grizelda, Alberto, and Gomez spun around in the opposite direction in time to see her and Earl, who'd come on the run at the sound of the shots, separate and disappear into the maze of equipment crowding the barge deck.

Grizelda's reaction was immediate. "Get them!" she yelled to the five bodyguards, and launched herself after the fleeing pair like a sprinter coming out of the blocks.

Chapter Twenty-Four

Earl dodged around a rack of oxygen bottles, moving with considerable speed and agility for a man his size, and made it past the inboard end of the ROV control van just as the first gunman pursuing him threw up his sawed-off pump shotgun and fired. The triple-ought buckshot punched a close group of holes in the thin steel near the van's corner, sending paint dust and metal chips flying and making the entire structure ring like a struck gong.

The bodyguard cursed and ran forward, jacking a new shell into the shotgun's breech. He rounded the corner of the van in time to see Earl, about ten feet away, in the posture of having just thrown a heavy object, two-handed. His eyes flickered upward, catching movement, but did not have time to focus before the nitrogen cylinder—six feet and one hundred and fifty pounds of heavy steel—smashed into his face and chest. It knocked him backward, past a following gunman, and into a deck winch. He had the misfortune to fall just so: his cervical vertebrae shattered in a hangman's break on impact, killing him instantly.

Acting on sheer instinct, not thinking about the fact that he had nowhere to go while aboard the dive barge,

Earl leaped past the next corner of the ROV van and ran smack into Posey as he stepped out the door.

"What the hell hit my shack like tha—" he blurted, and then Earl swept him along in the crook of one huge arm.

"Git movin'!" the big man yelled, throwing a punch on the fly at a third bodyguard who'd just appeared on the opposite side of the van. The ham-like fist took the man—the weasely one named Miguel who liked to smoke *basouko* on guard duty—flush on the side of the jaw, and he went down like a poleaxed calf, his eyes rolling up white in his head.

From somewhere in the middle of the barge, Grizelda's rasping bawl echoed above the persistent growl of the multiple on-deck diesels: *"I want the woman alive! The others—get rid of them!"*

Whatever personality defects Gerald Posey might have had, slow minded he wasn't. Hunching low, he sprinted along at Earl's shoulder as the huge man dashed pell-mell through the maze of deck machinery. They rounded a double pallet of fifty-five-gallon gasoline drums—fuel for the various two-stroke engines aboard—and stopped.

There was nowhere to go. They were at the stern of the barge.

The second gunman appeared beside the last compressor, leveling his shotgun from the hip. In tandem,

Earl and Posey dove behind the gasoline drums and rolled toward the stern rail as the man fired.

The gasoline drums exploded. An immense red-and-black fireball engulfed the stern, spraying burning fuel halfway up the deck. The gunman who'd fired the shot was roasted to a cinder instantaneously in the scorching flash. The fireball tumbled up into the sky, boiling with black smoke, buoyed by its own heat.

At the opposite end of the barge, Sass paused momentarily in her cat-and-mouse game with Grizelda, Alberto, and the two remaining bodyguards to stare wide-eyed at the fiery spectacle. Seeing the rain of flaming gasoline sweep toward her, she ducked under a metal awning of corrugated steel that sheltered the on-deck welding area—and tripped over Gomez, who had taken cover beneath the grinding bench only seconds earlier.

He seized her by the left ankle with both hands, screeching *"I've got her! I've got her!"* and Sass kicked him in the mouth with her right work-boot. The lawyer made a sound like *MMpffghpffmm!* and clapped his hands to his smashed lips and teeth. Sass left him rolling around on the deckplates, wailing, and headed for the metal steps that led up to the sat shack.

Reaching the top just as Grizelda appeared beside the bell-launching skid, she bolted through the door, slammed it shut and locked it. Heavy feet began to pound up the access stairs as she lunged for the descrambler radio.

"Ben!" she screamed. *"Get into the bell right now! Don't ask why! GET EVERYONE INTO THE BELL AND SEAL IT!"*

She screamed again as a shotgun blast blew a hole in the door near the lock, spraying her with fiberglass shards and bits of insulation. This was followed immediately by a heavy battering that shook the damaged door in its frame—but amazingly, the lock held. Sass dashed to the far end of the shack as the battering continued, and flung open the window that overlooked the sat pot and mated bell.

She was out the window like a scalded cat and dropping to the curved top of the big chamber when she heard the second shotgun blast. Without looking back, she sprinted to the end of the chamber and slithered down between it and the bell.

"I said don't shoot her, idiot!" Sass glanced up in time to see the musclebound woman with the red hair seize the barrel of the shotgun being aimed at her and jerk it skyward as it discharged. Something else was shouted, but she missed it in her haste to bleed the access trunk and disengage the bell.

Oh, please, she implored silently, her thoughts racing and her hands flying, *let them be in the bell. Please, God, let them be sealed in the bell.*

She broke the locking clamps free before the trunk had completely vented. There was a blast of water vapor as the mating surfaces separated, and the bell jerked forward several feet on its trestle. She took a quick look inside the trunk before lunging for the A-frame controls, and nearly cried with relief when she saw the sealed hatch. They were inside. She caught a glimpse of Ben's face in the tiny porthole, his expression furiously questioning, just before she slammed forward the lever that controlled the hydraulic rams. Their eyes locked for a second, and then the bell was dragged violently off the trestle by its lifting cable.

It swung outward like a wrecking ball, and at the fullest extent of the arc, Sass released the freewheel brake. The bell hit the water with a jarring splash and sank, the cable slithering after it through the sheaves of the crane block. The heavy umbilical that supplied unlimited gas, hot water, electrical power, and communications had been disconnected by Earl for routine maintenance after the last dive and lay like a great twisted python on the deck plates beside the launching skid.

Sass seized a short crowbar from a bracket on one of the skid uprights and rang it over the head of the bodyguard who had suddenly appeared behind her. The man staggered past her in an agonized stoop, clutching his bleeding scalp with both hands and groaning. Sass hit him again, a homerun swing to the ribs this time, as the bell continued to sink. Out of the corner of her eye, she saw Grizelda and Alberto come around the far end of the sat pot.

Whirling, she brought the crowbar down on the winch controls with every ounce of strength she had left. Again. And again. As the internal electronics of the steel control box became progressively more damaged, the secondary safety overrides kicked in, jamming the winch at Full Stop.

There was a loud **POP!** and a slug sparked off the deck between her work boots. She hit the control box once more for good measure and froze in place, trying not to tremble. Slowly, she looked across the deck. Alberto had his pistol lined up on her, aiming low. Beside him stood Grizelda, looking particularly simian with her muscles inflated and her lips pulled back in an angry sneer.

"I can shoot you without killing you," Alberto called. "One in the thigh, for instance. Or perhaps the knee. Or you can stand still. Take your pick."

Sass let the crowbar slip to the deck with a loud clatter. Straightening, she turned to face Alberto and his sister head on. "I'm standing still."

They approached, carefully.

"That's good," Alberto said. "Now then, we weren't properly introduced when we got here, were we? You were too busy, I think. I'm Alberto Ramos. This is my sister Grizelda."

He smiled. "She likes you. We both like you. So please don't make me shoot you."

*****

Inside the crowded confines of the diving bell, forty-four feet below the surface, Ben, Vern, and Pierre were all fighting down individual attacks of barely controllable panic. Even for the three highly experienced divers, the sudden bizarre sequence of events—from the thunderous detonation somewhere on the barge to Sass's screamed order to enter the bell to the violent, crashing launch and free-falling descent—combined with the complete lack of information from their support crew to produce the worst state of mind possible for a saturation diver: an intense, claustrophobic feeling of being both utterly trapped and utterly unable to do anything about it.

They knew the cure. Sitting quietly around the trunk hatch, eyes closed, they willed their heartbeats to slow and their breathing to deepen. Willed away the awful, suffocating panic.

It took several minutes. Pierre was the first to speak.

"*Merde.* What has happened?"

Ben blew out a long, slow breath. "I don't know." He looked over at Vern, touched him on the shoulder. "Vern. All right?"

The big man kept his eyes closed, breathing very deliberately in through his nose and out his mouth, and nodded in response. "Yeah. Ah'm fine."

"Okay," Ben said quietly. "Let's just all stay cool, eh?"

"Absolument," Pierre concurred, his customary exuberance replaced by a studied calm. In their current circumstances, a subdued demeanor was critical: one person's excitability could easily re-escalate into panic, and panic was more contagious than typhoid. In a hollow steel sphere barely six feet in diameter, occupied by three men, there was no room for that.

Ben looked at the gauges. "No pressure on the surface-supplied side of the gas rack," he said. "No topside electrical power, either. The umbilical's not attached. We're on our own D/C battery power to keep the CO_2 scrubbers running—and any lights we're stupid enough to turn on."

"And no radio communications," Pierre added.

"Right. No radio."

"How 'bout," Vern muttered, his eyes still closed, "we shut down one scrubber? Draw half the battery power an' use half as much absorbent soda. We might need it, y'all. Long as we don't git to huffin' an' puffin' in here, one canister oughta wash out enough CO_2 that we don't choke, huh?"

"You're right, Vern," Ben said. "Good thinking." He reached over his shoulder and pulled the power cable of the nearest scrubber out of its moisture-proof connector. Inside the stainless steel housing, the unit's circulating fan stopped rotating.

"I am speechless, *mon ami*," Pierre told the big man. "A wise suggestion."

Vern opened one eye and smiled at him. "Ah ain't as dumb as Ah look, froggy."

"Evidently not, which is a great relief, I assure you." A restrained Gallic shrug. "Of course, I would have thought of it myself in only a few more seconds, you realize."

"Yeah. You or Ben. Ah ain't debatin' it."

"Bien. Talking too much generates carbon dioxide, *n'est-ce pas?"*

"Yeah. What you said."

Ben unscrewed the top of the scrubber housing and extracted the soda canister, a two-foot-long clear plastic tube full of white, pea-sized granules. Some of them were tinged with pink, which indicated that they had already absorbed a certain amount of CO_2. He passed it across the bell to Pierre. "Bag this, will you?"

The little Frenchman nodded and put the canister into a sealable plastic sleeve, isolating it from the surrounding atmosphere and halting the CO_2-absorbing reaction that consumed the soda.

Ben replaced the top of the scrubber, sat back on it, and looked out one of the two tiny portholes.

"See anything?" Vern rumbled.

"Water," Ben said. "Some horse-eye jacks. The bottom of the barge. That's it."

He fell silent, continuing to peer out the port. The only sound was the quiet whir of the single operating scrubber-fan.

"What the hail d'you think happened?" Vern said finally. "Sounded like World War Three out there for a moment. Then we git bounced around like we did. That ain't no way to launch a bell."

Ben shook his head as he gazed out into the blue void. "I just don't know, Vern. Something's gone very wrong."

"We cannot open the hatch at this depth," Pierre said, stating the obvious. "Even if we could physically do it, we would all expire—*pouf!*—from explosive decompression—as if you need me to tell you."

"Well," Ben stated, "somebody up there better do something soon, because we're going to need more makeup oxygen eventually. Either they've gotta pick us back up, swim down themselves, or lower us down to hatch-depth at twelve hundred feet so we can get out of here and open the valves on those reserve O_2 bottles."

"One way or the other," Vern muttered, his voice very low, "Ah got a feelin' we're gonna see some more action here in a few minutes. Ah just hope it turns out to be the kind we want."

*****

Grizelda walked slowly around the sat system's launching skid, eyeing the deployed A-frame and the bell's supporting cable. Then she stepped over to the starboard rail and peered down. The bell was visible as a pale greenish blob in the Windex-blue water, dangling nearly fifty feet beneath the barge.

Sass was standing beside Alberto, pale faced and silent, her hair falling over one eye and a smudge of dirt on her right cheekbone. Behind her was one of the two remaining bodyguards—the man who'd fired his shotgun through the sat shack door lock—his weapon supported in the crook of his elbow and trained on her back.

Grizelda traced the cable back through the A-frame block to the main winch, then did the same with the electrical conduits to the main control panel. She wiggled the smashed levers—to no avail—and then stared over at Sass, running her eyes up and down her from head to toe.

"Did a good job on these crane controls, didn't you?" she grunted. "Now—why would you do that?"

Alberto made a fluttery gesture in the air with his gun hand. "Isn't it obvious? We can't get at them down there . . . at least for the time being. This lovely creature"—he reached out and stroked Sass's shoulder, prompting her to jerk away in disgust—"thinks the cavalry is coming, evidently."

There was a muffled groan from behind a nearby compressor and the bodyguard Sass had whacked over the head with the crowbar limped into view, one hand clasping a bloody rag to his damaged scalp, the opposite arm clutching his aching ribs. He glared daggers at her as he made his laborious way over to Grizelda.

"There is no sign of the other two, Senorita Ramos," he reported, between moans. "But I found Javier. He's dead—his neck was broken. Miguel is unconscious beside the second control van. And I also found Sanchez. At least, I *think* it was Sanchez." He paused to grind his teeth and emit a whimper of pain. "The thing I found looked like an overcooked enchilada— wearing Sanchez's big emerald ring. He must have been caught in the explosion."

Grizelda scowled. "No great loss." She fixed him with her cold black stare. "The other two must be somewhere if you can't find their bodies."

The bodyguard automatically shook his head, which made him wince in pain. "I—I believe, Senorita Ramos," he said, "that they were burned up in the fireball. They must have been right in the heart of the blast. Anything left of their bodies would probably have been blown into the water. There was so much heat that the entire stern had the paint charred off it."

Sass felt a stinging pang behind her eyes, and her throat tightened. Earl, the efficient, good-natured giant, was gone. So was the awkward but surprisingly human ROV tech, Gerald Posey. And Gene. They'd already loaded his body, covered by a dirty tarpaulin, into the Boston Whaler.

She looked from Grizelda, to Alberto, and back to Grizelda again. "You've just killed three people," she said, her voice hoarse. "For *what?*"

The musclebound woman stepped forward, until her hot, heavy breath was on Sass's face. "For disappointing me," she whispered. "And for arguing about it." Then she grinned and stroked the outside of Sass's right breast with two fingertips.

Sass flinched back, her face reddening with anger, and the bodyguard behind her jammed the muzzle of his shotgun into her lower spine. She froze.

Alberto gestured with his Beretta at a pile of nylon and neoprene lying inside a coil of dive hose on the deck. "What is that?"

"It's a hot-water suit," Sass said. "A spare for the bell."

"Oh? I've never heard of such a thing. What's it for?"

Sass cleared her throat, thinking that as long as he was talking, he wasn't shooting. "Keeping a diver warm when he's down deep, where it's cold. Heated seawater gets pumped into the suit."

"From what?"

Sass pointed at the idling hot-water machine, steam rising from its vented tanks. "From that. It sucks up seawater through the intake hose, heats it with a kerosene burner, and pumps it down to the diver."

"You don't say."

Alberto strolled over to the machine, located the intake hose, and followed it across the deck to the opposite side of the barge. Sass could just barely see him between two large racks of helium gas. He stood at the rail, where the hose went into the water, for several minutes, looking down.

When he returned, smiling the oiliest smile Sass had ever seen, he took his sister aside and began to converse with her in low tones. As he did so, Gomez reeled into view around the end of the sat pot, holding a towel to the lower half of his face. Seeing Sass gazing coldly at him, he stumbled over toward the Ramoses and extended a shaking finger in her direction.

"Sshbrrmmdffff!" he gurgled into the towel.

Alberto and Grizelda stopped talking and regarded him with amused interest. "Repeat that," Alberto said.

Gomez removed the towel, exposing the bloody pulp of mashed flesh and tooth splinters that had previously been the generating apparatus of his thousand-watt attorney's smile. *"She bwoke my teef!"* he reiterated, comprehensibly this time.

"I see that," Alberto nodded. "And did a good job of it, too." He threw Sass an admiring glance. "I adore capable women—like my sister. They're so . . . *stimulating."*

Sass locked her knees to keep her legs from shaking. The expression on Alberto Ramos' face was that depraved.

Gomez replaced the towel, quite obviously offended by the lack of sympathy forthcoming from his two employers, and wobbled over to an oil drum to sit down. Grizelda crossed her arms and stood beneath the A-frame, watching Sass.

"Is this suit ready to go?" Alberto asked her. He pointed at the backup hot-water rig.

Sass nodded silently.

The slender man with the lubricious smile redirected his index finger at the spare dive helmets hanging on the side of the equipment van. "I want you to hook up a helmet to this hose and prepare the suit for a dive."

"Do it yourself," Sass said.

Alberto's smile faded. He brought the Beretta up again, sighting low. "Such pretty legs," he murmured. "Which kneecap would you prefer to have blown off?"

Sass swallowed, hesitated, then started toward the suit. "All right. All right."

Alberto lowered the pistol. "I can talk to the diver by radio, like you do? And hear him as well?"

She nodded, pulling the end of the hose out of the coil and checking the bronze fittings. "If you like. I can hook this hose to an on-deck radio." Her internal organs felt as if they had suddenly turned to ice. "You're not diving?"

The slender man's cold smile returned. "No," he said, waving the Beretta at Gomez. "He is."

Chapter Twenty-Five

"It's getting hard to breathe in here," Posey whispered. "We're using the oxygen and building up carbon dioxide."

"That's a fact," Earl grunted, spitting seawater. "The air's downright thick."

He looked over at the ROV tech, whose wet face was illuminated by the soft blue light that suffused the water beneath the barge. He had lost his steel-rimmed glasses in the initial tumble from the stern rail as the gasoline drums had exploded, and was now blinking myopically in an attempt to see the details of his surroundings.

Not that there was much to see. He and Earl were treading water inside one of the barge's disused seachests—a water-intake alcove in the underside of the hull near the stern. The intake orifice of this one had been welded shut years ago, when the barge had been depowered and no longer required raw cooling water. All that remained was this small depression in the hull, less than eighteen inches deep and three feet in diameter, that caught a pocket of air whenever the barge was underway in calm weather. Eventually, rough seas would displace it, but fortunately for Earl and Posey, who'd stroked downward under the stern to escape the inferno above, conditions hadn't been rough since the passage through the Yucatan Channel days earlier. Earl had discovered the little sanctuary by accident, groping along the hull plates, and dragged Posey up into it with him, half-drowned.

It was a temporary refuge at best, albeit out of the line of fire. But there was no time—or even air—to discuss what had just happened or why. There was only one pressing issue: how to get clear of the homicidal maniacs roaming the deck above. They didn't doubt that if they popped to the surface alongside the barge— anywhere—they would be in imminent danger of having their heads blown off by a shotgun blast.

"We have to get out of here," Posey said, his breathing raspy. "We're going to pass out and drown if we stay."

Earl nodded in the glowing blue light. "You got that right. Any ideas?"

There was a light splash and the tech held something up—something made of yellowish plastic, about the size and shape of a large television remote. "Yep," he replied, blinking. Although he could barely see, he managed a thin smile. "Glad I made this unit water-proof—and that it didn't fall out of my pocket." He squinted at the device and pushed a button. There was a beeping sound, followed by the red flash of an LED. "I might need you to help me see the display screen. Let's try calling a ride."

*****

Sass stood back from the helmet and hot-water suit she'd just rigged to the dive hose and regarded Gomez with a certain amount of pity. The lawyer was standing in his shiny maroon-satin boxer underwear, still holding the bloody towel to his face, looking like a hundred and sixty pounds of soggy milquetoast without his designer garments. He'd managed to regain partial control over his power of speech, despite a nasty lisp, and turned to Alberto and Grizelda yet again, pleading:

"I—I don't underfftand why you want me to do thiff. Why can't you jufft cut the cable fwom up here?"

Alberto waved his pistol around haphazardly. "I told you. My sister and I have decided that your contributions to our business thus far have been entirely too . . . sedentary. Too exclusively—ah—*cerebral*. It's time you exerted yourself a little."

Beside him, Grizelda let loose her deep giggle. "Yes. I think I want to see that. In fact, I insist on it."

Sass drew herself up, her face very pale. "Did he just say *cut* the cable?"

"Yes," Alberto said. "I believe he did."

She swallowed hard. "You promised me, if I ran Gomez's dive, that you would hook the crane up to the bell, lift it back on deck, and let me decompress those men."

"Yes, I did, didn't I?" Alberto turned and smirked fawningly at Grizelda. "Actually, I just thought it might be entertaining to watch what would happen to the human body if I shot out the bell's portholes. As I understand it, going from over a thousand feet of saturation to sea level in, oh, thirty seconds or less, would have a rather extreme effect on a person's well-being."

"It would be murder," Sass said flatly.

"HAAH!" Alberto shrilled out his sharp, high-pitched laugh. "Well, what's another of those, more or less?" He shook his head. "Mr. McCluskey should not have annoyed my sister . . . and he most certainly should not have attempted to put his hands on her—not in my presence, at any rate. But there's no sense in crying over spilt milk, eh?" He grinned. "Now we just have to tie up the loose ends. My sister and I hate loose ends. If you don't *tie* them up, they tend to *trip* you up. Isn't that right, Gomez?"

"Er—yeff," the lawyer replied, struggling to get his legs into the hot-water suit.

Sass stepped forward, her face lined with strain. "If you cut that cable," she said, "the bell and those men inside will sink all the way to the bottom, one thousand two hundred feet down. They'll die down there." Another step. "Please. Let me rig another crane line to the bell—pick it up onto the deck and decompress them. They won't have a chance if you do this." She halted as she felt the hard muzzles of two shotguns dig into her back.

"That's close enough, I think," Alberto said. "You know, if you hadn't dropped that bell into the water and then smashed the A-frame controls, it would be easy to pick them up now." He appraised her with suspicion. "Why did you do that, anyway?"

Sass looked stricken, her lower lip trembling. "I—I just thought I needed to get them away from—from you. From the guns. They're vulnerable while they're under pressure. I was afraid you might—do something . . . like shoot out one of the sat pot portholes."

"Hurry this up," Grizelda growled at Alberto as she paced back and forth. "These people have wasted enough of my time."

"Please," Sass said, her eyes glistening. "Let me pick them up."

Grizelda stopped pacing and stared at her. "No," she rasped. "Too much trouble." She glared at her brother. "They're divers—so let them dive. *Sink* them."

Sass sagged to her knees with a despairing sob and buried her face in her hands.

Alberto yawned. "Such melodrama. I hate melodrama." He wiggled his Beretta at Gomez as he stepped toward Sass. "Hurry up. Finish zipping that suit shut and get ready for the helmet."

He reached down, stroked Sass's blonde hair for a few seconds, then grabbed a fistful of it and forced her to her feet. Her face was anguished, and she was choking out little sobs—but oddly enough, her eyes were dry. Alberto suddenly became rather impatient with her.

"Stop it!" he hissed. He propelled her roughly toward Gomez. "Get over there and help him put the helmet on."

She stumbled across the deck, bent down, and picked up the yellow fiberglass dive hat. In accordance with her halting instructions, Gomez pulled the hat's neck dam down over his head and adjusted it. Sass tried not to look directly at him—the lower half of his face resembled a bloody eggplant.

When she attempted to lower the heavy helmet over the lawyer's head, he cried out in protest and blocked its descent with both hands. "I—I can't do thiff, Alberto! I'm hurt, I'm—I'm claufftrophobic! I have a—a—chronic ear condiffion!"

Abruptly, the slender man strode across the deck and leveled the pistol at him, aiming directly between his eyes from less than a foot away. "You'll have a chronic hole in your head if you don't put that fucking helmet on right now, counselor." Behind him, Grizelda giggled.

The part of Gomez's face that was not bloodied and purple turned ashen. Slowly, he removed his hands. Sass lowered the hat into place, locked it onto the neck dam, and stepped back. The lawyer's shoulders sagged under the weight of the heavy gear.

Alberto nodded, lowering the Beretta. "Very good. Is the hot water on?"

"Not yet," Sass told him. "I have to open up a valve over there."

"Can he turn it on and off underwater?"

"No, not the way this suit's rigged. There's no in-line valve he can reach. If he wanted to stop the hot water going into the suit, he'd have to locate the quick-disconnect at the hose fitting and break it free."

"Gomez doesn't even know what a quick-disconnect is," Alberto told her. "In fact, he barely knows what a hose is."

Sass said nothing.

"Now," Alberto continued, "the water isn't too hot? I don't want my attorney parboiled—although it's not an altogether inappropriate fate for the majority of lawyers I've met."

"It's mixed down to about seventy-five degrees on this line," Sass said. "But he doesn't need hot water for a dive this shallow, you know."

Alberto ignored her last comment. "Good. I want to talk to him. After you."

Sass led him across the deck to the small topside dive station—radio, air rack, and hot-water valves. The two bodyguards followed, keeping their shotguns trained on her. Beside the starboard rail, apart from everyone else, Grizelda paced back and forth, scowling down at the water with her muscular arms folded.

Sass indicated the radio, showed Alberto the TALK button and how to actuate it. He depressed it and bent down near the speaker. "Gomez."

"Wha—? What?" The response was muffled and distorted by static.

"You have a wrench and wire cutters tied to your harness. Get down on top of that bell and break loose the shackle that connects it to the cable."

"All . . . all wight." A pause. "You'll pull me back up wight away, after I'm done?"

Alberto smiled slowly. "Of course. Now get in there."

The attorney waddled across the deck, dragging hose behind him, and stopped at the starboard rail. The hat tipped forward as he stared down, weaving slightly.

"Thiff iv too high up to jump, Alberto," he said, his voice taking on a whining quality. "I'm too heavy! I'll ffink! I'll—*EEEYAAAGGHHH!*"

One second after Grizelda shoved him off the edge of the barge, his scream of alarm was cut short by an ugly, belly-flopping impact with the water.

*****

"Someone's on top of the bell," Ben said. "Listen."

Pierre and Vern looked upward, straining to hear. There it was again. A metallic clunking noise, like that of a wrench on a hex nut.

The little Frenchman jumped to his feet and pressed his face against the scarred Lexan of the nearest porthole. *"Tabarnac,"* he swore, "I cannot see anyone."

Ben, looking out the other port, shifted sideways as Vern stood up. The big man's shoulders nearly filled the upper part of the bell. "Sorry," he muttered.

"That's okay, Vern," Ben said. "Have a look. Maybe you can see something I don't."

"Thanks." They traded places. "Huh. Ah don't see nothin' neither."

Ben slid back down to a sitting position. "Well, I can sure hear him." He glanced from Pierre to Vern. "I hope that's one of our people out there, doing something good for *us*—like getting the umbilical hooked up so we can talk to Gene and find out what the hell's going on."

"Sapristi!" Pierre exclaimed, still looking out through the Lexan. "Why doesn't he come to a port-hole and signal us, eh? Let us know his intentions!"

"Ah was just thinkin' the same thing, froggy," Vern rumbled. "That's a mite . . . strange."

Pierre sucked his teeth in irritation and snatched up a chipping hammer from the bell's floor grating. "Ayy, *imbecile!*" he shouted, rapping hard on the uppermost curve of the sphere. *"Attention!* Show yourself, you dry-land farmer, you! There are men in here who need to know what is happening!"

They waited. "That hammering would bring a response from anyone on our crew," Ben said. "Earl, Gene, Sass—even Gerald. Anyone."

They watched the ports in growing exasperation, listening to the continuous sound of tools being employed on top of the bell.

Vern slid back down beside Ben. "Well," he said, "whatever happens next, it can only be one of two things."

Pierre glanced down at him. "And what are those?"

"A good thing," the big man replied, "or a bad thing."

There was a sudden metallic snap. The bell jolted to one side . . . then began an odd, gentle gyration that grew increasingly more pronounced. Outside the portholes, the cheery blue glow of filtered sunlight began to fade.

Pierre slid down to a sitting position opposite Ben and Earl, his fingers white on the edge of the trunk hatch. *"Mon dieu,"* he whispered.

They all recognized the motion. It was the sway of an untethered free-fall.

The bell was sinking.

As the ambient light coming through the ports ebbed away, Ben caught one last glimpse of the rack-mounted depth gauge.

"Three hundred and forty feet," he said into the darkness, his voice hoarse with tension. "And increasing. We're going to the bottom."

*****

Gomez watched in horrified fascination as the bell dropped away beneath him, leaving him clinging to the cable he'd just unshackled. The big steel sphere wobbled as it sank into the blue abyss, becoming smaller and smaller, its color changing from bright orange to dull brown to gray . . . to . . .

And then it was gone, without even a trail of bubbles to mark its descent.

My god, the lawyer thought, there were actual *people* in there.

Then his better instincts took over.

Fuck it. Better them than me.

He began to haul himself up the cable, hand over hand. It was all he could do to climb six feet. The weight of the gear—helmet, weight belt, suit, and tools—was just too much for his office-softened arms to handle. Panting hard, which hurt his damaged mouth like fury, he hung in place and croaked out a request:

"Pull—pull me up on the hove. I can't do it myffelf."

He looked up. The bottom of the barge loomed above him like a huge, dark roof, his hose dangling slack from one edge. He looked out to his left and right, something he hadn't yet done. The first thing he saw was a school of small silver jacks cruising past like a benign living cloud. The second thing he saw was a fourteen-foot great hammerhead shark, a shoal of striped pilot fish fluttering just ahead of it as it swam—directly toward him.

Every muscle in Gomez's aching body went into seizure.

"AAAAGGHH!" he shrieked into the hat's oral/nasal mask. *"FFHARK! Pull me up! Pull me up!"*

He began to claw his way up the cable again, making little progress. The shark, which had spent the night feeding on the buoyant carcass of a dead pilot whale, was not at all hungry. In fact, it had merely been making an inspection pass. But it found the sudden thrashing of the bubble-blowing creature interesting. It quickened its swimming motion and veered in closer, both curious and wary.

Gomez's bowels were squirting. Every ludicrous Hollywood cliché he had ever absorbed about killer sharks came rolodexing up out of his subconscious. Absolute terror imbued his flabby deltoids with preternatural strength, and he dragged himself up to a depth of twenty feet, wheezing like an asthmatic.

The shark continued to circle at a distance of about four yards, planing up lazily as Gomez climbed, staying level with him. Its great black eye, situated at the end of its head-lobe, roved over the floundering lawyer. The frenetic motion was just too stimulating to ignore, even for a shark thoroughly sated by a bellyfull of whale meat. It would continue to observe the performance for as long as it lasted.

Gomez took this behavior for a death sentence.

"It'ff coming for me!" he screamed, when in fact the shark was not. *"Jeffuff, help me! Get me out of here! GET ME OUT!"*

*****

Alberto sighed and gestured to one of the remaining bodyguards. "Pull that idiot up, Carlos." He waved Sass back from the radio with his Beretta. "Excuse me."

He depressed the TALK button, cutting off the flow of terrified whimpering from the speaker. "Gomez."

"Pull up on the hove! Why iffn't anyone pulling up on the hove?"

"Gomez. Listen to me."

"Oh, god—what?"

"Do you remember the name Joachim Strasser?"

"AAGGH! THE FFHARK! THE FFHARK'S COMING CLOFER!"

Alberto glanced up at Carlos, who was now at the rail beside Grizelda, slowly recovering Gomez's dive hose. Catching the bodyguard's eye, he motioned for him to speed up slightly. Then he bent down to the radio again.

"We're picking you up. Now, answer my question. Do you remember the name Joachim Strasser?"

"Ahh, god, at lafft. Ffhank you . . . ffhank you . . . hurry . . ."

"Gomez, if you don't answer my question, I'm going to let you sink back down to the end of the hose and stay there."

"NO, NO! Affk me again! Affk me again!"

"For third and final time: do you remember the name Joachim Strasser?"

"Yeff, of courffe," the lawyer panted. "He waff chief finanffial conffultant to Manuel Noriega in Panama. Head fftrategifft for ffeveral of the biggefft naffional bankff."

"Correct. Would you say he was adept at handling money? Moving it, legitimizing it, keeping it out of sight?"

"He waff one of the greatefft money laundererff in hifftory."

Alberto glanced up from the radio again as Gomez appeared at the top of the dive ladder, looking like a half-drowned spaceman in the heavy dive helmet and bulky hot-water suit. Grizelda grinned at her brother, nodded, and began to walk across the deck toward the far side of the barge as Carlos helped the exhausted lawyer up the last few rungs and onto the starboard rail.

"God," Gomez said, gasping. "What a terrifying exffperienffe." He fumbled at the locking mechanism of the dive hat's neck dam. "Help me, pleave. I have no idea how to get out of thiff equipment."

Alberto held up a hand toward Carlos. The body-guard backed away, smiling. Gomez continued to pluck ineffectively at the cam-lock of his neck dam, heated seawater pouring out of the cuffs and vents of his suit.

"I ffaid I need help," he repeated. "I'm getting ffteamed in here."

From the opposite rail of the barge, beside the in-take hose of the hot-water machine, Grizelda waved a dip net on a ten-foot-long extension pole at her brother, and proceeded to lower it over the side.

"Joachim Strasser had a serious downturn in his for-tunes a while back," Alberto said into the radio, "thanks to George Herbert Bush and Operation Just Cause. When Noriega went, so did the lucrative appointments enjoyed by all his cronies. Strasser really got screwed, because at the same time the US Marines were rooting out old Manuel, financial SWAT teams from the DEA, the FBI, the CIA, and several other governmental agencies too secret even to have acronyms were freez-ing and seizing millions of dollars in Panamanian assets. Including the bulk of Strasser's own fortune."

"That'ff too bad," Gomez said. "Now, can ffome-one pleave—"

"So a few months ago, my sister and I decided to hire him—since we were aware of some serious accounting problems within our organization. We asked him to use all his expertise to track down what we perceived to be an inexplicable leak in our cash flow."

Despite the hot water coursing around his body, Gomez's blood suddenly ran cold.

"You'll never guess what he concluded in his report to us. That our principle lawyer-slash-accountant—that would be you, Gomez—was effectively skimming between twelve and twenty-one percent off our gross income *each month,* and depositing it into his own secret accounts. And had been doing so for nearly three years." Alberto paused to grin across the deck. "How about that, eh?"

Gomez's eyes were boggling with fear as he stared back at his employer through the dive helmet's faceplate. "If—if you kill me," he stammered, "you'll never be able to acffeff your money. I've hid—hidden it too well."

Alberto laughed and waved a hand. "Oh, good heavens, don't worry about that! Mr. Strasser is most efficient. He's already found ninety-five percent of it. But thank you, Gomez, for your concern."

He laughed again and waved a hand at Grizelda, who immediately did something over the side with the long-handled dip net.

Gomez stepped forward, arms outstretched, staggering under the weight of the helmet and suit. "Pleave,"

he said, "there'ff been a mifftake . . . a miffunderfftand-ing...I—*YAAGGGGHHH!*
YEAAGGHGHGHGHGH!"

The back-to-back shrieks that came out of the radio jolted Sass like high-voltage electricity. She lurched away, clapping her hands to her ears, as Gomez threw himself to the deck and went into a series of frenzied contortions, his hands ripping and tearing at the hot-water suit.

Alberto smiled and pressed the TALK button. "What seems to be the problem, counselor?"

"YEEEAAAAAAGGGGGGHHHH!"

"Oh, I see. Well, send me a report on that at the end of the month. In triplicate."

He snapped the radio's power switch to the off position. Gomez's agonized screams were cut off instantly.

Sass teetered back, wide-eyed, her hand to her mouth, until she came up against the side of the sat pot. Alberto sidled back near her, his Beretta held loosely at his side, watching the now-silenced man in the dive helmet and suit flog himself against the steel deckplates with bone-cracking violence.

"What . . . what's wrong with him?" she managed to ask.

Alberto held up the pistol. "Just wait."

Gomez flopped around on the deck like a dying fish for another two minutes, clawing at the suit and banging the helmet on the steel plates. Gradually, his frenetic gymnastics ceased, and with one final agonized tremor, he sagged onto his back and lay still.

Alberto crooked a finger at Sass. "Come."

He walked over to the stricken man, Sass trailing behind him. "Undo that helmet and take it off him," he ordered. When she hesitated, he pointed the Beretta at her. "Now."

Her hands shaking, she uncammed the neck dam, took hold of the hat's top handle, and pulled it off the lawyer's head. At the sight of him, she gasped and nearly dropped the heavy helmet on her toe.

Gomez's face was swollen to such a degree that he was almost unrecognizable, as if he had been force-injected with latex foam. His skin was waxy and shot through with tiny purple veins that seemed to have bloomed from his flesh like threadworms. His eyes were swollen completely shut, and his blue-gray lips were stretched back over his teeth in a grimace of death.

Sass set the hat down. "What happened to him?" she asked, trying to keep her voice from trembling.

Again, Alberto smiled and crooked a finger. "Allergic reaction. Follow me."

He led her over to the far side of the barge, where Grizelda was still standing with the dip net. Looking very pleased with himself, he pointed down at the water. "Observe."

Sass came forward and peered down. The seawater intake hose for the hot-water machine extended below the surface about two feet. Around it, supported on a ring of Styrofoam floats, was a four-foot-diameter basket made of fish netting. And all along the port side of the barge—its windward side—bobbed the shiny, blue-pink bladders of dozens of Portuguese Man O' War, borne in by the slight wind and current.

Sass had put the netting basket around the end of the intake hose herself, to prevent stinging jellyfish of any kind from being sucked up into the hot-water machine—and subsequently pumped on, in pulverized but still-toxic form, to an unsuspecting diver.

"Here's a good one," Grizelda said, and dipped. The big invertebrate, its football-sized bladder shimmering translucent blue, came up in the net like a lump of wet, hairy Jello. A Gorgon's mop of purple tentacles dangled beneath it, some of them trailing off into the water for twenty feet or more.

Grizelda inverted the dip net and dropped the animal in beside the mouth of the intake hose. Instantly, it was sucked up and disappeared.

Alberto burst out with his neurotic, high-pitched laugh. *"HAAH!* I guess Gomez didn't feel that one." His sister joined in his mirth, giggling in her odd, low tone.

Sass backed away, staring at them in disbelief. Sick wasn't the word for these two. She stopped once again when she felt the shotgun in her back.

Alberto wiped the tears from his eyes with the back of his gun hand as his laughter died away to a chuckle. *"Hee-heeee hee!* Too funny. All right . . ." He motioned to the two bodyguards. "Make sure all the bodies are in the speedboat. We're going in to the island to dispose of them. We leave them floating around out here, chances are they'll wash up half-eaten on some resort beach and alarm the tourists. We don't need any law enforcement types, from any country, sniffing around asking questions. Move!"

As the two bodyguards turned and hurried off across the deck, Alberto put the Beretta on Sass again. "Hey. Do you know why that man-eating shark down there didn't eat our lawyer?"

Sass shook her head slowly, watching the gun.

The slender man giggled. "Professional courtesy," he said.

Chapter Twenty-Six

Sligo had missed everything. The gunshots, the gasoline-drum explosion, the wild deployment of the bell, Gomez's spastic death-by-jellyfish—everything. He'd missed it because, thirty seconds before Alberto's first two shots had signaled the murder of Gene McCluskey, he'd snuck over the seaward side of the *Cucaracha*—attired in the shiny yellow suit, heavy custom-plumbed dive helmet, and monstrous backpack assembly of Kronos Industries' DOA-9000—and slipped beneath the gentle Caribbean swells, dragging his bulky air-lift bag with him.

Nothing had gone right after that.

Fumbling to get dressed in after Alberto's departure, taking him at his word that he would not be back until the following day, Sligo had neglected to hook up the few systems within the highly-advanced rebreather that were not permanently plumbed. He'd skipped most of the part of the manual entitled *Pre-Dive Checks* in favor of snorting up two very big lines of coke before camming the helmet down onto his head. Just to calm the nerves. Not that he was nervous or anything.

He'd filled the backpack's reserve cylinders with the right gases. He'd made sure that its two onboard batteries were charged to capacity. He'd looked over the diagram in the centerfold of the manual so he'd have some idea of how to put the gear on correctly. He'd skipped the final chapter in the big instructional volume—the one entitled *Deep-Diving Applications and Extreme Exposures*—because it had started with a technical word containing nine syllables.

There was just too much crap to read. Dammit, there was *gold* waiting for him down there! And if he didn't hurry up and get wet, those commercial divers were going to grab it all. Which would be a major bummer.

So, after turning on the unit's master power switch (it was a weird, toggle-like doodad with a locking ring), over the side he'd gone.

Shploonk.

"Beep," the DOA-9000 had said into dive helmet's ear speakers.

Immediately, a heads-up light display had appeared in the upper right-hand corner of his faceplate, hyper-focused so that it could be read by a human eye only an inch or two away. **Negative Buoyancy** the display flashed. And below that, in more personal terms: **You Are Sinking**.

No shit, Sherlock.

After dropping thirty feet, frantically equalizing his ears and groping for the right control button on the rebreather's chest console, Sligo had discovered the

399

first system he'd failed to hook up: the DOA-9000's integral buoyancy compensator. He'd kept his cool, though. He hadn't started screaming as he tumbled downward through the empty, frigid darkness until he'd reached about four hundred feet.

This had largely been due to the fact that the size and intricacy of the heads-up display had been increasing exponentially as he sank, distracting him with a cornucopia of technical alerts and dire warnings in an attractive assortment of vibrant neon colors:

Danger—Descent Rate Excessive. Slow Down. Negative Buoyancy. You Are Sinking. Exceeding Recommended Surface Decompression Limits. Switching To Trimix Blend. Adjusting PPO$_2$. Negative Buoyancy. You Are Sinking. Entering Extreme Exposure Zone. Danger—Descent Rate Excessive. Depth Hazard. Inadequate Gas Reserves. Surface Supply Umbilical Required. Surface Supply Umbilical Not Detected. Adjusting PPO$_2$. You Are Too Deep. Go Back.

Etcetera.

"Beep," the DOA-9000 had said. "Beep."

Sligo had been so consumed by the display—and by scrabbling frantically at the chest console controls, trying to get the goddamsonofabitchin' piece of junk to do something he wanted it to do—that he hadn't noticed the fourteen-foot hammerhead that had followed him down to nearly two hundred feet, the pod of false killer whales that had sideswiped him at three hundred, or the nine-meter-long juvenile giant squid that had scooted out of his path at seven. He hadn't noticed a single thing—not even with the aid of the powerful hat light that the DOA-9000's computers had automatically switched on at a mere twenty fathoms.

Now, passing eight hundred feet, it was all over but the screaming—and even that release was beginning to elude him. It was difficult to vocalize strenuously while gasping in a breathing mix that was more than twenty times the density of air at sea level. But Sligo did have two things going for him, both cocaine-related. First: the membranes of his sinuses and oral-nasal passages were so eaten away by his lifelong snorting habit that his facial cavities and ears tended to equalize themselves automatically as he sank. And second: the anaesthetic effect of the blow that was coursing through his system cancelled out the musculoskeletal pain of overly rapid compression.

The wizardly computers of the DOA-9000 did the rest, mixing and re-mixing the component gases in response to the ever-increasing depth, until the actual percentages of nitrogen and oxygen he was breathing, along with the bulk helium, were miniscule—and absolutely ideal for his depth at any given moment. No matter how extreme the conditions, no matter how

grievous the lack of sound dive planning and judgement, the Kronos Industries DOA-9000 was not going
to let him die—not if it could help it.

"AAAAAAAAAAAAAAAAAGGHH!" Sligo declared,
plummeting in total darkness past nine hundred feet.

"Beep," the DOA-9000 responded cheerfully.

*****

Earl resurfaced in the sea chest beside Posey, blowing like a whale, and pushed the hair out of his eyes.
The atmosphere within the little alcove was almost
unbreathable now—heavy with humidity and carbon
dioxide, nearly devoid of oxygen.

"Can you see it?" Posey asked.

Earl's lungs were working like a blacksmith's bellows in the bad air. "Yeah . . . just like you said . . . it's
hoverin' about fifteen feet below the barge. Just about
. . . die-reckly underneath your . . . launchin' davit."

"Excellent," Posey said. "With any luck, they
didn't notice it auto-disconnect from its tether and sink
out of sight." He squinted hard at the little LED screen
of the remote. "Good thing I'm more nearsighted than
farsighted. I can just make out the readings here."

"Ah'm dee-lighted . . . to hear that," Earl panted.

Posey glanced at him. "I won't be able to see where it is as we swim to it. Do you think you can get me there and hold me onto it as I engage the main drive?"

"Ah'll sure try."

"Good. I've preset the vehicle's internal compass for a course dead south. Hopefully they won't be looking in that direction. We'll hold our breath for as long as we can before I bring the unit to the surface. Then we'll repeat the procedure until we're far enough away from these people that we can turn toward the island."

"Sounds good," Earl said. "Let's do it."

Together, they hyperventilated in the thick air three or four times, then ducked under the water and pushed off the bottom of the barge. Posey stroked blindly, seeing only a soft blue haze and the blurry form of the man just ahead of him, but Earl could make out the torpedo-shaped silhouette of the ROV hovering some forty feet away.

By the time they reached it, their lungs were already aching from lack of oxygen. Straddling the unit with Earl close behind and holding him aboard, Posey hit the drive button on the remote. Immediately, the ROV began to move forward, slowly at first, then picking up speed until the slipstream threatened to peel them off the slick black hull. The shadow of the barge disappeared as they cruised out from under it and into the sunlit open water.

Manipulating the remote's buttons with his thumb, holding on like a limpet, Posey took a knot or two off the vehicle's speed. Desperate for air, he angled it up toward the surface. *Just don't be looking south, you bastards,* he prayed. *Just don't be looking south.*

*****

"Wait a minute, Luis." Alberto looked over at Sass as the fifth bodyguard—the only one to escape death or injury aboard the barge—halted in the act of escorting her down the deck toward the Boston Whaler. "We're forgetting something. Isn't there a man in the outer lock of this big chamber?" He pointed at the sat pot. "McCluskey said a diver had been injured and was being taken out of saturation."

Sass's heart sank. She'd hoped that Chris Toricelli would remain forgotten in the confusion. Before fleeing the sat shack through the sliding window, she'd ripped away the radio wires that could have enabled him to attract attention to himself by speaking, then opened the bleed valve on the lock to achieve the maximum safe depressurization rate. There was a chance, she'd thought, that the hatch would pop when no one was around, and Chris would be able to suss out the situation and call for help: the Coast Guard, the US forces at Guantanamo Bay—anyone.

No such luck, apparently. Sass barely managed to conceal her bitter disappointment. He must have seen what was going on through the port of the outer lock when he couldn't get anyone to talk to him, figured out what was happening, and had the sense to lie back quietly on his bunk while the lock continued to bleed up toward the surface. If only Alberto hadn't remembered .

. .

Alberto strode past Carlos—whose skull was still bleeding from the love-tap Sass had given him with the crowbar—as he struggled to drag Javier's body over to the Whaler. Miguel—the *basouko* affecionado who'd barely survived his encounter with Earl's pile-driver of a fist, was attempting to help him. With one hand clapped to his swollen and probably broken jaw, his heart was clearly not in his work.

Alberto jumped up on the framework of the sat pot's support skid, shielded his eyes, and peered into the porthole of the outer lock. "Aha," he announced. "There is indeed a gentleman inside. He does not appear to be all that impressed with my appearance. He's just lying there looking up at me. Goodness gracious"—he paused to lick his lips—"this is a rather handsome young muffin, to say the least."

"Let me see," Grizelda growled, stepping up on the skid and shouldering her brother aside. She stared through the thick Lexan, squinting to see into the lock's dim interior. "Mmmmm."

Alberto jumped off the skid onto the deck, looking petulant. "She's so *pushy*," he said to Sass, who was standing nearby with Luis's hand clamped around her upper arm. "Always has to be first in everything."

Grizelda turned and leered, showing her teeth. "I like him," she said.

"Well, so do I," Alberto told her. "We'll just have to share this time."

The musclebound woman gave him her basilisk stare and stepped down off the skid. "You," she grunted at Sass. "How quickly can you get him out of there undamaged?"

"Twenty-five days," Sass lied. "Saturation divers are decompressed on a specific schedule. Exceed it and they die. They can only be bled to the surface at three feet per hour, and for only sixteen hours out of every twenty-four."

"What?" Alberto exclaimed, annoyed. "That's— ummm—let me see . . . er . . ."

"Three feet times sixteen hours equals forty-eight feet per day. They've been pressurized to nearly twelve hundred. Twelve hundred divided by forty-eight gives you the number of days it'll take: twenty-five." Sass paused for a moment, letting it sink in. "There's a US Navy dive manual in the sat shack. Go look it up if you don't believe me."

Just don't look hard enough to find out where I'm exaggerating, she thought. And especially, don't look in the updated decompression schedules we're using— the ones that use shifting gas percentages in the breathing mixes to get a guy out of a thousand-foot sat in seventy-two hours or less.

"Hmm," Alberto mused. "Hmm. This calls for a change of plan, don't you think, big sister?"

Grizelda stopped running her eyes up and down Sass and snapped them over onto her sibling. "Yes. This barge can't stay anchored out here for the next month. It and its crew will be missed."

"We could always just sink it," Alberto suggested mildly, "like we intended. And just forget about the diver in the outer lock. Call the whole thing a tragic accident, if it's ever discovered. A catastrophic loss caused by a sudden explosion. We saw it from the house, were helpless to do anything . . ."

"Who'd ask anyway?" Grizelda snarled. "The whole thing could disappear, like the diving bell, and who'd know whether it sank or just took off for Brazil?"

Sass's heart felt as if it was about to stop beating. She had to think of someth—

"Except that," Grizelda continued. "I really, *really* like the looks of that one in the outer lock. He would be worth waiting a few weeks for."

Alberto smiled rapturously at his older sister. "I agree. So this is what we'll do: we'll have Sligo use the *Cucaracha* to tow this barge into the lagoon. We'll moor it under the trees and cover it with palm fronds—in case any search-and-rescue air patrols fly over us. She"—he pointed at Sass—"will complete his decompression. And in the meantime, we'll attempt to convince her that being a cooperative houseguest and . . . becoming our very good . . . *friend* . . . is really in her best interest. If she doesn't, of course, we can always amuse ourselves by shooting out the window of that outer lock before the decompression is completed—and watching what happens to the young man inside."

Grizelda directed a lascivious grin at Sass. "I like that idea."

"I thought you might." Alberto said. He turned to Miguel and Carlos. "Get a couple of acetylene torches fired up and cut all four of those anchor cables. I'm going back aboard the yacht and have our worthy captain start the engines."

*****

The worthy captain had still not regained his breath after tumbling downward a total of one thousand one hundred and ninety-two feet, landing headfirst on the foredeck of the *Arista*—fifteen feet above natural bottom—and crashing through the rotten planking into the wreck's forepeak. The momentum of his plunge had carried him on down into the tiny compartment until he had become jammed, upside-down, between two unyielding wooden surfaces, like a bung in a beer keg. He tried to shriek, his legs kicking wildly above the broken deck, but his helium-shriveled vocal cords would not permit a truly robust caterwaul. What came out was Donald Duck squealing in falsetto.

A kaleidoscope of brilliant neon colors flashed and blinked before his eyes. Virtually the entire faceplate of his dive helmet had become littered with technical data and safety warnings, to the extent that he could hardly see his hand in front of his face. It was like some horrible acid flashback—a swarm of hyper-real poly-chromatic locusts coming to eat his brain.

"Beep," the DOA-9000 said, doing its high-tech best for him. "Beep."

Struggling to free himself, vibrating like a live fish clamped between two cutting boards, Sligo managed to extract his left arm and reach upward. His gloved hand landed on something flat and hard—the horizontal surface of whatever was pressing against his chest and stomach. He heaved back, trying to pull himself out the way he had come in—and his hand punched through the surface as if it was made of thin cork. It didn't penetrate far, however, before his knuckles drove into something that felt like coarse gravel.

Gasping and straining, Sligo backed himself out of the crevice into which he was wedged and glanced around, trying to get his bearings. His hat light bounced over dark, splintered wood, yellow-and-red marine encrustations, sea fans, sea worms, sediment particles, more splintered wood, a crawling bone-white crab the size of his palm, black water, more sediment particles, more black water . . .

His foot was caught. Panicking, he looked down, trying to yank it free, and his light illuminated the lid of the big wooden barrel through which he'd shoved his hand.

From under the broken, waterlogged panel, and all around his shiny black Kronos Industries glove, there came a luminous, warm, silvery-yellow glow.

Sligo stopped breathing and stared down. Slowly, he pushed the remnants of the broken lid away. Even through the cluster of multi-colored lights on his faceplate there was no mistaking the barrel's contents.

It was full to the brim with gold chain.

In that instant, everything else was forgotten. The overwhelming darkness, the penetrating cold, the terrifying depth, the alien surroundings, the aching in his joints, the choking heaviness of the gas he was breathing—gone. All that existed in Sligo's world, for the better part of fifteen seconds, was a gleaming, gorgeous, marvelous, magical, *stupefying* pile of G-O-L-D.

YEAH, baby!

A shiver passed through his body and he was suddenly aware again of his immediate situation. Holy Jesus. It was absolutely *freezing* down here, and as black as the inside of a cow. But here was the payoff. The swag. The brass ring. The literal pot of gold at the end of the fucking rainbow! And all he had to do was get it to the surface.

Snuffling up a cokey post-nasal drip, he swallowed and squinted past the neon squiggles on his faceplate, assessing the barrel's size. It was a little smaller than a fifty-five gallon oil drum. Good thing he'd brought an extra-large lift bag with him.

In actuality, the bag had arrived on bottom with him by accident. It had been the first thing he'd let go of after realizing that he couldn't control his buoyancy, but its straps had somehow gotten wrapped around his lower legs, upended him, and kept him in that inverted orientation all the way down to the foredeck of the *Arista*—as if he'd had a drogue chute attached to his ankles.

Well, he was glad of it now, if not then. Working quickly, he finished disentangling the lift bag straps from his legs and began to cinch them around the barrel. The pesky little neon characters in the heads-up display flickered and changed at a furious pace, but Sligo, intent on his task, barely noticed them.

"Beep," the DOA-9000 said, chagrined at being ignored. "Beep."

Sligo's coke/greed/depth-addled mind was racing in high gear—his ownself talking to his ownself. Get the straps on good! Get 'em on tight! Get the bag pushed through the hole and spread out on deck! Get the damn thing inflated with the CO_2 cartridge! Get the load rising free and clear! And don't forget to hang on so you   can . . .

Get the fuck out outta Dodge!

He hadn't noticed it at first, but it was *really* goddamn scary down here. Black and lonely and freezing and weird and creepy—nothing like the warm tropical shallows he was accustomed to frolicking in. Suddenly, that twelve hundred feet to the surface—the same distance a fast Jamaican in track shoes could run in forty seconds—seemed longer than a trip to the next galaxy. His mind squirmed on the verge of a full-blown attack of claustrophobia.

Keep it together, Sligo! Keep it together! You're nearly outta here with the swag!

He locked his right hand around one of the lift bag's straps and hit the valve of the CO_2 cylinder with his left. There was a hollow *whoosh*, the small cylinder jumped, and the heavy open-bottomed bag began to inflate. It rose from the rotting deck of the *Arista* like a collapsed ghost coming back to life.

Yeah, baby! *YEAH, baby!*

Abruptly, the bag went vertical, swinging up on its straps. Sligo, sitting on the edge of the hole, felt the barrel of gold shift under his feet. The cylinder whooshed on.

And then . . . the lift bag began to move upward. Powerfully. Inexorably. The barrel rose with it—and with the barrel came Sligo, his feet planted in gold, clinging with both hands now to the canvas straps. There was a cracking sound as the barrel caught on the edge of the hole, then broke through the rotten wood of the foredeck and ascended into open water.

Sligo was beside himself with glee. As the open CO_2 cylinder continued to dump its contents into the lift bag, he went into a nearly auto-erotic state of self-congratulation. It lasted all of thirty seconds, when he realized that the entire assembly was now moving *much* too fast. CO_2 gas was billowing out the bottom of the bag as the cylinder emptied, and it was becoming difficult to hold on in the slipstream.

What the fu—

413

The strap he was hugging with all his strength tore away. As he fell back from the skyrocketing lift bag, which was spewing excess gas like a Gemini booster, he nearly broke both ankles on the rim of the barrel. Only the stiffness of the top-quality Kronos Industries dive boots saved him. The last thing he saw in the glare of his hat light, as he tumbled back down into the abyss, was the bag-and-barrel rig spiraling up into the darkness in the opposite direction, burping clouds of gas, getting smaller and smaller . . .

And then it was gone.

"AAAAAAAAAAAAAAAAAAGGHH!" Sligo declared, thrashing as he sank.

"Beep," the DOA-9000 replied, ever cheerful. "Beep."

Chapter Twenty-Seven

Alberto was beside himself with rage. *"Where is that asshole Sligo?"* he screamed down at the two bodyguards on the foredeck of the *Cucaracha*. Miguel and Carlos looked up toward the flybridge and shrugged, trying to look blameless as well as clueless. *"God-DAMN it, that unreliable degenerate pisses me off!"* He spent the next twenty seconds pounding both fists on the steering console, like a child in the throes of a temper tantrum.

"He may have been caught in the explosion, too, *Jefe*," Miguel said, speaking carefully so as not to exercise his injured jaw. "I saw him near the stern of the yacht as we were chasing the big American. The blast could have reached him; there are burn marks on the transom."

Gradually, Alberto calmed down. "Fine. Fine then. *Fuck* him! He's never around when I need him, so *fuck* him anyway! Are those anchor cables cut?"

"Yes, *Jefe.*"

"Then I'll pilot the yacht and barge in. Make sure those lines holding them together are tight. And add on a few more, too."

He turned the ignition keys and the *Cucaracha*'s twin diesels roared into life. Blue smoke filled the air above the transom. Alberto let the engines warm up for less than a minute before slipping them into gear and hitting the throttles. The mooring lines stretched and creaked, white foam churned out from beneath the yacht's stern, and very slowly the barge began to move forward. As it gained speed it turned toward the island, leaving a broad, bubbling wake on the azure-blue water behind it.

Alberto looked back toward the dive site as Grizelda joined him on the flybridge. She was in her usual state of cold, self-involved distraction, her empty eyes scanning the island and the horizon beyond. Alberto pursed his lips and spat.

"What a waste of time and money." He gazed resentfully at his sister. "And all these complications. Don't you think you've put enough energy into tracing our ancestor's gold? And that business of the bloodlines: does it really matter if the descendants of the man who killed him are living on the next island? I mean, what's the difference? They're nothing but a collection of uneducated peasants who smell like fish."

"Finding them makes a difference to me," Grizelda said, staring across the strait.

Alberto rolled his eyes. "Well, genealogy is interesting, I suppose. But you take everything to such extremes. How about that dithering egghead Fuentes? How much did it cost you to have him run those DNA tests on the bodies you found in the old chapel? And do the comparisons on you and me and the people from the village? That was pretty clever, by the way, getting DNA samples by giving them free medicine and taking cheek swabs." He chuckled. "They actually thought they were being immunized against smallpox, the fools. I wonder if bulk cough syrup actually has any medicinal properties."

"Who cares?" Grizelda said. "And by the way, Fuentes decided to give me a discount, in the end. He waived his fee."

Alberto smiled at her. "I won't even ask," he said. "But, knowing you, I'm sure it was creative."

She grinned at the horizon. "It was . . . satisfying."

The barge and yacht had a tendency to wander off course to starboard. Alberto cut back the rpm on the port engine and tweaked the wheel slightly to compensate. The petulant expression returned to his face. "You have to admit," he muttered, "it is disappointing about the wreck. Personally, I never thought it would really amount to anything, but you insisted . . ."

Grizelda rotated her head and stared at him, on the verge of one of her lethal mood changes. "That's right, little brother. I *did.*"

"Well, it was worth investigating, anyway," Alberto said hastily. He turned and looked over his shoulder at the far end of the barge's long, curving wake. "I'm only saying that all this expense would have been justified if there'd been something of real value down there." He pursed his lips and turned back to the wheel. "One miserable gold nail. Treasure ship, my ass. More like a worthless pile of old junk."

As he looked away, the dive site's calm surface—now more than four hundred yards astern—was suddenly disrupted by an explosion of white water, a bulge of yellow fabric, and a furious boiling of gas. Alberto and Grizelda continued to gaze toward their island, oblivious to the commotion behind them.

Sligo's extra-large lift bag wobbled on the surface for a few seconds like a giant yellow thumb. Then, as another support strap slipped off the barrel below, it laid itself over, gently, on the calm blue surface of the sea and burped out its remaining CO_2.

Two seconds later, the barrel of golden chain was hurtling back down toward the wreck of the *Arista*, much faster than it had come up, the deflated lift bag flapping behind it.

*****

Sligo had landed on his back in the mud after tumbling nearly one hundred and twenty feet, which was as far up as the lift bag had carried him before he'd lost his grip. That his ascent had been so limited was fortuitous: he had not risen high enough in the water column to experience decompression problems. Despite this backhanded stroke of luck, he was not feeling particularly fortunate. He was, in fact, in a state of blind, blubbering, semi-deranged panic.

He clawed his way to his feet, literally weeping with fear and self-pity at the injustice of it all. The faceplate of his dive helmet, in addition to being decorated with colorful neon squiggles, was almost completely fogged over with condensation. The cold was extreme, penetrating even the Ultra High Efficiency ThermaLint™ lining of the Kronos Industries Deepwater Exposure Suit—not to mention the sub-liner of identical material that Sligo wore like longjohn underwear. Though the DOA-9000 recirculated the trimix gas he was breathing, retaining his body heat, and even added a certain amount of warmth to the loop as a by-product of the chemical reaction in the unit's internal CO_2-scrubbing soda canister, it was not enough to counteract, over time, the pervasive chill of the deep ocean. He was less than ten minutes away—among his other pressing difficulties—from going fatally hypothermic.

He spent a frantic forty-five seconds madly punching and re-punching every button on the rebreather's chest console, triggering a flurry of kaleidoscopic activity on the heads-up display, but accomplishing little in the way of positive buoyancy. His fingers going numb, he tried to rub away the condensation that was obscuring the faceplate, but of course it was on the inside.

For want of anything better to do, he began to run, floundering along with arms akimbo, taking one sucking, mud-encumbered step after the other. It was like trying to sprint through molasses. Though he had no way of knowing it, he was less than ten feet from the crest of the sediment bank traversed by Ben, Chris, Pierre, and Vern during their sorties from the bell to the *Arista*. His rediscovery of the wreck occurred when he cracked his shin against a half-buried ship's timber, fell on his face, and looked up through his fogged, neon-speckled faceplate to see his hat light playing over a wall of encrusted wooden hull strakes.

It was almost like meeting an old friend. Staggering to his feet, he stared wild-eyed up at the wreck, started forward, then felt a strange rush of water against the backs of his legs. He stopped. Turned.

His High-Output Kronos Industries Dive Light illuminated a mottled expanse of gray-green skin. Illuminated a four-foot-wide mouth with broad, scowling, Edward G. Robinson lips. Illuminated a pair of forward-staring, protruding eyes the size of small bowling balls. Illuminated a set of pulsating gills an eight-year-old boy could have climbed through. Illuminated two huge, sculling pectoral fins that were each the size of an unfolded New York Times, Sunday edition.

Before Sligo could open his mouth to scream yet again, the giant jewfish—all thirteen feet and two thousand eight hundred pounds of it—opened *its* mouth, flexed its gills, and inhaled his right leg up to the groin.

"AAAAAAAAAAAAGGGHH!" Sligo commented.

Having issued his by-now-standard response to unexpected downturns of fortune, he proceeded to beat frantically on the forehead of the giant fish. It reacted to this by swiveling its bulging eyes in apparent annoyance and swimming slowly off with him, as if clearing its home area of trash.

"AAAAAAAAAAAAAGGGHHH!" Sligo repeated, in case the fish hadn't heard him.

He was being partly dragged, partly carried over the bottom. *Bump.* The back of his helmet hit something hard. *Bump. Bump.* Flailing like a captured insect, he twisted around and caught a glimpse of several large chunks of wood sticking out of the sediment. *Bump.* He hit another one. The jewfish was dragging him around the periphery of the wreck.

His leg didn't hurt at all. Having no teeth, only a sandpapery mouth lining like that of a bass, the jewfish did not bite into or chew whatever it inhaled. It simply swallowed the item whole. Alternatively—as in Sligo's case—it often clamped down hard on a trespasser in order to make a point about territoriality.

The jewfish dragged Sligo leisurely through a pile of broken planking—*bang, crunch, scrape*—the discomfort of which prompted him to writhe and flail with increased energy. Lashing his arms around, he inadvertently smacked the huge animal in the left eye with one hand. Abruptly, the jewfish braked, spreading its paddle-like pectoral fins. Then it convulsed, flaring its gills, and spat Sligo out like a hundred-and-sixty-pound loogie.

The force of the ejection plastered the smuggler against the bow of the *Arista*, knocking the wind out of him and seriously irritating the electronic brain of the DOA-9000. The polychromatic locusts of the heads-up display swarmed anew before his dazed eyes as he fought for breath.

"Beep," the DOA-9000 said in protest. "Beep."

Sligo sagged forward into the cold mud on his hands and knees. Then he looked up. Less than four feet away, the giant jewfish was sculling just above the bottom, examining him, its glassy, globular pop-eyes swiveling independently. Despite his ongoing panic, the pouting lips and jowly cheeks and gills reminded Sligo of someone.

"Winston Churchill," he croaked aloud into his oral-nasal mask. "I'm being gummed to death by fuckin' Winston Churchill."

The jewfish flared its gills, gaped its enormous maw, and inhaled him head first—helmet, shoulders, and upper arms. Sligo's world instantly became dark—except for the attractive neon colors of the heads-up display—and a ring of squeezing pressure clamped around his shoulders and biceps. It was not unlike being jammed forcibly into an old car tire.

Fortunately, his breath had returned. *"AAAAAAAAAAAGGGHHH!"* was the only remark that seemed appropriate, as the great fish flexed its maxillary musculature around his upper body.

He could feel his legs and feet dragging along the bottom as, once again, the jewfish began to swim.

*****

The diving bell had been resting on the seabed with its clump weight buried in the mud, all lights off to conserve battery power, for nearly fifteen minutes. Ben, Pierre, and Vern had been taking turns inspecting the various life support systems and gas reserves, sitting quietly around the trunk hatch and passing a pressure-proof flashlight back and forth. Their breath came out in streams of condensed vapor; without the umbilical to

423

supply hot water to the radiant heaters, it was getting very cold.

"Okay," Ben said, shielding the flashlight with his fingers, "I figure we've got plenty of helium and nitrogen, and at least three days of metabolic oxygen. Plus four cylinders of that special mix that's supposed to decompress us faster than normal. Pierre?"

"Zut alors," the little Frenchman said. "The CO_2 buildup will become a problem, *mes amis*. We have only two cylinders of absorbent soda left, in addition to the one we are using now. With three of us . . ." He shook his head. "Maybe fifty hours."

Ben nodded slowly. "Vern?"

"No damage to the bell, 'far as Ah can see," Vern drawled. "Leastways, not in here. Plumbin' is all good, gauges is workin'. An' we got maybe four days of battery juice left." A thin smile spread over his face in the soft glow of the flashlight. "We might could even turn on a low-voltage light in here, now an' then."

"Mon dieu," Pierre said, "we are sitting on the bottom of the Caribbean Sea under twelve hundred feet of water, marooned in saturation and left to our own devices. I suggest strongly that we do not waste anything."

"Who said anything 'bout wastin' anything, froggy?"

"You did, you stegosaurus, you."

"Well, Ah know one way we could save a third of the oxee-gen, a third of the scrubber capacity, and take up a third—'scuse me, maybe a *fifth*—less space in here: pitch your French pygmy ass out through the trunk *right now.*"

Pierre snorted. "The same principle would apply ten-fold to you, you Quasimodo, you. Do not make it necessary for me to chastise you physically again. And by the way, you owe me—"

"Yeah, Ah know, Ah know," Vern groaned.

"—Twenty doll*air*," Pierre finished.

Ben ignored the exchange. Any kind of stress-relief right now was a good thing, and people in a tight spot who retained the capacity for banter were a long way from panicking. He got up carefully, leaned back against the scrubber, and glanced down at his two companions. They were good men, both of them. Cool and aware under pressure—literally as well as figuratively.

There were far worse people to be stuck with in a sunken diving bell.

He looked out the tiny porthole and cleared his throat. "I'm going to switch on the external floods for a minute," he said. "See if we're near the wreck. Maybe I'll even spot Gerald's ROV flying around us. Bringing us a backup cable."

425

Vern looked up at him in the dim glow of the flash-light. "Ah wouldn't hold mah breath," he muttered. "Some sumbitch swam down and unhooked us from our lift cable—let us sink on purpose. Less'n Gene's done got control of the situation up there again, Ah wouldn't count on help arrivin' any time soon."

"Mm." Ben blew out a long breath. He was right, of course. "Well, let me take a look out here, anyway." He hit the switch. Instantly, the powerful outer lamps came on, illuminating the sea floor for thirty feet around the bell. "I don't see the wreck," he mused, "but we must be close. There are a few chunks of timber sticking out of the mud right here."

"Try the other side," Pierre suggested.

"Right." Ben rose, stepped across the trunk hatch, and peered out the opposite port.

"Holy shit," he said. He blinked, rubbed his eyes, and stared out through the Lexan again. "I must be seeing things."

Pierre and Vern glanced up. "What gives?" the big man asked.

"There's a jewfish the size of a Volkswagen mini-bus swimming around the bell," he said. "And some guy's legs and feet are sticking out of its mouth."

*****

426

"Beepbeepbeepbeep," the DOA-9000 said insistently, trying its best to let Sligo know that at least half a dozen things were going seriously wrong with its electronic innards. Multicolored neon warning squiggles reproduced themselves like cancer cells all over his blacked-out faceplate. "Beepbeepbeepbeepbeepbeep-beepbeepbeepbeepbeepbeep . . ."

"AAAAAAAAAAAAAAAAGGGGHHHH!" the smuggler declared, for the twenty-seventh time since the giant jewfish had inhaled the upper third of his body. He felt the great lips and mouth plates gum him yet again, like an overworked piece of Juicy Fruit.

He raked his hands desperately along the animal's knubbly-slick cheeks, trying to gouge its eyes, but simply couldn't reach. His feet kicked and flailed in open water, kicked into the mud bottom, kicked something hard that hurt his toe . . .

*****

"Ah don't gawd-damned well believe it!" Vern exclaimed, flinching back out of reflex as the partially-consumed diver in the slick yellow-and-black suit kicked the toe of his boot into the Lexan port. The jewfish was that close now, apparently attracted by the bell's floodlights. "Where the hail'd he come from?"

All three of them were crowded around the tiny opening, heads jammed together, trying to see.

"That guy's still alive," Ben said.

"Bet he ain't happy, hoss."

"Tabarnac! He must have been sent to rescue us, *n'est-ce pas?* What else would he be doing down here, eh?"

Ben shook his head in bewilderment as the jewfish made another casual, unhurried circle within range of the lights, turned on a dime with the ponderous delicacy of a docking zeppelin, and hovered in place about ten feet away, its pectoral fins fanning the bottom. Its glassy, bulbous eyes stared straight ahead at the bell. The shiny yellow-and-black legs protruding from between its rubbery lips continued to kick feebly, resembling a pair of half-eaten dinner noodles.

"Ah think he's lookin' at us," Vern muttered.

"I do not think so, *mon ami.*"

"You blind, froggy? Lookit him, dang it. He's starin' right at us in here."

"Wherever he's looking," Ben said, "that guy in the yellow suit is in a bad way. Give me a hand getting dressed in. I'm going out to try to help him."

"What? What you think you're gonna do for him?" Vern demanded, watching the kicking legs.

"I don't know," Ben said, still at the port, "but I'm not just going to sit here and—"

Without warning, in front of their eyes, an object hurtled down out of the darkness above the giant jewfish and clobbered it on top of the head. There was an explosion of rotten wood, followed immediately by a cascade of silver-yellow chain that fell over the animal's eyes in a glittering metallic curtain.

The jewfish's entire enormous body shook, its gills flared, and in one massive convulsion it vomited out the yellow-and-black-clad diver like a cat hacking up a particularly nasty hairball. The hapless human sank into the mud in a heap, stirring feebly, and the jewfish took off into the surrounding darkness with frenzied sweeps of its immense tail, shedding the bright yellow chain as it went.

"Mon dieu, this is bizarre," Pierre whispered. "Like a Fellini movie."

Ben leaned back from the port and stooped down to grab one of the hot-water suits. "Come on, help me," he said urgently. "I'm going out to get the guy before that damn jewfish comes back."

Chapter Twenty-Eight

It took Ben only two minutes to climb into the hot-water suit, cam his dive hat on, and drop through the access trunk. Without any hot water circulation the cold was biting, but the suit provided a certain amount of insulation and he wasn't planning on being outside the bell for very long. The clump weight had sunk so far into the bottom that the end of the trunk was only six inches above the mud line, and to get all the way out, he was forced to burrow sideways like a gopher.

Emerging beside the bell, he yanked out an additional twenty feet of dive hose, got his bearings, and began to plod across the floodlit seabed toward the recently-regurgitated diver. The individual in the snappy yellow-and-black suit was lying splayed on the mud, his arms and legs sticking out from beneath a large lift bag—also yellow—that had settled over him like a shroud. Ben noted the bag's straps, the shattered barrel, the pile of gleaming golden chain, and concluded that what he and his companions had just witnessed was the result of a lifting operation gone awry. A poorly planned lifting operation.

Upon reaching the diver, he peeled the flaccid bag off him and seized the top handle of his dive helmet. Glancing around for any sign of the bad-tempered jewfish, he began to haul him back toward the bell like a sack of potatoes, his body leaving a long, smooth skid mark in the pale gray mud of the bottom. The individual was wearing some kind of Star Wars unit on his back, which—in the absence of a dive umbilical—was obviously his primary life support system and not just a glorified bailout bottle. Ben assumed that it was a rebreather. What the hell the guy was doing at a depth of twelve hundred feet, all alone, in one of those twitchy experimental rigs, was anyone's guess.

The yellow-suited diver was barely conscious, so after clearing away more mud Ben had to stuff him up into the access trunk like an overdressed mannequin. By the time Vern and Pierre got hold of the newcomer and hoisted him up into the bell, he was panting with effort and chilled to the bone. He squeezed up past the dangling yellow-and-black legs, popped the cam on his dive hat, and handed it to Pierre.

"I need to get out," Ben said, his teeth chattering. "I know it's too damn crowded, but I need to warm up."

"Come on, pardner," Vern replied, and lifted him physically out of the water by the straps of his shoulder harness. "Gotta git you outta that there suit and into somethin' halfway dry." He deposited Ben in a tiny sliver of space next to one of the useless radiant heaters.

Pierre located the cam locks on the limp diver's neck dam, popped them, and pulled the helmet off his head. The man looked like death warmed over, his narrow face sickly pale, his dirty-blonde hair plastered over his balding forehead. Eyelids fluttering, he tossed his head weakly from side to side and mumbled through bluish lips: *"Winston Churchill . . . Winston Churchill . . ."*

"What the hail's he sayin'?" Vern asked.

"Sounds like 'Winston Churchill' to me," Ben said.

"That's what Ah thought." The big man shook his head. "Never mind."

The newcomer was coughing now, his bloodshot blue eyes fully open and darting wildly around the bell's cramped interior. He began to thrash, forcing Pierre and Vern to seize an arm each.

"WINSTON FUCKIN' CHURCHILL!" the man shrieked, arching up.

Then his eyes rolled over white in their sockets, his body shook uncontrollably, and he collapsed back against the side of the bell with a long bubbling moan.

*****

The *Cucaracha* and the rafted barge were just gliding through the narrow channel that led into the Ramoses' boat-dock lagoon when Sass, taking decompression notes and switching out gauges at the side of the sat pot's outer lock, sensed a presence behind her. She spun to find Grizelda hovering over her left shoulder, smiling hungrily. Pulling back in alarm, she faced the chamber again and continued to enter figures on her clipboard.

Grizelda grinned and moved closer. "What are you doing?" she inquired softly.

Sass cleared her throat. "Recording pressures and checking the calibration of these gauges."

"You took the big one off and replaced it," the musclebound woman said. "What for?"

Sass turned and looked at her. "Because it was out of *calibration*," she replied, keeping her voice level. "I replaced it with a gauge that was accurate. When they're in use, particularly outdoors on the side of the sat pot, they're subject to heat from the sun and a lot of vibration from the on-deck engines. They tend to become inaccurate after a while, and it's essential that I know exactly how much pressure the man inside here is under at any given time during the decompression."

"Mmm." Grizelda eyed the gauge. "So he's at the equivalent of one thousand feet right now?"

"That's right."

"He still has a long way to go. A long time to be locked up. Like you said—a couple of weeks."

"Uh-huh."

Grizelda rolled her shoulder muscles like a boxer. "What's his name?"

433

Sass hesitated. "Chris."

"Chris." The big woman rotated her head, stretching her neck. "I like that name."

Sass said nothing. Turning again, she began to examine her clipboard.

There was a cheap hardback aluminum chair next to the chamber skid. Its legs scraped across the deckplates as Grizelda reversed it and sat down, straddling it like a man with her legs apart and her forearms propped on the vinyl-covered back.

"Something bothers me about you," she said.

Sass looked at her briefly. "Sorry."

Grizelda's stone-cold eyes were fixed unwaveringly on hers. "One of the men that we sank in the diving bell . . . he was your husband, wasn't he?"

"We're not married," Sass said.

"Don't split hairs with me. The one named Gannon—you and he have been together for a long time: yes or no?"

Sass nodded. "Yes."

Grizelda stared at her for a few seconds. "What bothers me is that we just left your husband to die at the bottom of the sea, but you don't seem particularly upset about it."

Sass's face was a hard blank. "What do you want me to do? Roll around on the deck sobbing? Would that change anything?" She forced the corners of her mouth to lift. "Maybe I was a little tired of him, anyway. Besides, keep yourself looking halfway sexy and men are just like houseflies—there are always a few of them buzzing around."

"Mm." Grizelda didn't smile, but her obsidian eyes softened imperceptibly. "Always." She paused. "How long can they survive down there without—what's it called?—surface support?"

Sass looked out through the lagoon entrance as Alberto maneuvered the yacht and barge up alongside the palm-fringed shore. "Is it more than half an hour since we left the dive site?"

Grizelda glanced at her watch. "At least. Maybe forty-five minutes."

Sass resumed making notes on her clipboard. "Then they're already dead," she said.

There was a scraping sound as the musclebound woman rose to her feet, pushing the chair away. She came in close, her breath hot on Sass's neck.

"One thing's for certain," she whispered. "Even if you're lying, there isn't anyone around to lower a cable and lift them back to the surface. So if they're not dead now, they will be soon." She laughed, an unpleasant, snarling sound. "Which is what anyone stupid enough to climb inside a hollow steel cannonball that gets dangled by a thread in deepwater deserves."

*****

Ben pulled the heavy sleeveless sweatshirt over his head and down around his torso. "Brr. That feels better." He shifted his feet carefully in the close confines of the darkened bell. They'd elected to turn off all lights, including the small flashlight, and work as much as possible by feel—something that, as commercial divers, they were accustomed to doing anyway. In addition, foregoing the ability to see removed the visual reminder that they were now four men crammed into a tiny space intended for two. It was tight; they were shoulder to shoulder, seated in a circle around the trunk hatch.

The only sounds were the gentle hum of the scrubber's electrical fan and the *drip* . . . *drip* . . . *drip* of condensation falling from the bell's roof to the floor grating. The darkness was total—almost peaceful. The three divers used it and the accompanying silence to compose themselves once again—to relax, clear their minds, and prepare for what lay ahead.

"No one is coming to get us," Pierre said finally.

"Doesn't look like it," Ben replied.

"Naw," Vern concurred.

Ben shifted his legs again, brushing those of the other men in the darkness. "Sorry, boys. Well, then—"

"Ohhhhhohhhohhhhhh," the mystery diver groaned, sandwiched between Pierre and Vern. *"Gy-yaaaa-eeeuughghhghh."*

"Dang, he's comin' around," Vern said. "How 'bout a little light, there, Pee-yair?"

The Frenchman switched on the flashlight and wedged it in behind a padeye, directing the beam straight up so that its illumination spread throughout the bell. The mystery diver, now out of the yellow suit and Star Wars backpack—they were hanging on equipment hooks over his head—tossed beneath the rough Army blanket Vern had tucked around him, moaning. His fancy red long john underwear was damp with sweat.

Ben leaned across the hatch and put a hand on the man's shoulder. "Hey. Hey, buddy. Take it easy. Just wake up slow. You're all right now."

The man's blue eyes fluttered open, goggled around at the bell's interior and the three divers hovering over him, and settled on Ben. "W-w-where am I?" he croaked.

"In a diving bell," Ben told him. "Safe, for the moment."

The man looked as if he was about to dissolve into tears. "I-I had a dream," he whispered. "I was Jonah—the dude from the Bible, ya know? And I got eaten, just like him. But not by a whale." He paused, blanching.

"By a big-ass fish that looked like a dead British politician."

Ben, Pierre, and Vern smiled at each other. "What's your name?" Ben asked.

"Jeremiah Sligo. Just Sligo."

"I'm Ben. This is Pierre and Vern."

"Yeah? Hiya." Sligo gazed around, still disoriented. "Where the hell are we? Shit, it's small in here! I-I-I . . . I wanna get out!"

"Whoa," Ben said, putting out his hand as Sligo tried to sit up. Beside him, Pierre and Vern laid hold of his upper arms. "Take it easy."

Sligo's eyes began to dart around very quickly, his panic increasing. "I wanna get out! When do we get out?"

"You need to calm down," Ben said. "We're stuck on bottom in this bell. Someone up top cut us loose on purpose. Sank us." Immediately, he wished he hadn't said anything.

"WHAT?" Sligo shrieked. He began to thrash in earnest. *"WHAAAAAT?"*

Vern swore as the struggling man knocked his elbow back into the side of the bell. When Sligo began to foam at the mouth and scream in full voice, he closed his hand as if preparing to knock on a door, seized him by the hair, bent his head over, and rapped him once behind the ear with his knuckles. The distraught smuggler went out like a light, keeling over onto Pierre's lap.

"Thank you," Ben said, sitting back.

"Don't mention it," Vern growled. "Little trick Ah learned when Ah was bouncin' at a bar in the French Quarter a few years back, durin' the oil slump."

"Is it myself, only?" Pierre remarked, looking down at the longhaired man drooling on his sweatpants. "Or have we perhaps rescued an unconscionable—how do you say it?—*asshole.*"

"Well, he isn't exactly at his best," Ben said charitably. "Let's let him sleep awhile. Give him another chance when he wakes up."

He cracked his knuckles. "In the meantime, let's work on getting out of here."

"Line it out, chief," Vern said.

"Okay. First of all, we took the cable winch off the bottom of the bell so we'd have room for all that extra deep-diving backup gas. Good thing we did, too, 'cause we're gonna need it, with four of us sucking oxygen in here. But that means we don't have any teth—"

"Ohhhohhohhhgghh," Sligo moaned, coming around. He put a hand behind his ear and struggled out of Pierre's lap.

"A miscalculation, *mon ami*," the Frenchman said to Vern, pushing the smuggler back against the wall of the bell with a look of disgust. "You appear not to have clonked this one hard enough."

"Sorry, froggy," Vern said. "Ah'll do better next time."

"Oh god," Sligo whimpered, staring around again. "Oh god. Oh fuck me . . ."

"Relax," Ben told him, without sympathy this time. "And keep still." He looked at Pierre and Vern. "As I was saying, we don't have a tether, but we don't want to be unanchored, so—"

"Oh god," Sligo burst out, terrorized. "We're gonna die down here! Oh Jesus. Oh fuck me . . . oh fuck me . . ."

"Hey," Ben said. "Will you shut up? Nobody's going to die."

"Unless you force my large friend to kill you for being annoying," Pierre added.

"All we need," Ben said, "is something we can use as a cable. Something to—"

"But we're stuck inside a ton of fuckin' steel on the bottom of the sea!" Sligo wailed. "How you gonna get a cable up to the surface to lift us, you jerkoff? Can't you *think* straight? Can't you see it won't work? Oh god, I'm trapped under a thousand fuckin' feet of water with a bunch of jerkoffs . . ."

Ben leaned forward and looked the trembling man in the eyes. "Before I let Vern put you back to sleep," he said, "there's something I need to tell you that you obviously don't know."

"What? Oh fuck me. *Whaaat?*"

"Just this," Ben continued. "A diving bell like this one might be made of a couple of tons of solid steel, but cut loose the clump weight . . ."

"Yeah? Yeah?"

". . . And it *floats.*"

Chapter Twenty-Nine

When Sligo woke up again he was mashed over on his right side with the blanket covering him from head to toe, *corpus delecti*-style. The tender spot behind his left ear throbbed painfully. Spluttering, he pulled down the rough wool and had a furtive gape around. The little flashlight was still on, propped up behind some piping. The first thing that caught his eye was a length of beautifully-wrought golden chain stretching down vertically from a snatch block on the bell's overhead lifting padeye and through the open trunk hatch near his feet. No—*two* lengths: one drum-tight, the other loose and dangling.

"My swag," he said weakly.

Ben looked up from the partially disassembled re-breather lying across his and Vern's upper legs. Sligo continued to gape. The two men were apparently gutting the unit piece by piece. Over here was its small green oxygen cylinder, over there the black helium reservoir. On Sligo's other side, the short guy with the foreign name—Pierre—was toweling his neck dry, stripped to the waist and blue with cold.

"What's . . . what's goin' on?" the smuggler mumbled.

Ben resumed his work with a screwdriver and small ratchet. "Nice unit," he said, "for a prototype. Too complicated to be reliable, though. That's the problem with all these computerized, high-tech rebreathers: you're fine and dandy until one of the chips goes bad and the gas mixer suddenly starts pushing you one hundred percent O_2 at three hundred feet."

"Or one hundred percent nitrogen or helium at *any* feet," Vern added.

Sligo blinked from one man to the other. "Huh?"

Ben shot Vern a glance. "Didn't you even think twice about diving this deep with a unit that had 'D-O-A' written on it?" He indicated the shiny yellow fiberglass cowl with its black Kronos lettering, now dangling from an equipment hook over Sligo's head.

"Crossed my mind," the smuggler said lamely.

"I'm assuming you came with the boat that brought our 'employer."

"Uh . . . yeah."

"What happened up there? They send you down?"

"Not exactly."

"I didn't think so. You had no surface support? No bell? Nothing?"

"Umm . . . no."

Ben shook his head, working with the screwdriver. "So all you had was a death wish, I guess."

443

"Well, I kinda thought—you know—I might pick up a little of the gold down here for myself, on the sly." Sligo shrugged, looking squirmy. "Runnin' a boat don't pay so good." An ingratiating grin. "You're a workin' man, you can understand that."

Ben didn't smile. "What gold would that be?"

Sligo waved a hand. "You know—the *gold*. The treasure. The swag that's layin' all over the bottom out here." He pointed at the thin chain hanging from the snatch block. "That stuff." His eyes narrowed suddenly. "That's mine, by the way. I found it."

"Then you found the only 'swag' out here besides one gold nail," Ben said. "And we're borrowing your chain. Pierre just went out and got it."

Sligo made the rapid calculation that he was more likely to prosper in the company of these people if he didn't make a big deal out of the chain right now. "Oh, sure," he said. "No problem. Whatever helps."

Ben put the screwdriver down and looked at him directly. "The situation we're in, I can't afford to worry about anything except the job of getting this bell to the surface and us decompressed properly. So I'm only going to ask you this once: is the blonde woman who was working with Gene McCluskey safe? Sass Wojeck's her name."

"Who?" Sligo said.

"The blonde woman who was working as a sat tech on the dive barge. Is she safe?"

The smuggler shrugged helplessly. "I guess so. I dunno. I never saw her. We arrived, the boss and his lawyer went over to talk to divin' supervisor, and I went into the water. I don't remember any blonde woman, honest."

Ben held his eye for a long moment, then went back to work with the screwdriver. "All right."

The smuggler shifted uncomfortably under his blanket, a steel projection of some kind digging into his back. He glanced around the interior of the bell again. It was an alarmingly small place, crammed with too much equipment and too many people. The atmosphere was damp, cold, and suffocatingly thick. All of a sudden, a ball of panic began to expand in his chest like a fast-growing tumor, sending out hot, stinging tendrils of fear that spread up the back of his neck, over his skull, and into his ears. He began to cower, sinking back against the curved steel of the lower hull, his eyes darting over the equipment. Up at the snatch block. Down at the open trunk hatch. Over at Pierre.

The Frenchman was gazing at him, frowning. "Vern," he said softly.

The human mountain sitting on the smuggler's left side scowled down at him. "Hey," it growled. "You ain't gonna start buggin' again, are you?"

"I . . . *urrghk* . . . I don't know. I don't feel so good . . ."

Like a schoolmaster lecturing an incorrigible student, Vern held up an index finger. It was the size of a small kielbasa. "You want me to rap you again?"

"No."

"Then sit still and shut up."

"O-okay."

"You start buggin', Ah'm gonna rap you."

"I . . . understand."

"Good."

Ben gave a grunt of satisfaction, removed a large plastic tube from the rebreather, and held it up. "Got it. The soda canister. Fresh crystals, Pierre." He shook the tube, examining the contents through the semi-transparent casing. "Looks like they're hardly consumed. Only a little pink tinge to 'em."

He passed the canister over to the little Frenchman. "How much longer do you reckon these give us before we all die of CO_2 poisoning?"

Sligo blanched.

Pierre turned the container over in his hands. "Hmmm. Another ten hours, if we try to restrict our activity and keep our breathing light. I will have to do the mathematics again, make a new estimate." He jabbed a thumb at Sligo. "I had not counted on the sudden appearance of this impressive specimen." His eyes roved over the smuggler with open dislike.

"Nothing we can do about that now," Ben said. "Look, if he hadn't shown up, we wouldn't be able to cannibalize all this stuff out of his rebreather. We've got another small cylinder of oxygen, another soda canister, and I'm going to be able to use the onboard batteries, too. They're twelve-volt."

Sligo's panic was subsiding. "I—er—we really gettin' back to the surface?"

Ben nodded. "Yeah. Pay attention, it'll take your mind off being in here. Here's the story: this bell floats once you disconnect the clump weight—the big rectangular block of concrete that hangs from two chains about three feet beneath the access trunk. Usually, if a bell breaks free of its lifting cable and umbilical, you just drop the clump, float back to the surface, and the support boat picks you up. You lock back onto the sat pot and decompress normally, on deck. If you're in a current, or you don't want to ascend blindly, you attach your emergency ascent cable to the clump and let yourself unspool slowly. That's what we want to do here, since we don't want to go drifting off into the open Caribbean while we're decompressing. We're deco-ing as we go because we can't trust the barge to recover us—something's obviously gone wrong up there or we wouldn't be in this situation in the first place.

"Trouble is, we took the emergency ascent spool off the bell so we'd have room for more onboard backup gas, since we're diving so deep. Without the spool, I figured we'd just have to float up uncontrolled and take our chances. Then I thought about your barrel of chain." Ben paused and caught Sligo's ferrety eye. "It came out of the *Arista*'s forepeak, didn't it?"

"Forepeak, forepeak," Sligo stammered. "Uh—yeah, now that I think about it."

Ben nodded. "I thought so. I read an old manuscript back in New Orleans that was written by one of the *Arista*'s officers. It described a mutiny that took place as she was sinking in a storm. A barrel of golden chain was seized by the captain as it was about to be thrown overboard in an attempt to lighten the ship and save her. He and his men dumped it into the forepeak. The rest of the gold went over the side or was lost from the main holds when she broke in two. But the barrel stayed in the hull's forward section. That's what you found."

Sligo's mouth twitched. He wasn't really following but . . . "Cool," he said.

"The manuscript said that each barrel contained one thin golden chain *eighty rods in length*. Do you know how long a rod is?"

"Um—a foot?"

Ben shook his head. "No. Five and a half yards. Sixteen and a half feet. So eighty rods would be one thousand three hundred and twenty feet. You know how deep the water is here?"

Sligo knew that number by heart—the distance a fast Jamaican in track shoes could run in forty seconds. "Twelve hundred feet," he said.

"Right. So your gold chain is more or less exactly the right length for us to use as an emergency ascent cable—all the way to the surface with a hundred and twenty feet to spare. If we don't get pushed off on the diagonal too far by a current, that is—that'd eat up some more chain. But there hasn't been much current out here that we've noticed."

Ben pointed at the chain. "One end of it's shackled to the clump weight on bottom. We fed it up through the open trunk and through that snatch block. That's what you call a *jamming* snatch block. It has a friction fitting on it that allows you to stop or slip whatever's running through it—chain, cable, or rope—as much or as little as you like. The rest of the chain's piled up on one of the outside gratings, with the extra gas bottles.

"We're slipping the chain a set number of feet every ten minutes, manually. I've worked out an emergency decompression ascent rate for us, using some special deco gas we've got. It's fast—maybe too fast—because we don't have enough soda for the CO_2 scrubber to last through a standard decompression. We might make it to within five fathoms of the surface and end up dying of the bends. But it's either that, *maybe*—or die for sure of carbon dioxide poisoning." He smiled thinly. "Some choice, eh? But we think it'll work."

Sligo's fear returned with such intensity that he thought he was going to be sick. "Oh fuck me," he whimpered. "Oh fuck me . . ."

Vern glowered down at him. "Don't be startin' that again."

Sligo's breath was coming fast and hard, his eyes goggling. "How long . . . before we reach the surface? *How long before we get-out-of-this-fucking-thing?*"

"Two and a half days, unless I can fudge these tables and recalculate a bit," Ben said. "So you might as well relax."

"WHAAAAT?" Sligo flailed the blanket off his body, screaming. *"TWO AND A HALF DAYS? YOU GOTTA BE JOKIN'! I AIN'T STAYIN' IN HERE TWO AND A HALF DAYS! I AIN'T STAYIN' IN HERE TWO AND A HALF MORE MINUTES! TAKE THIS THING UP! TAKE IT UP RIGHT NOW! I WANT OUT! I WANT OUT! DO YOU HEAR ME? I-WANT-TO-GET-THE-FUCK-OUT!"*

He groped wildly at the valves on the gas rack, spittle flying from his lips.

450

"Vern," Ben sighed.

There was a sound like knuckles knocking on an empty coconut.

"Ooooooooo," Sligo said, going limp.

Silence returned to the bell.

*****

"Ben," Vern said into the darkness. It had been more than an hour since they'd turned off the flashlight in order to save its batteries.

"Yeah."

"Ah was just thinkin'. How strong you figger that there chain is?"

Ben groped along the hull, located the flashlight, and switched it on. The dull glow permeated the bell's interior once again, turning the hot-water suits and other hanging equipment into looming silhouettes. In the center of all the rubber, nylon, stainless steel, bronze, plastic, and tempered glass, the old chain glistened a clean, pale yellow—a narrow metal spine running down the vertical axis of the bell.

Reaching out, Ben took hold of its running end and examined it for the twentieth time. The links were unusual, S-shaped rather than simply oval, and very small. Each one was less than three-quarters of an inch long, barely a quarter-inch thick, and interlocked with its neighbor in a way that reminded Ben of snakeskin—tight and flexible at the same time. It looked delicate, like jewelry. Certainly not like anchor chain.

Vern was right to be concerned, he knew. The bell had several hundred pounds of positive buoyancy. At some point near the surface, the last narrow link running over the sheave of the snatch block would be supporting not only the upward pull of the bell, but a downward pull of *another* several hundred pounds, at least—the weight of a thousand-plus feet of gold chain. There was an excellent chance that the thin metal would fail under the combined stresses; even a modern lifting cable sometimes parted under its own weight.

Ben exhaled slowly. They'd have to get the hatch shut quickly if the bell broke loose, or they'd all die of explosive decompression. And then, if they survived, they'd spend the rest of their deco table bouncing around on the swells of the open ocean—good weather didn't last forever—trying to bleed the bell down to sea level pressure through quarter-turn ball valves. Not a pleasant thought.

He rubbed his fingers over the chain. It was beautiful, as clean as the day it had been loaded aboard the *Arista*. Gold was called the Noble Metal because nothing reacted with it. It didn't oxidize. It didn't combine with other elements to create new compounds. You could melt it with other metals, like silver, and mix them together to make an alloy, but the gold would remain gold. It could be smelted back out anytime.

How strong it was depended upon the purity of the alloy. Being a welder, Ben knew enough basic metallurgy to get by, and he'd bought Sass a few baubles over the years. He smiled to himself, remembering. All women liked to be given gold—even down-to-earth types like Sass, though she would rarely admit it.

Ten carat gold was fairly strong. Fourteen was weaker, but made sturdy rings and everyday jewelry. Eighteen carat was soft enough to distort easily if subjected to minimal stress; many a wealthy woman had lost a nice stone from a ring because the claws that held it in its setting were made of eighteen carat gold instead of cheaper and stronger ten or fourteen carat alloy. Twenty-four carat gold was considered pure, and was soft enough to scrape with a thumbnail. It had no real strength in a structural sense.

"This looks like a pretty strong alloy mix, Vern," Ben said quietly, looking at the big man beside him. "Not pure, by a long shot. If it was, it would have pulled apart already. I'm thinking it's tough enough for what we need." He wasn't sure, but there was no point in being negative.

"Sure is purty, ain't it?" Vern said. "Look real good 'round a lady's neck." He smiled in the dim light. "Or maybe it's a little heavy for that."

On the other side of the bell, Pierre stirred. A little snore came from his open mouth.

"That dang froggy, he don't have no trouble sleepin', does he?" Vern's smile turned to an open grin.

"Nope," Ben said. "And while he's sleeping, he's making a lot less carbon dioxide, so let's let him stay like that." He glanced down at Sligo. "How's our guest?"

Vern reached out a big hand and patted the smuggler's head through the shroud of the army blanket. "Don't you worry 'bout him none. Ah done give him a real good sleepin' pill last time he got to fussin'."

The big man sighed and put his hand back in his lap. "What the hail you figger happened up top anyway, Ben? What we gonna find when we get up there?"

Ben reached out and snapped off the flashlight. "I don't know," he said into the wet darkness. "I just don't know."

*****

The sun was hanging low over the western horizon, partly obscured by streaks of purple cloud, as Posey and Earl began to approach the island's outer reef. They'd spent the entire afternoon astride the ROV, their combined weight pushing the torpedo-shaped vehicle just under the surface so that they rode waist deep, working their way slowly up the strait and away from the yacht and barge. The two rafted vessels had pulled off the dive site by mid-afternoon and motored into a small, well-concealed lagoon near the eastern end of the island's south shore. Posey and Earl had been able to make out the narrow entrance channel—just barely—in the distance.

Not wanting to risk being spotted, they'd elected to cruise along quietly in deepwater, staying at least two miles offshore, until they got closer to the island's western end. Even at less than a knot of forward speed, the trip had been an ordeal. Water pressure against their bodies constantly threatened to wash them off the slick hull, and vibration from the electric motor, even at minimal rpm, rattled their spines until their teeth buzzed. They were cold, tired, and utterly sick of having to hold on to the all-but-featureless ROV.

The deep, open waters of the strait had provided an added incentive to do so, however. From time to time, throughout the afternoon, large, elongated shadows had appeared alongside and behind the vehicle, rising from the depths like phantoms. Without diving helmets or masks, it had been impossible to tell for certain what they were—but it hadn't been hard to guess. Some of them were longer than the ROV itself.

Now the waters that washed against them were in-shore warm and increasingly emerald-green as the bottom rose beneath the vehicle. The wind had freshened slightly, building a two-foot swell throughout the afternoon . . . a swell that churned into foam as it surged over the top of the reef. Only a two-foot swell—but to the tired men on the ROV, eyeing it from the waterline, the light chop looked like a veritable maelstrom.

Posey increased the rpm on the main drive as the vehicle entered the bumpy water over the reef. Gritting their teeth, he and Earl held on like a pair of barnacles. Patterns of rich brown, ochre, and yellow flashed just beneath them, barely three feet down, as the ROV surfed easily over the jagged coral and into the calm waters beyond.

Posey took the electric engine out of gear. The ROV drifted to a halt, heaving gently under their weight. Two hundred yards away, across a glassy green flat of seagrass beds, the palm-lined shore of the island stretched off to the east and west, rimmed by a strip of white-sand beach. Heavily-jungled highlands rose immediately behind it, their lush continuity interrupted by sporadic cliff faces that gradually ran together farther to the east to become the dominant shoreline feature.

Breathing hard, Posey sat up straight and half turned to squint myopically at Earl. "Well, what do you think?" he asked. "All I can see is general surroundings: trees, beach, water, a few cliffs—without my glasses I can't make out any detail."

Earl reached out and slapped the back of his wet shirt. The ROV tech had shed his ubiquitous peacoat soon after hitting the water in the wake of the explosion on the barge's stern. "Don't you worry 'bout that, son. Ah kin see plenty good." He paused momentarily. "How 'bout we motor on over towards that big fallen palm tree yonder. Ah think there might be a little stream cuttin' through the beach right beside it."

Posey held up the remote control box. "Which way, Earl?"

"To the right. Git up a little speed an' Ah'll die-rect you."

The ROV began to slide through the water again, cruising over the grass beds like a long black shark. The turquoise-and-jade shallows were gradually losing their color as the lower curve of the sun's hot orange fireball sank below the western horizon. In the hillside ravines light mists began to form, drifting through the trees like curtains of gauze.

"Bear right a little more," Earl said. "That's good. Hold 'er steady, now."

Posey squinted ahead. "I see it. That's definitely a small stream coming out of the jungle beside that tree trunk. Think we can motor up it?"

"Looks like it might be deep enough from where Ah'm sittin'. Even if we cain't motor up, we can sho-nuff wade and walk this thang into the trees. At least—" Earl hawked and spat salt water. "'Scuse me. At least we'll be hid."

"Sounds good."

The ROV nosed into the outflowing water of the stream's miniature delta. Earl dipped a hand and tasted. "Mm! Fresh as a Smoky Mountain spring, son! Be nice to have a drink and git this salt off, eh?"

"Yep," Posey agreed. "If it's not so full of amoebas that we give ourselves terminal diarrhea."

Earl made a growling noise deep in his throat and drank the handful anyway. "Lord ha'mercy," he said suddenly. "What's that up ahead under them branches?"

"I don't see anything," Posey replied, tensing up and squinting.

As the ROV slid up the little creek and out of sight behind the encroaching foliage, Earl eased himself off into the thigh-deepwater and pulled the vehicle sideways onto a tiny midstream sandbar.

"Huh," Posey heard him mutter. "Stay low and quiet while Ah scout around some. What we got here is a dugout sailin' canoe, hid under some palm fronds. And there look to be fresh footprints in the bank right next to it."

Chains of Gold

Chapter Thirty

It was nearly half-past midnight when the door of the sat shack banged open. Sass, dozing in one of the padded office chairs with her feet up on the edge of the gas rack, awoke with a start. Through bleary eyes, she found herself looking at another Ramos bodyguard, a man she hadn't seen before. This one was nappy-haired and very dark-skinned, with contrasting light blue eyes and a long narrow nose. She guessed him to be Cuban.

"Yes?" she said, pushing a few strands of long blonde hair back off her face.

"You come," the man said. "Come up to house."

Sass shook her head. "I can't do that. I told the Ramoses that I have to stay here and monitor this diver's decompression."

"Heh?" the bodyguard grunted, his blue eyes narrowing.

"I-can't-come-up-to-the-house," Sass enunciated. *"No hacienda, comprende?* I have to stay here." She shook her head adamantly and pointed at the floor.

The bodyguard jerked up the weapon he was carrying—an odd-looking, snub-nosed submachine gun—and took a step forward. *"You come!"* he shouted. *"Vamanos!"*

Sass looked into the little black hole of the gun's muzzle and swallowed. "I told you," she said quietly, "I have to stay here." She shook her head once more, leaning back as the agitated man pushed the weapon at her. "What are you going to do? Shoot me? Do you think that would make your bosses very happy?"

For a man with limited English, the bodyguard seemed to understand that very well. He pulled back, looking confused. Then, slowly, he smiled. Flipping a selector switch on the side of his machine gun, he swung it toward the gas rack and fired.

The single shot smashed through the face of one of the oxygen-pressure gauges, through the rack's aluminum supporting template, and out the side of the shack itself. There was an ear-shattering blast of escaping high-pressure O_2.

"Hey!" Sass yelled, lunging forward. She slapped a hand on the blown line's upstream needle valve and twisted it shut. The high-pitched scream of oxygen died away.

Breathing hard, she looked over at the bodyguard. The dark-skinned man was grinning at her in triumph.

"You *asshole,"* she said.

He nodded happily and gestured with the machine gun. "You come to house," he repeated. When she didn't move he lined the weapon up on the rack again.

"All right, all right," Sass told him. "I-come-to-house."

They exited the sat shack and made their way across the darkened deck toward the gangplank that had been rigged to the shore of the lagoon. Overhead, the stars were hazy and dull in the black sky, and a warm, insistent wind was stirring the tops of the palm trees. The weather was changing.

Where are you, Ben? Sass thought, a pang of desperation stabbing through her. *Where are you right now?*

She paused by the side of the sat pot, stepped up on the skid, and peered through the port of the outer lock. Chris was asleep on his cot; a cheap gray blanket pulled up to his lower ribs, his splinted wrist lying across his stomach. She hopped back down and looked quickly at the lock's external gauges.

"Jefe want to know how deep man is now," the bodyguard grunted, struggling with the words. "You show me. Then we go."

"He's at eight hundred and thirty-seven feet," Sass said, pointing at the gauge she'd replaced earlier with Grizelda leering over her shoulder. "See?"

The man leaned in close, squinted at the gauge, shrugged, and nodded. "Hokay. Now we go." He motioned with the machine gun again, stepping back.

Sass walked forward obediently, taking a last look at the gauge she'd de-calibrated to read four hundred feet deeper than the actual pressure within the lock. Eight thirty-seven minus four hundred. Four thirty-seven. Chris would be popping a hatch in just over thirty-six hours. And the gauge, in case anyone happened to be looking, would still be reading four hundred feet. Might give him a little time to get to a single-sideband radio and put out a long-range distress call. The guards weren't letting *her* anywhere near a transmitter.

If she could just handle these Ramos lunatics until then . . .

If Ben was just doing what she'd known he could do all along, once the bell had been cut loose and sunk . . .

She looked up at the misty stars again as she and the bodyguard trudged along the thin strip of beach toward the dock. *No bad weather for two more days,* she prayed. *Please. Just two more days.*

There was a battered yellow jeep sitting at the end of the road that led up to Alberto and Grizelda's *hacienda*. Sass could see the house through the trees, a dark, blocky shape high up on the crest of one of the island's central ridges, dotted with enough lights to make it stand out against the night sky.

A sudden cold breeze wafted along Sass's bare neck as she reached the jeep, making her shiver. The bodyguard waved to another gunman strolling along the dock, then slid into the driver's seat, his machine gun across his knees, pointing at the passenger's side.

"You get in," he ordered.

*****

The boy had watched the events of the preceding day with considerable interest. First there had been the horrific killing of the pudgy man who'd run down the jeep track onto the dock. Then, after returning to the house and cleaning off the gore that had drenched her, the red-haired murderess and several of her gunmen had departed by speedboat for the barge anchored in the strait. The boy had positioned himself atop a cliff several hundred yards east of the lagoon in order to get a good offshore view. To his amazement, soon after the woman's arrival, the unmistakable *pop-pop-pop* of gunshots had sounded across the calm water, followed by a tremendous explosion. A huge ball of fire had boiled up into the sky, and the barge's stern had disappeared behind a pall of black smoke.

An hour later, the big white yacht called the *Cucaracha* had motored into the lagoon with the barge tied alongside. The boy had never seen so much exotic equipment in one place. He didn't recognize any of it: great hinged frameworks of tubular steel, hoses and cables running everywhere, and immense tanks—big enough to hold a dozen men—with hatches and portholes all over them. It was a baffling array.

The *narcotista*'s gunmen had removed two bodies from the speedboat tied alongside the barge—one of them a guard he recalled seeing on the house terrace, the other an older white man who looked, by his size and dress, to be an American. The dead men had been carried off into the jungle about two hundred yards and hastily buried.

The boy had also followed something else. Not long after the explosion, his keen young eyes had caught a strange object moving away from the barge, all but submerged. It was heading up the strait about three miles offshore, parallel to the island's southern coast. He couldn't be sure, but it almost looked as if there were two men sitting on something long and narrow, hunched low in the water.

The *narcotista* and her brother—the boy had seen him before, at the house—had gotten into a yellow jeep and driven up the winding road to their hilltop *hacienda*. Several bodyguards had remained behind on the barge, apparently keeping an eye on a slender blonde woman wearing shorts and a checkered work shirt—a person the boy did not recognize. Like the older man who'd been buried in the jungle, she appeared to be an American. She was tall, athletic in her movements, and—as far as the he could tell from a safe distance—extremely attractive. She carried a clipboard and walked repeatedly back and forth between one of the large tanks and the door of a nearby van, taking notes.

So there had been much activity. Just before dusk, as he'd jogged back along the cliff-top trail toward the fishing cave, he'd caught sight of a large, odd-looking object moving over the top of the outer reef, almost directly opposite the mouth of the little creek where he'd hidden his dugout canoe. Closer inspection had revealed it to be two men—Americans, once again—riding on top of a long black pipe with stubby wings and some kind of tailfin arrangement. They'd glided across the darkening grass flats inside the reef, looking all but exhausted, and proceeded on up the stream. Of course, they had to have found his canoe.

The boy shifted his chin on his forearms, gazing down from the safety of concealment in the mouth of the fishing cave. It was very dark now, well after midnight, but the dim starlight made it just possible for him to make out the two men who'd ridden in from the strait aboard the strange black pipe. After climbing to the cliff-tops, they'd spent nearly two hours bumbling around in the jungle highlands before discovering the trail that led toward the lagoon and house. They'd gotten as far as the marker rock—the tall pillar of coral limestone under which Fernando had been murdered—

before darkness and uncertainty had forced them to stop.

Now they were lying huddled at its base, apparently trying to get some sleep. Not very wise—they weren't exactly hidden from view, but with all the activity at the lagoon, it was unlikely that the *narcotista*'s gunmen would be along any time soon.

The boy nestled his head on his elbow and began to doze. The morning would bring new things. More activity, certainly.

More opportunities.

*****

"Ah, Mish Wojeck, pleashe come in." Alberto waved a limp hand from the far side of the *hacienda*'s living room, where he was curled up—female housecat-style—at one end of a large black leather sofa, sipping pink gin. His eyelids were booze-heavy. "Bumpy ride up that jeep track, ishn't it?"

Sass moved reluctantly forward, prodded by the blue-eyed bodyguard's machine gun. Across from Alberto, Grizelda was seated in her exotic Swedish armchair with her back to the living room entrance, staring into a darkened alcove near a pair of French doors. She did not turn around.

"Wait outshide, Felix," Alberto slurred.

The bodyguard nodded to Alberto and departed, leaving Sass standing a few feet behind Grizelda in the warm glow of the twin end-table lamps that provided the luxurious room's only light. She glanced around, taking in the pricey design work, the custom made furniture, and the various paintings and sculptures—all of which looked expensive, if rather tacky. Her wandering gaze came to rest on Alberto. Being a homicidal criminal paid well, evidently.

His wealth didn't do much for his sense of personal style. If his sister was a musclebound female troll who dressed like a cross between an aerobics dominatrix and an MTV video slut, he himself was no less idiosyncratic in his choice of wardrobe, if far less remarkable physically. He was wearing a hip-length peignoir of some sheer rose-colored material, mercifully devoid of any fuzzy pink faux-fur trim, and a leopard-spotted bikini thong—extra small. That was all. Sass could scarcely believe her eyes.

The nearly-naked man uncoiled his soft, bare legs and sat up, carefully manipulating his martini glass with its blush-tinted contents. He smiled the drowsy, contented smile of the sated alcoholic and patted the sofa cushion beside him with his free hand. "Don't be shy. Have a sheet."

He giggled at his own malapropism and sagged back, raising his glass. "You musht have one of theesh."

Sass stayed where she was, observing him with disgust. Grizelda's head turned slowly sideways to look at her brother, then rotated forward again. Her blue-veined hand rose off the wooden arm of the chair, and a steroid-lumpy finger beckoned. "Come in," she rumbled. The finger pointed to a small armchair sitting kitty corner to hers. "Sit down."

Something in the voice told Sass that it would be better to obey—at least for the time being. She moved around the big woman, eyeing the raccoon-tail tendril of hair that hung from the back of her neck, and cautiously eased down into the chair. Grizelda's post-midnight attire was simple: a short, blue-satin kimono and black Doc Martens combat boots. Across the room, on the other side of the huge, ornately carved coffee table, Alberto giggled like a mental case into his pink gin.

"She hash to tell you," he chortled, half to himself. "She'll tell anyone and makc 'em lisshen—even if they don't give a shh—shh—*shit.*"

Grizelda ignored him, slumped in her armchair and stared past Sass into the darkened alcove at the far end of the room. Her eyes had the blank soullessness of a marble statue. She raised her arm again and pointed into the shadows.

"Go turn that light on," she said. "The switch is on the wall by the doors."

Sass hesitated, then got up and walked across the room to the alcove. In the middle of it, sitting on a pedestal about the height of a kitchen stool, was a large stainless steel canister. When she flipped the switch next to the French doors, a recessed ceiling light came on directly above the container, illuminating it.

"There are four clips around the bottom of the canister," Grizelda said. "Pull them back and lift the metal cover off."

What the hell is this? Sass wondered. *Some sick new stunt?* Cautiously, she snapped back the four clips. Then she paused.

"Lift the cover off," Grizelda repeated, her eyes like droplets of lead.

Apprehension tingling in every nerve, Sass pressed her palms to either side of the container and lifted. The shiny metal cover came free of its base and slid upward, revealing a large glass urn filled with clear, colorless liquid.

Inside the urn was a man's head.

Sass gave an involuntary shriek and stumbled back several steps, dropping the cover. The thin metal cylinder clashed and clattered on the tile before finally rolling to a stop against the pedestal's base.

"Oopsh," Alberto said, and burst into a fresh fit of giggling.

The head stared out through the glass with eyes that were little more than opaque balls of yellowed tissue, the color of the irises long since leached away. The skin was wrinkled like that of a prune, and stained a dark brown, as if it had been tanned. Patches of what had once been coarse, dark hair still clung in frizzy clumps to the scalp, chin, and jaw. The features were clearly European: high forehead, heavy brows, broad cheekbones, long hawk nose, and thin-lipped mouth. The mouth hung half open, giving the withered face, with its fogged-over eyes and sunken cheeks, a look of mournful astonishment that it was no longer alive. A stump of neck, hacked through cleanly just below the Adam's apple, rested its tattered lower end on the bottom of the urn.

Still backing away, Sass bumped into one of the end tables and nearly fell. The lamp teetered but stayed in place, casting wobbling shadows around the room. Alberto snickered drunkenly into his pink gin.

"Sit," Grizelda ordered, pointing at the chair Sass had vacated. Unsteadily, she moved past the end table and complied.

The henna-haired woman fell silent again and flexed her bodybuilder's hands on the wooden arms of her chair, staring across the room at the spotlighted urn and its grisly contents. She appeared to slip into some kind of unquiet trance; a state of extreme focus in which she locked eyes with the disembodied head, exercised her facial muscles continuously, and attempted to reduce her chair's arms to sawdust by direct manual pressure. One Doc Martens boot tapped rapidly on the tile floor.

"Five hundred years ago," Grizelda intoned, "my ancestor, Captain Diego Ramos, was sailing from the coast of southern Mexico with a ship full of Aztec gold when he was caught in a storm. He tried to save his vessel, its crew and cargo, but was betrayed by his Master of Swords; a professional soldier named Sebastian Rodrigo Nunoz, who led a mutiny against him.

"His ship, the *Arista*, was lost. My ancestor and his loyal officers were captured by the mutineers as they abandoned ship, but managed to escape once they reached this island. They set up separate camps. Ramos tried to reason with Nunoz—convince him to repent and join forces with him, but the mutineer would not. Instead, he attacked my ancestor's camp repeatedly, trying to kill him and the other men who had remained loyal.

"Ramos eventually retreated to the next island, where he set up another camp. But Nunoz pursued him, attacking again and again, until finally all the loyal men had been killed and only my ancestor remained.

"He made a stand, alone, but the mutineers overpowered him by sheer force of numbers and dragged him before Nunoz. Ramos continued to fight like a lion, but they held him down so that he could not even struggle. When he felt safe enough, Nunoz stepped in close and murdered him by beheading him with his sword."

A look of psychopathic loathing passed over Grizelda's face, an expression so malevolent that Sass involuntarily drew in a sharp breath. The big woman's nostrils flared, her hands and arms flexed, and she continued:

"But both Nunoz and my ancestor were alive on these islands long enough to leave their genes. Some of the Indians here are blood relatives of Nunoz; some— like me—are related to Captain Ramos." She paused to nod her chin at the urn. *"That* is Captain Ramos. And the feud is not over. Not—"

"Thish is where she usually getsh dramatic," Alberto cut in. He fluttered a hand and gulped the last of his gin.

Except for pausing, Grizelda ignored the drunken interruption. "Not until the last of Nunoz's descendants are dead," she rasped, "and his line wiped off the face of the Earth."

"Drum roll pleashe," Alberto chortled, getting up in a whirl of pink gauze and lurching toward the wall bar with his empty glass. "There you have it: my shishter's obshession. Finding all the relatives of the man who killed our ansheshtor, taking revenge on them for shomething they didn't do . . . umm . . . oh, and getting the *Arishta's* gold, too . . . that wash in there shome-where originally, I believe."

He clinked the bottles on the bar top, fumbling with a cap. "Five hundred yearsh have gone by. Talk about holding a grudge . . ."

Grizelda stared blackly at the pickled head of Diego Ramos. "Get your drink and sit down, little brother," she snarled, "or big sister will get annoyed."

Sass was amazed by how quickly the man in the pink peignoir and leopard-skin briefs finished mixing his nauseating cocktail—pure gin with a dash of Grena-dine—and curled back up on the end of the sofa.

She pointed at the urn. "This . . . thing . . .is nearly five hundred years old? Where did it come from? And why hasn't it rotted away?"

"Out of respect for my ancestor," Grizelda said slowly, "the Indians preserved his head. A scientist who was my guest here just recently performed a laboratory analysis and told me how they did it. The head was immersed in a fire-glazed clay pot full of boiled sap, preservative herbs, and alcohol distilled from fermented *naga* vines. Then a clay top was molded on to seal the pot, and it was made air-and-watertight with several coats of mineral paint.

"They put the pot into a stone coffin, along with the rest of my ancestor's body, and the coffin was moved into a little Catholic chapel he and his men had built. Eventually, the traitor Nunoz was killed by his own men and put into a second coffin on the opposite side of the same chapel. For five centuries Diego Ramos lay next to the man who'd cut off his head, unable"— Grizelda raised her arms into the air, her fists balled and shaking—"to strike out . . . to take him by the throat . . . and choke the life out of him."

Sass watched silently. The woman ground out the words through foam-flecked lips, her facial muscles working, her eyes staring into the light above the glass urn. Alberto, Sass noticed, was not giggling.

"Diego Ramos was a great man," Grizelda went on, her tone becoming hushed. "A warrior who took what he wanted." She dropped her arms. "*And so am I.* If I can't have his treasure, I'll have his revenge on the last living descendants of Sebastian Rodrigo Nunoz— even if they *are* only Indian fishermen."

Her head nodded suddenly, as if the intensity with which she'd related her tale had drained her energy. Sass looked across the coffee table at Alberto. He was passed out on the sofa; mouth open and head lolling back. His pink gin had spilled into his lap, staining the crotch of his skimpy leopard-skin briefs.

Grizelda's head came up. She waved a lumpy finger at Sass. "You can go back to the barge now," she said. "One of the men will drive you down in the jeep." Then she smiled, her expression turning hungry. "Or you can stay. We have room upstairs." One hand strayed to her substantial cleavage, began to probe it lightly. "Until the diver Chris gets out of the chamber, the choice is yours. And by the way, the guards have orders to watch you twenty-four hours a day. I've also told them to shoot the ports out of the decompression lock if you give them any trouble."

She giggled deep in her throat as Sass got immediately to her feet, jaw set, and took a wide berth around her on her way out of the living room.

Chapter Thirty-One

The only thing worse than being cooped up in a small diving bell in the middle of a dangerously rapid emergency ascent and decompression was being cooped up in a small diving bell in the middle of a dangerously rapid emergency ascent and decompression with Jeremiah Sligo. He'd freaked out so often over the past thirty hours that Vern's knuckles were sore from slugging him behind the ear.

"Oh, no," Ben muttered, looking up from a notebook full of gas formulas. He pointed across the bell with his pencil. "He's waking up again."

"This ol' boy's a pain in the ass," Vern grumbled into the oral-nasal mask strapped over his mouth and nose. "As often as Ah bin hittin' him, you'd think his skull woulda caved in by now—but he got a headbone harder'n a monk's dick in a whorehouse."

"Tabarnac, that's pretty hard," Pierre said from the other side of the trunk hatch. Like Vern, Ben, and the semi-conscious Sligo, he was wearing a bulky rubber oral-nasal mask, its gas supply hose leading to a bank of valves just above Ben's head.

Ben finished solving the complex decompression equation he'd been working on and stuck the pencil in the notebook's spiral binding. "Let's give him a chance

. . . see if he's gonna behave himself before you risk breaking a knuckle on him again." He glanced at Vern, the crinkling crow's-feet around his tired eyes revealing the smile beneath his mask.

"Ah ain't gettin' mah hopes up," Vern growled.

"Oh, god," Sligo moaned, not even trying to sit up. *"Oh, fuck meeeeee . . ."* He put a hand to his head, winced as he touched the livid bruise behind his ear, and looked over at Vern reproachfully. "You've busted my bean, you overgrown bastard."

"Nawww," the big man replied, scowling at his blanket-covered feet. He was long past being even a little bit apologetic. Sligo had been that irritating. "Ah just rapped you. Howevuh"—he glowered at the smuggler—"if you'd like your bean well an' truly busted, Ah'd be more'n happy to oblige."

"Don't fucking hit me again, okay?"

"Then don't be buggin' on us again—*okay?"*

Sligo shifted his attention to Ben. "Jesus, man, I told you I don't like this thing on my face! I feel like I'm smothering!" He pawed at his oral-nasal mask.

"And I told *you,*" Ben said, folding his arms and eyeing him, "that you have to wear it so you can get your decompression gas. If you don't breathe in this special mix you'll take a bends hit for sure, at the rate we're coming out of saturation. Hell," he added, "we may all keel over dead in the next hour as it is."

Sligo made a whining noise and lifted the corner of the mask away from his cheek. "But I can't *handle* this fucking thing, man."

"Take it off again and I'll have Vern hit you so fucking hard you'll be picking your eyeballs off the deck like marbles," Ben said. Like his two companions, he'd had a bellyful of Jeremiah Sligo.

Sligo dropped his hand away from his mask and slumped back. He stayed quiet for about ten seconds then said, "I'm hungry."

"Join the club," Ben told him. He opened his notebook again.

"I'm thirsty, too," Sligo persisted. He looked at Pierre. "You guys told me that it was important to stay hy . . . hydraul . . .hydra—"

"Hydrated," Pierre said.

"Yeah!" The smuggler nodded triumphantly. "What you said! Hydrated. It's important to stay hydrated during decompression, so your blood don't gum up or something. Right?"

"More or less," Ben said, concentrating on his gas formulas.

"Well, I'm thirsty."

Ben sighed and looked up. "How much water have we got left, Pierre?"

The Frenchman inspected the half-dozen plastic bottles next to him. "About three liters."

"Let him have half a liter."

Pierre grunted and tossed Sligo a bottle, none too delicately. The smuggler seized it and unscrewed the cap. Then he looked at Ben. "Gotta take this mask off to drink it," he said, his tone brimming with the juvenile slyness of an adolescent who thinks he's maneuvered an adult into a contradiction.

Ben pointed his pencil at him. "Like I told you before: lift the mask, drink, put the mask back, and continue breathing. No one can swallow liquid and breathe at the same time, so you won't have to miss a single breath of that deco gas. Vern, if he fucks with me on this, put him to sleep again."

"Ah might break his thumb first," the big man rumbled. "Just for the fun of it."

Sligo's eyes widened and he slumped away, clutching the water bottle. "Hey, hey—no problem, guys. No problem."

While the smuggler drank, adhering to procedure, Ben checked his notes yet again. "You were right, Pierre. We used up the soda canisters faster than I thought. Too many people and no gas to vent the bell with. If I hadn't re-figured these decompression tables to the limit of the accepted error and added another fifteen percent, we'd never have made it to the surface." He paused, looking at his notes and shaking his head. "Damn. I don't care how good this new deco mix is.

There's no *way* a man should be able to come out of a twelve-hundred-foot saturation in only thirty hours. Not even if he's rolling the dice and cutting the times like we are. You guys sure you're feeling all right?"

Vern shook out his massive arms, which made Sligo cower away a bit further, sucking on his bottle with his mask ajar. "So far so good," he reported. "No niggles, aches, or pains yet."

"Moi aussi," Pierre said. "Me too. Nothing so far."

Ben looked at Sligo. "How about you?"

"Huh?"

"How do you feel?"

The smuggler shrugged, adjusting his mask over his mouth and nose. "Feel? Well, okay, I guess—considerin' I've been gummed half to death by a giant guppy, nearly drowned, and whacked in the head on a regular basis by Mr. Giggles over here." He jerked a thumb in Vern's direction. "I feel pretty good, I guess. Thanks for askin'. How about you?"

Ben rubbed his eyes. "You just don't have a clue, do you? Why don't you pay attention to what's going on once in a while? Do you have any sharp pains in any of your joints? Any dizziness, tingling sensations, or numbness? Anything abnormal at all?"

"Uh, no," Sligo replied, nonplussed.

"Good. Now breathe in your gas and suck on your bottle and keep quiet."

"An' watch who you're jabbin' your thumb at," Vern added. "Ah told you Ah had a hankerin' to snap one of 'em off."

"Okay," Ben continued, "we started the ascent and decompression thirty hours ago at twelve hundred and five feet. That was at twenty-one hundred hours—nine p.m. the day before yesterday. Now it's oh-three hundred hours on the morning of the third day and we're at thirty-five feet. And nobody's collapsed. I don't know what's going to happen in this last atmosphere of pressure, but maybe our luck will hold."

"Mon dieu," Pierre said slowly. "I have nev*air* come out of a one-thousand two-hundred-foot sat in less than . . . *twelve days."* He shook his head. "We should be dead."

"It's the new deco gas." Ben shrugged. "It's hydrogen based. And the oxygen partial pressures are varied all over the table. I don't know what to tell you. The theory is that it fools your body into offgassing more quickly. Don't ask me how."

"Theory, huh?" Vern remarked. "Well, we sure gonna find out how good a theory it is, ain't we?"

"Yeah, we are." Ben tapped his pencil on the notebook and glanced at his watch. "Almost time to slip that chain another couple of feet."

"Wonder what the weather's like up there," Vern muttered, pulling the blanket off his legs and preparing to get to his feet.

"I wonder *who* is up there," Pierre said. "If anyone."

Sligo was silent, huddled under his blanket, his ferrety blue eyes zipping back and forth between Vern and Ben.

As Vern rose to one knee, the bell took a sudden lurch. The thin gold chain, which had been drum tight against one side of the access trunk during the entire ascent, wandered across the opening; first one way, then another. The hanging equipment began to swing gently as the bell wobbled. Over Sligo's head, the needle on the external depth gauge began to creep up.

"Cut loose that chain and shut the hatch!" Ben shouted, scrambling out from under his own blanket. *"It just broke somewhere down below us! We're heading for the surface!"*

Vern was there first. Grabbing the small bolt-cutters they'd placed near the snatch block for just such an emergency, he positioned the jaws around the chain and squeezed.

There was a loud SNAP. The chain ends whipped down through the access trunk and disappeared.

Pierre slammed the inside hatch on the trunk a second later.

"Shit," Ben breathed. He tapped the interior pressure gauge. "We lost eleven feet in about five seconds. We're down to twenty-four feet equivalent pressure in here now. Everybody still okay?" There was a universal nodding of heads. "Okay, good."

The bell began to pitch and roll like a Popeye punching bag, and for the first time in nearly two days, foam, air, and star-strewn night sky shared space with water in the viewing fields of the two tiny portholes.

"Stay down low and hang on," Ben said. "The seas kicked up while we were away." He blew out a long breath inside his oral-nasal. "We've still got to bleed down to surface pressure for another couple of hours. We'll use the secondary vent valve."

"Dang," Vern growled, "Ah thought that chain was gonna take us all the way."

"Yeah, I know." Ben slapped his hand into the side of the bell. "It was holding us in position, too. I just hope we don't get swept out to sea past the island while we're decompressing, now that we're not anchored. Hey, what's wrong with you?"

Sligo was staring over the rubber skirt of his mask with stricken eyes. Staring at the closed hatch of the access trunk.

"My swag," he whispered in a voice tinged with horror. *"My gold."*

*****

The flash of lightning and its accompanying clap of thunder jolted Sass awake. Heavy raindrops were beginning to pelt the metal roof of the sat shack, signaling the onset of a sudden squall. As the scatter-shot dinging became a continuous tattoo, she propped herself up on one elbow and pushed her tangled hair out of her face. Every joint in her body was stiff from dozing on the shack's one small couch, and her clothes felt as if they had been stuck to her skin with wallpaper paste. The inside of her mouth *tasted* like wallpaper paste. She was long overdue for a shower and a change, but she was damned if she was going to return to the Ramoses' house for anything—and the guards had chained shut the hatches leading down to the barge's belowdecks living quarters.

She glanced at the small, inconspicuous gauge on the side of the gas rack that gave a true reading of Chris's depth in the outer lock: sixty-seven feet. There was another flash, another thunderclap, and the cacophony on the roof intensified. He'd be popping a hatch in less than six hours, according to the modified decompression table she was using.

She checked the pressure on his deco mix supply. There was still nearly a thousand pounds in the current cylinder—it would be several hours before she'd have to switch to another one. She thought about checking on him, began to lean toward the descrambler radio, then looked at her watch. Twenty minutes past three in the morning. He'd be asleep. She settled back against the wall of the shack, yawning.

Grizelda and Alberto had not put in an appearance throughout the entire previous day. There had been time to talk to Chris on the radio, in hushed tones, and tell him what had happened. The kid had taken it pretty well, hadn't blown his lid, though the news of Gene McCluskey's murder had hit him hard. Now he was waiting to pop a hatch, and would bide his time even after the seal broke. The plan was for him to stay put until he saw a clear opportunity, then board the yacht—which sported an array of long-rang antennae—and transmit a mayday message to the Coast Guard or U.S. Navy, along with the island's latitude and longitude.

Then he was to disappear into the jungle, arming himself if possible, and contact Ben, Vern, and Pierre if and when they managed to surface the bell and make it to shore. In spite of Chris's expressions of dismay and doubt, Sass had been adamant that they would show up, and show up soon.

There was a click and the door of the shack opened, letting in a gust of rain. It was the guard named Carlos: the man Sass had clocked over the head with the crowbar. He looked bad. The right side of his scalp was wadded with a huge gauze pad, held in place by a cheap blue-and-white bandana tied beneath his chin. The white of his right eye no longer *was*—it had become a blot of red, discolored by the rupturing of internal blood vessels.

He looked at Sass with pure hatred, dripping water on the floor, and banged the door shut behind him. Outside, the wind howled to a crescendo, then eased as the squall began to pass by. The hammering downpour lessened in intensity.

Sass gave him a thin smile, knowing that, like the others, he had orders not to harm her, but to restrict her movements by threatening Chris's safety. Her mocking attitude clearly enraged the man, but for the time being there was little he could do about it—and she was too tired and fed up to care.

So piss on him. And the other gun-toting *banditos* as well.

"What can I do for you?" she inquired, looking bored.

Carlos' dark face screwed up as if his big toe was being mashed in a vice. "Bitch," he snarled. "When Senorita Ramos and her brother are finished with you— if there is anything left—I will be waiting." He spat rainwater and hefted his sawed-off shotgun. "I'm going to start with the same crowbar you used on me. We'll see how much you smile then."

Sass settled back on the settee and stretched her arms over her head, fully aware that her checkered work shirt would ride up and expose her flat brown stomach. A little skin to keep the bastard off balance. It had the desired effect. The man's close set eyes focused on her belt buckle and his mouth went slack with distraction. She was almost certain she could have whisked the shotgun out of his hands if he'd been five feet closer. File that thought away for later . . . it might come in handy.

She glanced at the inner lock gauge again as she pulled down her shirt: sixty-six feet. With a final smirk at Carlos, she folded her arms, closed her eyes, and pretended to doze off. Chris would be free in just a few more hours.

And somewhere out in the dark, choppy waters of the strait, the bell was bobbing, the men inside—Ben, Vern, and Pierre—in the final stages of emergency decompression. Her only concern was, that since the cable spool had been removed, they would have had to detach the clump weight, float up, and do the entire depressurization on the surface. A bell could drift a long way in thirty hours . . . maybe too far from the island for them to be able to swim to shore. If they were ten miles out in the Caribbean . . .

She made herself stop right there. They weren't.

And even if they were, Ben would find a way back.

Her throat thickened and hot pressure welled behind her eyes.

He always came back.

*****

"Ah don't know 'bout you," Earl said, shivering, "but Ah'm dang near half froze."

"Me too," Posey replied. He rubbed his upper arms. "I was pretty close to being dried out yesterday, but I'm soaked again now. Sure wish I had my peacoat."

Earl could barely see him in the darkness, huddled beneath the dripping fronds of a low scrub palm. When the squall had hit, he himself had taken cover under the broad leaves of a banana tree. Neither afforded much shelter, but after spending the entire day scouting around the big house they'd spotted on one of the island's central ridges, creeping through steamy, bramble-choked ravines while trying to get close enough to learn something without being seen, they weren't about to do much blind dashing through the nighttime jungle in search of the perfect dry spot. The trees would have to suffice.

"You git any sleep before the rain ran us outta that little clearin' we was in?" Earl asked.

"Maybe an hour. Mosquitoes were eating me alive."

"Me too." Earl sighed and looked out past the dripping leaves at the black void of strait and sky. The squall mists were thinning; a few stars glittered through the overhead haze like random flecks of ice. "It'll be dawn soon. We might oughta check out that lagoon we saw from the ridge yesterday. Looked like there might be a dock or somethin' on it. Ah couldn't quite make it out through all the trees."

Posey sneezed. "Excuse me. Good idea. Maybe we'll find the barge nearby. That's if I don't die of pneumonia first, that is."

Earl managed a rueful grin. "Hang in there, son. Tomorrow's another day."

The tech sneezed again. "Aghh. It's already tomorrow," he said glumly. "And as the senoritas say in Matamoros when you buy them a drink that's too cheap: 'Already-I-don'-like-it-a-*lot.*'"

Chapter Thirty-Two

"Ohhhh, Jeeezuzz. . . ." Sligo groaned, his head lolling as the bell took another great wobbling roll in the trough of a wave. "I'm gonna be sick again . . . *ohhhhh . . ."*

"Cain't you just die an' git it over with?" Vern snarled, braced between the radiant heater and the gas rack. "You gawd damned sloppy pukin' sumbitch." He'd already had to strip one vomit clogged oral-nasal off the smuggler and get him into a backup.

"Don't puke in that new mask!" Ben said. He was wedged up next to Pierre, the two divers holding each other steady, his eyes flickering continuously between his watch and the bell's internal pressure gauge. The Frenchman had one hand on the big quarter turn ball valve that was venting the interior back to sea level, manually controlling the bleed rate. "You can't breathe in here without a mask! The atmosphere's got no oxygen in it, just helium and carbon dioxide. Pull the mask, puke, and put it back on or you're dead meat! We don't have the time or the means to revive you if you pass out, you understand?"

"Or the inclination," Pierre added.

Sligo responded by throwing up a pint of watery yellow stomach acid all over the Frenchman's bare feet.

It was the sum total of his stomach contents. None of them had eaten for nearly a day and a half.

"Merde!" Pierre cursed, kicking his soiled feet into one of the loose blankets.

With a muted roar, a breaking wave toppled the bell over onto its side. There was a sucking POP, and the trunk hatch jumped on its hinge. Water squirted out sideways all around the circumference of the seal.

Ben looked at his companions as the bell wallowed upright. "That's it!" he exclaimed. "Sea level. We're outta here!" He glanced at his watch. "Oh five-fifty. Maybe there'll be a little daylight out there so we can see the island. Get your escape bags."

Sligo stared up from his retching. *"What if we can't s-see the fuckin' island?"* he wailed.

Ben shrugged. "Then we're screwed," he said simply. The biceps in his tanned arms flexed as the bell took another sickening, corkscrewing roll. "Okay, Vern. Wait for the next trough and let's open the hatch. Pierre, you lock it back so it can't slam. Ready . . . *now!"*

They heaved and the heavy metal disk swung up with a clank. Seawater spewed into the bell like a geyser, stopping only when Ben hit one of the blow-down valves and pressurized the interior with the remaining onboard gas just enough to force the water back down the trunk shaft. With every surge, eardrums and sinuses squeaked and popped.

"Let's get the hell out of here!" Ben shouted, and stepped into the trunk, his small bag of escape gear slung by a strap over one elbow. The hard steel tube was no place to linger—not with the pounding the bell was taking. He took one more deep breath and pulled off his mask. "Meet you outside, on the top bumper rail!"

He dropped into the foaming black water and disappeared.

"Oh, fuck meee," Sligo moaned, his eyes half-crazed. He clutched the escape bag—facemask, makeshift snorkel, and jury rigged flotation aid—that Pierre had prepared for him, and got to his hands and knees, dry heaving energetically.

"Go on, froggy," Vern growled. "Ah'll stuff this lump o' shit on through to where y'all can git ahold of him."

"Tabarnac, mon ami," the little Frenchman exclaimed, "why bother?" He inflated his muscular chest, yanked the oral-nasal off his face, and slipped through the trunk opening with the agility of an otter.

The bell wallowed viciously back and forth as a series of crossing swells hit it. Sligo careened into the edge of the upright hatch, shrieking with pain as his elbow cracked into the steel, and Vern seized him by the seat of his bright-red Kronos Industries Ther-maLint™ Sub-Liner long john underwear. He lifted the gibbering smuggler up bodily, inverted him against his hip so that he hung head-down, ripped his breathing mask off his face—eliciting another agonized shriek—and jammed him down into the trunk like a piledriver going through a guide shaft.

*"AAAAHH*blub—" Sligo said, his rubber-bootied feet disappearing.

Vern followed a second later, dropping into the water feet first. Immediately encountering the smuggler at the trunk's bottom end—somehow wedged in the opening like a plug in a drainpipe—he stomped him the rest of the way out with half a dozen powerful kicks.

Holding his breath, Vern maneuvered himself expertly through the bell's external framework of gas cylinder supports and up the side of the heaving capsule. The water outside wasn't black, as he had anticipated, but a deep turquoise blue, which contrasted sharply with the international orange of the hull. So much color meant the presence of light. Dawn had to be breaking.

Out to his right, still five feet underwater, Sligo was kicking and clawing and rotating like a flashy red pinwheel, having lost his grip on the bell. Vern snatched a leg with one hand, yanked him in, and propelled him up toward the surface. Then, with a heave of his great arms, he drove himself upward as well.

His head broke the surface and he filled his lungs with fresh air—moist, briny, and clean; the first he'd tasted in many hours. Blinking water out of his eyes, he checked his surroundings. Ben was on the opposite side of the bell, his arms locked over the circular bumper rail that ran around the capsule's top. Pierre was closer, to his right. He was hanging on to the rail with one hand and trying to keep Sligo from floundering beneath the surface with the other. The smuggler didn't seem to have grasped the fact that in order to survive, he was going to have to hold his head above water long enough to breath.

Vern swore and grabbed him by the back of the neck. In one motion, he lifted Sligo waist-high out of the water and slapped him onto the bumper rail. The smuggler gasped, clutched frantically, grabbed, and hugged the rail to his chest. His long, dirty-blonde hair matted over his face like seaweed, interfering with his breathing.

"Hang on, idjit," Vern shouted. He glanced around again. Only the top curve of the bell was visible—perhaps ten percent of the capsule's total volume. Capping it like a thick steel halo was the circular bumper rail. Everything was awash in foam and wobbling like mad, although the seas were not as big as he'd first thought—less than four feet. Overhead, the shredded black remnants of squall clouds scudded across the silvery dawn sky. It was blowing clear.

"Well, what now?" Vern yelled to Ben.

"It's light enough to see the island," Ben called back. "I keep spotting it when we ride up on a swell. But I need to get a better look. Hang on a minute."

He waited for a trough and then heaved himself up onto the bell, clinging to the bumper rail for balance. Sitting up and craning his neck, he gazed off to the northwest. "There's the island! We're—" He paused. "Shit, we're being driven past the eastern point! The wind and waves are pushing us out into the open Caribbean!"

He slid back down into the churning water. "But the point is only about three quarters of a mile away." Foam sloshed into his face and he coughed and spat. "The bell's passing close by it on its way out to sea. We should be able to make the swim in less than two hours, if we don't run into any currents. But we have to go now."

"Whaaaat?" Sligo wailed, hanging on for dear life. *"We're goin' somewhere?"*

Pierre reached out and cuffed him on the side of the head. "That is for not listening, *imbecile!* You were told you have to swim! Now prepare yourself!"

Vern was already donning his facemask, snorkel, and fins. The small mesh gear bag he stuffed into the waistband of his sweatpants. Swiftly, Ben and Pierre followed suit.

Sligo dragged himself up onto the very top of the bell, as Ben had just done. He made no move to put on his swimming gear.

"We have to go *now!*" Ben yelled at him, pushing away from the capsule through the deep blue water. "We can't wait for you to make up your fucking mind! Come on!"

Sligo stared around at the driving swells and white-caps, his bloodshot blue eyes wild with fear. *"Are you crazy?"* he yelled back. *"We're in the middle of the fuckin' ocean! There's sharks everywhere! There's a fuckin' hurricane blowin'! I can't swim in this!"* He nearly lost his balance, groping wildly, as a breaking wave tossed the bell.

"We can do nothing for him now," Pierre panted, finning up beside Ben. "Either he comes or he doesn't."

"Amen," Vern growled, sculling up next to them. He adjusted his snorkel alongside his face. "He ain't gonna be able to hold on for more'n an hour, Ah'd say. Less if it gets any rougher."

Ben tried once more. "Let's go, for chrissake! You can't stay there!"

Sligo stared at him in desperation. *"I don't believe this shit!"* he screeched. *"Here I am floatin' around in the middle of the goddamn ocean again! It's the same as when I dropped those Arab terrorist assholes off on the NAOC-X! How can this shit happen to me twice in one lifetime?"*•

It was Ben's turn to stare. *"What* did you say?" he exclaimed in disbelief.

And then a rogue wave, twice as high as the running swells, broke between the three divers and the bell. It washed over them like a tsunami, tumbling them up and down in a welter of foam, and when they found the surface again, gasping for air, the bell was more than forty yards away. Drifting out to sea amid the driving whitecaps.

Atop it, perched in the middle of the circular bumper ring like a bright-red, longhaired garden gnome, was Jeremiah Sligo—still babbling at the top of his lungs. They could see his mouth moving, see his eyes darting around crazily, but they could no longer hear him. There was only swash of the waves and the moan of the wind.

The man was done. Vern was right: eventually he would tire, lose his grip, and be swept off the bell. It

---

• See *CRASH DIVE*, Ben Gannon's first adventure.

was only a matter of time. They took a last look. Then, as one, they positioned their snorkels in their mouths, turned face down, and began to kick hard toward the low cliffs that lined the island's eastern point.

Chapter Thirty-Three

Grizelda walked out of the bathroom of the hilltop *hacienda*'s master suite, toweling her short hair. She was naked, her red-brown skin even more florid than usual from the heat of her shower. Across the room, Alberto, also naked, lay sprawled on the disheveled king-sized bed, looking soft and wasted. Only his eyes appeared alive; they followed his sister's every move with dazed adoration.

"That was unbelievable," he mumbled. "All night long. I can't even move."

Grizelda let out a low giggle, continuing to towel her hair.

"It's always unbelievable," Alberto continued. "Don't you think?"

"Mm."

"Well, I think so," he said petulantly. "But it's so *long* between the times you want to do it with me. Why do you make me wait like that?"

Grizelda faced him, her lips peeling back into a slit of a smile. Slowly, deliberately, she wiped a few beads of water from between her big breasts. "Because, little brother," she said, "if I didn't, you might not think it was so . . . unbelievable."

Alberto's mouth hung slack. Then he licked his lips and swallowed. Languidly, Grizelda turned away and began to towel her back.

"What are your plans today?" Alberto asked, somehow finding the energy to stretch.

Grizelda stared out the bedroom's picture window at the blue Caribbean horizon. "Exercise," she said. "I feel fat." She scratched her left calf with the big toe of her right foot, and as she did so, muscle and sinew rippled from her hips to her ankles and veins stood out beneath her skin like worm trails.

The characteristic bark of shrill laughter erupted from Alberto's lips. *"HAAH!* Oh, yes, you're fat. An absolute porker, that's what you are, big sister."

Grizelda ignored his comments. "It's calming down. I'm going to the reef this morning. I feel like a hunt."

Alberto rolled onto his stomach. "I don't know where you get the energy. But whatever. If you must. Oh, and by the way: we don't need any more groupers with their heads blown off. The freezer is full of them, and I'm sick of fish."

"Don't worry," Grizelda said. "This is exercise only. I'm just going to kill a few things and let the sharks have them. Some big things. There's a juvenile jewfish that weighs about two hundred pounds out by the sunken ledges. He'll make a nice target for a power-head."

"Just as long as you don't drag the ugly beast home and try to make me eat it."

"I told you not to worry. By the way, I sent Luis to the mainland in the Whaler. He'll be gone the rest of the week, getting some fresh supplies."

Alberto wadded a pillow up against the headboard and sat up. "When can we bring our two guests up to play?" he asked, a depraved smile playing about his face. "I can't wait."

Grizelda pulled open a dresser drawer and extracted a black thong and athletic top. "I told you: not until the pretty boy in the saturation chamber gets out. Two weeks." She shook her head at him. "You are soooo greedy, Alberto."

Her brother pouted and crossed his arms. "How about the woman?"

"No. We need her to complete his decompression. We don't know how to do it, and I want him coming out undamaged, in good physical condition." She grinned. "His energy levels high."

"What if they don't want to play?" Alberto countered. "They might not, you know, after what we did to their friends."

Grizelda looked at him as she stepped into the black thong. "Of course they won't. We'll use the body tranquilizers in their food. That'll make them easy to handle."

Alberto smiled at his sister. "You're so clever. You want the woman first, don't you? You can have her, you know. I don't mind."

Grizelda pulled her top down over her jiggling breasts and moved up beside the bed. "Yes," she said, leaning in close. "I know I can."

"I love you, big sister," Alberto mumbled.

"And I love *you,* little brother."

They locked lips hungrily, chewing on each other for a good thirty seconds before Grizelda broke away and stood up.

"Go down to the barge when you finally get out of bed," she said, in a voice devoid of emotion, "and make sure that our edible little blonde bitch isn't up to anything the guards are too stupid to see." She headed toward the door, stretching her shoulder muscles. "Something isn't right about her, about the way she's cooperating. She's smart. And she's wily enough to outmaneuver those fools. Make sure she doesn't."

Grizelda paused in the doorway. "And then tonight, little brother, maybe I'll show you how much I appreciate it."

*****

"Dang!" Earl whispered, peering through the leaves. "That's Sass down there."

Lying beside him on the jungle floor at the edge of the little overlook, Posey cupped his hands around his eyes to block out the morning sun. "Goddammit to hell . . . I can't see that far away, Earl. I'll have to take your word for it."

"It's her all right."

"What's she doing?"

"Sittin' on a chair by the sat pot, takin' notes on her clipboard. Appears to me she's still decompressin' someone."

Posey blew out a long breath. "The divers. Ben, Vern, Pierre, and Chris. That's four more of us who are still alive."

He fell silent as Earl looked around some more. They had chosen a position high up on the hillside that sloped down to the lagoon's western shore. Directly below them, perhaps three hundred yards away, lay the barge and yacht. Farther around to the north, where the heavily treed shoreline became a narrow strip of white beach, a dock stretched out into the emerald-green water. Between the dock and barge, dark shapes were cruising back and forth, undulating lazily just above the shallow bottom.

"Sharks down there," Earl mused. "One of 'em's a tiger. Big sumbitch, too. See that squared-off head?"

Posey shrugged. "No, I can't."

"Yeah, yeah. 'Course you cain't. Sorry. But he's there."

"Then I hope we don't have to go swimming again. At least not in that lagoon."

"Dang it!" Earl said suddenly.

"What's wrong.

"Ah just realized: there ain't no divin' bell on the barge." Earl searched for a moment. "Nope. No bell anywheres."

"Well, they must have . . . lost it or something, eh?" Posey speculated.

Earl looked at him. "The dang thing was mated to the sat pot, last I saw. If it ain't there, someone must have launched it. An' if someone launched it, there were probably divers inside. Why would you launch an empty bell?"

Posey nodded. "I see what you're getting at. If there were divers inside . . ."

"And it ain't on board now . . ."

Earl's voice trailed off. "The bell's cable's hangin' loose on the A-frame crane. Ah wonder how many of our boys are in that pot." He chewed his lower lip. "Maybe it's just Chris, in the outer lock. He was the only man who couldn't have got hisself into the bell."

"But why would—" Posey began.

"Ah don't know," Earl said quietly. "Ah don't know why they'd have launched it, why they'd have cut it loose, or if there were any divers in it when they did. Ah just don't know." He glanced out to sea. "Hell, the dang thing could be floatin' around out there right now with three men in it."

Posey blinked. "That big ball of steel *floats?*"

"If you cut loose the clump weight."

"But you're talking about a ton or two of *steel*. A giant cannonball. That bell's heavy."

"So is that steel barge," Earl pointed out, "but it floats real good. Your ROV weighs a bunch, but it floats too."

The tech nodded slowly. "Huh. You're right. All these years working offshore beside divers and chambers and bells, and I never even thought about it."

Earl gave a short chuckle. "Don't worry 'bout it, Gerald. Ah do believe you done more'n enough thinkin' 'bout other things."

"I can't argue with that," Posey replied ruefully.

The big man rolled onto his side and slapped a mosquito that was feasting on his earlobe. "Well, what we gonna do? We need to get Sass outta there, but we cain't spring whoever's in the sat pot until their decompression's finished—and she's runnin' it." He turned his head and spat. "We get her clear, these assholes might kill the people they're still holdin'. There's maybe two, three armed guards down there."

"Right." Posey thought a moment. "You know, we didn't see any of our crew up at the house, but that doesn't mean anything. They could be locked up somewhere. Maybe Ben, or Pierre, or Vern"—he paused as a look of pain came into Earl's eyes at the mention of his brother's name—"or even Gene."

Earl shook his head. "Not Gene. I told you."

"Maybe he was only wounded," Posey ventured hopefully.

Earl shook his head again. "No. He was shot dead."

There was another pause as the ROV tech regarded the leaf litter. "Fucking hell. Those *bastards*."

"Pretty much."

"So what do we do? We can't try to take her away from them now. Do we just sit here in the goddamn jungle until the hatch pops, then charge in like the cavalry?"

"Ah don't think that'd be a good idea," Earl said. "Tell you what: let's scout down around that there lagoon, see how many gunmen there are. Maybe we can sneak aboard the barge or yacht—get a message out by radio. Get some dang *help*."

Posey nodded. "Lead on. Just remember: if it's not within twenty feet of me, I can't see it. Don't let me give us away by stumbling around."

"You just hang close an' keep your feet under you. If Ah need to let you set awhile, Ah'll tell you."

Together, they backed away from the edge of the little overlook, got to their feet, and began to pick their way through the dripping jungle in a downward traverse.

*****

Ben moved carefully, trying to place his hands on the sharp limestone without cutting them to ribbons. He looked down. At the base of the cliff he was climbing, blue-green water and white foam surged in and around the exposed reef formations that he, Vern, and Pierre had just navigated. The other two divers were right behind him, clinging to the vertical rock like a pair of waterlogged monkeys. It was a seventy-foot drop to the jagged reefs below, and at least forty to the cliff-top. And the limestone face was beginning to overhang, the handholds few and far between.

And they were tired. The three-quarter-mile swim from the drifting bell to the eastern point of the island had taken nearly two hours, and they'd had to fight a strong current running along the outer reef as they'd approached. Throughout the entire deepwater part of the journey they'd been shadowed by sharks—pelagic whitetips, mostly—that had glided through the bottomless blue void thirty, forty, fifty feet beneath them. None had made any threatening movements, but their presence alone had kept the snorkeling divers bunched up and kicking hard, if cautiously. It had been unnerving and exhausting.

Now they were all a slipped fingertip or two away from tumbling to a painful death on the spiked rocks at the base of the cliff. But there was no other way to get off the eastern point. The longshore current was flowing the wrong way, and would only have taken them out to sea had they attempted to swim further west along the island's southern coast. It was climb or nothing.

Ben leaned out, arms shaking with strain, and searched the cliff face above him. "Goddamn thing's getting smooth," he shouted, "and really overhangs at the lip. We need to try this crack over to the right, see if we can get some better holds and jams in it."

"Long as we do sumpthin' soon," Vern called up, his voice hoarse. "Ah'm too dang big to hang by mah arms much longer."

"Put your foot here, *mon ami,*" Pierre said. He was hanging from a single hand jam, his fist balled and wedged in a small crack, arm straight and relaxed, hips in, his neoprene-bootied toes planted securely on small bumps in the limestone face. "Do not try to hold yourself by arm strength alone, and especially with your arms bent. You will exhaust yourself very quickly like that." He took hold of Vern's right heel with his free hand and shifted his foot to a tiny ledge. "Put your weight on there. You see how it relieves your arms? Good. Now, observe. Concentrate on your foot place-ment, bend your knees, keep your hips in close to the rock, and straighten your elbows. Like me—*comme ca, eh?* Trust me on this. Back home in France, I climb rocks for fun."

"You gotta be shittin' me," Vern grunted, his arms trembling.

"No, *c'est vrai*—it's true. Rock climbing is a very big sport in Europe. Top climbers are national celebri-ties."

"Well, hoo-ray for them fuckers," Vern panted. "Look, froggy, Ah'm about to slip offa here."

"Give me your hand."

"What?"

"I said give me your hand."

"You'll fall too if'n you try to hold me."

"Non. That will not happen. Quickly, now—your hand!"

"Jeezus!"

As he fell, Vern locked wrists with the little Frenchman, swinging out away from the rock on one arm. Pierre grunted, flexing his legs as he took the sudden weight. But his jammed fist did not slip and his other hand did not let go. Vern swung up against the cliff just beneath him.

"Oof! Jee—Jeezus H. Christ!"

Above the pair, Ben had already moved to the wide vertical crack that appeared to travel all the way to the top of the cliff. He watched helplessly as Vern dangled in empty space, clawing and kicking at the smooth limestone. Pierre held his position like a human grappling hook, his powerful arms and legs quivering, veins bulging on top of whipcord muscle.

"Ah—Ah cain't git ahold of anything!" Vern groaned. "You gotta let go, froggy . . . no sense in . . . both of us fallin' . . ."

Pierre didn't move. Head down, jaw set and eyes closed, he squeezed Vern's wrist even more tightly. *"Non,"* he gritted, his entire body beginning to shake. "You owe . . . me . . . twenty dol*lair* . . ."

He gave a tremendous heave and with one arm dead-lifted the big man eighteen inches straight up. Vern's feet found a square-cut edge, got a purchase. The fingers of his free hand sank into a narrow fissure two feet above his head, twisted, and jammed.

"Ah got it," Vern gasped. "You can let go now."

Only when he was that sure Vern was supporting himself on the rock did Pierre release his wrist. He remained hanging from his own hand jam, head sagging onto his chest, his breath coming hard and fast, for nearly fifteen seconds.

"You guys all right down there?" Ben called.

"Yeah," Vern replied. "Barely." Pierre merely nodded, too exhausted to speak.

"Good work, Pierre," Ben said. "Good work." He looked up at the interior of the crack into which he had wedged his left shoulder, hip, and knee. "This crack widens about ten feet up, turns into a chimney of sorts. It looks pretty climbable, and goes all the way to the cliff-top. I can see daylight and green leaves up there. Can you make it?"

"Sure, why not?" Vern growled.

"Oui," Pierre replied, finding his voice at last. He glanced down at Vern, whose head was beside his left knee, and grinned. "We can make it."

"Good. I'm going up."

Ben wriggled upward, jamming the elbow, shoulder, hip, and foot on his left side until the crack widened out enough to accommodate his entire body. Once inside, he planted his back and buttocks against one wall, his feet and hands on the other, and began to work his way up using friction and opposing pressure. Unlike the outer rock face, the chimney was studded with small edges and irregularities, which aided his ascent.

He emerged from the small sinkhole that formed the mouth of the chimney after only five minutes. The cliff-top was overgrown with low, wind-beaten vegetation, and provided a panoramic view of the strait, eastern point, and southern shore of the island. Behind him, a narrow trail wandered off into the encroaching jungle in a roughly westward direction.

He turned his attention to the sinkhole as Pierre clambered out of the chimney, followed by a puffing and grunting Vern. The big man looked all but done in, his face pale and lined with strain. Ben and Pierre got a hand under each arm and helped him to a kneeling position on firm ground.

He sat on his haunches with his head bowed, silent, his great shoulders heaving as he gulped in fresh air like a human bellows.

"When you're ready," Ben said, "we'll follow this trail over here. There was a lagoon below that house we saw on the ridge before we went into sat. Maybe that's where the barge is. Or somebody."

Vern nodded, still getting his breath. After a few more seconds, he leaned forward and picked up a flat rock about the size and shape of a large poker chip. Then he located another fragment, triangular and sharp, and began to scratch the first rock with it. When he was done, he dropped the fragment, looked up at Pierre, and held out the first rock.

"Here," he said.

Pierre took the rock. On it, Vern had scratched **20—V.P.**

"Qu'est-ce que c'est?" the Frenchman asked, frowning. "What is this?"

"Mah I.O.U.," Vern replied, placing his hands on his knees. "Ah ain't got your twenty bucks on me right now."

He heaved himself to his feet without another word, and the three of them headed off into the jungle along the little trail, Ben leading the way.

Chapter Thirty-Four

Grizelda had developed an unconventional technique for spearfishing on the outer reefs west of the lagoon. Not particularly concerned with harvesting fish for sport and food, but rather with the physical exertion of snorkeling over a quarter mile offshore and the almost erotic sense of power she derived from killing virtually any marine creature that crossed her path, she carried a peculiar weapon on her reef safaris.

It was a custom made speargun nearly six feet long—a single piece of carved teak heartwood, inset along its length with stainless steel plugs that rendered it neutrally buoyant and perfectly balanced underwater. The cocking and firing mechanism was stainless steel as well, crafted by an Italian gunsmith to precise specifications. It shot a relatively short four-foot tempered steel spear, powered by three slings of extra heavy surgical tubing. There was no tethering line or breakaway gear on the spear and gun, for the simple reason that Grizelda had no desire to reel in or otherwise retrieve what she shot. The killing was the thing, and her spears were designed to do just that—with considerable violence and dramatic effect.

She carried a total of seven—six in a special quiver on her back and one in the gun—which was the maximum number she could swim with comfortably. She ordered them two hundred at a time, considering them disposable. Each spear was tipped with a powerhead: a metal tube about the size of a light-gauge shotgun shell that housed a greased .44 caliber pistol cartridge. The powerhead contained a firing pin, and when jammed against any reasonably firm surface—the living flesh of a grouper or shark, for example—the cartridge would discharge, firing the heavy-caliber slug into the target.

It made a very satisfying mess, Grizelda had found. The heavy spears would travel with great accuracy for up to twenty-five feet, and blow large, gaping holes— the result of both concussion and projectile force—in anything they hit. Even large sharks—such as bulls or hammerheads—were so damaged by the powerheads that they would do little more than shudder, turn belly up, and sink; or, if not killed instantly, wriggle off into the blue gloom in a frenzied death spiral. Grizelda rated the satisfaction of killing sharks in this manner just fractionally below that of manhunting on land with her twin knives.

She smiled, inhaling the damp morning air. There was just nothing like a hunt to get the blood flowing. To sharpen your killer instincts and revel in the certainty that you—and you alone—were at the top of the food chain. The *real* food chain: the one that included the rest of humanity.

She was jogging down the jeep track from the house with her mask, snorkel, and fins bouncing against her hips, clipped to her four-pound weight belt. Her left hand was tucked behind her, stabilizing the backpack quiver with its six spears as she ran, and in her right she carried the big speargun, loaded but not cocked. Strapped to the outside of her right calf was an eight inch diving stiletto in a black polyethylene sheath.

She could see the yacht and barge through the trees now, floating on the green-glass water of the lagoon about five switchbacks farther down. Hawking up a wad of phlegm, she spat forcefully and continued her fast trot down the winding road. The barge bothered her. At some point, the tug that had brought it would return. The barge couldn't be sitting abandoned and damaged in her private lagoon, the crew gone, when it did. The entire dive platform needed to be towed out into deep water and sunk; the evidence of what had taken place aboard it erased.

She'd have to make sure that the tasty-looking blonde with the sharp mind—Sass—was decompressing the diver in the outer lock as quickly as possible. She might be stalling, trying to buy time—

Grizelda jogged around the next-to-last switchback, looked up, and stopped in mid stride. Just emerging from the jungle less than ten yards ahead was a man she'd never seen before. An American, by the look of him, wearing a sleeveless gray sweatshirt, black track shorts, and neoprene dive socks. He was soaked to the skin; his tanned arms and legs smeared with mud and rotten leaves. Like her, he was carrying a mask, snorkel, and fins. He wasn't so much walking as stalking his way forward, clearly intent on not being seen.

The man—he was tall, six feet or more—suddenly turned and looked straight at her. For a second, the two of them stared at each other, frozen. And in that second, Grizelda thought of the lead diver Alberto had described to her: sun-streaked auburn hair, clean-shaven, tanned and very fit, a commercial diver's tattoo on his right   forearm . . .

"Gannon!" she bellowed and yanked back one of the speargun's rubber slings.

By the time she got the gun cocked and half-raised, Ben was across the road and leaping into the foliage. Grizelda brought the weapon up level and fired instinctively, without aiming. The slender steel spear zinged out of the gun with an accompanying snap of surgical tubing and flashed through the sunlit air above the road.

It shot through the leaves just behind Ben's fast-moving head and struck the three-inch-thick trunk of a young palm tree. There was a loud BANG, a burst of wood pulp and splinters, and the upper half of the tree toppled over.

"Gannon!" Grizelda roared again. Whipping out a second spear and inserting it into the gun, cocking all three slings this time, she charged after him with a wild shriek: *"YAAAAAGGHH!"*

*****

"Merde!" Pierre whispered, rising from behind the dense cluster of brambles that had prevented Grizelda from spotting him, a mere ten paces behind Ben. He looked over his shoulder at Vern—ten paces behind *him*—and motioned him forward. The big man was at his side in three seconds.

"Ben was right," Pierre breathed, scanning the road up and down. "We kept thirty feet between us, moved one at a time, and only the lead man was seen." He grimaced. *"Tabarnac!* We should go after him."

Vern shook his head. "Yeah, we should. But we're gonna stick to the plan. That's the way he wants it, an' that's what we agreed. *Oui?"*

The Frenchman nodded grudgingly. *"Oui."*

"Okay, then. We work our way down to the barge, slip into the water just up from where it's moored, and swim between it and the yacht. We counted only two guards with Sass when we scoped out the situation from back up the trail there, so we oughta be able to climb on board without them seein' us and give 'em both a fuckin' headache." Vern flashed a hard smile.

"I will enjoy that part hugely, *mon ami,*" Pierre said. "And once we have disposed of the armed baboons, Sass will be able to tell us what has been going on, eh?"

"Yeah," Vern replied, moving forward. "And personally, Ah cain't wait."

*****

Ben was running for his life. He'd seen the musclebound woman—bizarre; she looked like some kind of comic-book villainess—cock the big speargun and start to bring it to bear, and he knew a powerhead when he saw one. The hiss of the spear and the explosive detonation just behind his head confirmed her armament. Tired as he was, his legs felt as if they contained railroad springs. The last thing in the world you wanted to get hit by was a powerhead.

He'd found the continuation of the narrow, winding trail that he, Pierre, and Vern had taken west from the clifftop. It was following the contour of the lagoon; below him, through the trees to his left, he could see the *Cucaracha*'s white hull next to the rusty-black metal of the barge, less than two hundred feet away.

He hurdled a fallen tree, the rotting trunk draped with green velvet moss, and dodged around a small outcropping of white limestone. Behind him, he could hear his pursuer yelling in Spanish, most likely to the two guards on the barge.

Good. That would give Pierre and Vern an opening. Whether the gunmen joined the chase or not, they would be distracted by the commotion. And Sass was not slow to seize an advantage either. He grinned even as he ran. Seeing her alive and well had removed his greatest fear and given him a much-needed surge of adrenaline.

The slope the trail was traversing had increased to nearly forty-five degrees, and the footing was treacherous. His neoprene socks, not the best footwear for sprinting through wet jungle, slipped and skidded on mud and leaf litter as he clawed his way up a little rise, down into a hollow, over another rise . . .

And there the trail ended, at a little clearing bordered on both sides by twenty-five-foot limestone cliffs—too smooth to climb, even if there had been time. Straight ahead, the aquamarine patchwork of the island's inner and outer reefs gave way to the deep blue of the open Caribbean, which stretched off to the southern horizon. It was the equivalent of a box canyon—but a box canyon with a back door.

Ben hesitated for only a second. With the musclebound woman's footfalls pounding through the jungle behind him, he took half a dozen running steps and leaped off the twenty-foot coral cliff that formed the seaward edge of the clearing.

He hit the water with his legs together and plunged down nearly fifteen feet, sheathed in bubbles. Staying submerged, he slipped his mask on, cleared it of water with a quick exhalation, and jammed his feet into his fins. As air hunger began to gnaw at him, he visualized the big woman on the edge of the cliff, her howitzer of a speargun lining up on his submerged form . . .

No *way* he was surfacing right here.

He whirled three hundred and sixty degrees, surveying the underwater landscape. From the base of the cliffs to about thirty feet out, the water was surprisingly deep, as if a channel had been gouged parallel to the shoreline with a giant dredge. Ben estimated its depth to be around sixty feet. Farther to seaward, the bottom rose rapidly to less than twenty feet, giving way to the intricate coral topography of the inner reef.

The cliff, less than fifteen feet away, looked undercut—scooped, especially up at the waterline, as if wave action had eroded out a series of concavities. Perhaps the woman wouldn't have a clear shot if he surfaced there. He had little choice; he was about to black out from lack of air.

His chest burning, he kicked forward and made for the cliff, trying to stay deep. Three feet from the coral-covered rock face, he felt something brush the blade of his left fin. He looked back and below in time to see the gleaming steel shaft of a spear lose its downward momentum and begin to fall sideways, its trajectory traced by a thin arc of air bubbles. Neither the impact with the water's surface nor the grazing contact with his fin had been sufficient, apparently, to fire the power-head.

His vision starting to blur, his heart hammering behind his breastbone, he popped his head out of the water right next to the cliff, in what had seemed from below to be an area of shadow. It was a good choice. Wave action had indeed undercut the limestone a good six feet, creating a shallow, continuous sea cave that ran laterally east and west. The roof of the recess, barely three feet above his head, prevented him from being seen from the lip of the cliff.

He was sucking in air, his head clearing rapidly, and feeling a hint of relief at having temporarily outmaneuvered his pursuer, when a large, dark shape dropped into view below the upper edge of the rock. It was the musclebound, bikini-clad woman, a horrific sneer on her face, falling through the air feet first, facing the cliff. The speargun was level, cradled against her hip.

She and Ben locked eyes, and just before her feet hit the water, she fired.

Ben jerked sideways, and as he did the spear flashed by his right ear and struck the rock behind him. There was an explosion, a spray of limestone shards that stung the back of his head—and then he was underwater again, the spent shaft dropping past him toward the bottom with its powerhead trailing smoky bubbles.

Inverting himself and kicking furiously along the cliff at a depth of five feet, Ben glanced out to seaward. At the same depth, perhaps twenty-five or thirty feet away, the bizarre-looking woman was yanking her fins on, her mask and snorkel already in place, her speargun tucked under one arm.

If there was one thing Ben was sure of, it was that he wanted as much distance between himself and that powerhead-loaded gun as possible. He streamlined his body and kicked along the cliff with all his might, dismissing the possibility of arming himself by diving for the spear the woman had fired at him from the clifftop—the one that had not detonated. With her now in the water, clearly able to swim and maneuver at least as well as he could, there was nothing else to do but haul ass and try to survive by speed, endurance, and cat-and-mouse tactics.

The crevices and irregularities in the cliff, teeming with fish, along with the abundance of staghorn formations and domelike brain corals, gave him a certain amount of cover and some additional speed; he was able to accelerate every few feet or so by pulling himself along as well as kicking. His pursuer, despite her obvious strength, was encumbered by the large gun, which left her only one free hand, and the quiver of steel spears. And she was trying to track and overtake an elusive quarry that was already fleeing about as fast a human being could underwater. Not an easy task, Ben told himself, kicking and clawing his way through the sea fans and branching corals, scattering schools of blue surgeonfish, black-and-yellow sergeant majors, and green parrotfish as they drifted and grazed along the vertical undersea pasture of the rock face.

He broke the surface like a breaching porpoise, gasping in air, and finned past a wedge-shaped section of cliff that jutted out into the channel. Then he dove again, glancing back. Through the shafts of sunlight flickering through the azure-blue water, he could see the woman's bulky form. She was still coming, kicking like a mad thing; hunting him from the surface.

Swimming parallel to her, out in open water about twenty feet away, was a medium-sized shark—a lemon, Ben guessed, from its light coloration and the shape of the its tail—exhibiting the wary curiosity so typical of its kind. There was a lot of energetic thrashing going on along the cliff this morning: thrashing that often meant an easy meal. The shark, however, was not about to charge in and take on a large, mobile animal nearly as big as itself. It was too cautious for that.

But most people, Ben knew, were funny about sharks. Distracted by them. He stopped swimming, whirled around in the water, and pointed vigorously at the cruising animal. On land, the woman probably wouldn't have batted an eye, figuring the gesture for an attempt at the old 'look there!' trick. In the ocean, however, instincts are far different. When someone—anyone—swimming in salt water makes a frantic pointing gesture, other people tend to look. Ben saw her head twist sideways, the beat of her kicking falter, and the speargun swing away from him.

He finned forward again, on his back, watching the activity behind him. The woman was vertical in the water now, at the surface, her full attention on the shark. It had reacted to the change in her swimming pattern. Instead of pacing her, it began to circle.

Ben was an extra twenty fin kicks ahead of the woman when she fired. The spear streaked out of the gun and punched into the shark just behind the gill slits. There was an immediate explosion—*crump*—accompanied by a small cloud of expanding gas. The eight-foot animal shook violently, a huge, bloody hole blown in its forward body cavity, and went spiraling off into the channel with its white belly upturned, trailing internal organs and wriggling like an eel.

Ugly, Ben thought, and redoubled his kicking effort. One last look behind him revealed the woman placing another spear in the gun, cocking the slings, and finning forward as she picked up the pursuit.

Ben dove along the cliff face yet again, his leg muscles searing. He'd gained a little distance on her, but it wasn't much, and sooner or later he was going to have to slow down. Try to get out of the water.

Sooner rather than later.

*****

Sass's eyes widened as she saw Pierre's head and shoulders rise above the port rail of the barge. A couple of seconds later, Vern's huge frame emerged from between the barge and yacht next to him. Both men were dirty, stubble-bearded, and soaking wet. It was all she could do not to react, sitting on deck in the aluminum chair beside the outer lock of the sat pot. Catching Pierre's eye, she folded her arms and raised two fingers beneath her elbow in a gesture of caution. Then, very deliberately, she turned her head and spoke in a loud voice to the two guards who were standing ten feet in front of her:

"So. Have you two guys figured out why Big Momma was running through the jungle yet? Screaming at you to stay put and watch out for strangers?"

The guard named Carlos jabbed his submachine gun at her, his already confused face twisting even more. "Quiet! You don't talk!"

Sass shrugged. "Oh, hey—whatever you like. I just figured that with *only two of you on the barge*, you might be wondering why she didn't stop and explain things to you a little better."

Carlos stepped forward. *"Quiet!"* he shouted. "Why do you talk so loud?" He aimed his weapon directly at her forehead, scowling. *"You keep quiet!"*

"Sorry, sorry." Sass sat back, put up her open palms, and gave him a winning smile. "Just trying to be helpful, that's all. I mean, are you sure you heard right?"

"Heard . . . right?"

"Well, yeah." She leaned forward, showing him her cleavage down the open neck of her work shirt. "I mean, if she told you to stay put, you and Miguel are already doing what she wants, so you should just relax"—she sat back and let her tanned brown legs fall apart—"and take it easy."

The muzzle of the machine gun sagged a little as Carlos' small eyes ran up and down her body. Miguel drifted up behind his comrade, interested now, a slack grin on his lips. He carried his sawed-off shotgun loosely in one hand, its barrel pointing at the deck.

"Nobody's around," Sass went on, gazing at them. Her hand strayed up to the top button of her shirt. Casually, she popped it loose. Then the one below. Then the rest, until the garment was open all the way down to her belt buckle. She stretched her arms over her head and arched her back, letting them see some skin. Under the shirt she wore only an insubstantial blue bikini top.

"Hot out here, don't you think?" she drawled, and shucked the shirt off her shoulders in one smooth motion. The two gunmen crowded closer, their eyes riveted on her smooth brown arms, flat stomach, and firm, full breasts. She beamed up at them, showing her white teeth, and licked her upper lip.

"You know, a girl can really get bored, stuck on this barge day after day." She looked directly at each of them in turn, waiting . . . then pulled down her bikini top and exposed her breasts. "Look here, boys."

Carlos leaned in, panting, and Vern hit him just above the left ear with a three-foot length of cheater pipe. He went down as if guillotined. At the same time, Pierre brought a five-pound ball peen sledgehammer down on top of Miguel's head—CRACK. The man's eyes rolled up in their sockets and he promptly joined his associate face down on the steel deckplates.

Sass replaced her bikini top as she leaped out of the chair, hunched her shirt back onto her shoulders, and threw her arms around Vern and Pierre's necks. "Oh, *god!* Am I glad to see you guys!" When she pulled back, her eyes were damp. "Are you both all right? Is Ben all right?"

Vern toed the motionless Carlos. "As far as we know. He had to take off into the jungle. Some crazy woman was chasin' him."

Hurriedly, Sass buttoned her shirt. "Crazy woman? A bodybuilder type with short red hair? A couple of inches taller than me? Ugly as a goddamn gorilla?"

Pierre smiled. "Ah. You know her."

Sass nodded. "Grizelda Ramos. She and her brother Alberto are the ones we were supposed to be working for. They own this island." She nearly tripped over her tongue, the words were coming so fast. "A pair of cold-blooded killers. They killed Gene out on the barge. Shot him when they got into an argument."

Both Vern and Pierre were thunderstruck. "No," Vern said.

"It's true," Sass went on, her eyes glistening. "I dropped the bell because I figured it was the only way to stop them from killing you. They were ready to kill everybody on the barge, once Gene was dead. I sabotaged the lifting spool, because I thought they might just cut the bell loose and let you sink, if I steered them that way. I was pretty sure they didn't know it would float without the clump weight, and that you guys could probably save yourselves." A little sob escaped her. "They thought they were getting rid of all three of you at once by sinking it."

Vern hugged her around the shoulders, and Pierre squeezed her hand. "Easy, *cheri,*" he said. "You did well, and we will put things right now, *tabarnac.* Will we not, Vern?"

"You got that right," the big man growled. He let go of Sass, bent down, and seized Carlos by the seat of his baggy pants. "Let's lock these scumbags into that small surface decompression chamber, just for safe-keepin'. We can blow it down to ten feet and shut the vent valves. They'll never get the hatch open."

Pierre grabbed Miguel by the feet. "Good idea, *mon ami.*"

Sass pushed blonde hair back off her face. "What if they don't wake up in there?" she asked. "This guy's got blood running from his ears. He might die."

Vern looked at Pierre, then at her.

"Who cares?" he said. But when Sass frowned at him, his expression softened. "Okay, okay. We'll keep an eye on 'em. Check on 'em when we have time."

They dragged the two unconscious guards across the deck. Sass opened the chamber hatch, and Vern and

Pierre stuffed them into the entry lock, one after the other.

"Okay, cross it over," Vern told her, pulling the hatch shut.

There was a blast of air as Sass threw a valve and transferred pressurized air from the inner lock to the outer. The hatch sealed. She blew the lock to eight feet and stopped. "There. They can't get out. No sense in blowing them too deep and breaking their eardrums."

"You're nicer than me," Vern rumbled. "Ah'd have blown 'em down 'til their brains turned to mush."

"What about Ben?" Sass demanded. "We—we have to find him. That woman's crazy. She helped her brother kill their own lawyer when we were still out on the dive site—by *stinging* him to death with Man O' War tentacles!"

Pierre gave her a look that indicated nothing could surprise him at this point, bent down, and picked up Miguel's shotgun. "I will track them down. Vern will stay here with you while you go to that yacht and make a distress call. Then I think you shou—"

"I think you should all stand very still!" a voice shrilled.

The three of them spun around, staring down the gangplank toward shore. Leaning against a pair of twin palms at the water's edge were Alberto and the blue-eyed Cuban bodyguard, Felix. Both were holding submachine guns in the shoulder-firing position.

"Just to let you heroic gentlemen know: if anyone moves, the first one to get shot will be the lady!" Alberto stepped out from behind the palm, lowering his weapon to chest level, and moved on up the gangplank. Felix remained at his tree, sighting carefully.

Alberto had dressed down for the morning: khaki shorts, a black mesh tank top, and the kind of miniature gold-lamé cowboy hat usually worn poolside by society women with too much money and no taste. A pair of cat eye sunglasses with frames that matched the hat completed his ensemble. He waved Felix up as he reached the barge deck and stalked forward, keeping his machine gun trained on Sass. With a thin smile spreading across his face, he jerked the barrel toward the sat pot.

"Get over there," he ordered, his voice losing some of its neurotic chirp. "Out of the sun. It's too fucking hot, don't you think?"

Carefully, Sass, Pierre, and Vern backed away, watching the muzzle of Alberto's gun. He herded them under the superstructure that supported the elevated sat shack, then stepped into the shade himself and sat back on the lip of the pot's entry hatch. As Felix approached, covering the trio with his own weapon, Alberto relaxed slightly, resting the machine gun on his

533

knee. He glanced around the end of the big chamber at the outer lock's internal depth gauge.

"Pretty boy Chris is still at four hundred feet, eh? Well, one must be patient if one wants to play with quality items." He grinned lasciviously. "Some things are worth waiting for."

Sass edged sideways, pushing Vern and taking Pierre with her. Alberto's eyes narrowed. "Tut-tut." He tipped up his submachine gun. "Where are you going? Stand still. *Felix.*"

The guard stepped in and pushed the barrel of his weapon into Pierre's cheek. *"Estop!"* he snarled.

Pierre, Sass, and Vern estopped.

"Felix is a rather excitable individual," Alberto said mildly. "A street brute from Havana. I wouldn't antagonize him if I were you." He laid his submachine gun across his knees and rubbed his eyes. "All right. Who are you two, and how did you get onto the island?"

When neither Vern nor Pierre answered, Alberto's expression hardened. "You," he snarled at Vern. "You resemble a person who was working on the deck of this barge—another big, dumb animal like yourself. Your brother, perhaps?"

Vern said nothing, didn't move.

"Yes," Alberto said, his sharp eyes running over the big man, "I think so. The similarity is too great. Well,

I don't know what hole you and your friend were hiding in, but I'd like to tell you that your brother is currently *dead*—blown sky-high in an explosion. How about that, eh?"

Vern's face didn't even twitch. Not getting the reaction he wanted, Alberto became angry. "Didn't you hear me? I said your brother—"

"Ah heard you," Vern cut in.

Alberto frowned and adjusted his gold-framed sunglasses. "I think," he said, tapping a finger on his machine gun, "that you and this angry-looking midget represent two additional complications that I just don't feel like dealing with this morning. Stand apart from Miss Wojeck, please. Over there."

Vern didn't move. Neither did Sass or Pierre. They simply smiled.

"Didn't you hear me?" Alberto shrilled, his voice cracking. "I said—"

That was as far as he got before Chris, who'd soundlessly eased the sat pot's inward-swinging hatch open on its well-greased hinges, locked one muscular brown arm around his throat and yanked him back into the outer lock.

Simultaneously, Pierre swiped the barrel of Felix's machine gun away from his cheek. The weapon chattered off a short burst as both he and Sass drove the stunned guard back across the deck with their combined body weight. Vern went for the gun Alberto had dropped, catching it on the first bounce.

Felix's machine gun fired again, the staccato roar going on and on and on . . .

Chapter Thirty-Five

The boy ran along the clifftop trail, pausing every fifty feet or so to look down at the red-haired woman as she powered her way through the clear blue water with a tireless fin kick, speargun angling forward. The man she was chasing was visible from above only intermittently, diving and kicking and hauling himself along the very base of the cliff. The woman stayed farther out, perhaps twenty feet, and as the boy watched, she extended the gun at arm's length and fired it. A long steel needle streaked through the water just beneath the surface and hit the rock face behind the man's whipping fins. There was a muffled detonation, and the spear bounced back out in a cloud of coral dust.

The boy ran on, moving ahead of the pair. The man was a strong swimmer, fit and agile, but it was obvious that he was tiring, and the red-haired woman had a deadly weapon with a long reach. She wouldn't have to gain more than a few feet on him before it would be very hard for her miss with her high-velocity speargun. And, the boy knew, the cliffs were sheer and continuous for the next half mile. There was no beach or landing. No way out of the water.

Clenching his fists, arms and legs pumping, he fairly flew along the narrow, treacherous path, heading for the familiar coral pillar that stood in the little clearing only a few hundred yards ahead.

*****

Ben was all but done in. Each breath felt like an inhalation of red-hot tacks, and his vision was beginning to blur. His hands and knees were shredded bloody from clawing his way over and through sharp coral, and his ears were aching from the near-miss detonations of his pursuer's powerhead-tipped spears. She hadn't gained on him, but he hadn't outdistanced her either: he was just barely out of effective range of her speargun. He wasn't even sure if he'd been counting correctly—did she have two spears left, or three? At this point, did it even matter?

He dove along the rock face again and hauled himself over a huge dome of brain coral, scattering a school of yellowtail snapper. His hands were raw, stinging in the salt water. The desperate realization that he was going to have to change tactics or take a powerhead in the back began to manifest itself. He was going to have to slow down, let her get close enough to take another shot, *dodge* it somehow—and then charge her and hope he could close the distance before she was able to reload. The more he thought about it the worse it sounded.

And then he looked down.

Fifty feet below him and just ahead, from beneath a massive overhang of rock and coral, a small figure was waving. It was a boy, naked but for a pair of ragged cutoff shorts and a cheap facemask. He was so far down that he didn't look real; more like a doll than a human being.

Ben blinked and refocused. It couldn't be.

But it was. A young native boy, long black hair flowing around his head and shoulders, looking straight up at him and beckoning.

Ben broke the surface one last time, sucked in a huge chest full of air, and dove.

The channel was deep here, the blue void yawning down to an irregular bottom of jumbled shapes and shadows. Some of them seemed to move. To Ben's right, the rock wall swept down precipitously, cutting inward at the overhang under which the boy still waited, his legs pedaling, and continuing on down into the indigo gloom.

Ben cracked his jaw repeatedly, equalizing his ears as he drove deeper and deeper, feeling flinty little pains stab throughout his chest as the increasing water pressure compressed his lungs and rib cage. He was no breath-hold expert; no free-diving record setter with a high tolerance for having his thorax crushed. He was a commercial diver, accustomed to having all the air or gas he needed when working underwater, delivered at ambient pressure to keep his chest properly expanded.

I'll never make it back to the surface without passing out, he thought, reaching the overhang where the boy had disappeared seconds earlier. *Assuming there is a surface* . . .

But he flipped onto his back, got his gashed hands on the coarse rock, and pulled himself under the ledge. He kicked his way into the darkness perhaps two body lengths, then looked up.

Through a living storm of fish, swirling and fluttering in the cerulean glow, he saw the boy's legs kicking upward, more than twenty feet above him. He was in a great chimney of rock—at least forty feet across—that extended up to some kind of glimmering interface, far above, that *resembled* a water surface when seen from below.

Only one way to find out.

Swallowing convulsively, fighting to stay conscious, he kicked and pulled up through the billowing, darting schools of minnows, grunts, and pinfish. Larger animals—grouper and snapper—raced along the walls for cover, disturbed by his and the boy's passing. As he ascended, the glimmering, indistinct interface above did not look any more promising—there was no light filtering down from the sky; no indication of a true surface.

But the boy had come from somewhere.

Ben's heartbeat was hammering in his ears, his chest on fire, his vision shutting down, when his head suddenly erupted from the water into cool, moist, blessedly breathable air. On the verge of passing out, he floundered onto this back, clawing for something—*anything*—to hold on to.

His hand scraped over a flat rock; he flailed again and got a grip on it. Coughing and shaking, he hauled himself up onto what felt like a rough slab, awash just below the waterline. Exhausted, he rolled over, felt coarse rock against his spine, and sagged back, gasping.

Blinking salt water out of his eyes, he looked around, trying to penetrate the dimness. Gradually, the details of his surroundings emerged. He was in a great, domed cavern—a void in the limestone—that arched above the wide pool of salt water in which he'd just surfaced. Miniature terraces and natural landings extended around what he supposed was the landward side of the pool, separated by jumbles of broken rock. The entire space was illuminated by the muted blue glow of sunlight emanating up through the submarine chimney from outside.

Ben staggered to his feet, searching the fractured boulders and ledges for any sign of the boy. "Hello!" he called. "You there?"

The empty echo was short and sharp. There was no answer.

Ben stepped up off the water-washed ledge and onto a small terrace.

"Hey," he called again, looking up into the recesses of the cavern. "Where are you?"

Nothing.

The soft splash alerted him just in time. There was an elastic SNAP of surgical tubing as he threw himself sideways. The spear Grizelda had fired from less than ten feet away missed hitting him between the shoulder blades by a millisecond and smacked into the rock.

BANG!

The explosion was deafening in the close confines of the cavern. Rock chips sprayed into Ben's left shoulder and neck as he reeled along the boulders, losing his footing. He glanced down at the pool even as he fell. The woman was treading water about six feet from the edge of the landing on which he'd climbed up, her speargun angling up into the air.

Ben tried to get his feet under him, tried to redirect his momentum and dive on top of her before she could reload—but the rocks and the slime and the darkness would not cooperate. He toppled sideways off some kind of edge . . . turned in the air . . . clutching at nothing . . . and landed on his back and hip with a wet splat in a tight, partially flooded crevice. Pain shot through his ribs, forcing an agonized groan from his lips.

Desperately, he twisted around, trying to jerk his body free, but by the time he got one arm loose and his head turned so that he could look back the way he had fallen, the woman was standing over him.

Ben stopped struggling and locked eyes with her, as he'd done when she'd first leaped off the cliff into the sea, and again when he'd pointed out the lemon shark that had swum up on her flank. Her face, simian and coarse-featured in the blue light, had virtually no expression. Her eyes were so cold that they almost seemed to lack pupils—like the blind, unblinking orbs of a marble statue. She stood with her legs wide apart, every detail of her improbably-muscled body highlighted by the blue glow from the pool—bulging deltoids and biceps, flaring laterals that lent her torso an exaggerated V shape, turtle's shell abdominals, and massive, corded quadriceps and calves.

Her nostrils pulsed and her lips peeled back from her teeth in terrifying aberration of a smile. Reached back over her shoulder, she pulled the final spear from her quiver and balanced it in one hand, holding it mid-shaft, throwing style. The speargun she set aside to lean against a boulder.

She stepped forward one pace, down to a slab of rock directly above Ben. Her lips drew back even

more, her teeth gleaming blue-white in the eerie illumination, and she raised the spear, preparing to stab it
downward. From deep in her throat came an unearthly
baritone giggle.

Ben closed his hand over a loose chunk of rock, trying to work it free so that he could throw it . . . so that
he could do *something*. He tensed up . . . preparing to
take the awful, flesh-tearing impact of the powerhead . .
.

"Heueueueughhh . . ." the woman said. It sounded
like air rattling out of a balloon.

Ben stopped struggling and peered up. The woman
dropped the spear poised over her shoulder into the
water—*splash*. With goggling eyes, she stared down
between her breasts at a two-foot length of gore-slicked
steel that had suddenly sprouted from her sternum. Her
teeth bit into her lower lip and she clapped both hands
around it.

"AAAARRRGGH!" she screamed, and flexed her
massive arms and shoulders, trying to push it back
through her body.

The boy Ben had seen waving to him from beneath
the underwater overhang stepped out from behind her.
His intelligent young face was set, very serious, as he
backed away a couple of paces. His eyes were riveted
on the woman, observing her with a cool, dispassionate
interest.

The red-haired woman's legs began to shake. She wobbled sideways, and Ben could clearly see the full silhouette—blade, hilt, and handle—of the sword that had transfixed her from spine to chest. She bore down on the blade again, her fingers dripping blood, and tried once more to push it out of her body.

"AAAAAAAARRRRGGGHHH!" she screamed again, facing the pool. The sound was as chilling and inhuman as the howl of a werewolf. Her entire body was shaking now, trembling as if on the verge of epileptic seizure.

The boy stepped forward, grasped the handle of the sword, and raised his leg. In a single smooth motion, he planted his bare foot in the small of the woman's back and ripped the long blade free, simultaneously propelling her to the edge of the rock slab. Then he stepped back, watching.

The red-haired *narcotista* teetered on the slab's lip, clutching her chest. She turned, weaving, and stared at the boy in disbelief. Blood was bubbling from her mouth.

"Fernando is waiting for you," the boy said in Spanish, and pointed. "Down there."

Grizelda Ramos coughed once, spitting blood. Then her soulless eyes rolled up in their sockets, her arms sagged to her sides, and her head lolled back. She fell slowly, like an axed tree, and hit the pristine blue water of the pool with a smacking splash.

Ben struggled up out of the crevice, his ribs throbbing with pain, and stared at the body as it sank . . . drifting headfirst down into the depths, trailing a haze of red-brown blood . . . the silhouettes of fish whirling around it, dashing and darting like leaves in a windstorm . . . until, finally, it could no longer be seen . . .

He felt a hand on his shoulder. "Let me help you," the boy said.

Ben mobilized his street Spanish. "*Muchas gracias,*" he replied, and meant it.

By the time he got out of the crevice, he realized that he'd broken at least one rib, maybe two. The boy assisted him up over the lower boulders, and together they climbed up to a relatively large terrace that overlooked the pool from a height of about twenty feet. Here Ben sat down and rested, clutching his side.

His eyes had become completely accustomed to the dim blue light, and he took a moment to marvel at the immense natural amphitheater. Limestone concretions and stalactites hung from the domed ceiling; water streamed continuously down into the pool from several of the largest. Behind him, the broken rock sloped up to meet the ceiling in the shadows of the cavern's upper recesses. There was no sign of an opening anywhere that he could see.

The landing on which he was resting had clearly been used for some time as a bivouac site. A flattened sleeping mat of dry palm fronds lay in one corner, and several halved coconuts full of water—fresh, he assumed—sat at one end of it. There were a few other items: a hand-reel of fishing line, several fishhooks of varying sizes, a rusty fillet knife, and a small machete.

The boy picked up one of the coconut halves and sat down cross legged next to Ben. "Here," he said, holding it out.

Ben took it gratefully and drank. Rainwater, cool and smelling like a summer thunderstorm. He drained the coconut in four gulps. He hadn't realized how dehydrated he was.

The boy smiled at him and retrieved a second shell. "More?"

Ben returned the smile and leaned back against the rock. "You first, *amigo.*"

The boy sipped once and held out the coconut. "You have the rest."

Ben drank again, and as he did, the boy tore a small handful of leaves off his sleeping mat and began to clean the blade of the long sword that lay across his lap, frowning with concentration. He looked very serious about what he was doing. Ben shifted a little, trying to relieve his aching ribs, and regarded him.

"Thank you," he said again. "She was going to kill me."

The boy nodded. "Yes. She was a very bad person. She killed my brother Fernando. And another man, on the lagoon dock." He stopped rubbing the blade for a moment. "I think she killed many others, too, at different times. I don't *know* . . . but that is what I think."

"Wouldn't surprise me," Ben remarked. He studied the boy, then held out his hand. "Oh. By the way, I'm Ben Gannon."

The boy shook his hand with surprising timidity. "Hello." He seemed distracted, as if his mind was somewhere else. Ben was about to ask him his name but decided to wait, sensing that it might be better to let the boy tell him in his own time. Instead, he pointed at the sword. "Where did you get that?" he asked.

The boy began to narrate in a low, steady voice: "A very long time ago, two men from across the sea were shipwrecked on these islands. One was a good man, the other very bad. Each commanded a band of followers. They fought. The good man fled from this island to my island across the water, trying to stop the killing. But the bad man pursued him, and would give him no peace.

"Finally, after many people had died, the good man called the bad man out onto the open sand, where my

548

village is now. In front of everyone, he declared that there would be no end to the killing until one of them was dead, and that today was the day when all would find out which one that would be.

"The two men drew their swords and fought. They fought for hours under the midday sun, neither of them yielding. They fought until they were on their knees, still cutting at each other. The heat was sucking the life from both of them. A man cannot sustain such fury beneath our sun. Our sun will have its way with him.

"Then, as they were both about to collapse, a sudden rainsquall swept over the beach. It cooled them, refreshed them. They struggled to their feet to continue the fight. But the good man was quicker. With one great blow of his sword, he cut the bad man's head off his shoulders . . . and the battle was over." The boy lifted the blade that lay across his knees. "I think it was this sword."

Ben nodded gravely. "May I see it? It looks very old."

The boy passed it to him, hilt first. "Of course."

"So," Ben said, examining it, "the good man prevailed. He—"

"He prevailed," the boy went on, "but he did not live long. He was betrayed by one the bad man's followers, it is said, who stabbed him in the back as he knelt at his prayers in the little chapel he and his men had built. In memory of the great battle between the good man and the bad man, their bodies were preserved by the old arts, and they were both placed in great stone coffins in that same chapel, to lie opposite each other for all eternity. That is the story the elders of our village have told for generations.

The boy looked at Ben. "The sword you are holding came from the good man's coffin. The *narcotista*'s men stole it. I stole it back from her." He pointed at the base of the blade, where it joined the hilt and crossguard. "See? I think those letters must be his initials."

Ben turned the blade so that the blue glow from the pool highlighted the fancy etching.

"F-R-N," the boy said. "But I do not know what they stand for. No one in my village, not even the elders who taught me the story, knows his name."

Ben rubbed his thumb over the letters, looking closely and frowning. "This is a very old style of script," he said. "The same kind you'd see in Spanish documents and ship's logs from the sixteenth century. I was reading some just a few weeks ago up in New Orleans"—he glanced at the boy, saw his puzzled look, and smiled—"up in the United States."

"Ah, yes," the boy said, nodding. "America."

"Right, America." Ben tapped the sword with his index finger. "Anyway, this old-style letter here—the first one—it's not an F. It looks like one to us, but it's a fancy way of writing an S. So the initials are actually S-R-N."

The boy sat up, his forearms resting on his knees, and looked pleasantly surprised. "Oh!" he exclaimed. "Those are also *my* initials!" A broad smile spread across his face.

Ben put the sword down carefully on the rock. "Is that right? What's your name?"

The boy continued to beam. "Sebastian Rodrigo Nunoz," he said proudly.

Chapter Thirty-Six

It took Ben the better part of three hours to make it back to the lagoon along the clifftop trail, leaning on Sebastian most of the way. The near-vertical climb out of the cavern had played havoc with his broken rib, and by the time he and the boy emerged from the jungle on a rocky overlook about a hundred feet above the barge, every breath was giving him a sharp stab of pain. But it was endurable. A broken rib, he reminded himself, was far from fatal.

They were all there. The entire dive crew. Earl and Vern Pickens were standing next to each other beside the sat pot, both holding what looked like small machine guns. Gerald Posey was sitting just inside the door of his ROV van, typing away on a laptop computer. Pierre LeRenard, a cut-down shotgun under his arm, was standing on his tiptoes and peering into one of the viewports of the small deck-decompression chamber they'd brought along in case they had to do any surface-supplied diving. Chris Toricelli, his wrist wrapped in a white bandage, was walking across the barge deck toward a yacht called the *Cucaracha*, which was tied up alongside. And on the bridge of the yacht, talking into a radio hand-mike, was Sass. Ben's train of thought derailed when he caught sight of her.

She was the first one across the gangplank and up the slope to meet him once he and Sebastian had called out and begun to make their way down through the thick foliage. When she got her arms around him and hugged, crying softly and whispering into his neck and ear, he had to sit down hard on the leaf litter.

"Oof!" he grunted, stroking her hair. "Easy, girl. Damaged goods, here." Then he squeezed her until it was she who could barely breathe.

Everyone else was up the slope in Sass's wake in a matter of seconds, crowding around and helping Ben to his feet. They half-carried him, protesting, onto the barge and into the shade of the saturation unit's super-structure. There he was propped up on a foldaway deck lounger that Vern dug out of the equipment van, and given the medical once over by Pierre and Sass.

"That hurt, *mon ami?*" Pierre inquired, probing.

"Agh. Yes. Please don't do that again." Ben smiled through drawn lips as the Frenchman continued to run his fingers over the nasty blue-black swelling on his left side. Sass looked on, her hand on the nape of Ben's neck.

"Tabarnac," Pierre swore softly, "one rib gone, I think. Maybe one or two others cracked. You will need an X-ray to know for sure." He felt carefully with both hands. "Nothing is displaced, though. You have no lung pain, no organ pain. You are not coughing up

blood. So I do not think the bone pierced anything vital. We should be able to tape you up, and if you rest—and I mean *rest*, not run around like D'Artagnan—you will hold well until the U.S. Navy gets you to hospital in Guantanamo Bay."

"They're coming," Sass said. "I've been talking to them for the past hour. A helicopter lifted off the deck of a cruiser doing drug-interdiction patrols southwest of Jamaica fifteen minutes ago. Their ETA is seventeen hundred."

Ben glanced at his watch. "About an hour and a half. I can survive that long." He started to smile, then stopped. "Where's Gene?" he asked.

There was a general shuffling and lowering of eyes. Then Sass told him.

Ben was silent for a long moment. He put a hand up to his forehead and rubbed his brows, as if trying to massage away the painful news of Gene's murder. No one spoke, and after a while he dropped his hand into his lap and looked up at Vern, Earl, Pierre, Chris, and Gerald Posey in turn. "Do we know for sure where they buried him?" he asked.

"Ah think so," Earl said. "Sass gave us a good direction to look in. There's fresh-turned earth in the jungle over thataways, back in about two hundred yards."

"We're not leaving him here," Ben said. "When the chopper comes, that's the first thing we'll tell them."

"You bet," Vern growled.

Ben pushed himself into a more upright sitting position, gritting his teeth. "Where's this Alberto asshole, anyway?"

Chris stepped back and rapped his knuckles on the hull of the sat pot. "Right here," he said. "In the outer lock. Blown down to ten feet so he can't get the hatch open."

From inside the chamber, there came a dull pounding sound, very faint. The corner of Chris's mouth lifted in a thin smile, and he flicked on the power switch of the external descrambler radio.

"LET ME OOUUT!" a high, neurotic voice screamed. *"I'M CLAUSTROPHIC, DON'T YOU UNDERSTAND? AAAAAAAH! AAAAAAAAAAAH! I CAN'T STAY IN HEEEEEEERRRRRE—"*

Chris turned the radio off with a snap, cutting short the noise. "He's been in there for about three hours now," he said. "Ever since I yanked his greasy butt inside and put his lights out by slamming his head on the inner hatch a couple dozen times. But he woke up, I'm sorry to say." He looked genuinely disappointed. "We give him a vent of fresh air every half-hour or so, just to keep him alive. Same with those other three dickheads in the small chamber." Chris sucked his teeth in disgust. "You wouldn't believe what this guy was wearing on his head." He held up the gold-lamé couture cowboy hat. "Must be some kind of raging pansy-boy."

"What he is," Sass said, "is a murderer. And that's all that matters."

Ben looked at Posey. "What happened to you, Gerald?"

The ROV tech plucked a freshly lit cigarette from between his lips and adjusted his spare pair of steel-rimmed glasses. "Earl and I were blown off the back deck of the barge by an explosion. We rode in to the island on my ROV. For the past two days we wandered around trying to figure out what was going on, and what to do about it. As long as Chris here was in decompression, we couldn't try to steal Sass away from the barge—he'd have died, right? So we scouted around, waiting for an opportunity. We had no idea where you guys were, or if you were even alive.

"We were up at the house this morning, sniffing around, when Alberto and the only remaining guard came out in a hurry, got into a yellow jeep and left. We took the chance of entering the house and found a couple of shotguns. So that was good—at least we were armed. Then we heard machine gun fire echoing up from the lagoon. We didn't know it, but it was Vern and Pierre and Sass and Chris getting the jump on all three guards *and* Alberto. By the time we made it down to the barge, they had it all wrapped up.

"Yeah," Earl drawled, picking up the story. "We had a big dang reunion—Ah about did a blue-devil jig right here on deck—and then Sass went to that yacht over there and got the distress call through. Navy cruiser picked her right up. Then our only con-sarn was *you*."

"Yes," Sass said. "Where is that awful woman?" She pointed at the massive bruise on Ben's side. "Did she do that to you?"

Ben smiling, shifting on the lounger. "Indirectly. I sort of did it to myself."

"Where's that mega-bitch at, anyhow?" Vern growled. "You take care of her? She ain't gonna show up anytime soon, Ah hope."

"No," Ben said. "She's . . . gone." He looked at Sebastian, who'd been hovering silently in the background. "Gone for good. I'll tell you about it in a bit. But first, I'd like everyone to meet my new friend, Sebastian. Sebastian Rodrigo Nunoz. He saved my life."

Vern looked down at the top of the boy's head, raising an eyebrow. "That right?" He put a big hand on the Sebastian's shoulder. "Good job, son."

"Yeah, dang right," Earl added.

"Good job, kid."

"Nice to meet you, Sebastian."

"Yeah, me too. Great job, buddy."

The boy grinned at Ben under the shower of praise, and moved closer.

"We'll be returning Sebastian's favor, somehow," Ben said, reaching out and squeezing the boy's upper arm. "Once we get squared away. That's a promise."

There was a chorus of agreement, and then Earl held up a hand for silence. "Gerald an' me, we got something to show everyone," he announced. "Before the Navy boys get here." He walked away from the group, bent down, and fished a lumpy object out of the sat pot's support skid. "We found this up in the house, just before all that shootin' started. Ah threw it on my back 'cause Ah just couldn't see *leavin'* it."

He held up a small nylon backpack covered in dark brown stains. His arm muscles bulged; even for him, it was rather heavy. "Them are bloodstains, Ah figger. Don't know whose, though."

He carried the pack over beside Ben, set it down, and opened it. It was stuffed with U.S. currency, neatly bundled in inch-thick packets. Earl picked up a stack of fifties and handed it to Ben. "If they're all like this one, there's gotta be close to two hundred thousand in here . . . maybe more." He looked around at the ring of faces. "Ah don't believe this here is the kind of money anyone's likely to miss."

"It's blood money," Vern said. "If Ah ever saw it."

"Absolument," Pierre agreed. "No doubt."

"You know what the law enforcement boys'll do when they get here," Earl said. "Confiscate it and everything else on this island. Tell 'em, Gerald."

The ROV tech cleared his throat. "Earl's right. There's so much evidence of large-scale drug trafficking in that house—I mean records, maps, boat and plane schedules; the whole bit—that I think everyone from the DEA to Interpol to the Seventh Cavalry will be coming over the horizon to get a piece of the pie, once the Navy clues them in as to what's here."

Sass looked down at the money. "So what do we do with it?"

No one ventured an answer. Finally, Vern coughed and kicked his toe into the deckplates. "Ain't none of us wants that cash," he said. "It's drug money. We take it for ourselves, we're just stealin' what someone else stole. Ain't no way to make it right." He coughed again, grimaced, and spat. "An' right now, Ah don't want nothin' makin' me feel connected to the people that killed Gene."

The silence was even deeper. Abruptly, Sass dipped her head and covered her mouth and nose with one hand, her other arm folded across her chest. She choked out a sob, caught herself, and turned away. "I'm sorry," she said, wiping away tears. "It's just that . . . what happened to Gene. It was just so . . . *pointless.*"

Ben looked at her. Then at everyone else. "I'll tell you what," he said. "Here's what we can do with the money. Speak up if you don't agree.

"Sooner or later, this barge is going to be towed back to New Orleans. Earl—you take an acetylene torch and cut the top off that bollard on the starboard bow. You wrap this pack in an asbestos blanket and stuff it in there. Then you weld the top back on, clean it up with a grinder, and daub it with new black paint. Pull a few rusty cables around it and hit it with a length of chain a few times, and it'll look like it's never been touched.

"Then, when we get a chance, we open up the bollard in New Orleans and get the money back."

The men stirred, looking vaguely uncomfortable. "Well . . . *then* what do we do with it, Ben?" Earl asked.

"We give it to Chris," Ben said, "so he can give it to his father . . . so Gus Toricelli can pay for his cancer treatments." He smiled up at the young diver. "At least for a while."

All Chris could say was thanks. His eyes said the rest.

Earl was grinning. "Ah'll git right on that, chief." He closed the pack, picked it up, and stalked off across

the deck toward the bow. "Gotta take care of it before that chopper arrives."

"I'm going up on the yacht's bridge," Sass said. Her tears had dried, and she looked very much her in-control self again. "Do a radio check with the Navy boys." She turned and headed for the barge's port side.

Vern got down on his haunches next to Ben. "Good call," he muttered. "Wish Ah'd thought of it."

"Seemed the decent thing to do," Ben shrugged.

"All this trouble," Pierre said, standing beside Vern. "For nothing. Like Sass said. All for nothing. *Mon dieu.*"

"Well, you did find that golden nail," Vern reminded him. "An' we done rode up in the bell on a chain of gold." He shook his head. "Sure was pretty, wasn't it, though? Long too, and heavy. Would have been nice to have that, at least."

Ben chuckled, even though it hurt his broken rib. "You know," he said, watching Earl wrap the money pack in an asbestos welding blanket, "gold's fine. But I think when it comes right down to it, I'd rather have the price of a beer in my hand—any day—than a chain of gold on the bottom of the sea."

Epilogue

All things considered, it hadn't been a bad two weeks.

Once you discounted the raging thirst, the gnawing hunger, the searing sunburn, the festering salt-sores, the jellyfish stings, and the ass that was permanently deformed from lying on top of a bouncing, wobbling, constantly-awash dome of heavy steel—not to mention the almost minute-by-minute attacks of paranoia, rage, self-pity, and sheer terror that consumed every waking hour—there was a genuine upside to the situation.

He was fucking *rich.*

Jeremiah Sligo groaned and shifted his aching buttocks to a position where the diving bell's main lifting padeye wasn't trying to poke its way up his rectum. He was lying spread-eagled on his back inside the bumper ring, arms stretched out limply from his sides in the standard crucifixion pose, still resplendent in his bright-red Kronos Industries ThermaLint™ Sub-Liner long john underwear. He had spent most of the previous two weeks in this position—tied in place with a length of half-inch manila rope he'd scavenged during one of his infrequent underwater sorties to see if there was anything *inside* the bell that he could use *outside.*

He turned his head slowly on the bumper rail's hard steel tubing, eyeing the triangular dorsal fin of the shark as it completed yet another leisurely circuit around the bell. The sea was dead calm this afternoon, so Mean Sardine, as Sligo had nicknamed the fish, was easy to keep track of. The large oceanic whitetip had adopted the bobbing capsule ten days into its rapid northeasterly drift across the Caribbean, and had rarely disappeared for more than an hour at a time ever since. The animal's presence made diving to the trunk hatch and popping up inside the bell to get one of the water bottles that were kept full courtesy of passing squalls a bowel-squirming exercise—particularly since Sligo could not *stay* in the bell; not even for one breath.

The problem was that the atmosphere inside would not support life. It was a humid bubble of helium, carbon dioxide, a miniscule amount of nitrogen, and no oxgyen. Without a compressed air source, there was no way to flush out the bad gas. There was no battery power or absorbent soda left with which to operate a CO_2 scrubber, and no metabolic makeup O_2. The interior of the bell, which could have provided a far more sheltered, comfortable, and safe drift across the Caribbean, was basically unusable—a death trap.

Earlier, Sligo had found that out the hard way by sticking his head up inside, puffing a few times, and passing out as if he'd been anaesthetized. Only the shock of reimmersion, as he'd sagged out the bottom of the trunk, had revived him enough that he'd been able to grope his way to the surface. Afterwards, even *he* had been able to put two and two together and figure out the problem, and as a result had been limited to using the bell's protected interior for little more than water bottle storage.

But goddammit, he was fucking *rich!*

He turned his sun-blistered face back up toward the sky and licked his lips, his dry tongue dragging over cracked, peeling skin. His one functioning eye stared around like a mad blue marble, looking for rain clouds. The other had swollen shut days before, when a particularly nasty salt pustule on the side of his nose had ruptured and become infected. He'd used up all of his drinking water trying to clean the thing, which in retrospect had been a bad idea. His nose was still infected and now he was desperately thirsty to boot.

"Rain, you fuckin' bastard," he croaked to the sky.

The sky ignored him, burning down hotter and bluer than ever.

He pulled his feet—which due to constant soaking looked like two pale lumps of beef tripe—out of the water as Mean Sardine completed another circumnavigation of the bell, coming in closer than usual. Sligo struggled to a half-sitting position, which required considerable effort, and watched him. As he sometimes did, the whitetip drifted away, planing downward on huge, scythe-like pectoral fins, and disappeared into the sapphire-blue abyss.

"Haaa-haha-haaaaaa," the smuggler wheezed, keeping his good eye on the shark as it vanished. Even to his own ears, his laugh sounded like a rasp of an asylum lunatic. But he wasn't crazy. Oh no.

He was dyed-in-the-wool, honest-to-god, balls-to-the-wall *rich!*

He leaned over the bumper rail and looked down alongside the bell. He had come to love quiet weather because, in addition to not feeling like he was going to die every other second, he could look down through calm water and actually *see* it.

It was the golden chain from the *Arista* on which the bell had ascended. The golden chain *he'd* salvaged, goddammit. The big diver—the one who'd kept slugging him in the head, the cocksucker—had cut it free during the final rush to the surface. But what no one had noticed at the time was that the end had whipped down through the trunk, taken a weird lurch, and half-hitched itself around one of the supporting struts of the external framework.

It was there now . . . he could see it: a long gleaming thread of gold that hung down into the depths beyond his range of vision. It must have broken far below—maybe right at the bottom—because during a frantic, greed-driven dive to secure it using the binding hook of the bell's lifting come-a-long, he'd tried to pull up on it. It had been like trying to lift the Eiffel Tower. So most of the chain's twelve-hundred-foot length was, in all likelihood, still there.

He was rich.

The reason he felt secure in his newfound wealth was that the Isle of Youth—a landmass silhouette he recognized from his numerous Caribbean drug-smuggling trips—was sitting on the horizon to the north. And, as had been the case for several days now, it was getting larger. The currents that had swept him, in a state of petrified funk, across the upper half of the Caribbean Sea had carried him within a stone's throw of the southern coast of Cuba.

There was no doubt in his semi-deranged mind that he was mere hours away from washing up gently on the shore of Castro's kingdom, his golden chain trailing out obediently behind the bell as it grounded on talcum-soft white sands, and proceeding to live the life of Riley as the owner of several hundred pounds of antique *oro*.

Yeah, baby!

Just a few more hours. A day at most.

Squirming with pleasure at the thought despite his ravaged physical condition, Sligo drifted off to sleep under the orange-blue resplendence of a quiet Caribbean sunset.

*****

BLAAAAAAAAAAAAAAAAAAT!

This time, Sligo didn't even have time to scream. He thrashed awake, opened his mouth—and a wall of boiling white water cascaded over him. There was a thrumming, roaring, pounding noise; a sense of being inverted; and a loud underwater BONK as something hit the bell—_hard._

"_AAAAAAAAAAAAAGGGHH!_" Sligo finally articulated. Underwater, it came out more like "blrbrrbllrrbbrrllbrlb." His fingers tore at the slipknot he'd used to tie himself to the bumper rail.

BONK. Sligo's body whiplashed like a wet noodle at the impact, slamming him against the hull of the bell.

"Blrbblrlbrlb . . ." he commented again, before running completely out of air. The slipknot came free.

BONK-BONKETY-BONKBONK-BONK went the bell, catapulting Sligo off into the churning darkness.

The diving bell continued to skip along the side of the _Ivanovich_ as the big Russian freighter made top speed toward the Windward Passage, loaded to her plimsoll line with pineapples, sugar, and hand-rolled cigars she'd taken on in the Cuban port of Santa Maria. The vodka-pickled watch officer who'd blown the horn because he thought he might have seen something resembling a fishing boat in the water just ahead shrugged and went back to his seventh shot glass of 180-proof Potatopopoff.

The bell walloped its way along the underside of the freighter, burping helium, until it had finally traveled the length of the hull and was sucked into the whirling twin screws—giant cast-bronze propellers twenty feet in diameter—at the stern. One great blade clipped the steel capsule with a bang, taking a chunk out of its leading edge and sending it tumbling like a top.

The golden chain lashed toward the surface, wrapped in the port screw, and began to spool up on the spinning prop shaft. It snapped free of the bell in the first second. In the next ten, the entire twelve hundred feet was reeled up by the high-speed rotation. And as the fifteenth second ticked past, the over-bound, over-tightened, over-stressed ball of golden chain exploded, sending thousands of glittering fragments cascading through the dark evening waters toward the bottom more than three thousand feet below.

The diving bell, still tumbling in the whirlpools of the ship's wake, burped its last ten cubic feet of gas and sank.

Sergei Blutonov, the *Ivanovich*'s night cook, squeezed his blubbery three-hundred-and-forty-pound, five-foot-five-inch frame out through the aft door of the galley, dragging two large plastic garbage bags that contained the day's leavings, and paused by the rail to gasp for breath and light another Sobranie filterless cigarette. When his lungs felt sufficiently irrigated with the sour black smoke, he heaved the two bags, one after the other, over the side, picked his nose for luck, and waddled back into the galley to prepare the midnight meal. He didn't wash his hands.

Sligo was feeling bad. Air was the first priority, and after an eternity of floundering submerged in the black, post-sunset water, he managed to locate the surface and screech in a lung-full of something other than brine. The whirlpools and crosscurrents of the *Ivanovich*'s turbulent wake continued to knock him around like a pinball long after the freighter had become only a distant stern light against the purple evening sky.

Hyperventilating, he thrashed around three hundred and sixty degrees, looking for the bell. But it was gone. There was nothing to be seen but flat, black ocean. Which, like the sky, was becoming blacker by the minute with the coming of night.

"WHY ME?" Sligo shrieked up at the newborn stars. *"WHY MEEEEEEEEEE?"*

A huge dark object loomed up on his left side, eliciting another shriek and a spate of violent cringing. When he had finished drinking two or three more gallons of salt water, he calmed down long enough to take a good look at it, and realize that it wasn't alive.

It was one of the garbage bags from the *Ivanovich*. Gasping with relief, Sligo clawed his way on top of it, got it under his chest . . . and proceeded to dangle there at the surface, hugging the impromptu life preserver like it was Trixie Hendrix from *Hawgs & Ta-Ta's Magazine* herself.

After several minutes, he raised his head from the reeking plastic and looked around.

To the west, the last purple-red vestiges of the sunset were giving way to the blue-black shades of night.

To the south, the Caribbean Sea and sky were a vast, empty panorama of ebon gray, bisected by a single, indistinct line of horizon.

To the east, darkness had fallen so completely that, were it not for the white pinprick of the *Ivanovich*'s stern light, the horizon would have been impossible to locate.

Sligo blinked, rubbing salt water from his eyes.

To the north, the lights of the Isle of Youth winked warmly in the distance.

With an almost overwhelming sense of *déja-vu*, Sligo focused his one good eye on the far-off glimmering and began a slow frog kick, keeping his peripheral vision honed for any sign of the Mean Sardine.

THE END

About the Author

Before his untimely death in 2016 John McKinna was an Underwater Technical Supervisor and Operations Manager, responsible for overseeing upkeep of the main structure and support systems of the Key Largo Undersea Park home of Jules' Undersea Lodge. A former offshore commercial diver of twenty years' experience, he came on the Jules'/KLUP team as an adjunct to his primary line of work, that of internationally-known novelist and local musician. Like his wife Teresa, he was an avid free-diver, spearfisherman, lobster hunter, and cruising sailor. RIP John McKinna

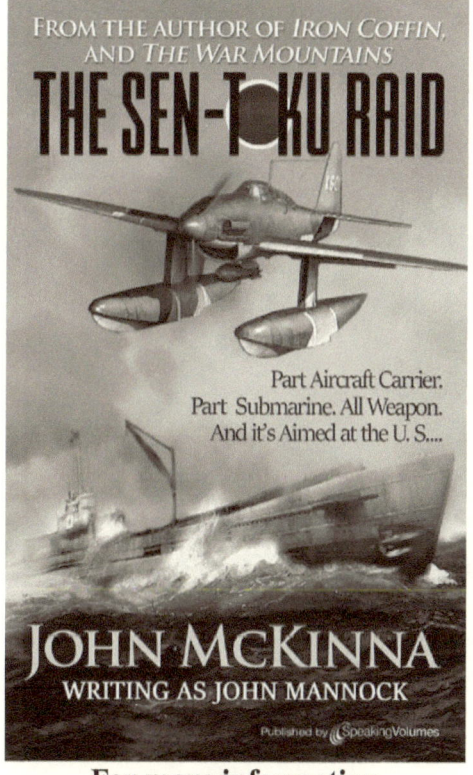

On Sale Now!

**Far below the surface.
Far from the fatherland.
And too close to the enemy for comfort...**

**For more information
visit:**